08/02/16
KT-171-147
04271028

The Constant Star

Out of the gloom behind her a young auxiliary fireman appeared. She could hardly make him out through the fog and, dazed, thought at first that he was her brother.

'Ah, Ronnie,' she said. 'There you are. I do believe I'm missing a shoe. Will you help me find it?'

'Girl 'ere needs 'elp,' the fireman called out.

Then she realised that it wasn't Ronnie, or Larry or Basil or the handsome Mr Powers, who'd asked her out to lunch at the Savoy, and, trembling uncontrollably, surrendered to the hands that passed her down and down into the care of nursing staff three floors below.

Also by Jessica Stirling

The Spoiled Earth
The Hiring Fair
The Dark Pasture
The Deep Well at Noon
The Blue Evening Gone
The Gates of Midnight
Treasures on Earth
Hearts of Gold
Creature Comforts
The Good Provider
The Asking Price
The Wise Child
The Welcome Light
A Lantern for the Dark
Shadows on the Shore
The Penny Wedding
The Marrying Kind
The Workhouse Girl
The Island Wife
The Wind from the Hills
The Strawberry Season
Prized Possessions
Sisters Three
Wives at War
The Piper's Tune
Shamrock Green
The Captive Heart
One True Love
Blessings in Disguise
The Fields of Fortune
A Kiss and a Promise
The Paradise Waltz
A Corner of the Heart
The Last Voyage
The Wayward Wife

JESSICA STIRLING

The Constant Star

HODDER

First published in 2014 by Hodder & Stoughton
An Hachette UK company

First published in paperback in 2014 by Hodder & Stoughton

1

Copyright © 2014 by Jessica Stirling

The right of Jessica Stirling to be identified as the Author
of the Work has been asserted in accordance with the
Copyright, Designs and Patents Act 1988.

All rights reserved. No part of this publication may be
reproduced, stored in a retrieval system, or transmitted, in any form
or by any means without the prior written permission of the publisher,
nor be otherwise circulated in any form of binding or cover other
than that in which it is published and without a similar condition
being imposed on the subsequent purchaser.

All characters in this publication are fictitious and any resemblance
to real persons, living or dead is purely coincidental.

A CIP catalogue record for this title
is available from the British Library

ISBN 978 1 444 78059 8

Set in Plantin Light
Typeset by Palimpsest Book Production Limited, Falkirk, Stirlingshire

Printed and bound by CPI Group (UK) Ltd, Croydon, CR0 4YY

Hodder & Stoughton policy is to use papers that are natural, renewable
and recyclable products and made from wood grown in sustainable
forests. The logging and manufacturing processes are expected to conform
to the environmental regulations of the country of origin.

Hodder & Stoughton Ltd
338 Euston Road
London NW1 3BH

www.hodder.co.uk

PART ONE

Midnight Matinee

1

Susan Cahill was twenty-four years old, good-looking, well-spoken and, on the surface at least, amazingly self-confident. She had already notched up, in no particular order, one husband, two lovers and a responsible job in broadcasting but by October 1940, a month after the blitzkrieg on London began, she would willingly have traded it all for a good night's sleep.

Nodding off while leaning against the studio door, snoozing in a chair in the producer's office or huddled on a lumpy mattress on the floor of the BBC concert hall, which had recently been turned into a dormitory, were no substitutes for clean sheets, fleecy blankets and enough space to stretch your legs without sticking your foot in some grumpy stranger's ear.

She had been camping in her friend Vivian's mews house in Salt Street since her flat had been wrecked by a high-explosive bomb but the demands of producing a twice-weekly radio programme, *Speaking Up for Britain*, meant she was seldom there. Added to the unremitting ferocity of the German bombing raids, it was hardly surprising that she no longer dreamed of soft lights, sweet music and dancing until dawn but only of a comfortable bed in a quiet room far from the dust and rubble of a city under siege.

In September the journalist Robert Gaines, *Speaking Up*'s American announcer, had suddenly upped sticks and returned to New York. Since then the programme had been making do with guest announcers, none of whom came close to filling Robert's shoes.

The board's first choice to take over from the renegade was a pompous Scotsman, recently transferred from Edinburgh. Unlike Susan's gruff Glaswegian husband, Danny, he trailed with him all the affected airs of the Athens of the North and producer Basil Willets, Susan's boss, would have none of him.

The next candidate was a former ballet critic of *The Times* who had sought refuge from the obscenities of war by pulling a few tutu-strings to obtain a staff job with the BBC. His florid style and mellifluous voice might go down a treat with elderly ladies in palm court hotels but, said Basil, not with hard-bitten station managers on the other side of the Pond – at which point the board lost patience and, behind Basil's back, appointed to the post a talented young broadcaster from the Bristol studio.

Susan had been on the telephone all afternoon trying to engage with jammed exchanges and her tolerance was wearing thin.

Mr Weymouth, a producer in Talks, had agreed to present the Tuesday programme and write a piece on 'Good Manners in Air-Raid Shelters' to leaven the gloom. The massing of Russian troops on the Rumanian border was a bit of news that couldn't be brushed aside, however, and Susan's task was to find a military expert who would make sense of the latest developments without boring the pants off the listeners.

Basil, who was married to Susan's friend Vivian, had nipped home to Salt Street to pick up a couple of shirts and have Viv pack some clean clothes for Susan. Alone in the office, Susan failed to hear the knock on the half-open door. Only when she glanced up did she realise that a stranger was watching her.

She covered the mouthpiece. 'What can I do for you, Mr . . .?'

'Powers, Stuart Powers.'

'I don't believe we've met,' said Susan.

'I don't believe we have. I've just arrived from Bristol. I'm here to speak with Mr Willets.'

Susan took her hand from the mouthpiece, said crisply, 'Thank you,' and replaced the receiver in the cradle. 'Basil – Mr Willets – shouldn't be more than ten or fifteen minutes. Please, have a seat.'

Stuart Powers was tall and slim, with a lock of fine fair hair spilling across his brow and eyes of the palest blue Susan had ever seen. She watched him pull out a chair, seat himself and stretch out his incredibly long legs. He wore a sports jacket over a roll-collar pullover, grey flannels and, on his feet, a pair of none-too-clean brogues. His casual style was appealing, a perfect fit for someone so tall and – yes – handsome. Remembering her manners, Susan squeezed out from behind the corner desk and offered her hand.

'I'm Susan Cahill, Mr Willets's assistant.'

She was all too aware how seedy she looked. Her hair needed washing, she'd neglected her make-up and had been wearing the same skirt and blouse for four days. He, in contrast, looked as fresh as if he'd been striding over Hampstead Heath all morning, not rattling about in a crowded railway carriage.

'May I smoke?' he asked.

'By all means,' Susan said.

He tugged a bashed cardboard pack of Du Maurier from his pocket, together with a box of matches, held out the pack and let her take one of the cork-tipped cigarettes. He struck a match and, cupping the flame in his palms, leaned down to light it.

'Am I right in thinking you used to be Vivian Proudfoot's Girl Friday?' he said. 'Plain Susan Hooper in those days.'

'I was, indeed, Viv's personal secretary for a year or two,' Susan answered. 'How do you know Vivian?'

'I don't. I was chummy with her former agent, Mercer Hughes, before he went abroad. He told me all about you.'

'Did he?' Susan abruptly changed the subject. 'More to the point, I take it you listen to our programme?'

'Of course I do.'

'Your opinion?'

'It hasn't been quite the same since the American left.'

'Fair comment,' Susan said. 'Robert was really one of a kind.'

'You must miss him?'

'I beg your pardon.'

'Mr Willets, I mean, must miss him.'

'Oh, he does. We all do, though Robert wasn't the easiest person in the world to deal with.'

At that moment the siren wailed, signalling another daylight raid, the third of the day. Stuart Powers stubbed out his cigarette.

'Where do we shelter, Mrs Cahill?'

'Fourth floor, Studio B. I wonder, awfully, if you'd mind carrying my typewriter. Where I go my typewriter goes too, on the off-chance I might get some work done.'

He hefted up the heavy Underwood, tucked it under one arm and offered a hand to Susan, as if she, not he, were unfamiliar with the maze of corridors, control rooms, offices and studios that filled the massive half-million-pound building.

'Which way?' he asked.

'This way.' Susan led him out into the corridor. 'We only use the basement shelters at night. The studios are safe enough during daylight raids, which never last long anyway.'

'I hope that isn't a case of famous last words.'

'Trust me,' Susan said and, glancing over her shoulder, flashed him a sample of her winning smile.

Some members of staff believed that the Luftwaffe was dumping bombs on the Borough of Marylebone simply to bring the BBC to its knees but knowledgeable chaps in the Air Ministry were not convinced that German pilots were all that clever or that accurate.

Broadcasting House was certainly a prominent target. The white walls had been painted drab grey to make them less visible from the air and the mammoth steel pillars that anchored the core of the building were so solidly embedded that folk working in the basements rarely heard the explosions that shattered windows and pitted the building's outer shell with shrapnel.

Daylight raids, while inconvenient, were too light and scattered to disrupt the putting out of programmes. Scriptwriters, editors and one or two musicians were milling about in the cramped studio while typists, machines balanced on every level surface, did their best to keep pace with producers' demands. The atmosphere within the soundproof room was overheated, the racket deafening, but there was no sign of panic, only the sort of organised muddle that Bob Gaines had dubbed typically English.

Mr Powers looked for a place to set down the Underwood

and, finding none, cradled it, like a baby, in the crook of an arm while Susan, toting a sheaf of scripts, snatched a chair from under the nose of a rival from the Empire Service.

She dumped the scripts on the chair and nodded to Mr Powers to put the typewriter on top, though she doubted if she would do much work until Basil got back. Not for the first time she'd failed to find a pundit willing to interpret breaking news. Fortunately, she'd had the sense to drag in ever obliging Professor Cobbold, at half past eight that morning, to record a talk on the Prussian character which would fill the programme gap.

In a couple of hours the *Speaking Up* team would gather in the listening room next to the third floor's Studio C to broadcast for pick-up by stations in America. Mr Weymouth was already in the building. Sir Hugh Everett, from the Ministry of Defence, was always punctual and his talk on 'Invasion: What Now?' had already been rehearsed. Three items, a session of question and answer, two minutes and twelve seconds of recorded music and the Tuesday hour would be over and, with luck, Susan thought, she might make it back to Salt Street for a few precious winks of sleep.

'Tell me a little more about your time with Vivian Proudfoot,' Stuart Powers said. 'Was she really one of Mosley's supporters?'

'No, she was never a fascist,' Susan said. 'Why are you so interested in Vivian?'

'I'm not. I'm interested in you. If we're going to be working together then we should probably get to know each other.'

'Basil may not take you on, you know.'

'Basil has no choice.'

'You mean, you're it.'

'I'm it – like it or lump it.'

'I trust you haven't been sent to corrupt our sober contribution to the airwaves with rumba bands and catch-phrase comedians.'

'Far from it.' He hesitated. 'I take it you haven't heard?'

'Heard what?'

'Can't say, at least not until Mr Willets has been informed,' Stuart Powers said. 'By the way, since you're not Hooper but Cahill now, I assume you are married.'

'What if I am? What business is it of yours?'

'Is your husband in the forces?'

'With the monitoring unit in Evesham, if you must know,' Susan said. 'We don't see much of each other these days.'

'What does he do at Evesham?'

'Editor. He has poor eyesight and – don't laugh – flat feet. When the opportunity to join the BBC presented itself, he took it, mainly because the army wouldn't have him.'

'Where are your folks?' Stuart Powers enquired. 'I'm not being nosey, just making conversation.'

'Of course, you are,' Susan said, thinking, Yes, I know your type, Mr Powers. You're not making conversation, you're fishing for a bed-mate. 'My mother's been dead for years,' she said. 'My father and his lady friend decamped to the south of Ireland. I doubt very much if they'll come back to London until the war's over. My brother – well, Ronnie, poor soul, was killed while trying to remove an unexploded bomb from the vicinity of a school. More fool than hero, you might say. Now' – she paused – 'what else do you need to know about me? Do I have a flat of my own? Do I live alone?'

'Do you?'

'I thought that might interest you.'

'I will need some place to rest my weary head for a day or two,' Stuart Powers admitted, 'until I find permanent digs.'

'I'm sure we can find you a ticket for the concert hall floor.'

'I've already spent quite a bit of time sleeping on floors in Bristol. I'd prefer something a little less communal, if possible.'

'My flat took a direct hit and appears to be beyond repair,' Susan told him. 'I'm lodging with Vivian and her husband who, as you no doubt know, is also our admirable producer. I suppose Vivian might be prepared to let you sleep on the sofa – a davenport actually – if it isn't going to be for long. Assuming, that is, you get the job with us in the first place.'

'I already have the job,' Stuart Powers informed her. 'It's just that Willets doesn't know it yet.'

'How long have you been with BBC Bristol?'

'Six months.'

'Six months? Is that all? Why aren't you in uniform?'

'Apparently I'm of more use to the BBC than I am to the army. I didn't apply for the presenter's job, if that's what you're thinking. I was told to show up today and briefed—'

'Briefed? Who briefed you?'

'In due course all will be revealed.'

'A man of mystery,' Susan said. 'Now I am intrigued.'

'There's nothing mysterious about me,' Stuart Powers said. 'What you see is what you get.'

The door of the studio flew open and a warden blew a shrill whistle to signal the all-clear. There was instant chaos in the crowded room and a general rush for the door.

Stuart Powers hoisted up the Underwood. 'You know, I'm becoming quite attached to this machine,' he said. 'I take it we're going downstairs again.'

'We are,' said Susan. 'Let's hope Basil's back.'

'Let's hope he is,' said the mysterious Mr Powers.

*

The late-blooming romance between Basil Willets, a middle-aged widower, and the writer Vivian Proudfoot had taken everyone by surprise. Shades of youthful passion had mellowed over the years to a point that had led to friendship and a wartime wedding. Vivian needed someone not just to share her life but to organise it, a role that Basil Willets, new-pin neat and a model of self-sufficiency, was only too willing to undertake in exchange for companionship and, Susan supposed, the joy of finally sharing a bed with his childhood sweetheart.

Basil was a wiry little man, not physically prepossessing, but with such a surfeit of energy that he could impose his will on his superiors and cajole those below him in the pecking order into doing his bidding without seeming like a tyrant. A recent expansion of the North American Service, however, had brought with it so many new rules and regulations that Basil was afraid that *Speaking Up* might be considered too staid for the tenor of the times and would wind up being strangled by red tape.

He was seated behind his desk when Susan arrived with Mr Powers in tow. He had hidden his shirts in a desk drawer, stowed the brown paper parcel of female garments in the stationery cupboard and, feet propped on the desk, was going over the scripts for the night's broadcast with a stop-watch and blue pencil.

'There you are, Susan,' he said, looking up. 'Did you find someone last-minute to cover the Rumanian thing?'

'I'm afraid not. We're stuck with Professor Cobbold.'

Basil offered no criticism. He scribbled a few hieroglyphs on the typed sheet and swung his feet to the floor. 'You'd better let Larry know,' Larry being the programme's sound controller. 'He'll slot in the recording before Sir Hugh's piece. Is Everett here yet?'

'No, but it's a little early.'

'He'll be here,' Basil said. 'A few Jerry bombs won't stop him making his voice heard.' He leaned his elbows on the desk, rested his chin on his hand and gave Stuart Powers the once-over. 'And who, may I ask, are you?'

'Your new announcer, sir.'

'Are you, indeed? Do you have a name?'

Mr Powers stepped forward, introduced himself and, reaching over the desk, shook Basil's hand.

'You used to write for the *Mail*, didn't you?' Basil asked.

'I did – still do now and then.'

'Good stuff, very sharp,' Basil conceded. 'Who sent you?'

'He's from Bristol,' Susan put in.

'Well, we won't hold that against him,' Basil said. 'Am I to take it, Mr Powers, you're being foisted on me whether I like it or not?'

'Haven't you received a memo from Personnel?'

Basil laid a hand on the pile of papers on his desk. 'If I have, I haven't found it – which is, I confess, remiss of me. On the other hand, it may not have turned up yet.'

'Do you mind if I sit down?'

'Please do.'

Susan watched Mr Powers fold himself elegantly on to the wooden chair. The window that looked down on the street had been boarded over. There was no light in the room save the electrical fitting overhead and the lamp on Basil's desk. The urgent sounds of emergency vehicles, bells and klaxons were clearly audible, a noisy accompaniment to the clatter of heels in the corridor.

'Are we being cancelled?' Basil said, then promptly answered his own question. 'No, if we were you wouldn't be here.'

'I do wish you'd received the memo,' Stuart Powers said. 'It isn't my place to tell a senior producer what's going on.'

'All right,' said Basil. 'What is going on?'

Stuart Powers said, 'You'll be invited to a panel to tender your views in due course, I expect, but what it boils down to is that Walter Boscombe isn't happy with *Speaking Up* being re-broadcast to America in early afternoon. He's arranging studio space for a midnight broadcast from here. What's more we'll be going out three nights a week, on Monday, Wednesday and Friday, as from—'

Basil jumped in. 'I can't possibly produce three late night programmes with the staff I've got.'

'I'll provide linkage and scripted interviews,' Stuart Powers said. 'I also have contacts in Fleet Street we might call on for a bit of extra ooomph.'

'Ooomph?' Basil's lip curled. 'Oh, so it's "ooomph" we're after, is it? What did you do in Bristol, Mr Powers? Write for Max Miller?'

Stuart Powers did not appear to take offence. 'I've only been in Bristol for a little while.' He hesitated. 'Before that I was the coordinator for the Canadians in the New York office.'

'I see.' Basil nodded. 'You're a big gun, a young gun but a big gun, none the less. I'm not sure whether I should take it as a compliment or an insult that Boscombe has stuck you here.'

'Three hour-long programmes a week with a guaranteed suppertime audience in the States?' Stuart Powers said. 'I really do think you should take it as a compliment, Mr Willets.'

'Given that I've no choice, I think perhaps I'd better.' Baz emerged from behind his desk and shook Stuart Powers's hand again. 'I look forward to working with you, Mr Powers.

Welcome to *Speaking Up for Britain*. I assume you'll stay to hear our broadcast tonight? We go on the air at eight.'

'I'd like that,' Stuart Powers said.

'Do you have accommodation? A place to stay?'

'I don't, as a matter of fact.'

'Susan will fix you up, I'm sure.'

'Will she?' said Mr Powers.

'Yes, with a mattress on the concert hall floor,' said Susan.

It had been a beautiful October day without a cloud in the sky. A full moon rose through curtains of smoke and, as night fell, bathed the city in brilliant moonlight. Unsurprisingly, the German planes came early and the first warnings sounded just after seven.

In Broadcasting House, news crews retreated to the basement and lifts were crowded with pages escorting the evening's guests to safety. Safety was the last thing on the minds of producers who had programmes slated for transmission. There was no mass exodus from the studios. It was, after all, just another air raid and nothing to get excited about.

The *Speaking Up* team was drinking tea and munching biscuits when Sir Hugh Everett arrived looking, Susan thought, just a mite more flustered than usual. He sipped tea, took three puffs on his pipe and, thus soothed, followed the producer to the listening room where Larry was checking sound levels.

The whistle and thump of falling bombs was audible in the corridor, though not the drone of aeroplane engines or, save as a pulse in the eardrum, retaliatory fire from the guns of the anti-aircraft battery in Hyde Park.

High on top of Broadcasting House fire-watchers were on the lookout for incendiaries, land-mines and parachute bombs. Below, at the Duchess Street entrance, an armoured car stood ready to transport newsreaders to a stand-by studio if 'the fortress' took a direct hit that put it totally out of commission, which, given the nature of its defences, was exceedingly unlikely.

At eight minutes to the hour Mr Weymouth came up from his lair in the basement, greeted Stuart Powers warmly, collected his programme material and went into the studio. He adjusted the mike, poured a glass of water from the jug that Susan had filled, placed his cigarettes, lighter and ashtray where he could reach them, squared his script and glanced up at the clock.

In the listening room, Susan experienced a flutter of anxiety, a common enough syndrome, until she heard Mr Weymouth offer greetings to the people of America and launch into his introduction, after which she relaxed and settled to enjoy the broadcast.

'Weymouth's only a nom de plume. He was a doctor before the war,' Basil whispered to Powers. 'Army Medical Corps in the last show. Did some broadcasting for us on and off. Dashed fine writer. How would your friends in CBC put it? Very "on the ball". We're lucky to have him.'

'Yes,' Stuart Powers said. 'I know you are.'

'Oh!' said Basil. 'Is he one of your crowd?'

'I do have friends in broadcasting,' Stuart Powers said, 'but I'd hardly call them a crowd. I've no more than a nodding acquaintance with Mr Weymouth, as it happens.'

'I'm not sure I believe you.'

'You mean you're not sure you can trust me.' Stuart Powers touched Susan's shoulder. 'What about you, Mrs Cahill? Do you think I'm trustworthy?'

'I'm sure you are,' said Susan guardedly.

She had started her affair with Robert Gaines not out of

trust or fellowship but from boredom and a desperate need for excitement, as if being caught in the middle of a war weren't exciting enough. The war was everyone's excuse these days; she was no exception. Uncertainty, tedium, drama and suffering, the sudden loss of values that had shored her up since childhood; she might not wear a uniform but the war had liberated her just as surely as any VAD or WRAC or debutante land girl. She wondered if Stuart Powers might be 'her destiny', as her sister-in-law Breda would put it, or if he was just another opportunist out for a good time.

A muffled growl, like distant thunder, penetrated the walls of the listening room. The floor shook slightly and a trickle of dust hissed down from the slant of the ceiling.

'What the devil's that?' said Sir Hugh Everett.

'Sounds like a bomb to me,' said Larry.

Mr Weymouth's talk on 'Good Manners in Air-Raid Shelters' continued without pause. The trickle of dust from the ceiling ceased.

Basil said calmly, 'It's nothing.'

'I didn't sound like nothing,' Sir Hugh said.

'I wonder if they heard it in Washington?' Stuart Powers said.

'Somehow I doubt it,' said Basil. 'May we have music, please?'

Weymouth's talk concluded and the strains of a string quartet playing Mozart emerged from the loudspeaker.

'See if he's all right in there, Susan,' Basil said. 'In fact, you may as well take Sir Hugh in now, if that's all right with you, sir. We've a recorded talk up next. Eight minutes and you're on.'

The door to the studio lay adjacent to the listening room. Susan peeped through the little glass porthole, opened the door quietly and ushered Sir Hugh into the studio. Mr Weymouth lit a cigarette and sat back from the microphone.

'Hugh,' he said, 'have you come to keep me company?'

'Unless you've anything better to do.' Sir Hugh took his seat at the table. 'I take it you were the one who vetted my material?'

'I was,' said Mr Weymouth. 'Do you really think Adolf's played his trump card regarding invasion or are you being your usual cautious self?'

Susan left them to it and slipped out into the corridor. Through flapping swing doors she could make out two men in blue uniforms and a duty officer huddled in conversation; beyond them, running, one of the secretaries from the Talks Department.

She was about to step back into the listening room when the duty officer spotted her. He left the uniforms and pushed through the swing doors. There was dust on the shoulders of his suit, a fine pinkish dust, a sprinkling in his hair too.

'Who's in the studio?'

Susan told him.

'Control?'

She told him that too.

'Have you seen the Director General?'

'No,' said Susan, surprised. 'What's up?'

'Something about a bomb on the fourth floor. I really' – he was already turning away – 'must find the DG,' then over his shoulder, 'Steer clear of the outer offices in the meantime, please.'

'Why?' Susan called after him.

'It may not have gone off yet.'

'What may not have gone off yet?' said Basil when Susan relayed the news.

'I assume he means a bomb,' Susan said.

'If there is a bomb,' Basil said. 'You know what duty officers are like. Lose some glass on the North Tower and the next thing you know the building's falling down.'

'Sounded a bit close for comfort, though,' said Larry.

'If there's any danger then someone will tell us to clear out. Not,' Basil added, 'that I've any intention of clearing out in the middle of a broadcast. Powers, might I impose upon you to trot along to central control and see if you can find out just what's going on. Put all our minds at rest.'

'I'm not sure I can find central control.'

'Susan,' said Basil, rather testily, 'go with him.'

Men were striding purposefully along the corridor and in one of the outer offices a secretary was hammering on a typewriter, presumably preparing script for a late-evening programme.

Stuart Powers took Susan's arm. 'Upstairs or down?'

'Down,' Susan said. 'There's no sign of the floors being evacuated. I expect it is another false alarm.'

They were halfway down the staircase when a policeman and two firemen, coming up, stopped them.

'Where do you think you're going?' the senior fireman asked.

'To the central control room,' Susan answered.

'From the third floor, are you?' said the copper.

'Yes, Studio C.'

'North American Service,' Stuart Powers put in. 'Mr Willets's programme, *Speaking Up for Britain*. We finish at nine.'

'How many on the crew?'

'Five. Look, what—'

'Is the Director General up on three?'

'His office is on the other side,' said Susan. 'Why?'

'He's got the Colonial Secretary with him,' the policeman said. 'I have orders to escort them out of the building.'

Crowded together on the half landing, three bulky men in heavy serge uniforms, two burdened with fire-fighting equipment and the other, the copper, with a truncheon clenched in his fist; Susan was aware of the strange, sour odour of men under pressure. Stuart tightened his grip on her shoulder as if he thought the uniforms might carry her off as a hostage.

'Are the lifts defunct?' one of the firemen asked.

'I don't think so,' Susan said. 'No.'

Stuart and she were looking down, the men in uniform looking up, all of them uncertain. Stuart said, 'What station are you from?'

'Manchester Square,' the fire officer told him. 'We've sent a dispatch rider to fetch the Divisional Officer from Bryanston Square. Big blaze there. We've a trailer outside but your roof fire's already been put out.'

'And the bomb?' Susan said.

'We've a crew searchin' for it right now. Look, we can't dawdle here all day,' the fire officer said. 'I suggest you alert your staff that there's a bomb what hasn't gone off and get them down to the basement. Now, please, make way.'

Stuart drew Susan aside and the men swarmed on upstairs just as another duty officer came leaping up from the second floor.

'Mr Carse,' Susan said, 'can *you* tell us what's going on?'

'Susan! What, yes,' Mr Carse said. 'A five-hundred-pounder came through the window on seven. It's lodged in the music room on four. I'd get below ground if I were you.' Then, like the firemen before him, he pushed past them and hurried on.

'Do as you're told and go down to the basement,' Stuart said.

'Where are you going?'

'Back up to tell Willets the news.'

'Basil won't break off transmission on the strength of a rumour, you know.'

She ducked under his arm and headed upstairs. He tried half-heartedly to catch her, then, shaking his head, followed her up to the third-floor corridor.

'You're enjoying this, aren't you?'

'Of course I'm not enjoying it.'

'You really should go down to the basement, you know.'

'Why?' Susan said. 'I'm not afraid of what might happen if that thing goes off. If it's my time to wave goodbye, so be it.'

'Oh, God, not another fatalist.'

'Stoic,' Susan said. 'I'll settle for stoic.'

'Or just plain stubborn,' Stuart Powers said and steered her ahead of him back into the listening room.

'If the London Fire Brigade can't shift a bomb without it going off . . .' Basil began, then instantly apologised. 'I'm sorry, Susan. I didn't mean to insult your brother's memory. Are you all right?'

'I'm fine. I just wish everyone would stop fussing.'

She hadn't mourned for Ronnie, not properly. There had been no body to bury, nothing left of him. She'd loved her brother dearly, though she'd thought him mad for running off to join the International Brigade and fight in Spain and even madder for marrying Breda Romano when he could have done so much better.

Water under the bridge now, all gone, like the shabby terraced house in Shadwell where she'd been born and raised and in which, latterly, Ronnie had lived with his wife and son. It was nothing but a heap of rubble, a gaping hole in the ordered line of the street; a hole in her life, too, now that her father and Nora Romano, Breda's mother, had scuttled off to Ireland and Danny had found Breda and her son a billet in Evesham; Breda and Danny all cosy in some rustic Eden, sleeping soundly, safe from falling bombs.

Sir Hugh Everett's voice from the loudspeaker said, 'Invasion is now a gamble for Herr Hitler and, if he is wise, he will listen to the advice of his generals. Much too depends on the Russian-German pact and whether it will hold firm over the course of the winter.'

Basil was oblivious to distractions. 'Six minutes and twenty to wind up,' he murmured into the cup-shaped microphone that connected him to Mr Weymouth's headphone.

'. . . possessed by two strong men each dedicated to expansion and backed by massive military might,' said Mr Weymouth over the speaker. 'We may have the will and the stomach for the fight, Sir Hugh, but do we have the means?'

Susan listened to the Defence Minister's answer with half an ear. She could hear nothing of what was going on outside. Stuart stood very close to her, looking not at the wall clock or the speaker but at her, a curious little smile on his face.

'Will you have dinner with me?' he said.

'Along with five hundred other staff members fighting for fish-cakes in the basement canteen, you mean?'

'I was thinking of a quiet dinner in, say, the Savoy.'

It was on the tip of her tongue to say, 'And then what?' but she was afraid he might take her seriously. She said, 'Our chances of reaching the Savoy tonight are absolutely nil.'

'Tomorrow then. Lunch tomorrow?'

'You don't waste much time, do you?'

'We may not have much time, Susan. Say you will?'

'Will what?'

'Have lunch with me tomorrow?'

'If it will make you happy . . .'

'It will. It'll make me very happy.'

'All right. Lunch tomorrow it is. Your treat?'

'My treat,' he promised.

The sprightly piece by Mozart floated airily from the loudspeaker and Basil, finger wagging, counted off the seconds. The music died. Larry at the control panel switched to the nine o'clock news in time to catch the last stroke of Big Ben. The newsreader's distinctive voice filled the listening room.

'Susan,' said Basil, puffing his cheeks in relief, 'will you fetch our guests from the studio.'

She went to the door, opened it and, hesitating, glanced back at Stuart Powers who, hips resting against the edge of the control panel, certainly looked more like a gentleman than a rogue.

Lunch, she thought, would be a pleasure and lunch, perhaps, would be the least of it.

She stepped out into the corridor.

And, on the floor above, the bomb went off.

The sound of the explosion and the blast wave were virtually simultaneous. Susan barely had time to cover her face with her forearms before the swing doors vanished in a torrent of debris and a gigantic hand picked her up, threw her bodily down the length of the corridor and left her sprawling at the top of the stairs.

She saw nothing in that moment but a strange electric-blue flash that faded instantly to crimson as a curtain of brick dust and plaster rushed towards her. Deaf and almost blind, she rolled on to her belly and drew her knees up to her chin. The wave broke over her, peppering her with stinging fragments.

Bizarrely, a typewriter, quite intact, whizzed past and vanished into the maw of the staircase, clattering away as if it, a mere machine, were seeking escape. She cupped her hands over her nose and mouth and sucked air into her lungs. Her hair, her unwashed hair, lifted as if a fist had tugged it, then her skirt and underskirt lifted as a second wave, driven by the fall of the corridor ceiling, shrouded her in more choking dust.

She lay quite still, waiting for darkness to close over her.

Shouting, screaming, a draught along the floor brought noises that sifted through the hissing in her ears. Papers swooped towards her, typed pages, a great rustling shoal that flapped past and, like the typewriter, vanished into the mouth of the staircase.

On hands and knees, she crawled to the stairs and, using the wall for support, hauled herself upright. Her stockings were ripped, buttons missing from her blouse and her knickers were soaking wet. She thrust a hand between her legs; pee not blood, thank God. She ran her hands down her legs and felt her face and head for wounds, then, hobbling, realised she'd lost a shoe, a precious, perfectly serviceable brown nubuck shoe.

Out of the gloom behind her a young auxiliary fireman appeared. She could hardly make him out through the fog and, dazed, thought at first that he was her brother.

'Ah, Ronnie,' she said. 'There you are. I do believe I'm missing a shoe. Will you help me find it?'

'Girl 'ere needs 'elp,' the fireman called out.

Then she realised that it wasn't Ronnie, or Larry or

Basil or the handsome Mr Powers, who'd asked her out to lunch at the Savoy, and, trembling uncontrollably, surrendered to the hands that passed her down and down into the care of nursing staff three floors below.

2

Until she'd arrived in Evesham, Breda Hooper's notion of a farmer was a rough-looking bloke in a smock and muddy boots who spent most of his time leaning on a gate with a straw in his mouth.

Five minutes in the company of Fred Gaydon had swiftly dispelled that idea. Mr Gaydon might not be exactly the white-tie-and-tails type and his boots were invariably caked with something worse than mud but he was clean-shaven, neatly dressed and not a day over thirty-five. More than that, he was constantly in motion, lurching about the fields on a tractor or clipping along the narrow lanes in a small, horse-drawn cart or, if no other means of transport was available, pedalling a rickety old bicycle that, Danny said, was only one step up the ladder from a penny-farthing.

Breda was willing to bet that Mr Gaydon had never spent more than a couple of minutes leaning on a gate in his life. Even when he paused to exchange a few words with her his mind seemed to be elsewhere and his feet anxious to follow.

The only time he ceased fidgeting was when he hunkered down to talk to Breda's son, Billy, and show the boy something interesting he'd found in a ditch or a hedgerow: owl pellets, the skull of a shrew, a blown egg from an abandoned nest and, once and best, a live mole he'd brought along in his hat, a soft, blind creature with a twitching snout that he'd allowed Billy to stroke and, on Billy's insistence, had put back on one of the molehills that had appeared on the edge of the stubble field behind the Nook.

Several of Mr Gaydon's trophies had wound up on the shelf above Billy's bunk in the converted railway carriage that Breda now called home. A speckled egg, a tiny skull and a collection of furry grey owl pellets were odd substitutes for the Dinky toys and lead soldiers that had been buried in the ruins of their terraced house in Shadwell. Even now, a full month after that frightful night, Breda shed tears into her pillow before she drifted off to sleep and offered prayers of thanks to a God in whom she no longer quite believed; tears for her husband, Ronnie, who had been killed in the line of duty and prayers of gratitude for the heavy rescue squad who, miraculously, had dug her mother and son, alive and relatively unharmed, from the smouldering heap that was all that was left of her house after the German bombers had passed.

Mr Gaydon was familiar with Breda's history and knew that Billy hadn't been told that his fireman father was dead. Being a gentleman as well as a farmer, and the father of two small daughters of his own, Mr Gaydon said nothing to disillusion the boy when Billy assured him that his daddy was fighting the Germans 'overseas' and would come home when the war was over.

Three shillings a week Mr Gaydon charged in rent for the rackety old railway coach, a sum that Breda had initially considered highway robbery. Three bob a week for a carriage propped on bricks and wooden sleepers with peeling paint and weeds growing under it and the niff of the outside toilet mingling with the stench of Calor gas and smoke from the iron stove and paraffin lamps.

The coach had been empty since Mr Gaydon's stockman had gone off to enlist in the RAF. Given that Evesham and all the villages surrounding the town, including Deaconsfield, had been invaded by weird BBC types from the monitoring unit at Wood Norton and hordes of evacuees from Birmingham, she'd been bloody lucky to find anywhere at all, Danny had told her, and had assured her that within a week or two the place would smell just like home.

The only flaw in Danny Cahill's character, as far as Breda was concerned, was that the beggar was seldom wrong. In fact, the only serious mistake he'd ever made – and what a whopper that had turned out to be – was in marrying Ronnie's sister, Susie Hooper, who any dolt could see was far too ambitious ever to settle down and be the sort of wife that a man like Danny needed.

Breda had been in love with Danny Cahill ever since one rainy night almost fifteen years ago when, fresh down from Glasgow and thoroughly lost, he'd wandered into Stratton's Dining Rooms, a posh name for the café her mother owned. Her mother had offered him supper and a bed for the night and Danny had stayed on as a paying guest until bleedin' Susie Hooper had sunk her claws in him.

Susan Hooper had been her rival as long as she could recall but now that she, Breda, had what the clever blokes on the wireless called 'territorial advantage' she couldn't bring herself to make the most of it and had too much respect for Danny, if not for Susan, to take up the running. After all, Danny hadn't brought her to Deaconsfield to have his wicked way with her. He was just being Danny, decent and responsible, and making sure that Billy and she were safe out of London and had a place to stay.

There was a lot to be said for living in the country and three bob a week soon seemed cheap for 'Shady Nook', the name some cove with a sense of humour had given the railway carriage. At least the Jerries weren't raining bombs down on your head night after night, though snuggled in bed in the Nook she sometimes heard bombers, the distant thud of guns and the whine of RAF fighter planes in the distance.

Surprisingly, she missed the East End hardly at all. She already had more friends here than she'd ever had in Shadwell, what with Mr Gaydon dropping by, and Mr and Mrs Pell, Danny's landlords, and Silwyn Griffiths and his fiancée, Kate Cottrell, who shared digs with Danny and were colleagues at Wood Norton.

The only person she didn't see enough of was Danny who worked long hours at the editing table and couldn't skive off just when he felt like it.

She, and Billy too, had settled quickly into a weekday routine. At half past seven each morning she took Billy to the Pells' house and left him tucking into a second breakfast while she and Mr Pell hoofed it to the factory out on the Shay Bridge road. There, looking rather out of place in the midst of rolling fields and orchards, the grey flat-roofed sprawl of Orrell's Engineering Works gave employment to a couple of hundred men and women under contract to the Naval Ordnance Board.

At half past eight Madge Gaydon and her girls picked up Billy at the Pells' house and escorted him to school where, in a classroom bulging with evacuees, he learned his ABCs, ate his dinner and played games until three o'clock when Mrs Gaydon and her girls returned him to Mrs Pell who kept him safe until Breda's shift knocked off at four. The arrangement suited everyone, not least

Mrs Pell who, unlike many of her neighbours, loved having young folk about the place. She fussed over her lodgers, Danny, Griff and Kate, like a mother hen, and not long after Breda arrived in Deaconsfield invited her to join 'the gang' for Sunday lunch.

Squeezed around the table in the Pells' living room they tucked into a splendid lunch washed down with beer and cider. Griff did his impersonation of a German reciting 'The Highwayman', Kate sang a jaunty song in French, Mr Pell told jokes and everyone joined in several rousing choruses of 'The Quartermaster's Store'. Breda, Billy on her lap and Danny at her side, was happier than she'd been in a very long time.

When dusk came creeping in around five and the party broke up, Danny insisted on seeing Breda home. Carrying Billy on his back, he used his shaded pocket torch to pick a way through the lane and along the footpath to the Nook. Only after she opened the door of the railway coach, drew the blackout curtains and lit a paraffin lamp did Breda, without warning, begin to cry.

'Hey, what's up wi' you, lass?' said Danny, concerned.

He unloaded Billy on to a bunk, put an arm around Breda and let her sob into his chest.

'Is Mummy sick?'

'Just cold,' Danny said. 'Tell you what, why don't you poke the stove an' stick on some coal nuts. Can you do that for me, Billy?'

'Yus.' Hopping from the bunk, Billy applied himself to the task while Breda detached herself from Danny's arms and took off her hat, scarf and overcoat.

'Careful you don't burn your fingers,' she said, as Billy knelt before the stove, opened the little door with an iron hook and stirred the embers with a poker.

Leaning against the door of the larder, Breda dried her eyes.

'I'm sorry, Danny. I don't know what come over me.'

'Guilt, is my guess.' Seated on Billy's bunk, he reached across the width of the aisle, took her hands and brought her to him. 'You don't mind it here, Breda, do you?'

'No, I like it.'

'Did you have fun this afternoon?'

'Yer, I did.'

'You're not betraying Ronnie by enjoying yourself, you know.'

'I feel bad about being 'ere with Billy and you,' Breda said. 'No, I don't mean bad, I mean lucky.'

Tears flowed again, making a right old mess of her mascara. Her nose ran. She sniffed and fumbled in Danny's top pocket for the handkerchief he always kept there.

Still kneeling by the stove, Billy looked round.

'It'll soon blaze up, Mum. I'll soon 'ave us all warm.'

'See, two guys to look out for you, Breda,' Danny said. 'What more could you want?' Then he added softly, 'Yeah, I know, I know.'

She rested against his knees, wiped her eyes and blew her nose, then, handkerchief balled in her hand, leaned and kissed his brow.

'Can you stay for a while?' she asked.

'I wish I could, sweetheart,' Danny answered. 'But I'm on duty, seven till seven. I'll need to push off in a minute.'

She knew better than to try to dissuade him. Work was no longer something you did to earn your daily bread; it was your contribution to defeating the Germans, your duty.

'Will I make you a sandwich? I've Spam in the cupboard and a jar of pickles,' Breda said.

'Nah, thanks all the same.' Danny got to his feet. 'The kitchen at Hogsnorton has finally got itself organised.'

Billy still found the nickname for Wood Norton amusing, though he'd heard it often enough. He tapped the poker against the lid of the stove and chanted, 'Hogsnortin, Hogsnortin, Hogsnortin,' interspersed with piggy squeals and honks until Breda told him to shut his noise which, being basically an obedient wee chap, he did.

'The Russians are lined up on the Rumanian border an' the Germans don't like it one bit,' Danny said. 'The air waves'll be buzzin' all night long an' there'll be no rest for the wicked.' He stooped and lifted Billy into his arms. 'Gotta go now, son. You take care o' your mammy, you hear?'

Billy bounced from Danny's arms on to the bunk.

'I lighted the fire, see,' he said jubilantly.

'So you did.' Danny rubbed the boy's tousled hair by way of farewell, opened the carriage door and stepped down on to the grass outside. He looked up at a clear night sky, already studded with stars. 'I'm glad I'm not in London tonight,' he said.

Breda followed him from the carriage. Light spilled across the patch of grass but she doubted if there was a warden within a mile of Shady Nook or, for that matter, a stray German bomber searching for targets along the River Avon. She raised herself on tiptoe and kissed his cheek.

'You be careful now.'

'Careful of what?'

'Anything,' she said. 'Everything,' then, alone in the puddle of light, watched him set off down the footpath and, with a final wave of the hand, vanish into the darkness.

*

Until the early summer of 1939 Orrell's Engineering Works had made parts for industrial washing machines. Then some bright spark in the Admiralty had stuck a pin in a map of the West Midlands and come up with the notion that Shay Bridge would be an ideal place in which to manufacture torpedo components. The reasoning behind the decision, Mr Pell explained, was based on the principle of not putting all your eggs in one basket and removing elements of ordnance production from obvious target sites like Woolwich and Portland, which seemed, to Mr Pell at least, a jolly sensible idea.

Orrell's little factory, out there in the wilds, was transformed by the building of four new sheds, heated and lined, and the installation of machines designed for turning out torpedo tail units. In Shed No. 3 experiments with some top-secret device related to gyroscopes were going on but not even Mr Pell knew much about that. The chaps on Orrell's workforce who hadn't been called to arms were retrained, Mr Pell among them. Well over a hundred and fifty new hands were brought in, mainly from the Birmingham area, and found billets along convenient bus routes in the small towns and villages north of Evesham.

The packing and dispatch section was staffed by women but in the main sheds all the machinists were male. In the catering department, in which Breda was employed, not one knob was to be found, as Mrs Trudy Littlejohn, a vicar's wife, put it, unless you counted – which Mrs Littlejohn emphatically did not – Mr Archie Jackson, former manager of a Salford Co-op, who was now the catering manager and in charge of provision purchase.

Trudy and Mr Jackson did not hit it off, which was hardly surprising given that Mr Jackson didn't hit it off with anyone, though, to be fair, he was a master in the art of manipulating Food Office inspectors, Food Control agents and probably the only person outside Whitehall who understood the in and outs of datum quotas and supplementary ration requirements.

Trudy Littlejohn and Archie Jackson had been at loggerheads long before Breda arrived on the scene. Trudy professed to be devoted to husband, parish and church. Archie, a godless socialist, had so far failed to find a mate godless and socialist enough to take him on. It didn't help that sleek and shapely Mrs Littlejohn towered a good six inches above Mr Jackson who, though no midget, was no man mountain either. The couple did not snap and snarl across the pastry board or in back of the potato masher but each adopted a tone of frigid politeness that made their exchanges seem even more venomous.

'May I enquire, Mrs Littlejohn, what became of the ham hocks that were delivered last evening? I have toured the cold room and can find no sign of them.'

'If you will cast your eyes to the bill of fare, Mr Jackson, you will no doubt remark that today's main course is Rustic Stew, a tasty and economical dish, well within our per capita allowance, and one for which ham hocks are regarded as an essential ingredient.'

'Thank you, Mrs Littlejohn. One cannot be too careful with meat products, particularly those of the pig which, I regret to say, have been known to trot off the inventory never to be seen again.'

'If you are implying dishonesty on my part, Mr Jackson . . .'

'I am implying no such thing, Mrs Littlejohn. My comment was generalised. I am satisfied with your explanation.'

Trudy Littlejohn was not prepared to let Archie slip so

easily off the hook. She stretched out a leg to block his escape and said, 'If any doubt lingers in your mind as to the fate of the ham hocks, may I suggest you invite Miss Hastie to open the pots, extract the strips of meat and weigh them, allowing, of course, for a degree of shrinkage in the cooking process.'

'Now, now, Mrs Littlejohn, there is no call for sarcasm.'

'No sarcasm is intended. I'm sure Miss Hastie would be only too pleased to uncover her hocks to satisfy your curiosity.'

Morven Hastie was even more shapely, if marginally less sleek, than Trudy Littlejohn, and several years younger. There wasn't a man or boy in Orrell's who wasn't half in love with little Miss Hastie or, at least, with her cookies and buns.

Mr Jackson knew when he'd been bested.

Flushing, he snapped, 'No need, no need to bother Miss Hastie,' and, vaulting over Trudy's leg, beat a retreat to the manager's office where, for a short time at least, he'd be safe from the legion of insolent women into whose midst the winds of war had blown him.

Breda was known as a 'half-shifter'. There were several such on the cooking, serving and cleaning staff in Orrell's canteen. Breda did not regard a forty-four-hour week as a 'half shift' in anybody's book but she knew there were men, and some women too, who, with overtime, clocked up sixty hours, and she was too grateful for the thirty-two shillings that her grade as a kitchen assistant brought in to utter a word of complaint. The hours were convenient, except on Saturdays when she had to drag poor Billy out of bed and, feeling like a traitor, dump him on the Pells for the morning.

One benefit of being employed on the day shift was that she enjoyed a fifteen-minute tea break and a half-hour break for dinner. The one disadvantage was that dinner had to be taken before first serving and it took her a couple of weeks to adjust to scoffing a main meal at half past ten in the morning. There was no separate staff room. Cooks, servers and cleaners all ate at two long tables in a corner of the dining room. It was during dinner breaks that Breda really came into her own.

Despite being a widow with a small son, she was looked upon as a sophisticated big city girl and thus an arbiter in discussions on the effectiveness of vitamin shampoo and toning rinses, if Amami curls went well with headscarves and if Dr Cassell's famous tonic tablets really did make every nerve in your body tingle and every organ throb, though, on this last point, Breda deferred to Trudy Littlejohn who claimed to have more experience with flagging organs than the rest of them put together.

Trudy might be married to an Anglican vicar but she was sufficiently worldly to recognise that, in time of war, fidelity was a two-way street and that while your Tom or Harry might not be having it off with mademoiselle from Armentières there was a fair to middling chance that he was having it off with her English equivalent. This mordant view was shared by Breda whose dear daddy had managed what amounted to a knocking shop for randy servicemen in a lane behind Victoria station, until the cops had nabbed him under the Undesirable Aliens Act and had sent him off to Canada on a ship that had been sunk by a U-boat with few survivors, Leo Romano not among them.

Brought up in the Church of Rome, Breda had encountered her fair share of aggressive nuns and shady priests and it didn't take her long to realise that Trudy Littlejohn's campaign against the male sex wasn't underpinned by religious prejudice but was, in fact, an addled fascination with sex itself.

'This man of yours, Breda,' Trudy Littlejohn enquired, 'does he take care of your needs?'

'He isn't my man,' said Breda, 'not the way you mean.'

'Oh, and what way would that be?'

'Look, I've known Danny since I was eight years old. He's more like a brother than anything. Anyroads, he already has a wife.'

'When did that ever stop them,' Trudy Littlejohn said. 'It's part of man's nature to want to scatter his seed.'

'Danny ain't that sort.'

'He's stationed with the BBC at Wood Norton, is he not?'

'I don't see what that's got to do with it.'

'A hotbed of intrigue down there, so I've heard. I mean, all those foreign types, swarthy men with no morals and too much time on their hands. I've heard all about the scandalous things that go on at the club they have in Evesham. Have you been there?'

'No, I 'aven't,' Breda said. 'I don't know where you get your information. The BBC Club's just a place where they can 'ave a meal and a tipple when they comes off shift. I wouldn't pay no heed to gossip if I was you, Mrs Littlejohn.'

'You're right, of course,' Trudy Littlejohn said. 'One shouldn't set much store by what comes out of the village pump. The tales I hear from Stanley's parishioners would make your toes curl. I'm their confidante, you see, their mother confessor, repository of all their grubby secrets, which is what a vicar's wife is for, I suppose, the cross I have to bear.' She slid a hand on to Breda's forearm. 'If there's ever anything you wish to tell me, any matter in which I can offer advice . . .'

'I'll be sure to let you know,' Breda promised, quickly drew her arm away and, from that moment, was on her guard against Trudy Littlejohn. Who might be a mother confessor to the folk of Shay Bridge parish but, within the walls of Orrell's Engineering, bore all the hallmarks of a Nazi spy.

Cloud had come in from the west and the fine spell of autumn weather seemed to be fading into winter at last. The wind slapped little waves against the piling of the bridge and plucked loitering leaves from the four tall oak trees that stood sentinel at the north end of Deaconsfield Road. In two of the three council-owned, semi-detached houses that formed the heart of the hamlet lights were lit, rectangles of warmth in the gathering gloom that would soon be extinguished by shutters and blackout curtains.

The rumour that a small German spotter plane had been brought down in a field a couple of miles east of Shay Bridge had got the girls in catering all excited. But Mr Lauchlin, senior Civil Defence Officer, had told Mr Jackson that the rumour wasn't true and there was no point in anyone galloping out there to see the wreck and hunt for souvenirs and, much to everyone's disappointment, Mrs Greevy, cook on the evening shift, confirmed Mr Lauchlin's report.

Breda felt the wind on her cheeks as she headed for the Pells' house to pick up Billy. In Shadwell the breeze from the Thames, funnelled by dock walls, warehouses and rows of tenements, always had an abrasive edge to it but here in the Vale of Evesham the wind was clean and invigorating.

She had quickly become conscious of the rhythms of

country life and remarked the changes in weather and landscape with the same attention she'd once given to the new season's frocks in the windows of the Whitechapel Co-op or posters for the latest Clark Gable picture plastered outside the Empire or the Palace.

She noticed at once that the field adjacent to Deaconsfield Road was under the plough, a host of gulls and rooks noisily trailing the tractor. Mr Gaydon had told her that strict new laws imposed by the Ministry of Agriculture meant that fields under grass since the Norman Conquest were being torn up and planted with wheat, beets and potatoes to replace grazing for beef cattle which were considered a land-rich luxury now that imports had dried up.

The straggle of women emerging from Orrell's gate had been left behind and the machinists' shift didn't change until six. There was no one at all along the length of Deaconsfield Road unless you counted Mr Turberville's old retriever who spent the day lying like a log in front of the gate and rose only to greet passers-by with a thump of the tail and a lolling tongue which, Mr Turberville claimed, was the canine version of a friendly hello.

In an hour or so she'd be snug inside the Nook, safe and sound with Billy, the coals in the iron stove beginning to glow and the tiny gas-fired oven purring as it cooked the pie she'd been saving for tonight's supper. Later, she'd write a long-overdue letter to her mother in Limerick and persuade Billy to sign it with a kiss for his granny. She was thinking of what she might tell her mother in the letter when she noticed Danny standing by the Pells' garden gate.

She gave him a cheery wave but became apprehensive when he didn't wave back and, quickening her pace, called out, 'What is it? What's up?' He advanced a step or two towards her, prodding at his spectacles as he usually did when he was agitated about something. Her apprehension mounted. Bad news was always just around the corner these days or, as now, waiting for you at the gate.

Voice rising, she said, 'What's wrong, Danny?' Then, 'Oh, God, don't tell me it's Billy? Has something 'appened to Billy?'

'Naw, naw, Breda, nothin' like that. It's Susan.'

'Susan?' Her relief was overwhelming. 'What about 'er?'

'The House took a direct hit last night.'

'The House?'

'Broadcasting House,' Danny said. 'Seven killed.'

'Was – was Susan . . .?'

'No, she's okay.'

'Well, thank God for that,' Breda said with as much sincerity as she could muster. 'There was nothing about it in the papers this morning.'

'The evening editions might run a para or two,' Danny said, 'but they won't tell us much. We don't want the Jerries to know they hit an important target an' give them a chance tae crow about it.'

'When did you find out?'

'Came down the wire last night just after ten. We knew there was a raid on but we never thought much about it until all our internal lines including the teleprinters went dead. Our boss got through to the newsroom eventually and we learned it was a bomb, a big bugger, that had landed in the main building.'

'Are you sure Susan's all right?'

'Fairly sure.'

'Have you spoke to 'er?'

'Not yet. Only bits and pieces of information trickled down throughout the night. Seven dead: no names. Forty or fifty injured. I asked for a line but was told it would be useless tae even try for a connection. Soon as our shift finished Griff whisked me off tae the club where there's a public phone, but it had a queue at it a mile long.'

'Where is Susie right now? Is she one of the injured?'

'I think she's back in Vivian's, or should be by now,' Danny said. 'We picked up some up-to-date news at the club. Fourth floor of the House badly damaged. The music room totally destroyed. Pile of damage on the third floor too, right under the explosion. I couldn't raise Susan at the BBC but I did get through to Vivian at Salt Street. She told me Susan's okay. Few cuts an' bruises but she was still up in Portland Place tryin' to sort things out. Basil, her boss, was in the BBC infirmary. Vivian had on her stiff upper lip but I could tell she was worried an' wouldn't be happy till she was allowed to see him.'

'Are they still broadcasting?'

'Oh, sure. Takes more than one bomb to stop the BBC.'

'I meant Susie's programme.'

'I don't know about that.'

'Danny, I'm sorry, so sorry. Really, really sorry.'

'I haven't told Mrs Pell, which is why we're out here,' Danny said. 'Frankly, I don't know what tae do for the best.'

'What do you mean?'

'I can't take more than a day off 'cause I've got leave saved up for Griff an' Kate's weddin' next month,' he said. 'What do you think I should do, Breda? Should I try to get down to London to see how she is – or will I just be in the way?'

'In whose way?'

'I mean, will Susan want to see me?'

'That's not the question,' Breda told him. 'The question is, Danny, do you want to see 'er?'

'Aye,' he answered without hesitation, 'I reckon I do.'

Breda sucked in a deep breath.

'Then go, you idiot,' she heard herself say. 'Just go. Right now.'

3

According to Fritz on Radio Frankfurt a thousand German planes had laid waste to London in the course of Tuesday night. A check with the Air Ministry, however, suggested that the number involved in the raid was closer to four hundred and that eighteen, possibly nineteen, enemy aircraft had been brought down. Figures were one thing and eye-witness evidence quite another. Heading east from Paddington, Danny was inclined to believe that Fritz's claim was closer to the truth than the Air Ministry's version and his heart sank when he entered Portland Place and saw the devastation the raid had wreaked on Broadcasting House.

He'd had trouble enough wending his way up from Evesham with prolonged stops at darkened wayside stations while army personnel hopped on and off. The train had been due to arrive in London at 11.20 p.m. on Wednesday night but had been held for hours in a siding awaiting an all-clear and hadn't crept into Paddington until half past seven on Thursday morning.

Fortunately, Danny was wrapped against the cold in a bulky sheepskin coat that Griff had loaned him, one of Kate's university scarves, a pair of knitted mitts from Mr Pell's extensive collection and a fur-lined balaclava that, added to his spectacles, made him look, Kate said, like Baron von Richthofen. He carried his gas mask and, in a greasy haversack, a change of underwear, one clean shirt, a packet of squashed fish paste sandwiches, one edible apple, a pear beyond redemption, a bar of Fry's chocolate, and a bulky brown bottle of Bulmer's cider that he shared with two very young, very raw RAF conscripts who were passing through London en route to somewhere in Norfolk.

The last time he'd been in Paddington was just after an air raid and he was gratified to see, through bleary red-rimmed eyes, that the station was open again, even if it was still missing most of the roof.

Portland Place, though, was a mess.

Papers were strewn everywhere, sheet music, files, letters, memos and reports blown out of the news and music rooms. There were gaping holes in the fourth- and fifth-floor walls and shattered windows in the third-floor offices, in one of which Susan had worked. Police, CD officers, ARP wardens and half a dozen soldiers armed with rifles were milling about a cordoned area that stretched almost to the top of Regent Street and within which a number of forlorn gentlemen in suits were picking over the scattered stationery like crows on a rubbish dump.

It was hardly surprising that the sergeant on duty was reluctant to let Danny through. Bedraggled, unshaven and dopey with lack of sleep, he resembled a tramp rather than an employee. Only after close inspection of his BBC pass was he escorted to the main door where an elderly commissionaire gave him the once-over and allowed him to enter.

The impressive reception hall was impressive no longer. Blast waves plunging down the lift shaft had caused the baffle wall to bulge ominously and carpenters were busy erecting shoring beams. Puddles of dirty water marred the marble and cleaners, all female and none young, were mopping and scrubbing as if their lives depended upon it, while typists, secretaries and production assistants trooped down the staircase lugging boxes, typewriters and files.

Extra staff had been drafted in to help at reception. Wardens stood by to supplement the squad of pages who had surrendered to the forces of disorder and were shouting, actually shouting, across the hallowed hall in search of instruction as to who had gone where and what offices were open. And this, Danny reminded himself, was the morning *after* the morning after the night before. Heaven knows what it had been like yesterday when fires were still burning and firemen and rescue squads were labouring to free the injured from the rubble. He approached the reception desk cautiously, cleared his throat and tried to catch the eye of an austere-looking woman who bore an uncanny resemblance to the King's mother.

On his third attempt at eye contact, she deigned to notice him and, leaning like the Tower of Pisa, said in regal tones, 'Whatcha want?' adding as an afterthought, 'Sir?'

'Miss Susan Hooper?' said Danny. 'Naw, hang on: Mrs Susan Cahill. She's my wife.'

'Is she?' said the dowager. 'Programme?'

'*Speaking Up for Britain.* Basil Willets is the producer.'

The woman shook her head. 'He's gone, I'm afraid.'

'Gone? Not – not dead?'

'No, his wife took him away about an hour ago.'

'And Miss Hooper – Mrs Cahill?'

The woman was clearly not familiar with protocol and, Danny thought, had probably been dragged in from Variety Rep on short notice. She looked down her snoot at him and said sternly, 'Now, which is it? Hooper or Cahill? What is she – a typist?'

'Production assistant.'

'Raaalllph,' the woman called out in a voice that reminded

Danny of the Dragon King in *Where the Rainbow Ends*. 'Chappie here looking for a Susan somebody. Mr Willets's assistant. Is she on the casualty list, or what?'

Ralph had high cheekbones, white hair, a waxed moustache and wasn't a day shy of sixty. He displayed a fusion of superciliousness and patience that suggested long service in some corner of the Corporation that dealt with nuisances and mischief-makers. He slid along the desk and peered at Danny.

'You're not Michael Foot, by any chance?'

'Naw,' said Danny. 'I'm not Michael Foot.'

'Well, I know you're not Mr Bevan,' Ralph said, while the King's mother stood by, nodding agreement. 'Is your name on Mrs Cahill's list?'

'What list?' said Danny.

'The guest list for tonight.'

'You mean, she's puttin' out a programme *tonight*?'

'Of course,' said Ralph. 'Are you, or are you not on the list?'

'He's the husband,' the woman chipped in.

'Ah! I see,' said Ralph. 'Right-o. Try the Calcutta.'

'The what?'

'The old Calcutta Cinema in Scobie Street,' Ralph explained. 'Never did find out why they called it that. I did hear it was supposed to be the Taj Mahal till somebody found out the Taj was actually a tomb but' – he shrugged – 'who knows. In any case, it's one of our temporary studios and that's where you'll find your wife. Do you know where Scobie Street is?'

'Off the King's Road?' Danny suggested hopefully.

'Soho,' said Ralph. 'Top end of Dean Street.'

'And if you can't find it . . .' said the King's mother.

'Yeah, I know,' Danny said. 'Ask a policeman.'

*

The nether end of Oxford Street was closed. Buses, motor-cars and pedestrians were being siphoned off into Regent Street. A huge land-mine had blown a corner off Leicester Square and taken out the Perroquet restaurant and Thurston's billiard halls and demolished a taxi rank and the torn and twisted chassis had not yet been removed. A friendly ARP warden directed Danny into Shaftesbury Avenue.

It seemed strange to be rolling up Shaftesbury Avenue at that hour of the morning with the theatres, those gay, grand palaces, standing empty under a soft pink-tinted sky. There were plenty of folk about, though, some emerging from shelters and Underground stations and others, clerks, agents and shop assistants, picking their way to work.

Danny paused at a snack bar on the corner of Wardour Street to purchase a cup of tea and a slice of toast and ask the guy behind the counter where he might find the Calcutta Cinema. By way of reply, he received a potted history of the picture house that, in time of peace, had, it seemed, screened a continuous round of cartoons, travelogues and blurry documentaries about Swedish nudist camps with, as the café owner ruefully put it, never much more than a glimpse of tit or a fat bare bum for yer tanner.

Revived by the tea, it took Danny less than five minutes to reach Scobie Street, which was really more of a lane than a street. Hunched and furtive, the cinema's quasi-Indian façade was blackened by smoke and pitted by shrapnel. The windows were boarded over and the doorway flanked by threadbare sandbags that leaked mud over what passed for a pavement. The sliding gates, once gilded, were open, though, and a board over the ticket kiosk displayed a peeling poster of a lovely blonde girl hugging a beach ball under the headline *The Maidens of Malmo: Unclad and*

Unabashed which, Danny thought, might have lost something in translation.

A BBC van blocked the width of the street. A Morris Oxford saloon was parked on the pavement. A couple of guys in brown overalls were unloading equipment from the van. Danny put a hand to the gates and gave them a shake. One of the overalls, a big chap with a roll of cable tucked under one arm, bawled, 'Hoy, you, 'op it. Ain't nothin' for you 'ere these days.'

Danny dug his BBC pass from his pocket and held it out at arm's length. 'I've been fifteen bloody hours on the bloody train an' I'll have no lip from you. Susan Cahill, where'll I find her?'

'Inside,' said the big guy, chastened. 'Downstairs.'

The number of aspirin tablets she'd consumed, added to quantities of coffee, had irritated her stomach and done nothing to ease the neuralgia that affected the left side of her face. Larry said the stitches had inflamed the nerves and it would soon pass off. Susan was not convinced. After a second restless night on a bunk in the newsroom, she'd gathered up a few bits and pieces rescued from the wreckage of Basil's office and had gone to the canteen and forced down a breakfast substantial enough to keep her stomach quiet and see her through the rest of the day.

She'd first set eyes on the Calcutta Cinema yesterday afternoon when it had been swarming with carpenters stripping out seating and removing projectors and the noise of hammers, saws and drills had been deafening.

'You can leave the technical side to the engineers, Mrs Cahill,' a chap from the Master of Works Department had shouted. 'What do you need to get yourself started?'

'Basic minimum,' she'd told him, 'two mikes and a clock in the studio, chairs and a table. I can manage without a separate listening room but for the office – a chair, a desk, a typewriter, and at least one telephone. Oh, and an electric kettle would come in handy.'

The Wednesday night raid had started just before eight, by which time Susan was installed in the manager's office and had 'nailed' two speakers, one from the American embassy and a journalist from the *Daily Mirror,* to discuss what Roosevelt's election for a third term might mean for Britain. She had also managed to borrow a guest announcer from Edward Murrow's CBS stable. Then, at Larry's insistence, they had risked life and limb by scuttling back to Broadcasting House to catch some sleep.

By half past eight on Thursday morning she was back in the windowless little office thirty or forty feet below the Soho cobbles.

The banging and hammering had largely ceased. Stage and screen areas had been left untouched, seats cleared from the vicinity of the projection room and the two small offices that flanked it. There was a lavatory with a washbasin, a cold-water tap, toilet paper, soap and a roller towel. The electricians had slung up extra lights, had fixed the extractor fan and were in the process of replacing the crusted old wall-plugs and checking out the fuse-boxes behind which rats had been happily nesting, undisturbed, for the past eighteen months. It was cold, though, very cold, a damp, skin-crawling sort of cold that made Susan's face ache.

The CBS guest announcer had promised to drop in around ten. Meanwhile, Susan was trying to locate a censor to approve Thursday's material without drawing attention to the fact that she, a mere female, was in sole charge of the production.

The telephone was working but switchboards across the city were unreliable and she'd been drumming her knuckles on the desk for five minutes awaiting a line to Mr Weymouth who was also a licensed censor.

'You don't look too good,' said a familiar voice.

She glanced up, more annoyed than surprised. 'You're not exactly a fashion plate yourself, Danny. What are you doing here?'

'I came tae see if you were okay?'

'Well, I am. I'm perfectly fine, thank you, just very, very busy.'

'Aye, I can see that much,' her husband said.

He took off the balaclava and scarf, draped them on a chair and put his gas mask and haversack on the floor, clearly intending to stay. The ache down the side of Susan's face flared. She held the receiver away from the crescent of fine stitches that decorated the fleshy part of her ear. She'd combed her hair over the wound and hoped he wouldn't notice but, of course, he did.

'Is your hearin' affected?' he asked. 'Are you deaf?'

'No, it's a superficial flesh wound,' she answered. 'I'm told it'll heal without leaving much of a scar.'

He seated himself on the edge of the desk. 'Any other damage?

'No, none.'

The line to Portland Place was active. She could hear the background chatter of switchboard operators and the mantra, 'We are trying to connect you. We are trying to connect you,' repeated over and over again.

Then a voice said, 'Henson here. May I be of help?'

'I wish to speak with Mr Weymouth.'

'I'm afraid he isn't here. Who am I talking to?'

'Thank you. I'll try again later,' Susan said curtly and

dropped the receiver into the cradle. She reached for the mug of coffee perched on the script folders.

Danny lit two cigarettes and passed one to her.

May I smoke?

By all means.

She felt again the sticking sensation in her throat, like a fragment of food that she couldn't swallow.

She drank a mouthful of coffee.

'How long will you be in London?' she asked.

'Goin' back on the two forty-two,' he answered. 'I'm on duty tonight, if the train gets me there on time.'

'Why are you really here, Danny? Is it to discuss a divorce?'

'A divorce? Heck, no!' he said, surprised. 'I just came to see if you were all right after what happened on Tuesday.'

'As you can see' – she blew smoke – 'I'm fine.'

'What about Basil?'

'Cracked ribs and torn muscles. Vivian's taking him off to the country to recuperate.'

'Where were you when the thing happened?'

'In the corridor outside the listening room.'

'Bloody lucky you weren't in the listening room, Susan,' Danny said. 'What about Gaines?'

'He's long gone. Don't you ever listen to *Speaking Up*?'

'The Pells do. I'm usually on duty,' Danny said. 'Has Gaines gone for good?'

'How can I possibly answer that?'

'So who's your new announcer?'

'We don't have a regular announcer yet.'

You mean, you're it?

I'm it – like it or lump it.

She drank the dregs of the coffee and said, 'What about your girl, your Miss Cottrell, how is she?'

'Kate isn't my girl. Never was. She's marrying my room

mate, Griffiths, next month. Nice wee do up in Coventry. Guess who's been asked to be best man?'

'Sporting your kilt, of course?' Susan said.

'No kilt. Clean shirt, blue suit.'

'Will Breda go with you?'

'Nah, it's a family affair.'

'While we're on the subject,' Susan said, 'how is Breda? Is she enjoying country life?'

'No complaints so far.'

'I wish you'd looked after me as well as you look after her.'

'You don't need lookin' after, Susan.'

'I suppose that's true.'

'What's happenin' about the flat?' Danny asked.

'Soon to be demolished,' Susan answered. 'There doesn't seem much point in looking for another place at the moment.'

'You're probably right.'

'Vivian's happy enough to let me stay with her meantime.' She hesitated, then blurted out, 'This is my chance, Danny, an opportunity to prove myself capable of producing . . .'

'Come off it, Susie. The powers that be aren't gonna let a twenty-four-year-old girl take charge of anything much beyond a pencil sharpener let alone a transatlantic broadcast.'

'Why must you always do me down? I'm more than capable of holding the show together until Basil's back on his feet.'

'I don't doubt it. But this is the BBC we're talkin' about and women, as you know, are only tolerated because there aren't enough guys to go round any more.'

'I can do it,' she said angrily. 'I know I can.'

'Well, sweetheart, all I can say is good luck.'

He reached for the haversack and gas mask case and strapped them over his shoulders just as the telephone rang.

'Are you leaving so soon?' said Susan.

'I'd offer to hang around an' take you to lunch but I can see you're up tae the eyes. Now I know you're all in one piece I reckon the best thing I can do is push off an' leave you to it.'

Lunch then. Lunch tomorrow.

The telephone rang and rang.

Somehow she managed to ignore it.

'Did you really come all this way just to see me?'

'Sure. Why wouldn't I?' he said.

The telephone abruptly stopped ringing.

'I'm sorry, Danny,' she said.

'For what?'

'That I don't have more time.'

'Sure,' he said again. 'I understand.'

She got to her feet, reached over the desk and offered her cheek. He kissed it lightly, avoiding her ear. He swathed the scarf around his neck and stuffed the balaclava into the pocket of the tattered sheepskin overcoat.

The telephone rang again.

She said, 'I'd better . . .'

'Of course.'

'Danny.'

'What?'

'Thank you for thinking of me.'

He nodded. 'See you around, Susan.'

'Will do,' she said brightly and watched him pass along the darkened aisle and vanish on to the stairs before she lifted the receiver and tentatively answered the call.

The mews house in Salt Street had so far escaped major damage and on that passive October morning had a self-satisfied look to it. He had met Vivian several times and

Basil Willets once or twice but he was still nervous about turning up unannounced on the doorstep.

He rang the doorbell and waited, swaying a little. His feet hurt and his calves ached, which wasn't surprising given the miles of London pavement he'd covered in the last few hours. He half expected a cute wee maid in a black dress and lace cap to open the door and had to remind himself that this wasn't Bloomsbury.

He was just beginning to wonder if the couple had already left for the country when the door opened and Viv peeped out at him.

'Danny,' she said. 'How lovely to see you.' She threw the door wide, wrapped both arms around him and hugged him to her ample bosom. 'I'm afraid Susan isn't here.'

'I know,' Danny said. 'She told me about Basil. I thought I'd drop by an' see how he is. I hope you don't mind.'

'Mind? Why would I mind?' said Vivian. 'Come in, come in. Have you eaten?'

She was a large woman, broad in bust and beam, but Danny was dismayed to see how gaunt her face had become and that her alert, intelligent eyes were ringed with shadows of fatigue.

She led him not into the long, low-ceilinged living room but into the office where, aided by Susan, she'd written the controversial books that had made her name. The desk was littered with papers but the typewriter was shrouded with an oilskin cover as if, Danny thought, it had been put to bed for the duration.

She held him at arm's length and looked him up and down.

'I don't think much of the coat,' she said, 'but, that apart, you seem well enough. Are you still locked up in Wood Norton?'

'More so than ever,' Danny said.

'I take it you saw Susan at Broadcasting House?'

'Nope, I had to track her down to a place in Soho,' Danny said. 'It's an old cinema the Corporation's leased as an emergency studio.' He hesitated. 'Basil doesn't know about it, does he?'

Vivian lowered her voice. 'No, and I'd rather you didn't tell him. I don't want to give him another excuse for fretting about his precious programme. If he asks – and he will – just tell him everything's under control; not, of course, that he'll believe you. Like all men, he regards himself as indispensable.' She put a hand on the desk top and leaned into it. 'He is indispensable, of course, but only to me. The BBC can replace him: I can't. Oh, God, Danny, I really thought I'd lost him.' She fought back tears. 'Inches, a matter of inches and I'd be just another weeping widow. Did Susan tell you?'

'Susan didn't tell me much.'

'It's all very well pretending to be fearless but when the chap standing beside you has his brains splashed all over the floor and you – Basil, I mean – are pinned down by a piece of concrete with your nose in a puddle of blood . . .' She shuddered. 'Basil won't talk about it. Can't say I blame him. What *did* Susan tell you?'

'She didn't tell me someone on Basil's crew had died.'

'Powers was his name. He'd just arrived on a transfer from Bristol. Poor devil was in the wrong place at the wrong time. A chunk of concrete dislodged by the explosion fell into the listening room. Larry, the sound controller, walked off unscathed, and my husband was struck but this Powers chap was standing right beneath it and his head was crushed. He never knew what hit him, so Larry told me. What a damned lottery life is these days. I can't imagine what Mr

Powers's wife must be going through, left alone with two small children.' Vivian puffed her cheeks and rested her backside against the desk. 'I'm just glad it wasn't Basil. Is that selfish of me, Danny?'

'No,' he told her. 'Hanging on to our own is what we do tae survive, otherwise we'd go nuts. How badly is Basil hurt?'

'Four cracked ribs. He's heavily strapped. The arm's the problem. He was pinned by his right arm and, thinking that the roof was about to come down on him, he wrenched it free with such force that he tore all the muscles and tendons. He'll be in a sling for two to three weeks but all he's fussed about is how soon he can get back to work. That,' Vivian said, 'is why I'm carting him off to the country whether he likes it or not.'

'Where in the country?'

'Gadney, a small village not far from Hereford.'

'Is that your brother's place?'

'Lord, no! I wouldn't lodge with David even if he did have space. He has land girls swinging from every rafter which, naturally, pleases him no end. To give him his due, he did find us the cottage on very short notice and insisted on sending a car to fetch us. It should be here presently, in fact, but if you need a place to stay, Danny, you're welcome to the run of the house.'

'Kind of you tae offer, Vivian, but I'm heading back to Evesham on the half-two train. I just popped up to make sure Susan was okay.'

'How "okay" is she? I mean, was it worth the journey?'

'She seems to be under the impression she'll be producing *Speaking Up* until Basil's back in the saddle.'

'Fat chance of that happening,' Vivian said.

'I know. Unfortunately I made the mistake of telling her.'

'She wouldn't take kindly to that.'

'Put me in worse odour than I was in before,' Danny said. 'Between you an' me, I don't know what tae make of Susan. She's changed so much since she left Shadwell all those years ago.'

'Wasn't that the intention?' Vivian said. 'By which I mean, her father was hell-bent on pushing her up the ladder. Oh, she's a smart girl, no question of that, but she is still young and hasn't yet learned to grapple with reality.'

'Your lot didn't help much,' Danny said. 'All those writers an' fascist sympathisers she consorted with gave her a false idea of what reality really is.'

'Now, now, don't blame me because your marriage failed.'

'I wouldn't dream of it,' said Danny. 'I knew what I was gettin' into when I asked Susie to marry me – or thought I did. Maybe if the war hadn't come along we'd have been all right.'

'Do you still love her?'

'I honestly don't know. I thought I was over her until that bloody bomb went off. Soon as I heard the news, first thing I thought of was Susan, is Susan all right. As my pal, Griff, put it, "There's love for you, boyo." Perhaps he's right.'

'Susan is still your wife, Danny,' Vivian reminded him. 'It's only natural you're concerned for her health and welfare.'

'You make her sound like a deservin' cause, Vivian. I'm not so sure she is deservin'.'

'He's gone, you know: Gaines. He cheated on her, she caught him at it and then – what's the expression? – he hightailed it back to the States. Susan was very upset about the whole thing.'

'Aye, I'm sure she was,' Danny said, 'but you can't expect me to give her much sympathy.'

'You've every right to be bitter.'

'I'm not bitter,' Danny said, 'just puzzled how she thought

she could have her fun with the American and stay married tae me.'

'Some women,' Vivian said, 'have a talent for separating cause from effect. I fear Susan might be one of them.'

'You mean she thought I was soft,' Danny said. 'Well, I suppose I am in some folk's eyes.'

'Or,' Vivian went on, 'perhaps she misjudged her own sex appeal and assumed you'd forgive her just to have her back. I suspect what shocked her more than Gaines's cheating was that you took her sister-in-law – what's her name?'

'Breda.'

'That you took Breda back to Evesham with you.'

'What was I supposed to do? Leave Breda an' the wee guy in Shadwell with London being bombed tae hell every night. Somebody had to take care of them.'

'Altruism: I doubt if Susan even knows the meaning of the word. I was much that way myself until I married Basil,' Vivian admitted. 'I'd no consideration – or very little – for anyone other than myself. It's a character flaw you find in some women; not vanity or a desire to be sought after, which is perfectly understandable, but a dark area on the outer edge of selfishness when you actually believe that the only reason the sun rises in the morning is to shine on you. It takes a very special kind of man to break down that belief but when it happens, when we're called upon to pay the piper, it comes as a shock to the system.' Viv tugged the cable-knit cardigan over her bust and grinned. 'If you ever dare breathe a word of what I've just told you to Mr Willets I will hunt you down, dear boy, and strangle you with my own bare hands.'

'I didn't come here just tae ask your advice about Susan, you know,' Danny said.

'Nonsense! Of course, you did,' Vivian said. 'It's actually

quite a relief to talk about someone else's problems instead of dwelling on my own. Now, let me make you an omelette. I've half a dozen eggs in the larder and there's no sense in them going to waste.'

'You could leave them for Susan,' Danny suggested.

'When it comes to fresh eggs, Mr Cahill,' said Vivian, 'altruism takes a back seat. Coffee or tea?'

'Coffee, please.'

'I'll have to help his lordship dress and make ready for the road shortly but if you promise not to get him over-excited, perhaps you'd like a few words with him. Talk about the Russians, the Balkan conflict or just when the Italians will invade Greece but, please, please, don't tell him that your dear little wife is in sole charge of his programme or, morphine or no morphine, he'll have another fit.'

'My lips are sealed, Vivian, I promise,' Danny said and followed her across the hall into the bedroom where producer Basil Willets, in dressing gown and pyjamas and a very large sling, was sitting up in bed just waiting to pounce.

As soon as he stepped through the door of the makeshift studio Susan knew the game was up. The few sensible cells still lurking in her exhausted brain had told her that Danny, more honest than tactful, had been absolutely right when he'd said that she'd never get away with it. Her last, faint hope of producing even one programme vanished as soon as Walter Boscombe, with the insolent Eton-bred drawl that every secretary in Broadcasting House loathed, removed the clipboard from her hand and said, 'Thank you, Miss Cahill. I'll take over from here.'

'I had hoped I might . . .' she heard herself say.

'Might? Might what, Miss Cahill?'

'It's Mrs Cahill, sir.'

The 'sir' slipped off her tongue involuntarily. She cursed herself for kow-towing to the martinet in the hand-tailored suit who, though only eight or ten years her senior, somehow managed to convey the self-righteous pomposity of a much older man.

He had the rugged jaw, cleft chin and thin lips that made all Lord Boscombe's sons instantly recognisable when they turned up at Ascot, Henley or Lords and that rendered them so distinctive that no door was ever closed to them, no post considered out of reach.

One brother was already in parliament, another in Naval Intelligence and Leonard, the youngest, was a fighter pilot with the RAF defending Britain in fierce air battles over the Channel but, being a Boscombe, would no doubt survive everything the German aces could throw at him and live to be crowned a hero.

It was no mystery why Walter had gravitated towards broadcasting. Broadcasting offered access to power on a grand scale. When the war was over and victory won, Mr Walter Boscombe would be in an ideal position to govern one of the world's most influential institutions. Right now his gaze was not on the far horizon but firmly fixed on what might be wrought in a smelly studio in Scobie Street, Soho, by taking over responsibility for a programme that the PM himself had praised as 'valuable' and that had all the potential to become a springboard, as Walter saw it, for shaping history which, after all, was what being a Boscombe was all about. Such grandiose ambitions were not shared by Susan whose aspirations were much more modest and in that dizzy hour of a dizzy day added up to little more than having her head patted by a man she heartily despised.

'I don't see Michael Foot on your list, Mrs Cahill.'

'Mr Foot was unavailable, sir.'

'Luke Williams?'

'Correspondent for the *Mirror*, sir.'

'Is that the best you could do?'

'Given the circumstances . . .'

He handed her back the clipboard with a flick of the wrist. She knew then that the informality of her relationship with Basil Willets was a thing of the past and that the sort of rapport she might have established with Stuart Powers, if he'd lived, would be impossible with this cold-blooded autocrat.

'The circumstances are immaterial, Mrs Cahill,' Walter Boscombe said. 'Is Foot available for Tuesday?'

'I really couldn't say, sir.'

'Didn't you ask him?'

'I only spoke with – I think it was his wife.'

'You think?' said Walter Boscombe. 'Don't you know?'

'The line was very bad.'

He sighed. 'Well, I suppose we'll have to struggle on with the programme as arranged for this evening, but Tuesday can, I'm sure, be saved.'

'Saved?' said Susan, through her teeth.

'Improved. Now, do I have an office?'

'There's my office, sir. I mean, an office.' She corrected the gaffe at once but not, it seemed, quickly enough for Mr Boscombe.

He said, 'Your office, Mrs Cahill? Since when did production assistants become entitled to have offices to themselves?'

'Mr Willets . . .'

'Mr Willets is *hors de combat* and will not be returning for quite some time. Meanwhile, we'll be using the Calcutta to transmit programmes to the North American networks until repairs on the House are completed. I will be overseeing all programme planning and personally producing *Speaking Up for Britain* on an expanded slate of three sixty-minute programmes each week. There will be no broadcast on Thursday evening next week but we will proceed at once to the new time. Our own little midnight matinee. I trust the late hour will not intrude upon your beauty sleep. In future North American transmissions will go out from 9.15 p.m. to 4.45 a.m. every night, and we will contribute to the schedule from here.' He paused, then added, 'I'll want all those seats out and the stage cleared for singers and bands as soon as possible.'

'Bands?'

'Must you repeat every word I say, Mrs Cahill? It's a thoroughly annoying habit and one I hope you'll break if we are to work together.'

'Work . . .' Susan began, then, 'May I take it I'm being kept on?'

'I assume you *can* type and take dictation?'

'Yes.'

He snapped his fingers. 'Then fetch your notepad and follow me, Mrs Cahill, and we'll set about making this dismal hole as habitable as possible.'

Susan was not deceived into believing that Mr Boscombe's bark might be worse than his bite and directors of the North American service wielded enough power to get things done in a hurry when it suited them. By six that evening, she was set up in a cubby with a telephone, a typewriter, a desk, a chair with a moth-eaten cushion, a filing cabinet that took up far too much space, a well-stocked stationery drawer, a catering-sized tin of Nescafé and two pounds of sugar in a sealed glass jar that, said Mr Boscombe, would give the rats something to think about before they succumbed to the poison that the electricians had put down for them.

Guest announcer Jack Cavill was a genial chap with a Tom Sawyer sort of grin. He knew Walter Boscombe well, apparently, and, to Susan's surprise, greeted her new boss with a most un-English bear hug. Jack hadn't been one of Bob Gaines's crowd of hard-drinking journalists from Lansdowne House but he had dined there often enough. If she hadn't been so tired Susan might have asked him for news of Robert but while she was not ashamed of how her less than glorious affair had begun she regretted how it had ended and wished only to put it behind her.

The engineers had done their job well. All links and connections were in place before eight when the red light came on and the hospitable American presenter read his introduction while Larry, Walter Boscombe and Susan crouched anxiously in a temporary listening booth and tried to ignore the muffled sounds of the air raid that filtered down from above.

When the programme ended there was none of the usual scramble to tidy up and join the queue in the canteen. Walter Boscombe thanked the engineers, put on his overcoat and hat, and invited Jack Cavill, Luke Williams and the embassy official to join him for a drink at his club, as if high-explosive bombs were no more threatening to life and limb than recorded sound effects.

He paused long enough to confront Susan at the door of the studio and ask when she was next on call. She told him that she was always on call if needed but that, it seemed, cut little ice with the new producer.

'I won't be in tomorrow,' he said. 'Have Friday off. You look as if you could use a break. I'll expect you at your desk on Saturday no later than eight thirty.' Then, without a thank you or a goodnight, he shepherded his cronies upstairs.

A dead rat held by the tail in one hand and a bottle of Scotch in the other, Larry appeared at her shoulder.

'Supper for two all right with you?' he said.

'Do not be disgusting.'

'What do you still have to do, Susan?'

'Fill in the log and tote up the fees for Finance.'

'Are you really keen on making a run for Portland Place? It's pretty heavy out there right now.'

'What's the alternative?'

'Having a snifter with me and my little friend here.'

'I'm not averse to sharing a bottle with you, Larry,' Susan said. 'But I'd prefer it if your friend found somewhere else to do his drinking. Besides which, I think he's had a drop too much already.'

Larry lobbed the corpse in the direction of the stalls where it landed with a soft thump.

'Hail fellow,' he said, 'well met. Your room or mine?'

'Mine.'

'Oooo,' said Larry. 'Will I have to fight for my honour?'

'Not a chance, me old mate,' Susan told him, smiling. 'Not one chance in a million.' And Larry, pulling the cork from the bottle with his teeth, followed her into the cubby.

The all-clear went off at half past four. Larry, sprawled over Susan's desk, didn't hear the signal but Susan, dozing in a chair, did. They shared a mug of coffee before going upstairs into the street. Smoke purled over the Soho rooftops and in the direction of Westminster the sky glowed red but Scobie Street was uncannily quiet. They climbed into Larry's sister's Morris Oxford and, en route to his sister's house in Kennington, Larry dropped Susan off at Salt Street. She kissed his hairy cheek by way of thanks, stumbled out of the motorcar and walked unsteadily down the narrow mews.

After days and nights indoors fresh air was welcome. The ache in her face had eased. She felt light, floating, still a little tipsy. There were fire-watchers on the roof of the insurance building that loomed over the mews. She could hear voices, male and female, drifting out of the darkness and, high overhead, the whine of fighter planes heading for home stations She fumbled the key that Viv had given her from her coat pocket, unlocked the front door, stepped into the hall and, leaning back, closed the door with her hip.

The darkness within was complete, the silence utter. She rested against the door, waiting for Vivian's sleepy shout, 'Is that you, Susan?' or Basil's cheerful 'In here,' from the kitchen. There were no sounds in the deserted house, however, no appetising smells, nothing and no one to greet her.

She found the light switch and flicked it up and down several times. The bulb in the hall did not come on. She felt her way across the hall to the living room and tried the main switch. No light: no electricity. Crouching, she felt for the line of the carpet. Then, overtaken by a vision of Vivian and Basil sprawled on the floor with their brains oozing on to the carpet, she shot upright and groped in a blind panic for a wall, a door, a window to give the room dimension and annul her terror of being alone in the dark.

She bumped her knees on the davenport, pressed her chest against the cushions, found the cord of the blackout curtains and gave it a tug. The curtains grated on the rail, opened a piece, stuck, then opened again. There was no sign of daylight but the window shape showed grey against black.

On her knees on the davenport, she cradled her head on her arms and let out a whimper of relief, a nasal sound that reverberated in the bones of her skull. She wept drily for a moment then bent her legs, tucked her elbows into her chest and, in that awkward position, fell asleep.

Broad daylight, a fine sunny morning; shafts of sunlight lit the familiar furnishings of the Willets' living room. The bulb in the ceiling fitting had come on but seemed inconsequential now. She rolled from the davenport and planted her feet on the floor. She was chilled, had a foul taste in her mouth and a ringing in her ears, a persistent ringing that, after a moment of confusion, she identified as the telephone in the office across the hall.

She lifted an arm and peered at her wristwatch: twenty past ten. She leaped to her feet, lurched across the living room, through the hall and, fearing that the ringing would cease before she reached the telephone, hurled herself into the office and snatched up the receiver.

'Mrs Cahill speaking,' she said breathlessly.

'At last,' said a delightfully irascible voice. 'It's about bloody time. Where have you – Viv, will you kindly hold the receiver up a bit. I'm not a damned dwarf, you know. Susan, are you there?'

'Yes. Where are you?'

'In a public phone box in the middle of nowhere. Wait – what's that? Gadney, Vivian informs me. The bustling metropolis of Gadney.'

'How are you feeling?'

'Sore. No telephone, no wireless at this cottage place. Dear God, I'd be better off in Pentonville. Can you hear me?'

'Not awfully well.'

'The broadcast, how did it go?'

'Fine, it went fine. No problems.'

'Which studio did you use?'

'We're in a temporary studio in Soho.'

'Soho!' said Basil. 'I didn't know we had a studio in Soho.'

'We have now,' said Susan.

'Did you find an announcer, since poor old Powers – since we lost poor old Powers?'

'Ray Cavill of CBS stood in.'

Susan pressed her stomach against the edge of the desk and squeezed her knees together. She heard the rattle of coins being fed into the box and Basil cursing, then, 'Look, you'll have to find a regular announcer. You can't go on scratching about for . . .'

'It isn't up to me,' Susan said. 'We've a new producer.'

'What? Who?'

'Mr Boscombe.'

'Walter Boscombe?'

'Yes.'

'Oh, bugger!' Basil said and then, with a noise like bacon frying in a pan, the connection faded out.

Ten minutes later, with no more word from Basil, Susan tumbled into bed and, within seconds, was dead to the world.

4

It was all Steve Pepperdine's idea and a pretty crazy one at that. But that was Steve Pepperdine for you, a forty-two-year-old boffin with a brain the size of a barrage balloon and enough letters after his name to fill a page of *Wisden's* who, far from being shy and retiring, had promoted himself, quite unofficially, into the role of Entertainments Officer for Orrell's Engineering Works.

'I don't care if he is a genius,' Morven Hastie said. 'I think he really wants to be George Formby. If he keeps strolling round the canteen strumming that blessed banjo much longer I won't be responsible for my actions. Doesn't he ever do any work over in that shed of his?'

'Oh, yes,' said Trudy Littlejohn, who was, without doubt, Mr Pepperdine's number one fan. 'He's the top man in his field. Stanley says we're exceedingly lucky to have him.'

'What,' said Morven, 'is his field?'

'Gyroscopes,' Trudy promptly replied.

'My cousin has one of those,' Morven said. 'My cousin can make it dance on a bit of string. What's so special about gyroscopes?'

'It's all very hush-hush,' Trudy Littlejohn confided, though she had no more idea of what really went on behind the closed doors of No. 3 Shed than anyone else. 'The Germans would love to get their hands on Mr Pepperdine.'

'Maybe we could trade him for Lord Haw-Haw,' Morven said. 'Serve the Jerries right if we landed them with "Our Stevie". He could be our secret weapon. Surrender, or I'll warble another chorus of "When I'm Cleaning Windows".'

'How ignorant you are,' said Trudy Littlejohn haughtily. 'It isn't a banjo; it's a ukulele. Being Scotch, I don't suppose we can expect you to understand traditional English folk song.'

'If that's traditional English folk song give me Harry Lauder any day,' said Morven. 'Who made this soup?'

'Don't look at me,' said Trudy. 'It's one of Mrs Greevy's specials.' She dipped her spoon into her bowl and sipped delicately. 'It tastes all right to me. Mulligatawny, isn't it?'

'Your guess is as good as mine,' said Morven. 'Seeing as how there's no rice and practically no mutton in it, it might as well be dishwater. An extra spoonful of curry powder wouldn't have done it any harm either.'

Mrs Littlejohn was unwilling to argue soup with Miss Hastie who, when it came to cooking, had no peer in Orrell's kitchens, a fact acknowledged by the murmurs of approval that greeted any of the dishes over which Morven had waved her ladle.

Trudy prudently changed the subject. 'If you're all so down on Mr Pepperdine,' she said, 'then no doubt you won't be attending the auction he's arranged to start off our Spitfire Fund.'

'What auction?' Breda said.

'What Spitfire Fund?' said Morven.

Trudy smiled smugly and dabbed her lips with a napkin that she carried in her handbag for just that purpose. 'Oh, now we're interested, are we? Well, I take it you – even you, Morven – know that institutions that collect enough money to buy a Spitfire can ask for their name to be painted on the fuselage.'

'Whose name would that be?' said Breda.

'Steve Pepperdine's,' Morven suggested. 'Available for weddings, funerals and lunchtime concerts?'

'Orrell's Engineering Works,' Trudy corrected.

'The Navy Board'll never stand for it,' said Breda. 'Buyin' a plane for the RAF is bad enough but advertising a top-secret establishment on the fuselage could 'ave us all in jail.'

Morven said, 'If we really want a Spitfire of our own why don't we give clever wee Stevie a few bits of canvas, a pot of glue and an old car engine and he can knock one up for us.'

'I can see you're not taking this seriously,' said Trudy.

'I am,' said Breda. 'What's going under the 'ammer?'

'All sorts of things,' said Trudy. 'Greene's of Evesham are putting up a free perm, for instance. The manager of the Clifton has offered four tickets for any film of the winner's choosing.'

'Oh, wonderful!' said Morven. 'How about something useful?'

'Small barrel of beer, home-brewed, from Mr Smethurst,' Trudy responded. 'Six bottles of cider from Bradshaw's. Basket of fruit from the Groves. Knitted helmets from my mother-in-law – Stanley's mother, that is – suitable for children up to six.'

'Really?' said Breda, sitting up.

'Shoes . . .'

'Oh, yer?' said Breda, sitting up higher still.

'Beautiful shoes,' said Trudy, 'from my very own wardrobe.'

'Still hot from the anvil then?' Morven muttered.

'Red suede with ankle straps and diamanté buckles, if you must know, made by Bally of Switzerland, and never worn,' Trudy went on. 'Far too good for the likes of you, of course.'

'What size?' said Breda.

'A little too large for me,' Trudy replied, 'which is why they haven't been worn. I've a very dainty foot, you see. You *might* be able to squeeze into them, I suppose, at a pinch.'

'Didn't you try them on before you bought them?'

'They were a gift,' said Trudy wistfully, 'from a special friend.'

'How much,' said Breda, 'do you want for them?'

'They're not for sale. You have to bid against other people and highest bid wins.'

'I do know what an auction is,' said Breda.

'When is this auction thing taking place?' Morven enquired.

'Saturday week at two thirty.'

'Where?' said Breda.

'In the church hall. Stanley's church: Shay Bridge St John's. Stanley's involved, you see. He and Steve—'

'Steve, is it?' said Morven. 'Pal of yours, is he?'

'A good friend,' Trudy said, 'of the church.'

'Let me guess,' said Morven. 'He plays the ukulele at Sunday School outings.'

'And Harvest festivals,' said Trudy, oblivious to sarcasm. 'He'll be compering the Christmas concert.'

'Oh, joy!' said Morven as Mr Jackson appeared in the side door of the kitchen and tapped his watch to remind them that the mid-morning dinner break was over. 'Perhaps he'll do some tricks with his gyroscope.'

The women rose to clear the table, carrying bowls, plates, cups and cutlery with them into the kitchen.

Breda hovered by Trudy Littlejohn's elbow. 'Them shoes,' she said, 'what are they liable to fetch?'

'If they go for a penny less than thirty shillings I'll be amazed.'

'Thirty bob!' said Breda, frowning. 'Blimey, they must really be something special.'

'Oh, they are, I assure you,' Trudy said. 'Are you interested in bidding for them, Mrs Hooper?'

'Nope,' Breda lied, 'just curious, that's all.'

The shift system at Wood Norton's monitoring unit was flexible in the extreme. Breaking news, a babble of reports broadcast from different foreign stations in a dozen different languages, required not only accurate translation but evaluation too. At the long table in the editorial hut, Griff and Danny helped compile a weighty daily news digest to circulate to all the government departments where decisions hung upon up-to-the-minute information. Kate crouched in a cubicle in the monitoring hut with earphones, a notepad and recording cylinders interpreting the unending chatter that poured from the foreign stations. It was, therefore, unusual for all three of Mrs Pell's 'guests' to be at home together.

Mrs Pell coped with the erratic timetable without a word of complaint. She was always on hand to rustle up a plate of toast, a pan of chips, a bowl of soup or a mug of hot cocoa. She seemed to thrive on five hours' sleep a night and a catnap in her armchair after lunch. She was no gossip, no chatterbox and held herself aloof from the often malicious tittle-tattle that passed for neighbourly conversation in Deaconsfield. She respected her guests' privacy but was always delighted to be taken into their confidence and, when asked, to give them the benefit of her opinion.

The snug little back kitchen was even more snug than usual that October morning. For once. Kate, Griff and Danny would set off together for the trek to Wood Norton just as soon as they'd stoked up on coffee and French toast. The wireless in the living room was turned up to full volume but it was too early for the eight o'clock news and, thanks to a bit of crafty tuning on Griff's part, provided a soothing background of dance music from a ballroom somewhere in Holland. With a slice of toast in one hand and a coffee mug in the other, Griff performed a nifty little *pas de deux* with his sweetheart and kissed her cheek.

Mrs Pell said, 'Now, now, enough of that, this time of the morning,' not because she objected to displays of affection between the happy couple but simply to spare Danny's feelings.

She was well aware that Danny had a crush on Kate Cottrell and had suffered a bruised if not a broken heart when she, Kate, had fallen for Griffith's charm and agreed to become his wife. Danny had sulked for a while after the engagement came to light but he was too fond of Griff and Kate to bear a grudge for long.

The wedding would take place in Coventry. Kate had taken two days' leave to travel up to Coventry to be fitted for a wedding dress and Griff and Danny had arranged leave for the wedding itself. Kate would go up a day in advance, Danny and Griff arrive together on the evening before the ceremony. Danny would return to Evesham as soon as the wedding was over but Silwyn Griffiths and his new bride would slip off for a forty-eight-hour honeymoon before returning to their duties at the monitoring unit. All the plans were in place, the sailing, on the surface at least, smooth. What worried Mrs Pell, however, was what would happen afterwards.

There had been heated exchanges with the district billeting officer who was all for transferring the newly-weds into married quarters in one of the houses up by Shay Bridge but Griff wouldn't have it. Danny, he declared, could surely move across the landing into the small bedroom currently occupied by Kate, and Kate and he would take the larger room that he presently shared with Danny. The arrangement made sense in theory but in practice, Mrs Pell thought, might turn out to be awkward, not least for Danny.

In the crowded kitchen that morning the chat was not about the latest news from Europe or the up-and-coming American presidential election, or even the Coventry wedding. Griffiths and Mrs Pell had had little opportunity to talk with Danny since his return from London and Kate hadn't seen him at all.

'Now we have a moment,' Griff said, 'albeit just a moment, how were things in the big bad city?'

'Depressing,' Danny answered. 'It's a relief to be back.'

Kate said, 'Much damage to Broadcasting House?'

'Quite a lot,' said Danny. 'Fourth an' third floors took the worst of the hit an' some programmes have been moved out to temporary studios, my wife's among them.'

Casually, Kate asked, 'How is your wife?'

'Lost the tip of an earlobe an' a bit of blood but still firin' on all cylinders. She's okay, I reckon. I didn't see much of her.'

Mrs Pell, breaking eggs into the frying pan, said, 'What about your house in London?'

'The flat?' Danny held his coffee cup in both hands and blew into it, steaming up his glasses. 'It's being demolished. Susan'll have some cash coming but we rescued nothin' from the wreckage. That's my fault. If I tried harder, I might . . .' He shrugged, laid the cup on the dresser and wiped the steam from his glasses with his necktie. 'It's a hell of a mess up there, an' no sign of things lettin' up. I didn't go down tae the East End. There's nobody there I care about now an' nothing much tae see except destruction.'

'Oh, Danny,' Kate said softly. 'I'm sorry.'

Danny shoved the glasses on to his nose and lifted his coffee cup. 'Nothin' to be sorry about,' he said. 'It's like another world, another life. What happened then has no connection tae what's happening here an' now. If it wasn't for Breda an' the wee boy, I'd wonder if it ever happened at all.'

'That's very philosophical of you, old son,' said Griff. 'Living in the moment is the only thing for a chap like you to do, I suppose.'

'A chap like me?' Danny said.

'Unattached,' Griff said. 'Well, at least semi-detached.'

'I've two more slices of French toast, if anybody's interested,' Mrs Pell put in hastily. 'Best grab them before Mr Pell comes downstairs. You'd better shake a leg if you don't want to be late. Are you going for the bus?'

'Bikes,' Danny said. 'I'll trot alongside.'

'No, it's my turn to trot.' Griff lifted one of the slices of eggy toast from the plate that Mrs Pell held out and bit off a corner. 'What happened to that job in the newsroom in HQ that seemed to be coming your way, Daniel? Did you talk to anyone about that when you were up in the Smoke?'

'Naw,' said Danny curtly.

'It's a leg up, isn't it?' Griff went on. 'A stepping stone to bigger and better things within the Corporation. Weren't you offered it after all?'

Danny hesitated. 'I turned it down weeks ago. I've no desire tae work in London right now.'

'I thought you might want to be near your wife,' Griff said.

'You're dripping, Silwyn,' Kate informed him and, seizing a drying cloth from the rack by the sink, held it under his chin. 'Please don't eat and argue at the same time.'

'Wasn't arguing,' Griff said through a mouthful of toast.

He stood upright and allowed his intended to wipe a smear of butter from his lips. 'I was asking Danny a simple question. I know if I were offered an editing post in the newsroom in Broadcasting House I'd jump at it.'

'And leave me behind?' said Kate.

'Good Lord, no,' Griff said. 'I'd take you with me.'

'What if I didn't want to go?'

'Then I'd have to think twice about it, wouldn't I?' Griff said.

'You wouldn't catch me going to London if I didn't have to,' said Mrs Pell. 'I'd be too frighted of all them bombs.'

'Quite right,' said Griffiths. 'On the other hand I don't share Daniel's sufficient-unto-the-day view of life. How can I when I'll soon have a wife to take care of? Now's the time to get a foot in the door before the chaps come flooding back looking for jobs in the BBC.'

'And when will that be – boyo?' said Danny.

'Three years, four years,' Griff said. 'What does it matter? I have absolutely no intention of waiting for the future to catch up with me. As far as I'm concerned an editing table in Wood Norton is just the first rung on the ladder. Broadcasting's the way of the future and that's the future for me – for us, dear, for us.'

'Assuming we win the war,' said Kate.

'Of course, we'll win the war,' said Griff. 'When we do, I want to be poised to take full advantage of the victory.'

'If I were you, Griffiths,' said Mr Pell from the doorway, 'I'd get myself poised to pedal off to work. Been a touch of frost overnight und the road'll be slippy.'

'Duly noted,' Griff said.

Swallowing a last mouthful of coffee, he buttoned his sheepskin overcoat, slung a scarf around his neck and, waiting for no one, not even Kate, threw open the back door and stepped out into the cold, dark morning air to check the tyres on the bicycles and make sure the hooded lamps were charged.

Kate buttoned her overcoat too, put on her beret and pulled it down over her ears. 'You mustn't mind him, Danny,' she said, as they went to the door. 'He gets carried away with himself from time to time and doesn't know what he's saying.'

'I'm used to it,' Danny said. 'Anyroads, you've got tae admire his optimism. At least he knows where he's going.'

'Or thinks he does,' said Kate and, shivering a little, took Danny's arm and stepped out into a yard silvered with the first faint frost of winter.

The siren sounded an air-raid warning shortly after three. Madge Gaydon, Billy and the girls came haring down Deaconsfield Road and ducked into the Anderson shelter that Mr Pell had buried in his back garden where, bearing cups of milky tea and a plate of scones on a tray, Mrs Pell soon joined them.

Mr Pell had made a very good job of building the shelter and, for added protection, had turfed over the curved metal sheets that stuck out of the ground. He had fitted steps, a stout wooden door and, below, two bunks and a bench. He had stocked it with blankets, pillows, lamps and bottled water which so far had not been needed.

There was no sign of German aircraft over the Avon but the pumping of an ack-ack battery on the side of the hill behind the hospital indicated that something was up there, apart from the fish-shapes of two barrage balloons far off in the distance.

Madge Gaydon and Mrs Pell stood at the door of the shelter scanning the sky and listening intently for the sound of aeroplane engines but there was nothing to see and nothing to hear save the faint puttering of a tractor whose driver had obviously decided to ignore the warning.

In the shelter Mrs Gaydon's daughters tucked into scones and milky tea but Billy crouched on a corner of the bench with his knees drawn up to his chest and his thumb in his mouth.

'What's wrong with him?' Dorothy Gaydon asked.

'He's scared,' her sister, Linda, answered.

Billy took his thumb from his mouth. 'Ain't scared.'

'He looks scared to me,' said Dorothy.

'There, there, boy,' said Linda, a precocious seven-year-old. 'You got nothing to be scared of. You want that tea?'

Billy shook his head.

Linda placed her empty cup on the tray and took up the full one. She sipped daintily, eyeing the gruff, untidy little boy with more curiosity than sympathy. Her sister reached for the last of the scones with the sort of superior smile only a pretty six-year-old can deliver.

'He's scared, he is.' She dabbed a crumb from the corner of her lips with a pinkie. 'I unt scared. I unt a cowardy custard.'

From a north-easterly direction two Hurricanes, flying low and fast, passed over Deaconsfield. Mrs Gaydon and Mrs Pell, shading their eyes with their palms, nodded approvingly as if the planes had been mustered specifically to defend the folk of the Vale from the dastardly Hermann Goering.

'That'll sort 'um,' Mrs Gaydon said.

'Yes, it will,' Mrs Pell agreed. 'Serve 'um right too.'

A piercing scream emerged from within the Anderson shelter. The women stiffened, glanced at each other and dived for the steps.

Cups were upturned on the earthen floor, tray, plate and the remnant of a scone too. Billy and the Gaydon girls wrestled among the spillings, Dorothy, squealing, at the bottom of the heap, Billy on top of her. Piled on top of Billy, Linda had her arms around his neck and, just as her mother stooped to pull her off, sank her teeth into Billy's ear and worried it as a terrier does a rat.

Madge Gaydon caught her daughter by the shoulders and yanked her upright. Lips flecked with blood, Linda fought to return to the fray. It was all Madge could do to hold her back. Mrs Pell stepped in to detach Breda's boy gently from the tangle. Bursting into tears, he buried his face in her skirt, while Dorothy, sprawled on her back in the dirt, screamed blue murder.

'The brute, the little brute, what's he done to you?' Madge Gaydon cried. Dropping to her knees, she attempted to calm her hysterical daughter while Linda, panting, rubbed her wrist across her mouth and licked away the blood as if it were jam.

Although she was small in stature and Billy no light weight, Mrs Pell carried him up the steps. He clung to her like a monkey, legs twined around her waist, arms around her neck, face pressed into her breast, sobbing so hard she feared he would choke before she could get him indoors.

Far away the AA guns popped and the waspish hum of the Hurricanes faded into silence. The siren on the post by the schoolyard gate sang the all-clear. And little Mrs Pell carried her precious bundle into the house and slammed the door with her heel.

'How is he?' Danny looked down at Billy curled in the bunk.

'He's settled now, thank God,' said Breda. 'What a state 'e was in, though. Never seen 'im like that before. I gave 'im hot milk with a teaspoon of whisky and half a crushed Aspro. He was shaking like a leaf, poor lamb. I wrapped 'im in a blanket till the stove heated.'

'Did he eat anything?'

'Some tinned mince and mashed potato. What am I gonna do about tomorrow?' Breda said. 'I'm sure she won't take 'im to school, that cow – Madge Gaydon, I mean. Mrs Pell says she'll do it but she's done enough already. 'Sides, what 'appens when he gets there? I mean, with those girls?'

'What did the girls say to him?'

'Called 'im a coward.'

'That'd do it,' Danny said. 'That an' the siren.'

'She bit 'im, you know, that little cow bit 'im.'

'Does Mrs Gaydon know what happened to Billy?'

'I doubt it,' Breda said. 'I told Mr Gaydon but not 'er.'

It was after nine before Danny had arrived at the Nook; a cold night, no longer clear and star-studded. She'd known he would hear the tale from Mrs Pell and come at once; that was Danny, her Danny.

She said, 'I ain't seen you since you got back from London.'

'Been on two straight shifts,' Danny said. 'We didn't even lift our heads when the siren went off this afternoon.'

The siren had wailed its warning in Orrell's too. Wardens and fire-watchers had galloped to their posts but there had been little interest shown in the raid in the canteen kitchen and no one had stopped work. Deftly shaping fish-cakes in one of the bays, Morven had called out cheerfully, 'As my old granny used to say, "Whit's fur ye will no' go by ye," and she lived to be ninety.' Ten minutes later the all-clear had sounded, the back-shift staff had trailed in and Breda had left to pick up Billy from the Pells.

She'd bobbed down Deaconsfield Road with her head full of red shoes with ankle straps and diamanté buckles. She'd had a pair like that – though not Swiss made – when she'd been a fast young thing and showered with gifts from assorted boyfriends. Presents were one thing, cash quite another. She'd never taken a penny from any of them, not even the flash Harry to whom she'd first given her all – and a damned painful all it had been too – in a hotel room in Margate three weeks before she'd turned sixteen. When Mrs Pell had opened the door and she'd seen the expression on Mrs Pell's face, however, all thought of shoes, past and future, had fled.

She was afraid to let Billy out of her sight now even for the five minutes it took her to draw water from the well behind the railway carriage. Everything was tainted by a fear that Billy would be plucked away like his dad, that even here among quiet fields and market gardens, he wasn't safe from the terror from the skies.

'Did you see Susie?' she asked.

'Aye, for all of five minutes,' Danny answered.

'Didn't you stay over with 'er?'

'She was busy, like she always is.' Danny seated himself on Breda's bunk. 'You don't have to be polite, sweetheart. I know you don't give a damn about Susan right now. Tae tell you the truth I don't give much of a damn about her either. Susan can look after herself.' He put an arm about Breda's shoulder and let her rest her head against his chest. 'I'm a lot more worried about you.'

'Doncha think I can look after myself?'

'You can't fool me, Breda. I've known you too long to be taken in. You're scared an' won't admit it.'

'I'm scared for Billy, not myself.'

'The worst kinda fear is the one you can't control. That's why your ma says her prayers every night and gallops off tae church to ask the good Lord to do what she can't do for herself. I used to think His eye was on the sparrow,' Danny said. 'That's what the nuns told me, an' I believed them. As long as God had His eye on the sparrow He didn't have His eye on me, which was just Jim Dandy.'

She wanted him to kiss her, make her forget her stupid fears, sweep them away on a tide of passion, as if this were a serial in *Red Star Weekly*; the sort of counterfeit passion that excluded things like knickers and brassieres and small boys who'd been buried alive, a lovely, dreamy fleshless passion that remained unconsummated, on the page at least, one in which the hero didn't kiss you while blathering about God and sparrows.

She snuggled closer. 'Did you ever try to find out who your mother was, or your father?'

'Never did,' said Danny. 'Never thought much about it, an' after a while I didn't care. I had food tae eat, a warm bed to sleep in an' clothes on my back. Whether it was God or the nuns that cared for me was immaterial. I still write tae old Father Flanagan now and then. He likes to know how I'm gettin' on.'

'I wonder what he'd say if he could see you right now?'

Danny laughed. 'Lucky bugger, that's what he'd say. Old Father Flanagan always had a thing for a good-lookin' girl.'

'Do you really think I'm good-lookin', Danny?'

'Stop fishin', Breda. You know you're a doll.'

'I don't feel like a bleedin' doll these days, I can tell yer. I feel like an old bag most of the time. I'll bet she still looks like a million dollars, war or no war.'

'Fact is, Susie looks like somethin' the cat dragged in.'

'Really?' said Breda. 'Honest injun?'

'Honest injun,' Danny assured her.

'Well,' said Breda, 'that makes me feel a whole lot better.'

'Thought it might,' said Danny.

It was warm in the coach, a little too warm, perhaps.

Breda disentangled herself from his arms, got up and went to the water bucket, dipped the kettle in and put it on top of the stove.

'What,' she said over her shoulder, 'should I do about Billy? Knowing Madge Gaydon it'll be all over the school what a savage little tyke he is and he's bound to get bullied.'

'Bring him to Mrs Pell's as usual,' Danny said. 'I'll take him to school an' have a quiet word with the teacher.'

'What about your shift?'

'I reckon the BBC can survive without me for an hour or so,' Danny said. 'Griff will come up with an excuse. He's a plausible wee Welshman when it suits him.'

As it turned out there was no need for Griff to perjure himself or for Danny to be more than a few minutes late reporting to the editing room at Wood Norton.

Breda had risen even earlier than usual to put coals in the stove and prepare Billy his favourite breakfast of sausages, the last of her meat ration for the week. She made toast, slice by slice, on the toy grill that topped the Calor gas-fired oven, slathered the slices with margarine and set them on the side table tucked between the foot of her bunk and the larder. She poured warm water from the kettle into a baking bowl, soaked a face-cloth and, with the instrument of torture ready to hand, wakened her offspring and before he knew what hit him, washed his face, dabbed away the tiny spots of dried blood from his lug, and told him to get up and dress.

He seemed more subdued than usual but, gratifyingly, did justice to sausage, toast and cocoa while Breda pandered to her nerves with tea and a cigarette before she washed her face and combed her hair. Glumly, her son put on his shoes and struggled into a raincoat that was rapidly becoming too small for him.

'You near ready, Billy?'

The familiar truculent growl was muted: 'Yus.'

She had no idea whether he was simmering with anger, ashamed of how he'd responded to the girls' taunts or afraid to face his classmates. Danny would wheedle it out of him in due course, for Danny was good at that kind of thing. She fed a shovelful of dross on to the fire, closed and locked the little door, checked that the cock on the Calor gas tank was off then opened the blackout curtains and turned off the paraffin lamps.

The knocking on the carriage door startled her and, in her nervous state, made her jump.

'Who is it?'

'Gaydon.'

'What do you want?'

'I've come to give Billy a ride to school.'

'No, thank you. We can manage very well on our own.'

'Breda' – he had never called her by her forename before – 'Breda,' he said, 'come out.'

She opened the carriage door reluctantly and, with Billy peeping round her, peered down at Fred Gaydon and his daughters trapped in a ring of torchlight.

'I think,' said Mr Gaydon, 'Linda has something to say to Billy, if he's there.'

'Oh, he's here.' Breda drew Billy out from behind her and held him against her skirts. Billy looked not at the farmer or his daughters but down at the ground at their feet.

The girl was not shy. If she resented being made to apologise she gave no sign of it. She threw back her head, tossed her thick blonde plait, and, as clearly as if she were reading a lesson in chapel, said, 'I am very sorry for what I did. I hope you may find it in your heart to forgive me.'

'Billy?' Breda administered a nudge with her knee. 'What do you 'ave to say to Linda?'

'Yus. Sorry.'

'Dorothy,' said Mr Gaynor, 'your turn.'

'You unt a cowardy-custud, not when you was bombed.'

Billy nodded gravely, stuck out his under lip, knitted his ferocious brows and said magnanimously, ''S'okay.'

'There we are,' Fred Gaydon said. 'All friends again. Now, if you're ready for the road, Mrs Hooper, I'll give you a ride in the cart as far as the Pells.'

'It's a bit early for school, ain't it?' Breda said.

'Mrs P will keep them for half an hour or so and see them to the school gate. Madge will collect at three as usual.'

'Is she – I mean, all right, your wife?'

'She is now,' Fred Gaydon said.

Breda found Billy's schoolbag and helped him into it. He stepped down from the railway carriage and stood awkwardly, staring at his shoes, until Linda, taking charge, reached for his hand.

'Fall in,' said Mr Gaydon. 'Column of route. All set.'

'All set, Daddy,' said Dorothy.

'Quick march.'

Breda, hastening now, slipped into her overcoat, pulled on her hat, stepped down from the carriage and closed the door.

It was still dark, though a broad seam of daylight showed just above the hedgerow. The ground was firm with frost, weeds and grasses glistening in the beam of Mr Gaydon's torch. He took her by the elbow to help her find her footing and then by the hand, as if she too were a child.

'He's all right, isn't he?' Mr Gaydon said.

'Yer, he's all right,' Breda said. 'How did you do it?'

'The girls know there's a war on, of course, but just what

it means and how people are suffering we've kept from them until now. Last night I showed them copies of *Picture Post*, nothing too gruesome, just photographs of the London blitz, smoke and ruined buildings and children like Billy sitting on piles of debris hugging a doll or a teddy bear. Even Dot, young as she is, understood. When I told them what had happened to Billy, Linda was appalled. It hadn't occurred to her what *blitz* really means or what the boy who lives in the railway carriage had gone through.'

'I hope you didn't tell them about his dad?' Breda said.

'No, they're only kids and we don't want that coming out.'

'And your wife?'

'Madge was unaware of Billy's ordeal. When I told her of it she calmed down at once. I heard her talking to the girls in their bedroom. It was her idea to have them apologise.'

'I don't quite know 'ow to thank you,' Breda said.

'I'm sure we'll think of something,' Mr Gaydon said.

PART TWO

All the Nice Girls

5

It soon dawned on Susan that the reason the Boscombes might be favoured by society was that they were darned good at whatever they chose to do. Her admiration increased in the run-up to the first midnight broadcast of *Speaking Up for Britain* which promised to be livelier than anything that she, or Basil for that matter, could possibly have dreamed up. Even cynical Larry was impressed by Walter Boscombe's vision, though less so by the condescending manner with which he treated his staff.

The third-floor studios in Broadcasting House remained out of commission. Now that time and money had been spent equipping it, the cinema-studio would continue to be used for the time being. The Calcutta also had the advantage of being forty feet below ground and relatively safe during air raids. Partitioned cubicles served as offices, a snack bar of sorts was set up and, within a week, Mr Boscombe's propaganda bridgehead was up and running.

On afternoons of the late night broadcasts Susan arrived at four and signed off officially at 1 a.m. On Tuesdays, Thursdays and Saturdays, she worked from noon until seven. With no family or friends in London, now that Viv and Basil had gone to the country, the unsocial hours suited her. She slept in her own bed and had time to do laundry, shop and cook a decent supper – or was it breakfast? – in Vivian's spacious kitchen.

To celebrate, she had her hair done, purchased a new brown wool tweed suit from Bourne & Hollingsworth and two pairs of silk stockings that she hoped would impress her boss.

Larry greeted her with a wolf whistle but, to her disappointment, Walter Boscombe appeared not to notice her remodelled look.

'Ciphers, that's all we are, love,' Larry Baines informed her. 'Let's face it, to the imperious Boscombe we're only myrmidons employed for his greater glory. If you showed up in your birthday suit I doubt if he'd turn a hair – which is not to imply that our Walter prefers boys to girls. It's common knowledge he's a devil with the ladies.'

'You're worse than an old wife, Larry,' Susan said. 'Where *do* you get your information?'

'From the *Tatler,* the *Mail* and the *Star*,' said Larry. 'Nowt wrong with a bit of juicy gossip about the upper crust to titivate us peasants. If I wasn't so deuced fond of champagne I might even sign on as a Trotskyite.'

'And give up your chance of a knighthood?'

'Good point, Susan, good point.'

News, Walter Boscombe declared, was the bedrock of broadcasting, its *raison d'être*. Henceforth *Speaking Up* would provide as much raw news as possible, flanked by talks, interviews and comments. He would not, however, attempt to beat the American broadcasters at their own game by introducing on-the-spot reports from London rooftops or the decks of cargo ships, nor would he surrender to the public's taste for dubious tales of heroism and miraculous escapes from death.

He was much concerned with 'voice', with the inflexions

that elevated a good script into a great one. He rehearsed each speaker personally, no matter who they were, and a rumour went around that he had once corrected the Archbishop of Canterbury's pronunciation of 'Deuteronomy', though that was never proved.

Finding a regular announcer was no easy matter. After several interviews, Mr Boscombe settled on Zach Gillespie, a middle-aged Canadian liaison officer on the Empire Service who was keen to do more broadcasting.

Mr Gillespie was small, dapper, completely unflappable and, unlike so many of his colleagues, not in awe of Walter Boscombe. He had a warm and friendly delivery and enough experience of broadcasting to have no fear of the microphone. He sported a neat moustache, a spotted bow-tie and a range of plaid sports jackets that were the envy of half the young men on the crew. His only flaw, if flaw it was, was his infernal politeness. He was indiscriminately polite to everyone, from tea-ladies to sound technicians, and, within a few days of his arrival, knew everyone by name which, said Larry, was one in the eye for aloof old Boscombe.

Geraldo's Orchestra was employed to record the programme's musical introduction: thirty-six bars of an up-tempo number that most certainly wasn't Mozart and sixteen bars of a haunting saxophone solo for fade out. Then, with everything finally in place, on the stroke of midnight on Monday, 28th October the restyled programme finally went on air.

Susan wasn't in the least surprised that the telephone was ringing at half past six on Tuesday morning. She let herself into the mews house and, following the beam of her blue-bulb torch, made her way into Viv's office to answer the call.

'Yes, Basil,' she said wearily. 'What can I do for you?'

'You can begin by telling me what the devil Boscombe thinks he's up to?' Basil shouted into her ear loudly enough to make the scars from her stitches ache. 'Seven items, seven items and that damned jazz band blaring away.'

Susan pulled out a chair and slumped at Viv's desk. 'What are you doing up at this hour, Basil? I thought you were supposed to be convalescing.'

'Don't change the subject.'

'Surely you're not in a phone box in Gadney?'

Vivian claimed a share of the mouthpiece. 'Unfortunately, we've acquired some new-fangled short-wave wireless that can receive the American Service,' she said, 'and, as if that wasn't bad enough, David's had a telephone installed in the cottage.'

'How is he: Basil, I mean, not David?'

'Not at all well.'

'Give me that damned phone, Vivian, please. Susan?'

'I'm still here.'

'Well, talk to me?'

'Of course. Sorry. We've a regular announcer starting on Wednesday. Zach Gillespie, a Canadian. He's a very nice chap with lots of experience.'

'I know Gillespie. He's all right. I can work with Gillespie.'

'When are you coming back?'

Vivian claimed the mouthpiece again. 'Whatever he tells you, don't believe a word of it. He's nursing an infection. Something in the lung. Fluid. Doctor isn't happy . . .'

'Quack. Damned quack.'

'. . . isn't happy at all. Is the house still intact, by the way?'

'Yes, I think so. I've only just got in.'

'Vivian, give me the phone. Thank you. Susan?'

'Yes.'

'Is there going to be a place for me on *Speaking Up*?'

'The proper place for you right now,' said Vivian in the background, 'is your bed.'

'I honestly don't know, Basil,' Susan told him. 'It's not the sort of thing Mr Boscombe discusses with me and I've heard nothing on the rumour mill. I'm sorry you didn't like the programme.'

'Flashy, it's flashy, that's what it is. I knew this would happen as soon as Boscombe got control. He's nothing but a blasted liberal with fancy ideas about what listeners want.'

'He'd be surprised to be called a liberal,' Susan said. 'As for what listeners want – well, we'll just have to wait for the postbag.' She hesitated. 'It's something new, Basil, and I rather like it.'

'That's because you're a silly young woman.'

'Basil Willets!' Vivian yelled. 'How dare you!'

'Yes, yes, I apologise. I'm not quite myself these days. Susan, forgive me. I just don't want to see things reduced to the lowest common denominator and vulgarians like Walter Boscombe undermining the integrity of the BBC.'

'Tosh!' said Vivian loudly. 'From what I heard – and reception wasn't the best – it came over as something bright and original. I know I'm just an old crone and not supposed to have an opinion, let alone the right to express it, but – Basil, are you all right?'

'Actually, I do feel a trifle peculiar.'

'Here, give me the telephone. Susan, I'm putting him to bed. He's been fuming since you went off air and now he's had his say – Basil, if you're going to be sick please use the bowl. Listen, I have to go, Susan. I'll try to call you later.'

'I'll be here until . . .' Susan began but Vivian had hung up.

She rested her head on her arms on the desk. She'd known that Basil would resent losing control of his programme.

She felt disloyal to her old mentor for preferring Mr Boscombe's approach, stripped, as it was, of stuffiness. The press hacks would have their say, of course, but the acid test would be the letters that trickled in via the BBC's New York office.

Meanwhile, she was glad to have a job that promised excitement and relieved that she no longer felt the need to have a man calling the tune; no man, that is, but the autocratic Walter Boscombe who surely had no interest in shabby girls from Shadwell.

Susan had just emerged from the bath when the doorbell rang. The water had been tepid, the air in the bathroom chill and, clad in nothing but a damp towel, she'd scurried into the living room. She was kneeling before the electrical fire warming her vest and pants when the bell sounded. Her first thought was that the person at the door must be a chap from Civil Defence or, possibly, a Water or Gas Board official come to warn her that a main had been damaged and the mews was about to be evacuated.

The clock on the mantel told her it was ten minutes to eleven. She would be pushed to finish dressing, scoff some toast and make it to Scobie Street by noon.

She hesitated, hoping that the caller would go away.

The bell rang again.

Danny? she thought. Could it possibly be Danny? What her husband might be doing in London she couldn't imagine. She recalled the last time she'd come out of a bathroom clad in nothing but a towel and had found Danny standing in the living room of their flat and her lover, Robert Gaines, emerging, trouserless, from the door of the bedroom.

Once more the doorbell rang.

'All right, all right,' she shouted. 'Give me a minute.'

Muttering under her breath, she hurried into the Willets' bedroom and snatched Vivian's old woollen dressing gown from the hook behind the door. Barefoot and bare-legged, she padded into the hall and, pulling the dressing gown tightly over her body, slipped the catch and opened the door an inch or two.

Commanders in the Royal Navy, especially those in uniform, seldom looked sheepish but somehow Derek Willets, Basil's brother, managed it. He was eight or ten years younger than Baz, tall, lean and weather-beaten. He should have been a model of authority but, for an awkward moment, appeared as embarrassed as a schoolboy.

Then he grinned and held up a bottle.

'Milk, Mrs Cahill?' he said. 'One pint or two?'

'Oh!' Susan exclaimed. 'I'm afraid Vivian isn't at home. Do you want to come in?'

'You don't sound too sure?' Derek Willets said. 'Do you have someone with you?'

'What?' Susan exclaimed. 'Lord, no! What am I dreaming of. Come in, do come in.' She drew open the door, crouching behind it. 'If you'll excuse me, I'll finish dressing.'

'Of course.'

He tucked the milk bottle under his arm, picked up a small suitcase, a leather attaché case and his gas mask from the doorstep and waited while Susan gathered up her clothes and sought refuge in the master bedroom.

Seated on the bed, she pulled on her garter belt, pants and stockings. She could hear him moving about in the living room.

She called out, 'Please make yourself at home.'

'Have you had breakfast?'

'No.'

'I've some reasonably fresh Irish bacon in my dunnage

if you'd care for a rasher or two?' He was close to the door, just outside. She waited tensely for the door to open and Commander Willets to catch her on the bed in her underclothes, like a tart awaiting a client. He said, 'Tea, or would you prefer coffee?'

'Coffee would be lovely. There are a couple of eggs in the larder, I think. I shan't be long.'

'Take your time,' he said, and went away.

She finished dressing and, seated on the stool at Viv's dressing table, combed her hair, applied a dab of powder and a touch of Vivian's lipstick, then, drawing herself together, darted across the hall to her own bedroom to fetch her shoes.

She could hear fat sizzling in the frying pan and, above it, the odd sound of a high-ranking naval officer humming to himself. Smoothing her skirt, she braced herself and went into the kitchen.

The table was set for two. The kettle was beginning to boil and, having shed the jacket of his uniform, Commander Derek Willets was busy at the stove. He glanced over his shoulder, tapped an egg on the rim of the pan, decanted the contents expertly into the fat, dropped the shell into the bucket by the stove, tugged the tray from under the grill and deftly flipped over the slices of bread that were toasting there.

'I thought you were at sea?' said Susan.

'Still refitting. Shore leave.'

'Have you heard what happened to your brother?'

'Vivian sent me a telegram which somehow managed not to go astray. How is the old buzzard?'

'He's not all that well, I gather,' Susan said. 'They're down in Herefordshire, place called Gadney.'

'Vivian's brother's place?'

'No, though it isn't far from David's farm.'

'You've been there, have you?'

'Not since the war started.' She took a seat at the table and watched him slide a fried egg and three rashers of bacon on to a plate. 'I can't say I much care for David Proudfoot. I think, actually, he's lucky not to be in prison.'

'Friends in high places,' Derek Willets said. 'He was mixed up with Oswald Mosley's crowd but slipped the net, I believe, by turning his town house in Mayfair over to the government before it could be requisitioned. Rather fitting that the mansion of a fascist sympathiser should be occupied by the offices of a Jewish Resettlement Bureau, don't you think?'

He added a slice of buttered toast to her plate and put the plate before her. He filled his own plate, poured boiling water into the coffee percolator and took a seat at the table.

'Tuck in,' he said.

Susan lifted her fork, pierced the crown of the egg and let the yolk spill softly on to the bacon. 'Is David Proudfoot – I mean, is he a friend of yours?'

'Heavens, no. Never met the fellow and have no wish to,' Derek Willets said. 'I wouldn't go as far as to say he's a prisoner on that farm of his but the authorities keep a weather eye on him.'

'How do you know these things?'

He chewed, swallowed and tapped the side of his nose with his forefinger. 'My love-struck brother is married to Proudfoot's sister so, naturally, I made some enquiries – or, to put it more accurately, enquiries were made of me.'

'Really?' said Susan. 'I had no idea the security services were so thorough.'

'I'd hardly call them thorough,' Commander Willets said. 'They are nervous, however, exceedingly nervous. Churchill is not alone in having a bee in his bonnet about the enemy within. Vivian's new book raised a few eyebrows, I can tell you.'

'What?' Susan put down her fork. 'How can that be? It isn't published until April. I don't think she's even had a proof yet.'

'It was offered for extract to the editor of *The Times* who, by the by, has been "advised", shall we say, not to print a word of it.'

'My, my!' Susan said. 'You are in the know.'

'Any book with a title like *An Enemy in Our Midst* by a well-known radical author was bound to attract official attention.'

'The book's not all that radical.'

'Ah, you've read it?'

'Most of it,' Susan admitted. 'I helped out with some of the research. Basil thought he might do a programme or at least an item on it but somehow that didn't come to pass.'

'Internment of foreign nationals is one of those not-so-secret secrets that the government prefers to keep to itself.' Derek Willets gave the percolator a shake and poured a stream of hot coffee into Susan's cup. 'Vivian must surely have realised that the book would be controversial.'

'I'm not sure she did,' said Susan, 'not, at least, when she began writing it. Indignation got the better of judgement in the end.'

'In that case,' said Derek Willets, 'I'd better tread cautiously when we meet.'

'Are you going down to Gadney?'

'Tomorrow. My leave's up Friday. Would it be frightfully inconvenient if I put up here for a couple of nights? I mean, if you feel in any way compromised I'll check into a hotel.'

'Compromised?' Susan laughed. 'I've slept on the floor of a BBC dormitory with three hundred men *and* shared a bunk with beardless twerps from the BBC newsroom so, no, I really don't think spending a night or two under the same roof as a respectable naval officer is liable to make a headline in the William Hickey column. Take the master bedroom. There are clean sheets in the linen closet in the hall. Now, with the best will in the world, I really must scoot. What are the roads like?'

'Oxford Street's closed at Marble Arch but the buses are running. You should be all right for Portland Place.'

'Soho,' said Susan, rising. 'I'm working in Soho now.'

'A lady of the night?'

'More or less,' said Susan and, swallowing a last mouthful of coffee, hastily took her leave.

'If it's not too impertinent of me, sir,' said Larry, 'may I enquire what an Outside Broadcasting van is doing parked on the pavement and why it's being guarded by two soldiers?'

Walter Boscombe paused in his dictation of a letter to the Director of Military Intelligence inviting him to an informal lunch at the BBC. He slit the seal on a box of his special cigarettes, extracted a cigarette and lit it with a bullet-shaped petrol lighter.

He blew smoke, though not in Larry's direction.

'Close the door,' he said.

'Do you wish me to leave, sir?' Susan asked.

'No, but I do expect you to keep your mouth shut.'

Susan lowered her gaze to her notebook.

'If,' Walter Boscombe said, 'a word of this gets out before broadcast on Wednesday I will personally see to it that you are both sacked for insubordination.'

Larry took his hands from his pockets and stood up straight.

'Can – I mean, can you do that, Mr Boscombe?'

'Of course I can. I could have you shot, in fact.'

'Oh!' said Larry glumly. 'You're serious.'

'Never more so,' Walter Boscombe said. 'I've commissioned an item from a fellow who must remain incognito. He will shortly arrive by taxi-cab and immediately enter the OB van. Two recording engineers – not BBC staff – are already in the van. You, Baines, will supervise the recording and ensure that the disc is brought directly to me as soon as the recording is completed. Do you understand?'

Larry, with difficulty, refrained from clicking his heels.

'Sir,' he said.

Mr Boscombe dragged on the cigarette and pulled smoke deep into his lungs. 'Then I need you to adjust the playing speed to raise the voice pitch, to disguise it, in other words, without making the speaker sound like Mickey Mouse. I assume that's within your capabilities.'

Larry, lips pursed, nodded.

'No one else will be involved in the process. I'll see to it that you have exclusive use of the equipment. The rest of Wednesday night's programme will be built around the recorded talk. Gillespie, for his own protection, will not be in on the secret.'

'What,' said Larry, 'is the secret?'

'You're no doubt aware that Hitler and Franco recently held talks at a railway station in Hendaye up on the Spanish border.'

'No secret there, Mr Boscombe,' Larry said. 'It was splashed all over the newspapers. Lots of goose-stepping, saluting and flag-waving. The Americans covered it.'

'What is not known is how Franco responded to Herr Hitler's proposition that Spain join the Axis, or that Heinrich Himmler, who was part of the Nazi delegation, met privately with Franco's Foreign Minister and was handed a list of all the Jews in Spain.'

Susan closed her notebook and put it on the floor by her chair. She had learned a great deal about Spain's political divisions from her brother, Ronnie, and had kept abreast of what was happening in the country after Ronnie had died.

She heard herself say, 'Have you found someone willing to talk about it on air, Mr Boscombe?'

'I have. The introduction will not include his name, of course. We'll let the Spanish, not to mention the Germans, fret about who our correspondent might be. The script has been approved by the highest authority and sanctioned for broadcast. The report is revealing because it comes from someone who was actually on the spot, and by that I do not mean wandering about the platform in Hendaye railway station selling ice cream.'

'In other words, we're broadcasting a talk by a spy,' said Larry. 'Does the DG know what's going on, Mr Boscombe?'

'Yes, and he's not too happy about it, but not even he can ignore orders from Downing Street. Duff Cooper and Professor Cobbold have agreed to discuss the implications of the report, live, immediately after broadcast but they won't hear it in advance, nor will they be privy to the identity of the speaker.' Mr Boscombe ground his cigarette into the ashtray and got to his feet. 'That's all either of you needs to know. You, Baines, will be obliged to sign the Official Secrets Act, but it's merely a formality.'

'I bloody hope so – sir,' Larry said.

'Our anonymous guest should be arriving at any minute. Perhaps you'd better pop upstairs and be ready for him.'

'Won't you be joining us in the van, Mr Boscombe?'

'No.'

'So I'm to be the gentleman's only face-to-face contact with anyone in the BBC?' Larry said.

'So it would seem. Aren't you up for it?'

'Oh, yes, I'm up for it. Just one question, sir,' Larry said. 'Will we be using spies as correspondents regularly from now on?'

'Alas, no. This was a unique opportunity that I found impossible to resist.' He placed a less than avuncular hand on Larry's shoulder. 'You'd be surprised at what goes on behind all the red tape that Whitehall spits out. This isn't the first time, nor will it be the last, that the security services and the BBC feed from the same trough. There now, doesn't that stir the patriot in you?'

'It does, sir,' said Larry, 'but it doesn't surprise me.'

'You, Mrs Cahill, are you stirred by our clandestine affair?'

'I am, Mr Boscombe. I must admit, I am,' which, Susan realised, was no more than the truth. 'I take it that the talk has already been scripted?'

'It has, but only three copies exist and none of them will wind up in our filing system. Naturally, all requests to reveal our source will be firmly resisted. You're not sleeping with some Fleet Street hack, by any chance?'

'I'm not sleeping with anyone,' said Susan indignantly.

'Good, that's good,' Walter Boscombe said and, still with a hand on his shoulder, steered Larry out of the room. He closed the door and turned to face Susan. 'You're no fool, are you, Mrs Cahill? You do know what's happening here?'

'I think so, yes. You're putting *Speaking Up* on the map and giving it weight while avoiding the charge of producing propaganda. Jazz bands and quick pacing are just camouflage.'

'Yes, I fully intend to give those smug bastards on

European Round Up something to think about.' His hooded eyes showed a glint of amusement. 'You know all about propaganda, I suppose, since it's your husband's stock in trade. He's still labouring in the Evesham salt mines, I assume.'

'Yes, he is.'

'Editing the *Digest*?'

'I really couldn't say.'

'Why not?'

'He doesn't talk about it.'

'And, of course, you don't see much of each other?'

'That's true.'

'Tell me, Mrs Cahill, do you keep in touch with Bob Gaines?'

'No.'

'That's over, is it?'

'I really don't think that's any of your business, sir.'

'Oh, but it is,' Walter Boscombe said. 'I make it a point never to work with people I can't trust. I don't care what you think of me, Mrs Cahill, or what your friend Larry Baines and you say about me behind my back. What I require from you is absolute discretion and total commitment.'

'You have that, sir, I assure you.'

'Did you know that your husband had been offered a position in the newsroom here in London?'

'Yes,' Susan said. 'I did.'

'Why did he turn it down?'

'You'd have to ask him that.'

'I can fetch him back, if you wish,' Walter Boscombe said. 'The Overseas Service can always use a good editor. Wouldn't you like to have your husband by your side?'

Susan answered without hesitation. 'No.'

'Really? Why not?'

'He's safe where he is.'

'Safe is a relative term, Mrs Cahill,' Walter Boscombe said. 'I won't make the offer again. Are you sure?'

'Yes, I'm sure.'

'Good,' he said. 'That's good.'

Then, brusque and businesslike, he stepped behind the desk, settled in his chair and, almost before Susan had time to flip open her notebook, began dictating once more.

Searchlight beams converged on scudding cloud high over the insurance building and the familiar plaint of an air-raid warning sounded just as Susan entered the mews. She increased her pace, glanced anxiously up at fire-watchers on the parapet and heard a warden's whistle shrill in the crescent beyond the horse-posts.

A door in one of the mews' cottages opened and two women rushed out, followed by a man in uniform. Clutching bags and blankets, the women scuttled off to the shelter in the crescent. The man trotted past Susan without a nod or glance and vanished in the direction of Edgware Road. In the distance the crump of bombs was still too soft to be threatening and a flash of brilliant white light over Fulham faded quickly.

Huddled on the step, Susan fumbled in her bag for her house key. She was still fumbling when the door opened, a hand caught her arm and yanked her, none too gently, into the hall.

There was light in the living room – a table lamp – enough to outline the figure of Derek Willets, who, in a heavy roll-necked sweater and baggy corduroys, looked more like a down-at-heel artist than a naval officer.

'I'm not dressing for dinner,' he said, 'unless you insist.'

Something large and loud passed over the house. Susan and Derek Willets tilted their heads and stared at the ceiling.

'What is it?' Susan whispered. 'I mean, is it one of ours?'

'No, it sounds suspiciously like a Heinkel.'

'What do you want to do?' Susan asked.

'What do you mean?'

'There's an above-ground shelter at the far end of the mews if you want to make a dash for it,' Susan said.

'What's the alternative?'

'The cupboard under the stairs.'

'What does Basil do? Where does he shelter?'

'He doesn't,' Susan said. 'Vivian and he – well, it's more Viv's doing than Basil's – they don't take shelter at all. They brazen it out. Vivian sits in her armchair reading and Basil sits in his armchair doing *The Times* crossword, both pretending that nothing untoward is happening.'

'Perhaps we should try it.'

'I see no reason why not,' said Susan.

He helped her out of her coat and put it away in the hall cupboard and, Susan suspected, did a quick reconnaissance of the shelter while he was at it. She went into the living room, opened the sideboard and brought out a full bottle of gin, a half-empty bottle of tonic water and two glasses.

She heard him pad into the room.

'Will you join me?' she said.

'With pleasure. I take it we're *sans* lemon?'

'I'm afraid so. You're not in the wardroom now, Commander, surrounded by every luxury.'

'Hoh!' he said. 'You've obviously never set foot on a destroyer.'

'If it isn't a state secret what's the name of your ship?'

'*Constant Star*.'

'It's a nice name.'

'I suppose it is. Never thought of it before. She's not a particularly nice ship and no spring chicken as destroyers go. She's currently being modernised for the second time in a year.'

'What do you do in her? What's her role?'

'Bit of this, bit of that.'

'I'm sorry. Obviously you can't talk about it.' Susan held up a glass. 'How much tonic?'

'Less rather than more, please.'

She did the honours and gave him the glass. She was acutely aware that she was alone in the house with a reasonably handsome sailor old enough to know his own mind.

She held out her glass and let him touch it with his. She was already quite tipsy, not from booze but from the secret doings in the basement office in Scobie Street. She sipped gin and tonic and resisted the temptation to tell Commander Willets all about it. One broadcast was a flea-bite in the struggle against fascism, though, and to a man who ran the gauntlet of U-boats in the North Atlantic it would surely seem trivial.

She watched him drink half the contents of the glass, his Adam's apple bobbing.

Over the rooftop another plane went by, followed by three muffled explosions close enough to Salt Street to shake dust from the ceiling beams and make the coils in the electric fire sing. She spread her legs, shifted her weight on to her heels and looked at him over the rim of her glass.

'What *shall* we do?' she asked.

'I'm not much good at crosswords,' he answered.

The frantic clanging of a fire engine passing along the narrow street almost drowned out her response. 'We could have supper, I suppose.'

'We could. We've plenty of time to cook.'

'Unless the gas goes out.'

'In which case we should repair to the kitchen without delay.'

'Shall I bring the bottle?'

'By all means,' he said.

The first sortie lasted until midnight and was not intense enough to trouble them. They did justice to sardines on toast, mutton chops, mashed potatoes and tinned garden peas before settling to smoke, sip gin and drain the coffee pot.

They discussed the progress of the war and how the tide might be turned against Hitler, talked too of how life had been for each of them before the war. Derek told her something of the Willets family, once close but now scattered, and she, having little to hide, spoke freely of her girlhood in Shadwell.

Soon after midnight Goering's squadrons returned. Within minutes the kitchen was filled with deafening sounds and every dish, cup and plate, every pot, bottle and jar shook on the shelves.

Drawing her elbows into her ribs, Susan made herself as small as possible and slipped beneath the table where Commander Willets joined her. The light in the kitchen flickered and went out. It was pitch dark in the space beneath the table. She heard Derek strike a match and saw his face illuminated from below, grotesque and theatrical. He lit two cigarettes, passed one to her and blew out the match before it burned his fingers.

She smoked unhurriedly, relishing the intimacy of the situation, detached from the bedlam outside.

A whistling bomb fell through the darkness. Susan flinched. The bomb did not explode. She heard men's voices yelling in the street. Something rattled on the roof; an incendiary. A pinkish flush penetrated the blackout curtain above the sink. Voices rose and fell. The flush faded. It was dark once more, except for the glow of their cigarettes.

Susan said, 'Do you want to go out and help?'

'For once, I believe I'll leave it up to others,' he told her. 'I must say, you're taking it very well,' he said.

'I've been through it before. Haven't you?'

'Not quite like this, no.'

Overhead the drone of the bombers' engines diminished. She heard the rumble of a heavy lorry pass along the mews and a whooshing noise that might come from a fire hose.

Derek said, 'If I bend my knees a bit you can rest against my legs. It might be more comfortable for both of us.'

She rearranged her position and rested her shoulders against his legs. He put an arm about her. 'Is that better?'

'Much better.'

She waited for him to slip a hand to the buttons of her jacket or downward to her thigh but he did nothing more amorous than rest his chin on top of her head.

'Comfortable?' he said.

'Quite comfortable, thank you.'

'Do you broadcast on Thursday?'

'No, tomorrow at midnight.'

'Are you really working in Soho?'

'Temporary studio, for how long I don't know.'

'What time do you finish on Thursday?'

'Seven, or shortly after.'

'How would dinner suit you? A proper dinner.'

'Are you going to cook?'

'I was thinking of the Dorchester.'

'I've never been to the Dorchester. Is it frightfully posh? Will I need to find an evening gown?'

'Not if we go the Grill Room. Might be best if I picked you up – where?'

'The old Calcutta Cinema in Scobie Street. Do you know it?'

'If I did, I wouldn't admit it. I'll find it, never fear.'

Tomorrow night they were broadcasting the special report from Spain which, if Mr Boscombe was to be believed, might keep her chained to her desk late on Thursday. The sensible thing to do was ask Commander Willets for a rain-check but she had no idea when she might see him again or if she would ever see him again.

She hesitated.

'I'm sorry,' he said. 'I've put you in an awkward position.'

'It could hardly be more awkward than this, could it?'

'No, I mean – your husband.'

'Danny? Oh, Danny doesn't mind what I get up to.'

'More fool he,' Commander Willets said.

6

'I do wish you'd stand still, Danny,' Kate Cottrell grumbled. 'We haven't got all day, you know.'

'I don't see why we have tae do this right now?' Danny said.

'Because it's barely two weeks until the wedding and it takes time to make alterations, particularly as I don't have a sewing machine at my disposal.'

'No one'll be lookin' at me, anyhow. All eyes will be on the blushing bride.'

'And the blushing bride has no intention of being upstaged by the best man's trousers falling down. Is that better?'

'Aye, that's better.'

'Stick your thumb there – just there – while I find the pins.'

They were alone in the Pells' living room at half past ten on a Wednesday morning. Griff, just off night duty, was snoring in bed upstairs. Mrs Pell had gone by bus to Evesham to join the queue at the butcher's in the High Street who, rumour had it, had taken delivery of the carcase of a Tamworth pig that the owner had reluctantly slaughtered by order of the local Agricultural Officer.

The first fire of the day blazed in the grate and warmed Danny's calves. He shuffled uncomfortably and tried not to stare at the young woman who knelt before him fiddling with the waistband of the two-piece suit he'd purchased off the shelf at Righton's retail drapers in Evesham, an establishment better known for ladies' wear than tailoring for short-arsed gentlemen.

Kate reached behind her and fished in the biscuit tin that Mrs Pell used as a sewing basket. She found a packet of pins and brought it down to her lap. She put three of the tiny pins in her mouth, resting on her lower lip, picked one out and inserted it at an angle across a seam that required re-stitching.

'I don' – she removed the other pins from her mouth – 'I don't know what possessed you to buy a suit obviously intended for a farmer with a beer belly, not a skinny chap like you.'

'I'm not skinny,' Danny said. 'I'm sinewy.'

'Huh!'

'At least I'm not a tub o' lard like Griff.'

'Now, now, none of that.' She tapped his knee with an admonishing forefinger and, stooping still further, adjusted the turn-ups. 'Silwyn's sturdy, not fat. Climbing hills in the Brecon Beacons has given him lots of muscle.'

'I don't think I want tae hear about Silwyn's muscles.'

She thrust the last of the pins through the worsted and got to her feet.

Danny had known from the outset that Kate Cottrell would never be the girl for him. He was far too unpolished to compete with guys like Silwyn Griffiths. If it hadn't been for the upheavals that war had brought about, he doubted if even Griff would have been good enough for Katerina Cottrell or that he, an orphan from Glasgow, would have met either of them, let alone be lucky enough to call them friends.

'Take them off,' Kate said.

'What? Here?'

'I'll turn my back.'

'Naw, naw,' Danny said. 'I'm not changin' my trousers with a woman in the room.'

'In that case, to preserve your dignity, I'll pop into the kitchen,' Kate said. 'Just don't dislodge those pins – oh, and fold the trousers neatly over a chair.'

Danny waited until she vanished into the kitchen and closed the door. He peeled off the wedding trousers and, keeping all the pins in place, folded them over a chair back. He hopped into his old flannels and buttoned them up.

'Decent,' he called out.

Kate reappeared.

'As a matter of interest what's Griff wearing on the big day?' Danny asked. 'A claw-hammer jacket an' a dickie-bow?'

'A plain dark suit.'

'Let's hope it fits,' said Danny. 'Wouldn't want tae see poor Taffy gaspin' for breath while taking the vows.'

Kate lifted the wedding trousers from the chair and draped them over her forearm. The jacket of the suit was already on a wooden hanger in Kate's wardrobe, safely removed from the smoke of the boys' room. Danny liked to think of his suit in her wardrobe, sharing space with her frocks.

Almost as if she'd read his thoughts, Kate studied him for a long moment, frowning. 'Danny . . .' she began.

'What?'

'Oh, nothing,' Kate said. 'Nothing of any consequence,' and, carrying the trousers over her arm, crossed the narrow hall and disappeared upstairs.

Basil Willets opened his eyes and, without raising his head from the pillow, said, 'Dear God! It's the angel of death.'

'After that taxi ride from Hereford station,' his brother said, 'I feel like the angel of death. What on earth are you up to skulking out here in the back of beyond?'

'Breathing my last, apparently,' Basil said. 'According to my darling wife this is the sort of place where BBC producers go to die.'

'Oh, stop it, Willets.' Vivian moved to the bed and, slipping an arm behind the pillows, hoisted him into a sitting position. 'You're no more dying than I am.'

'I am, though. I'm dying of bloody boredom.' He shifted position, plucked at the pillow behind him and grimaced with pain. 'What are you doing here, anyway, Deckers? I thought you were out on the vasty deep playing hopscotch with German U-boats.'

'Compassionate leave,' Commander Willets said. 'I told the admiral I wished to see my brother one last time before his wife strangled him.' He pulled out the bedroom's only chair and perched upon it. 'You don't look too bad to me. From what I heard I expected to find you in an iron lung.'

'Heard,' said Basil, 'from who – whom?'

'Susan.'

'That Judas!'

The cottage was hidden in a coppice a half-mile down a rutted track from the last house in Gadney. At one time it might have attracted penniless poets or same-sex novelists in search of an economical retreat far – very far – from the madding crowd but, like all David Proudfoot's country properties, it had fallen into disrepair.

In a warped iron grate a smouldering log gave off no discernible heat. The double bed took up almost all the space but, Derek thought, the room was a deal less cramped than his quarters on the *Constant Star*. He kept that information to himself, however, for he was well aware that grousing was good therapy.

Vivian rested her hips on the ledge by the tiny window. 'I take it you stayed overnight in Salt Street?'

'I did.'

'With Susan?'

'Yes.'

'Oh hoh!' said Basil. 'Up to your old tricks, Deckers. I trust you didn't take advantage of my little Judas.'

'I do wish you'd stop calling her that,' said Vivian. 'She's not responsible for programming, as well you know.'

'Perhaps not,' Basil said, 'but she doesn't have to be so blasted enthusiastic about the advent of the almighty Boscombe. Did you share a bed with her, Deckers?'

'We slept together,' Derek Willets admitted.

'Oh, God!' said Vivian.

'Under the kitchen table.'

'What was wrong with the cupboard?' said Basil.

'We were caught unprepared,' the commander explained. 'We hid under the table until the all-clear, after which we retired to separate rooms for a couple of hours' shut-eye.'

'Is our house all right?' said Vivian.

'The sink's filled with broken glass,' Derek said, 'but as far as I can make out the roof's intact. Salt Street's a mess, though.'

'It's only a matter of time,' Basil said, 'until our house goes up in smoke. If the bombing goes on much longer there won't be a habitable house left in London.'

'All the more reason,' Vivian said, 'for sitting tight – at least until you're well again.'

'I'm not ill, not that ill, at any rate.'

'What about the lungs?' said Derek. 'Susan hinted that you were spitting blood and I don't think she meant metaphorically.'

'It's nothing,' said Basil. 'I'll soon heal.'

'That's not what the doctors say,' Vivian reminded him.

'Country doctors, what do they know?' said Basil. 'Scabies and rickets, that's all they ever treat.'

'Of course it is,' said Vivian, not soothingly. 'You didn't happen to bring down my mail, Derek?'

'Susan says she'll deal with it. One thing I can tell you: *The Times* has decided not to publish extracts from your new book.'

Vivian sighed. 'Can't say I'm surprised. I've half a mind to ask Routledge to withdraw the damned thing, though I suppose the royalties might come in handy if the war goes on for long.'

'Which it will,' said Basil. 'Are you still on destroyers, Derek?'

'Yes,' he replied, and swiftly changed the subject. 'By the by, I had a long rambling letter from Mother.'

'Mother?' Basil rolled his eyes. 'How is the old hag?'

Vivian rose from her seat on the window ledge. 'If you intend to spend the next half-hour slandering your nearest and dearest, I'll make myself scarce. Are you staying, Derek?'

'I have to return to London on the afternoon train. I've one or two things to do before my leave's up.'

'Susan included?' Basil Willets said.

'She's working tonight, all night.'

'Wednesday, of course,' said Baz. 'Oh, dear, I expect we'll have to endure another of Boscombe's jazzy fiascos. I just hope I can stay awake.' He sighed, coughed and lay back on the pillow. 'Tell me what Mama's up to these days. Is she still enjoying life in the fast lane in Scotland? Is she safe enough there, do you think?'

Shaking her head, Vivian escaped to the scullery to scare up something for lunch.

The sky had clouded over. A blustery wind stripped leaves from the branches and chased them along the track from which direction the taxi-cab would appear. Derek had been a sailor for half his life and was used to farewells but there was something about this parting that made him uneasy.

Basil had fallen asleep in the middle of lunch, drifting off with a mouthful of veal and ham pie that Vivian, deftly and without fuss, had removed from his tongue with her fingertips. It wasn't Basil's bad temper or his sudden need for sleep that disturbed Derek but, rather, Vivian's obvious concern for his brother.

She walked with him a little way down the track. The afternoon was closing in on an early dusk and the air bristled with the flavour of winter. He halted Viv with a hand on her arm.

'What's really wrong with him? Tell me the truth?'

'Whatever he inhaled under that pile of debris irritated the lining of his lungs. It's nothing to do with cracked ribs. There's a military hospital on the other side of Hereford. David has offered to arrange an X-ray examination there, but Basil won't hear of it. He's afraid of what an X-ray might reveal, afraid that he might lose his job with the BBC if it turns out to be something serious.'

'If it's a question of money . . .'

'Lord, no,' said Vivian. 'We're far from broke. If it comes to it, I can turn my hand to writing more articles or even another book.'

'How long can you keep him here, Vivian?'

'As long as possible. I don't much like it and I certainly

don't appreciate being dependent on my brother but, frankly, I see no alternative. You, Derek, where are you off to?'

'London.'

'I mean . . .'

'I know what you mean. Fact is, I don't know. We'll be another week or so in dock taking on supplies before I receive my orders, and then we'll be off.'

'For how long?'

'God knows.'

'It was good of you to come,' Vivian said, then unexpectedly hugged him. 'I hate it, Derek,' she blurted out. 'Oh, God, how I hate being afraid all the time. Afraid for Basil, for you, for myself. I'm no sniveller as a rule – but now – look at me. This damned war has reduced me to a blubbering wreck.'

The taxi-cab appeared, rocking on the ruts of the rough country road. The sound of the horn sent two wood pigeons flapping off, low and loud, under the swaying boughs.

'Wreck or not, Vivian, he's lucky to have you.'

'Hah!' Vivian sniffed. 'Try telling him that.'

'Oh, he knows it. Believe me, he does,' Derek said.

'You'd better skedaddle before I forget myself,' Vivian said. 'Give Susan my love.'

'I will,' Commander Willets promised and, stepping into the taxi-cab, left his sister-in-law alone in the gathering gloom.

No sooner had the broadcast ended than the telephones rang. It had happened once before when Basil had unwittingly picked up a German attack on a British air base in Holland and the world and his wife had been treated to the sounds of a genuine raid in progress. Robert had been the presenter on that occasion and had wrung every last drop of shock and sentiment from the interrupted broadcast. Even Bob Gaines might be a little out of his depth, though, with an unnamed correspondent chatting matter-of-factly about eavesdropping on Hitler and Franco and delivering the news that lists of Jews in Spain had changed hands under the table.

There was no congratulatory call from Mr Churchill. Susan suspected that the PM had sanctioned the recording and preferred to keep quiet about his involvement in such blatant propaganda. Mr Gillespie, who had not been warned in advance what to expect, took it all in his stride and orchestrated the discussion afterwards with professional aplomb. But, as soon as it was over, he'd grabbed his hat and, air raid or no air raid, had headed straight out of the studio before, as it were, the roof fell in.

What folk on the east coast of America thought of *Speaking Up* and what impression a report on a secret meeting on the Spanish border had made on them remained to be seen. It was, however, obvious that every journalist in Fleet Street had mysteriously got wind of Boscombe's coup and, abandoning wives, mistresses and drinking companions, had plastered their ears to shortwave radios and were up in arms about being kept in the dark.

'I'm sorry, I do not have that information.'

'Mr Boscombe is not available at this time.'

'I'm afraid we can't provide you with a transcript of the talk.'

'Mr Boscombe's assistant, as it happens – and I would be very much obliged if you would modify your language.'

'Yes, I will be sure to let Mr Boscombe know you called.'

'If you won't give me a name I'm afraid I can't help you.'

'No, sir, I do not have that information.'

Larry spiked a mug of hot coffee with a dash of whisky and put it on Susan's desk.

'Geeze,' he said. 'We have set the cat among the pigeons good and proper. I knew it was dynamite, of course, but I didn't think . . .'

'If the minister cares to call in the morning – yes, I do realise who I'm talking to but I'm afraid Mr Boscombe has gone for the night and I am unable to help you.'

Susan replaced the receiver and let out a groan. The phone immediately rang again. She ignored it, reached for the coffee mug, drank deeply and wiped her lips on her wrist.

'What the hell do they want?' said Larry. 'Nope, don't tell me. They want the name of the chap who stood behind Hitler like the invisible man while *der Führer* was busily carving up the rest of Europe. What a slap on the kisser for *European Round Up*. How our Walter got away with it is beyond me.'

'He's a Boscombe. He can get away with anything.'

'Where is he, by the by? Has he really gone home?'

'He's next door, with the door closed, putting out calls.'

'Putting *out* calls? God, the switchboard in Portland Place must be sizzling by now.'

'He has a private line.' Susan swigged the rest of the coffee and held up the mug for a refill. 'By the look of it, I'm going to be here all night. What's it like up top?'

'Bloody noisy,' Larry said. 'How's the schedule for Friday?'

'Watertight.'

'When are you in tomorrow?'

'Noon till seven.'

'Rather you than me, love,' Larry said. 'No rest for the wicked.'

'I'm asking for the evening off. I deserve it.'

'That you do. What is it? Heavy date?'

'No, just dinner with a friend.'

'Think Boscombe will let you go?'

'He'd better,' Susan said. 'I've something in my drawer I believe Mr Boscombe might like to see.'

'Really?' said Larry. 'And what might that be?'

'The chit that our mysterious stranger left in the OB van.'

'A chit? For what?'

'Expenses.' Susan grinned. 'Can you believe it? Our super-spy puts in a claim for expenses signed with his name and address.'

'You're kidding?'

'I'm not.'

Larry rocked with laughter, then, still chuckling, said, 'I don't suppose you'd care to tell me his name?'

'Betray my country, let alone Mr Boscombe's trust – never.'

'When are you going to show him what you've got?'

'Ten seconds before I ask for an evening off.'

Larry laughed again, then, mopping coffee from his necktie, shook his head. 'I know what he looks like and you know where he lives. By gum, Susie-pops, we could net a tidy sum by flogging that information to the right people.'

'Or the wrong people,' Susan said. 'Not that we're going to.'

'No,' Larry ruefully agreed, 'not that we're going to.'

The telephone on Susan's desk was hopping with rage and frustration like a duck in a Walt Disney cartoon.

Still sniggering, Larry made for the door.

'See you around, Mata Hari,' he said.

'Not if I see you first, Funf,' said Susan and, picking up the receiver, politely told the caller, 'No, sir, I do not have that information,' which, of course, was an outright lie.

*

The office was stuffy and reeked of cigarette smoke. Mr Boscombe had removed his jacket, unfastened his cufflinks and pushed his shirtsleeves over his forearms which, Susan noticed, were downed with black hair. He had positioned the telephone in the centre of his desk and stared down at it as if he expected it to explode.

He seemed weary, hooded eyes heavy.

He looked up when Susan entered.

'What time is it?' he asked.

'Quarter past four. It seems to have quietened down.'

'The raid?' He lifted his head. 'Has it?'

'I meant the calls.'

'Too late for the early editions,' Walter Boscombe said, 'but we'll be crucified or possibly lampooned in the noon editions, I've no doubt.' Susan placed the official pale blue expenses form on his desk and slid it towards him. 'What's this?' He peered at the form. 'Oh, Christ!' he said softly. 'Sometimes I think we don't really deserve to win this war.' He squinted at Susan. 'Who else has seen the signature?'

'No one, sir, apart, that is, from the bloke – from the person in the OB van who brought it to me.'

'Baines?'

'No, Larry knows nothing of it.'

'Did *you* read it, Mrs Cahill?'

'I did. I didn't realise what it was at first.' She paused. 'Are you going to take me out into an alley and have me shot?'

'Would you be missed?'

'Probably not,' said Susan.

'Well, reliable assistants are hard to find so perhaps I'll spare you. However, it would be best for all concerned if you forget that this piece of paper ever existed.'

'Mr Boscombe.'

'What?'

'May I have some time off?'

'Oh, God!' he said. 'You're blackmailing me, aren't you? How long and when?'

'An hour or so tomorrow evening.'

'An hour or so? Some blackmailer you are. Certain ladies of my acquaintance would have squeezed a long weekend in Brighton out of it. Yes, yes, of course, you may have an hour or two off tomorrow evening. Tell you what, come in at one and leave at five. I'd give you the whole day but I expect a flood of mail from one quarter or another and need you around. Is that all right?'

'Very generous, Mr Boscombe.'

'It's not generous at all. It's mean, damned mean, but I have a reputation to live up to, don't I?' He reached behind him, fumbled in the pocket of his jacket, which was draped on the chair back, and fished out the bullet-shaped lighter. 'I will now put myself further in debt to your conscience by asking you to witness the deliberate destruction of BBC property.'

He lifted the claims form between finger and thumb, snapped the lighter and held the flame to the paper.

'What about Mr – I mean, our anonymous friend,' Susan said. 'Won't he complain if his expenses aren't paid?'

'Expenses?' said Walter Boscombe. 'He'll get no expenses from me. In fact, if I ever run across him again, I'll wring his blasted neck.'

The pale blue paper blackened as flame spread over its surface and then, dropping the sheet into the ashtray, Mr Boscombe poked the flakes with his finger until nothing remained but ash.

'Gone,' he said. 'Gone, Mrs Cahill, as if it had never been.'

'What's that, sir?' Susan said. 'As if what had never been?'

He studied her for a moment, head cocked, then said, 'One o'clock tomorrow. And please, Mrs Cahill, do try to be on time.'

Shoes and dress didn't quite match but there was no help for it. She was lucky to have a decent pair of shoes at all. Most of her possessions had been lost when the flat she'd shared with Danny had been bombed. She should, she supposed, have made more of an effort to reclaim whatever the demolition squad had dug from the debris but she'd been too busy, too stunned, really, to bother at the time.

The court shoes, just back from repair, had been in a drawer in her desk at the BBC, together with one or two other items she'd kept there in case of emergency. The dress was new. She'd picked it up at a Marshall & Snelgrove autumn sale and had not so far had a chance to wear it. It was far too short to pass as an evening gown but after a bit of fiddling with the belt she felt sure she could get away with it and not embarrass her escort who, in the absence of anything more formal, would be wearing naval uniform.

Derek had been fast asleep when she'd arrived home shortly after five on Thursday morning and had been gone before she'd wakened at half past eleven. She'd left a note propped against the coffee percolator informing him that she'd be home by six and would not therefore require to be picked up at the Calcutta.

Even as she was writing the note it occurred to her that the arrangement had all the hallmarks of a fiasco with Derek wandering about Soho while she waited in Salt Street. But Derek's uniform was set out neatly on the bed in the master bedroom together with underwear, stockings and a spotless white shirt still in its tissue wrappings, all of which indicated that he would return to Salt Street at some point in the afternoon.

Reassured, and inspired by the commander's meticulous preparations, she laid out on the bed in her bedroom every stitch that she intended to wear that evening in the not too serious hope that he might peep in and see just what sort of girl he would be stepping out with, right down to the skin.

Four or five years ago she would have shrunk from the very idea of entering the famous hotel on Park Lane and hobnobbing with the cream of society. Three years as Vivian's friend and companion had changed all that. Having seen the so-called 'cream of society' up close she no longer nurtured any sense of inferiority. She had dined in some of London's best restaurants, danced in its nightclubs and lunched on more than one occasion in the Savoy all without making a fool of herself and, no matter what Walter Boscombe might think to the contrary, she was a lot more sophisticated than the daughter of a Cockney dock worker had any right to be.

It was after two before Mr Boscombe showed up at the Calcutta. He carried with him a folder of censored scripts and a bundle of that day's newspapers and looked, Susan thought, not just weary but haggard.

He went directly into his office and closed the door.

Ten minutes elapsed before the familiar bark, not much more than a croak, summoned her to his office where, to her surprise, she found him in one of Basil's favourite positions with his chair tilted back and his feet on the desk.

He peered at Susan, frowning, as if he could not remember who she was or, perhaps, that he had sent for her.

'Kippered,' he growled. 'I'm absolutely bloody kippered.' He spread his shoes in a vee and observed her through them, as if through the sight of a gun. 'I don't mind admitting, Mrs Cahill, that last night's little caper took it out of me. And being summoned to justify one's actions to two po-faced members of the Board of Governors and some chump from the Advisory Council at half past eight this morning does test one's powers of endurance.' He closed the vee then opened it again. 'Five, I think you said. You have to be off at five.'

'Yes, sir, if you please.'

'Well, I'm not going to last that long.' He hoisted his feet from the desk and made a vain attempt to appear alert. 'Edited scripts to a typist for final drafting. Moran and Mortimer haven't delivered but will do so first thing tomorrow.'

'Mr Moran is doubtful.'

'The devil he is. He's just being coy. Leave Moran to me.' The spurt of energy was already waning. 'These damned trade unionists are all the same, desperate to voice their opinions but afraid to actually say anything that might land them in the soup.' He cupped his hands, pressed them against his cheekbones and kneaded his eye sockets. 'I'm talking too much. Always a bad sign. I'm going home.'

'The mail, Mr Boscombe?'

'To hang with the mail. Look, just answer what you can under a signature block and make sure you're away by five. If anyone asks for me, tell them I'm dead – which is damned near the truth, anyway.' He squinted at her out of one bloodshot eye. 'And thank you, Mrs Cahill, thank you for everything.'

'He thanked me, can you believe it? He actually thanked me,' Susan called through the half-open door. 'Wonders will never cease.'

'He's obviously coming around to realising how valuable you are,' said Derek Willets from the bathroom. 'Boscombe's sort are never as independent as they'd like us to believe.'

She had slipped on Vivian's dressing gown and was waiting for the commander to finish shaving so that she could bathe. She could see light reflected in the mirror above the bathroom sink but nothing of the man himself. It was quiet outside, no noisier than an average London evening with a low grumble of traffic from the thoroughfare but no whistles or klaxons and, so far, no drone of enemy aircraft overhead.

They had shared a gin and tonic while he'd told her about his flying visit to Gadney and his concern over Basil's health. He had obviously been busy that afternoon: the broken glass in the kitchen sink had been removed, the floor swept and a large sheet of plywood, rescued from a dump at the street's end, had been nailed over the window frame.

He had offered her the bathroom but when she'd asked him how long it would take him to shave and he'd told her, 'Ten minutes,' she'd graciously conceded first dibs.

She leaned on the wall in the panelled corridor, dressing gown snug about her, sponge bag and towel under her arm, and listened to the scratch of his safety razor, a splash of water, then his voice, moistened by toothpaste, saying, 'If we hurry it along, Susan, we might make the Dorchester before Jerry comes over.' He gargled, spat and ran water into the basin. 'Are you still there?'

'Yes, I'm here.'

He appeared in the doorway, his vest tucked tightly into the waist of his corduroys. He carried a leather pouch in one hand and, holding the door open with his elbow, looked down from what seemed to be an imposing height.

'Half an hour?' he said.

'Half an hour,' she promised and, ducking under his arm, stepped gaily into the bathroom and closed the door.

The Dorchester rose pale and majestic out of the darkness. Figures were just visible on the balconies, figures on the roof, toy figures, not real. The forecourt flowerbeds had been replaced by ugly anti-tank traps. Hunched under the massive concrete ledge on which the building floated, the entrance was flanked by sandbags. A doorkeeper in smart pre-war livery sprang from the shadows to salute the commander and admit the couple to the glittering hall.

A heady atmosphere of money and privilege, the like of which she hadn't experienced since the war began, enveloped Susan. She should resent the elegant ladies in furs and the men in evening dress who dined on the fat of the land while the homeless of Shadwell, Whitechapel and a dozen other poor London boroughs scraped for food and shelter, but she experienced only a fleeting moment of irritation that vanished when the sweet sound of Lew Stone's band playing 'Anything Goes' drifted down the promenade from the ballroom.

En route to the Grill Room, she became aware that among the ermine and black ties were several sleazy individuals whose business here was probably as dubious as their place in society. She recognised a Cabinet minister who had delivered a talk on *Speaking Up*, an actor who had almost gone to prison for soliciting young boys and, slithering a little on the marble floor, one of Bob Gaines's foreign press gang from Lansdowne House accompanied by a snake-hipped young woman who, Susan suspected, would go to bed with anyone in exchange for a decent meal.

Derek and she were shown to a table for two, a table that

might have offered intimacy if it hadn't been for the clam-shell-shaped chairs padded in maroon-coloured cloth that swallowed her up completely. Even at that unfashionable hour the Grill Room was crowded. Perched on the uncomfortable chair, Susan studied the guests at nearby tables, while Derek, amused, studied her.

'I've no idea why the décor is so oppressively Scottish,' he said. 'I could see sense in it if they served only venison and salmon with the odd grouse thrown in but the bill of fare's international.'

Susan looked round at the tartan-clad walls and pulled a face. 'It is a bit heathery, isn't it? Does someone come in and play the bagpipes and do a sword dance while we eat?'

'Mercifully not,' Derek said. 'It's no more Scottish than fly, by the way. My mother would be "sair offendit" by it all, I'm sure.'

'Oh, your mother's a Scot, is she?'

'No, she's from Poole in Dorset originally. She married a Scots marine engineer and spent much of her life on Clydeside. When my father died, Basil, my sister and I were shipped off to schools down south and, for one reason or another, elected to remain in England. My mother still lives in Scotland.'

'Where do you stay, Derek? Where's your home?'

He shrugged. 'For fifteen years it's been on board one ship or another. I had a couple of settled years in Dartmouth as an instructor, but usually I spend shore leave bunking with Basil – or did until he married Vivian. My sister in Cornwall puts up with me now and then and, if the worst comes to the worst, I visit my mother in Troon which, candidly, is one of the dullest places on God's earth unless you happen to play golf, which I don't.'

'Pointless question, I know,' Susan said, 'but have you never had an urge to settle down?'

'Not until now.'

'Now? Why now?'

'The war, I suppose. It's not that I don't know how to command a fighting ship – I was trained for it – or that I've lost what passes for love of the sea, but . . .' He shrugged again. 'If you must know, Susan, I've already seen too many men die horrible deaths. Here' – he thrust the menu at her – 'what'll you have?'

She scanned the card.

'Woodcock?' she said, too brightly. 'My goodness!'

'Tasty, but there's never much of it.'

'Derek' – she leaned across the table and lowered her voice – 'I don't wish to seem impertinent but have you seen the prices? I mean, can you afford all this stuff?'

'Put it this way, I couldn't afford a suite upstairs but I don't think dinner for two will ruin me. Besides, who else do I have to spend my money on?'

'I – I don't know,' Susan said. 'Another girl somewhere?'

'Oh, come on,' he said jocularly. 'You can do better than that.'

'I suppose it was a bit ham-fisted.' She paused. 'Is there?'

'There was,' he said, 'but there isn't now.'

She longed for him to add, 'just you,' but that, she realised, was asking too much from a solitary sort of man whom she barely knew. She was tempted to press for details about the girl he'd abandoned or who had abandoned him but she respected his reserve and read the menu in silence.

'What do you recommend?' she said at length.

'I don't eat here often enough to know what's good and what isn't,' he admitted. 'In fact, I've only been here a couple of times when Basil stood me lunch. The smoked eels might suit you?'

'Because I'm a Cockney, you mean?'

'I didn't mean that at all. Pork goulash? A grilled lamb chop? Dover sole? There's lobster, but I haven't trusted lobster since I had a bad experience with the beast in Gibraltar.'

She was only half listening. Her attention had been caught by a party of five men whose progress through the Grill Room was preceded by the *maître d'* and two waiters whose obsequiousness stopped just short of turning somersaults. The party were heading for a long table against the east wall where two distinguished-looking gentlemen waited to greet the new arrivals.

Resplendent in dinner suits, the five passed between the tables in a stately phalanx, ignoring the other diners with jaded hauteur as if acknowledging the stir of interest that their entry caused was beneath their dignity.

'My boss, Mr Boscombe. What on earth is he doing here?'

The commander raised his head and glanced at the group at the long table. 'Having dinner with his family, by the look of it. The tall one with the pure white hair is Lord Boscombe. The chap with him is the Foreign Secretary, Lord Halifax. He's a former Viceroy of India and was one of the appeasers until the war started. He was offered Downing Street but turned it down and threw his weight behind Churchill.'

'You're awfully well informed. Who are the others?'

'Boscombe's boys, I think. The young fellow in RAF uniform is almost certainly Leonard. The chap next to him – Guy – is something in Naval Intelligence. The other two – I haven't a clue who they are.'

'Perhaps they're spies?'

'What makes you say that?'

'Don't they look a little like spies to you?'

'If they look like spies they probably aren't. The thing about genuine spies is that they look just like you and me.' He tapped the menu card. 'It's time to order, Susan. What will you have?'

'Wait,' she said. 'He's spotted me. Oh, God! He's coming over.'

'Who's coming over?'

'Mr Boscombe.'

She had just enough wit to remain seated while Walter Boscombe weaved his way between the tables. Commander Willets got to his feet.

'Mrs Cahill,' Walter Boscombe said, 'what a pleasant surprise,' and then, unable to resist the taunt, added, 'Is this your husband?'

'A friend,' said Susan. 'Commander Willets, Mr Boscombe.'

'Basil's brother, I assume. A pleasure to meet you.'

Susan watched the men shake hands and heard them exchange pleasantries. Two handsome men, she thought, chatting casually over my head, the only two men in my life right now.

And Danny, of course.

Yes, and Danny.

7

Three hundred years of history were crammed into two streets at the heart of Shay Bridge and, if you ignored the tawdry villas that the twentieth century had dumped on surrounding acres, you might have been back in Cromwell's time or downing a tankard at Miller's Inn with one of Shakespeare's chums.

The old village lay above water meadows on a tributary of the Avon and was connected, so locals claimed, to the rest of Merry England only by the hump-backed bridge that gave the place its name. Thatched roofs, half-timbered walls and broad verges along the roadsides retained an old-world charm even in time of war and the church and adjoining manor-house seemed as timeless and tranquil as a painting by Constable.

There was nothing tranquil about the late-nineteenth-century brick-built hall that stuck out from the rear of the venerable church on that showery Saturday afternoon. It was thronged with women, children and a handful of men who'd been press-ganged into shifting chairs, putting up tables and erecting the gaudy signs that announced the inauguration of the Shay Bridge Spitfire Fund.

Few of the women who poured off the buses from Evesham and its neighbouring villages cared two figs about supplying the government with the wherewithal to build another aeroplane, provision of which, the ladies reckoned, was best left to those fools in London who had rushed wilfully into a war that was none of England's business.

Patriotism, or variations thereof, burned brighter in the girls from Orrell's Engineering who were well aware that the war had brought them well-paid work and who, like Breda Hooper and her friend, Morven Hastie, were not above blowing a few shekels on a good cause, provided they got something in return.

They were also curious to see Stevie Pepperdine in action and, in Breda's case, to eyeball Trudy Littlejohn's husband, Stanley, who, according to Morven, really had to be seen to be believed.

'Is that him? Don't tell me that's him.'

'Yup,' said Morven, 'that's him.'

'Blimey! He's ninety if he's a day.'

'If you heard him preach,' said Morven, 'you'd think he'd been on the right hand of Jesus when the Last Supper was served.'

'I wonder what Trudy sees in 'im.'

'I heard,' said Morven, drawing closer, 'it was a shotgun and she lost the baby before it reached term.'

'That,' said Breda, 'is sad, no matter what you think of Trudy.'

'*If* it's true,' said Morven. 'He doesn't look to me like he has the stuffing in him to make a baby.'

They loitered at the gate by the side of the churchyard within sight of the bus halt at Miller's Inn, awaiting the arrival of Madge Gaydon, Billy and the girls.

The churchyard was skirted by a lane that led to the door of the hall near which Reverend Stanley Littlejohn, in black duds and dog-collar, was glad-handing the local gentry, including Lady Ashcroft. She had generously agreed to open the fund by making a short speech and the first donation, a magnificent pair of cast-iron dragon's-head andirons that had been gathering dust in the cellar of Ashcroft House for years.

There was no sign of Trudy or of Steve Pepperdine who, presumably, were backstage somewhere.

Verger and churchwarden were fussily steering the queue into the foyer of the hall where a young curate on loan from another parish was collecting sixpence admission from every adult over fifteen, which diabolical liberty was, it appeared, the cause of considerable consternation. The barney failed to impinge upon Stanley Littlejohn. He continued chatting to the favoured few as if the clamour behind him was of no more moment than the cooing of doves.

'Can you imagine him in pyjamas?' Morven murmured. 'He'd need a stepladder to kiss Trudy goodnight.'

'And those wrinkles,' said Breda. 'Ain't seen that many wrinkles outside of a walnut. Here, is that our Archie? What's he doing 'ere? You'd think he'd get enough of us in the kitchens.'

Breda and Morven pretended to stare at the sky while giving Mr Jackson a right good butcher's. They watched him dismount from his bicycle, remove the clips from his trouser legs and, wheeling the bicycle before him, advance up the lane towards them.

'Mrs Hooper.'

'Mr Jackson.'

'M-m-m Miss Hastie.' He removed his cap. 'Are you well?'

'Why?' said Morven the merciless. 'Don't I look well?'

'Uh, yes, you look – uh – nice, very nice,' Archie Jackson mumbled and, sticking on his cap, hastened off to hide his bicycle behind the hall in the hope that no one would steal the bell.

'Strikes me you've made a conquest there,' said Breda.

'Better men than Archie Jackson have fallen at my feet,' Morven said, 'and been trampled into the carpet. One day my prince will come, but I can tell you now, Breda, it won't be Archie Jackson. Here comes the bus.'

Billy was already in thrall to Linda Gaydon and her sister or, if not in thrall, at best their prisoner. To Breda's amusement he allowed himself to be led off, meek as a lamb, to explore the accumulated junk displayed on the trestle tables below the stage upon which a lectern and a half-dozen empty chairs awaited the advent of the organising committee.

There were, around the hall, several card and picnic tables upon which the women from the Institute and the Guild had put out goods for sale: jam, of course, bottled fruit and pickles, sachets of herbs and a selection of knitted garments, including the woolly helmets that Trudy's mother-in-law had decided weren't suitable for auction and was selling at the bargain price of one and sixpence each.

Breda was tempted to buy one for Billy but she had in her purse exactly thirty-one shillings, half her life savings, and Billy had a balaclava and didn't need another one. She did, however, shell out sixpence for three toffee apples sufficiently sticky to shut Billy and the Gaydon girls up for a while.

Breda's experience of markets was confined to the bustling stalls of the East End but she had a sense that this was not the usual village bring and buy sale and that, with imports becoming ever more scarce, soon there would be nothing left to sell and even jam and toffee apples would vanish from the scene.

She followed Morven and Madge Gaydon down the hall to the trestles where, neatly set out and numbered, the lots were displayed. The Ashcroft andirons had pride of place. They were flanked by a large Oriental-style vase and, of all things, a beautifully made rocking horse that had already caught the attention of the dealers who had driven in from Evesham and down from Worcester to see what bargains they could pick up.

Paintings, framed, horses in one, the portrait of a sullen-looking girl in the other: who would buy those? Breda wondered. Books, including a run of encyclopedias bound in green leather and two massive volumes filled with coloured pictures of British birds; then lesser items like a keg of home brew, a case of cider, half sets of china and, lot number eighteen, the shoes, Trudy's shoes, mint in tissue in a box provocatively tipped up to show them off.

'Oh, God!' Breda sighed, realising that her goose was cooked. 'Oh, my God!' Her only hope now was that the gorgeous shoes, with their diamanté buckles and unblemished, flesh-coloured soles, wouldn't fit her plates.

She reached out a trembling hand and removed the right shoe from its nest, turned it this way and that and, with a sinking sensation in the pit of her stomach, knew that it had been made for her, just for her, by a jolly little cobbler in a Tyrolean hat sitting on top of an Alp.

'Why don't you try it on?' said Trudy Littlejohn from the edge of the stage above.

'May I?' said Breda.

'Of course, you may, my dear.'

Morven offered an arm and, thus supported, Breda shook off her old clodhopper and, reaching down, carefully slipped the red suede shoe on to her foot.

It fitted perfectly.

She raised her leg like a chorine and, hopping a little, admired the shoe which, even with the ankle-strap dangling, looked so elegant that it sent a shiver down her spine.

Morven glanced at Madge Gaydon and winked.

'Swanky,' she said. 'Very swanky.'

Breda did a little dance. 'Do you think so? Really think so?'

'Lovely,' Madge Gaydon said. 'When would you wear um?'

Practicality was the last thing on Breda's mind. She was entranced by the shoes, certain that mere possession would alter her life even if they never left the box but sat, like totems, on the shelf above her bed where she could admire them and dream of an evening when circumstances would conspire to allow her to wear them as they deserved to be worn.

From her stance on the platform Trudy Littlejohn said, 'They do suit you, Breda. Don't they pinch?'

'No, not a bit.'

'Put them back then,' said Trudy, 'and keep your fingers crossed no one else wants them.'

'Who else would want um,' said Madge, 'these days?'

Lady Ashcroft had been and, indeed, still was a fine figure of a woman. As the wife of a landed gentleman and the mother of four sons, all of whom were convinced that Worcestershire was the hub of Empire, she had long ago learned that flattery and brevity, in equal measure, were all that was required of her when called upon to open a fête, unveil a war memorial or, as now, give some hare-brained fund-raising scheme a kick on the derrière to get it started.

She shared the stage with Stanley and Trudy Littlejohn and the ubiquitous Steve Pepperdine who, having failed to convince his peers at Cambridge that not all mathematical geniuses need be self-lacerating introverts, had brought his ebullient alter ego into the land of the philistines where, in exchange for designing a sophisticated guidance system for torpedoes, he was handed a billet in the rectory and a captive audience upon whom to inflict his dubious talents as an entertainer.

'I trust you will all support this patriotic cause by bidding generously for any item that may take your fancy,' Lady Ashcroft concluded and graciously yielded the lectern to the vicar.

He promptly invited the assembly to bow its collective head and join him in prayer for all the brave young men – no mention of women – who were risking their lives to preserve the nation from Nazi oppression. He then launched into a reedy harangue that included reference to Midianites and Amorites and the selling of robes to buy swords that appeared to imply that God required nothing more than a single Spitfire with *Shay Bridge St John's* stencilled on the wings to notch up another crushing victory for right over might.

Morven nudged Breda's calf with the side of her foot and nodded towards the platform where Trudy and Steve Pepperdine were whispering like conspirators.

If Breda hadn't been captive to the red suede shoes she too might have remarked on the strange affinity between the vicar's wife and the boy genius. Mr Littlejohn's parishioners were apparently used to such behaviour and, being less savvy than city girls, dismissed the whispered conversation as a last-minute confab on how best to part fools from their money.

The vicar, oblivious to any hint of impropriety, droned on. 'And now a man who needs no introduction, our own, our very own, Dr Stephen Pepperdine, who will conduct the auction in his usual inimitable style. Stephen, if you would be so good.'

Trudy gave the doctorial kneecap a squeeze. Steve leaped to his feet and bounded to the reading desk with a beaming smile and a twinkle in his eye that was not reciprocated by hard-headed dealers or, for that matter, by the hard-hearted wives who had trailed in from the sticks.

In a voice that smacked more of Cambridge than Clitheroe and reminded Breda, vaguely, of one of the Western Brothers on the wireless, the doctor outlined the auction rules.

'Get on with it,' one elderly dealer was rude enough to call out. 'We ha'n't got all bloody day.'

'After the cider, sir, are you?' was Stevie's nippy response. 'You've had enough already, if you ask me. However, in deference to my friend in the bowler hat, lot number one: a fine pair of cast-iron andirons generously donated by Lady Anne Ashcroft – and won't her husband be surprised when he finds them gone, hah-hah. What am I bid? You in the bowler hat, may I start you at fifty?'

'Five,' said the bowler hat sourly, 'shillings.'

'That won't go far towards a Spitfire,' said Steve. 'May I remind you that we are here today to gather money for—'

'Three quid,' shouted someone from the rear of the hall.

'And ten.'

'Three pounds ten shillings I am bid.'

'And ten.'

A sticky hand tugged at Breda's skirt and, in a stage whisper, her son informed her, 'I need a pee.'

'Linda'll take him,' said Madge Gaydon.

'Nah,' Billy snapped, loudly enough to extract a frown from Dr Pepperdine. 'Nah, not 'er.'

Morven crouched and addressed Billy, man to man. 'Can you do up your own buttons?'

'Yus.'

'Come on then. I'll show you where to go.'

Billy scowled, then, to Breda's surprise, nodded.

'What about me? I need to do ut too,' said Dorothy Gaydon.

'All of you,' Morven said. 'Follow me.'

She detached the incontinent little band from the crowd in front of the stage and headed for the cloakroom.

'Thank you, madam,' Steve Pepperdine said. 'I can do up my own buttons,' a quip that, to Breda's consternation, drew laughter. 'Now, seventeen pounds, was it? With you, sir.'

The gentleman in question, not wishing to seem like a spoilsport, called out, 'Seventeen, it is. Knock me down quick 'fore the wife finds out.'

Steve Pepperdine rapped his hammer and, having warmed up the audience, moved swiftly on to lot number two.

One by one the items went, vase, rocking horse, paintings. The volumes of bird pictures fetched an astonishing one hundred guineas after an acrimonious bidding war between two shabby little booksellers who didn't look as if they had two pennies to rub together.

Breda's heart beat faster as lot number eighteen approached. She glanced round in search of her son but Morven had left him and his chums playing with the taps at the sink in the cloakroom where, she said, they'd be safe enough for a while.

'Lot number eighteen,' Steve Pepperdine announced. 'One pair of lady's shoes, Swiss made and split new. Who'll open the bidding?'

Madge Gaydon stood behind Breda, Morven at her side, an encouraging hand pressing into the small of her back.

Breda's arms were suddenly paralysed, her tongue stuck to the roof of her mouth. A strand of blonde hair popped from beneath her beret and bobbed on her damp brow. She flicked it away and heard Steve Pepperdine cry, 'A bid, we have a bid. What's that, madam? Is that a pound?'

Morven punched her lightly in the kidneys.

'Aaar,' Breda croaked.

'One pound I am bid for these exquisite shoes, suitable for dancing, hiking or digging the allotment. Guarantee waterproof – if it doesn't rain. Going at one pound, at one pound going . . .'

The hammer rose. Breda held her breath. Then, from her seat on stage, Trudy Littlejohn hissed, 'Steve?'

He turned and glanced over his shoulder, hammer aloft.

Trudy raised two fingers in a Victory Vee and, to avoid confusion, whispered something to dear Dr Pepperdine that only he could hear. He hesitated, lowered his arm, leaned an elbow on the slope of the lectern, pointed at Breda and informed her, 'Twenty-two shillings now is the bid.'

'What's Trudy playing at?' Madge muttered.

'The cow's running it up,' said Morven.

Breda thrust out her chest. 'Twenty-three.'

Steve Pepperdine received from Mrs Trudy Littlejohn another sign of victory. 'Five, that's twenty-five. Against you, madam.'

'Seven,' said Breda.

Craning forward, the vicar squinted at his wife in bewilderment and Lady Ashcroft so far forgot herself as to shake her head in obvious disapproval of Trudy Littlejohn's underhand tactics. 'And two,' said Trudy, smiling.

Breda didn't hesitate. 'Thirty shillings.'

'Thirty-five,' said Trudy Littlejohn.

'No, Breda, no,' said Morven urgently. 'That's enough. Let her keep the flaming things.'

'Madam, it's with you,' said Stevie Pepperdine.

And Breda, close to tears, shook her head.

The word 'lice' was never mentioned but at some point in their sojourn in the ladies' cloakroom Linda Gaydon decided that all Cockney children had them and Billy Hooper was no exception. She held his head under the tap while Dorothy scrubbed his scalp with a bar of carbolic soap someone had left beneath the washbasin.

Billy expressed his disapproval by screeching and kicking the wall until Linda kindly wiped the soap from his stinging eyes and, with Dorothy's comb, inserted a neat little parting in his hair before she returned him to his mother, nit-free and soaking wet.

'Billy, Billy,' Breda said, 'what 'ave you been up to now?'

'I told um, Mrs Hooper,' Linda said, 'not to play with the tap but he just wouldn't listen.'

Breda was too disconsolate to press for the truth. She took off her scarf, towelled Billy's hair with it and, sticking the scarf into her pocket and her beret on to her son's head, led him outside and down the lane away from St John's church hall and the humiliation she'd suffered there.

'It's a half-hour to the next bus,' Morven said. 'I think what we all need is a nice cup of tea. What do you say, Billy? Tea and a bun. Auntie Morven's treat.'

'Yus,' said Billy and took his new-found auntie's hand.

Shay Bridge's only tearoom was crowded with fugitives from the auction tucking into teacakes, muffins and the dainty lemon-flavoured sponge cakes that were the speciality of the house. Hunched at a corner table the two booksellers who had haggled over *Birds of Britain* were haggling still.

Three women from Orrell's staff gave Breda a wave while Morven claimed a table by the window. Taking Billy on her knee, she made room for Madge and the girls who had been given a good talking-to by their mother and were, at least temporarily, subdued.

Breda slumped despondently in a chair by the window. Through the bull's-eye glass she could make out blurred images of Shay Bridge's quaint black and white timbered houses, stark in the fading light. It would be dark before she got home to the railway carriage and, suddenly, she longed to be back in Shadwell, not stuck here among strangers whose notion of fun was to humiliate anyone who wasn't as posh as they were.

She sighed, reached across the table and adjusted the beret that had tipped over Billy's nose.

'Why'd she do it?' Breda said. 'I mean, buying back her own blessed shoes.'

'She has it in for you,' Madge Gaydon said.

'What 'arm have I ever done 'er?'

'Basically,' Morven said, 'I think she's just an evil bitch. Why did you want those shoes so badly anyway?'

'I don't know. I just did.'

'Pretty they were,' Madge said, 'but not much use hereabouts.'

The tea arrived. Morven poured cups for Madge and Breda and milk from the jug for the children. Madge set to with the jam dish, a spoon and spreading knife and the muffins disappeared as if by magic.

'I wouldn't want to be in your shoes – pardon the expression – on Monday,' Madge said. 'I barely know the woman but from what you've told me she's a nasty 'un and won't hesitate to rub it in.'

Morven wiped jam from Billy's mouth with her

handkerchief. 'If that is her game then she'd better be careful. By the time I get through with Trudy Littlejohn she won't know what hit her.'

'What *are* you talkin' about?' Breda said.

'Revenge, of course,' said Morven.

8

It was not in Derek Willets's nature to embroider the truth. He wasn't one of those sailors who, at the drop of a hat, will regale you with fantastic tales of derring-do in far-flung places. The only tangible evidence of his travels reposed on top of the piano in the drawing room of his mother's house overlooking the golf links in Troon: a random collection of ornaments from the odd corners of the world to which the service had carried him in the heady days before the Royal Navy began to prepare for war.

On Mama's piano there were no souvenirs from the Denmark Strait, from Narvik or Dunkirk or, now that the Italians had entered the fray, would there be trophies from long-haul trips escorting troopships to Egypt or the Far East. On that score Derek Willets lied by omission, by revealing nothing of the horrors of sea warfare or the perils that lay ahead, not least of which would be playing hopscotch, as Baz put it, with U-boats, E-boats and dive-bombers in the Western Approaches now that the French ports had fallen to the Germans.

Contrary to what Basil liked to believe, Derek was no swaggering salt with a girl in every port, though he had been less generous with the truth when he'd told Susan that he no longer had a girlfriend. First Officer Wren, Grace Alvarez, was currently serving in Gibraltar. It was almost a year since their paths had crossed. There had been no promises made, no commitment on either side and the affair hadn't ended; it had simply been put on hold.

For better or worse then, he had a lover far away and a C-class twenty-year-old destroyer sitting in a dockyard in Portsmouth awaiting his arrival. And, like it or not, Susan Cahill had a husband.

Even as he lingered by the bed in his brother's house in Salt Street looking down at Susan fast asleep, he knew that the one thing he must not do was fall in love. There would be time enough for that when he was Basil's age and the navy had done with him. He resisted the urge to kiss her and crept off without saying goodbye.

Walter Boscombe was far too downy a bird to follow the sensational report from Spain with anything controversial. Friday's *Speaking Up* was devoted to items of home news rounded out by a discussion of sorts between a trade unionist and a junior minister from the Department of Home Affairs who came armed with so many facts and figures that Zach Gillespie almost fell asleep listening to him.

The raid on London in the wee small hours was so intense that even Mr Boscombe was unwilling to run the gauntlet for the sake of a late supper at his club. He settled for ordering sausage rolls and tea from the snack bar for the guests while the staff, Larry and Mr Gillespie among them, toddled off to find corners to snooze in until it was safe to go home.

Susan had no particular reason to go home and, to judge by the explosions that rocked the Calcutta, might well find that she had no home to go to. She was relieved that Derek had left early on Friday and was, presumably, safe out of London.

She was filling in the daily log when Mr Boscombe brought her tea. He pushed the typewriter to one side, put the mug on the desk, then, stepping back, closed the cubby door. So far he hadn't mentioned their meeting in the Dorchester but she was well aware that wouldn't be the end of it.

She cupped the tea mug in both hands, waiting.

'You do seem to have your pick of the chaps, Mrs Cahill,' he began. 'Have you known Commander Willets long?'

'No, not long.'

'Met him through his brother, I suppose?'

'Hmm,' she answered.

'At the wedding, was it?'

'Yes.'

'How long have you known Vivian Proudfoot?'

'Quite some time.'

'Did you work on her new book, *Enemy in Our Midst*?'

'I helped a little.'

'It's quite critical of Churchill, I believe.'

Oh, Susan thought, so that's it. He isn't interested in me. He's fishing for information about Vivian. Cautiously, she said, 'Given that the book's not published until April I don't see how anyone can say what it's about, sir.'

He ground out his cigarette in the ashtray and promptly lit another. 'You may not be aware of it, Susan, but *The Times* has already turned down an opportunity to publish extracts.'

'I am aware of it.'

'In which case,' said Walter Boscombe, 'it's probably occurred to you that pressure was put on the editor, Dawson, not to print anything that might reflect badly on Churchill.'

'Pressure by Astor,' said Susan, 'or by Lord Halifax?'

'Unlike Dawson, I don't take advice from Astor *or* Halifax. Our programme might be called *Speaking Up for Britain*,

Susan, but by now you must be aware that it's really Speaking to America. I've no intention of sitting on my backside and letting the most persuasive medium ever invented remain mealy-mouthed just to placate the Minister of Information, that Bible-bashing hypocrite, Reith, whose ideas about probity and impartiality died a death the minute Poland was invaded. I'm planning a series of programmes on how we deal with traitors and Quislings. Eight programmes to start with,' Walter Boscombe went on, 'to give our friends across the Pond something to think about. What do you say? Are you with me?'

She pressed her knees together and, in as prim a voice as she could muster, answered, 'Yes, of course. What do you want me to do?'

'Persuade your friend Vivian to lead off the series.'

'That might not be so easy. Basil doesn't like what you're doing. He believes that once he's fit again he'll be brought back to produce *Speaking Up*.'

'There's no chance of that happening.'

'I know,' Susan said. 'Do you have a title for the series?'

'The Fifth Column: Who Are They?'

'That's really sticking your neck out,' Susan said. 'Whatever doubts she may have about Churchill, Vivian is no fifth columnist.'

'No,' Walter Boscombe said, 'but her brother is. Now, I suggest you catch some sleep. You'll have an early start tomorrow.'

'Will I?' said Susan. 'Where am I going?'

'To call on your friend Vivian.'

Hereford railway station seemed a lot less quaint than it had done the first time she'd stepped off the train from London six years ago. Stripped of sign boards and travel hoardings it was just as bleak as most other provincial railway stations, save for the stampede of RAF recruits heading for pubs and teashops to refresh themselves before reporting to the newly commissioned training station at Credenhill.

The broad high street was shrouded in misty rain and this time there was no David Proudfoot to collect her in his open-topped motorcar and carry her off to the sprawling Tudor-style farmhouse at Hackles where, perched on an umpire's chair that graced the tennis court in front of the farmhouse, Mercer Hughes, her first love and first lover, had been waiting for them.

The tennis court was probably a vegetable patch by now and the placid old cow, Daisy, would be gone, the pasture that looked out to the hills of Wales ploughed for cereal crops. She wasn't bound for Hackles, however. She was bound for Gadney, a village two or three miles from David Proudfoot's farm, to which, on a sleepy Sunday morning in what seemed like another age, she had accompanied the Proudfoot family to church.

She sheltered out of the rain in the station doorway until, eventually, a taxi-cab showed up. The driver, a small, pinch-featured chap well past middle age, peered out through the cab window.

'Credenhill?' he asked.

'Gadney.'

'Cost you.'

'I'm sure it will,' said Susan.

She bundled her overnight bag into the back seat and closed the door. The cab smelled faintly rancid as if someone had been sick inside. She sat back and lit a cigarette. The cab swung away from the high street. She glimpsed the cathedral, its outlines blotted by rain, and remembered, fondly, visiting it with Mercer.

'You a friend of his?' the driver called over his shoulder.

'What?' Susan said. 'Who?'

'Mr Proudfoot.'

'What makes you think that?'

'Take lots of folks out to Mr Proudfoot's place at Hackles, I do. His sister's staying in Gadney. Took a chap out there already this week. It's not much of a road.'

'I'm not a friend of Mr Proudfoot.' Susan hesitated. 'I am a friend of his sister, as it happens. I assume you know where she lives.'

'Oh, I know where she lives,' said the driver. 'You somebody famous?'

'No,' Susan answered, then, leaning forward, asked, 'What sort of people visit Mr Proudfoot?'

'That actress, seen her in the pictures – she's been here once or twice. Very nice. Tipped me three shillings when I picked her up one night. That big fellow in the government, Sir somebody, he comes down at weekends, him and his secretary. She's nice too.'

'Mr Proudfoot's daughters, do they ever visit?'

'Miss Eleanor? I hear she's in the army.'

'And the other one – Caroline?'

'She's at Credenhill. And she's got a feller.' He sniggered. 'The things they get up to in that back seat don't bear repeating. She's a naughty girl, she is.'

'Oh, really?' Susan said, then, suddenly weary of gossip, closed the window to shut him up.

Wearing a reefer jacket, a heavy sweater and flannel trousers, Vivian might have been one of Derek's ratings, not his sister-in-law. Gone was the make-up, the pretty clothes, the coiffed hair. She had assumed again the mannish appearance that had made Susan question her sexual preferences when Vivian had first interviewed her for the job of personal assistant.

Viv opened the cottage door while Susan was paying off the cabby. She leaned against the doorpost with a fist on her hip and a cigarette, without the ivory holder, dangling from her lip.

Her first words were, 'He isn't here.'

'Who isn't here?'

'Derek.'

'I know he isn't here. He's gone back to his ship.'

'I thought you were – never mind, you're here now.'

Viv pushed herself from the doorpost and made way for Susan to enter a tiny unfurnished hallway.

'Filthy day,' Susan said, taking off her hat and shaking it.

'They're all filthy days down here,' said Vivian. 'I'm constantly being informed that the summer was glorious and we should have been here in August. Is that luggage? You can't stay, Susan. We don't have room.'

'Well, I can't get back to London tonight,' Susan said, 'so you'll just have to make room.'

'I'm being rude. I'm sorry,' Vivian said. 'Here's your hat, what's your hurry. Come into the scullery. It's the only warm room in the house. At least we have electricity, which is something to be thankful for, I suppose, and a flushing lavatory. Peeing by candlelight never struck me as intrinsically romantic.'

The scullery was on the same miniature scale as the hall. Vivian nudged her way past Susan, flipped open the lid of a stove and fed in a small shovelful of coke from a bucket beneath the sink. She filled a large black kettle from the brass tap at the sink and dumped it on top of the stove, then, turning, forced a smile. 'Do pardon me, my dear. Evidence to the contrary, I *am* glad to see you. Give the kettle an hour or so to boil and I'll make us tea – unless you'd prefer cocoa.'

'Cocoa?'

'My hubby has reverted to a nursery diet: cocoa, custard, junket and raspberry jelly. He keens for a bowl of chicken soup but if you can find a spare chicken running round here you're a better man than I am. In any case, it's all moot given that he eats hardly anything. He's sick and won't admit it. He should be in hospital or at least have a specialist examine him. But will he budge? Oh, no, not my Basil. He doses himself with aspirin and cough lozenges, sticks his head under a towel and inhales Friar's Balsam as if it's nothing worse than a head cold. Frankly, I'm at my wits' end what to do with him.'

'Who's that in there?' said a voice from the hall. 'I'm not deaf, you know. Don't tell me it's another damned quack.'

Vivian sighed and opened the scullery door.

'Susan!' Basil exclaimed, then, delight waning, added, 'Have you come to tell me I've been sacked?'

'Don't be ridiculous,' Vivian said. 'You know perfectly well you can't be sacked when you're sick.'

'What's she doing here then?'

'She,' said Susan, taking his arm, 'is beginning to wonder that herself. Come along, you old grouch, give me the tour.'

He was clad in flannels, a dress shirt without a collar and a woollen dressing gown that hung from his skinny shoulders like rags on a scarecrow. A sling, fashioned from the belt of a trench coat, was draped about his neck but he had removed his arm from it and held it, the arm, down by his side, fist closed as if he were hiding something in his hand. He smelled strongly of medicines and faintly of sweat, hardly more than a ghost of the energetic man who had taught her the broadcasting ropes.

She hid her dismay as best she could and followed him three paces across the hall into a room that was both kitchen and parlour. She stood by while he eased himself into a rocking chair padded with a blanket and a threadbare cushion. He sat back, struggling for breath, and glared at Susan as if daring her to offer sympathy.

A table covered with a stained oilcloth, three wooden chairs, a stool and the rocking chair were arranged around a shallow stone fireplace in the grate of which smouldered a green log topped by a few lumps of coal. On the floor by the window was a wireless set, anomalously modern, and on the window ledge, a telephone.

From the doorway, Vivian said, 'All mod cons, as you can see. The lavatory is the door to the left of the hall. There are two bedrooms more or less tacked on at the back. Basil has the big one to himself. I repose on a camp cot in the little one. If you're still of a mind to share our luxurious accommodations, Susan, I'll bunk with Basil for one night – it won't kill him – and you can have the cot. Now, give me your coat and hat and make yourself comfortable.'

'What do you do for groceries?' Susan asked.

'David took our ration cards and sends a chap down on a cart every other day with food, fuel and cigarettes. I've asked him for books but so far nothing has materialised and I'm stuck with a load of trashy novelettes that someone left behind.'

'Doesn't David still have the library out in the barn?'

'No, that's gone.'

'Sold?'

'Stored somewhere safe for the duration, I expect.'

'Why doesn't he put you up at Hackles?' Susan said. 'Surely it would be more comfortable than here.'

'Hackles is a working farm now. My brother has actually been forced to get his hands dirty. I mean literally this time,' said Vivian. 'I'm grateful for all he's done for us but he has friends down from London almost every weekend and I've no wish to become involved with that bunch.'

'Hah!' said Basil wheezily. 'He's still a villain, I say.'

'He got you a wireless, didn't he?' Viv reminded her husband. 'And a telephone? If you weren't so damnably stubborn he'd have you in a proper hospital where you belong.'

'You just want rid of me, don't you?' Basil said.

'Absolutely,' Vivian said and taking Susan's coat and hat went out into the hall to find a place for them.

Basil gestured to Susan to come closer, then, glancing over his shoulder at the door, whispered, 'Tell me the truth. Has Boscombe sent you to sweeten me up before he gives me the boot?'

'More or less,' Susan said. 'Only it's not the boot.'

'What is it then? What does he want from me?'

'That,' said Susan, 'is what we have to talk about. He doesn't want you for *Speaking Up*, Basil, he wants a talk from Vivian.'

'Vivian?'

'To promote her new book.'

'Boscombe never promotes anyone but himself.' Basil sucked in two or three deep breaths. 'Whose side are you on, anyway?'

'It's not a question of taking sides,' Susan said. 'I'm doing my job, that's all. What would you have me do – resign?'

'No, of course not.' He paused, then, with a grimace, admitted, 'Boscombe certainly pulled something out of the fire with that Spanish report. I'd never have had the gall to do anything like it. What does he want with Vivian?'

'He's going after the fifth column and needs a lead to give the series momentum. I think he wants a piece from Vivian because she's a woman and an outsider.'

'If Vivian accepts Boscombe's offer, how long would she be away from home?'

'Overnight.'

'In London?'

'Of course.'

'Susan, I'm not fit to travel.' He glanced at the door again. 'Vivian's right. I am sick. I'm sick and I'm scared. If something happened to me, what would Viv do? No,' he corrected himself, 'I suppose what I really mean is what would I do without Vivian?'

'A question I often ask myself.' Vivian entered the kitchen bearing a tray of crockery. 'The walls in this place are paper thin. I heard every word.' She put the tray on the table and adjusted the cushion behind Basil's shoulders. 'This talk – what does it pay?'

'Fifteen guineas.'

'Expenses?'

'Yes, and expenses.'

'It's not to be sneezed at,' Vivian said.

'Dear God!' said Basil. 'You're not actually considering doing something for Walter Boscombe.'

'I wouldn't be doing it for Boscombe. I'd be doing it to help the country in time of war.'

'Hoh!' Basil spluttered. 'That's everyone's excuse.'

'I haven't agreed to do it yet, dearest. I'm simply mulling it over. Meanwhile, let's change the subject. Susan, what did you make of Commander Willets?'

'Every inch a gentleman,' Susan answered.

'Every inch?' Basil said.

'In a manner of speaking,' said Susan.

Supper at the Willets' country retreat was a far cry from dinner at the Dorchester. Vivian had never been much of a cook. The cheese and vegetable cutlets were lumpy, the custard too.

Basil ate one-handed and, to Susan's surprise, meekly allowed Vivian to chop up the cutlets for him. Between entrée and dessert, he suddenly fell asleep. One moment he was chatting and the next he was gone, eyes closed, breath rattling in his throat.

'Don't be alarmed,' Vivian said. 'It happens all the time.'

'Shouldn't we put him to bed?'

'He isn't comfortable lying down. He has dreams, nightmares. Best let him be, my dear. Finish your custard.'

'I think I've had enough.'

'Pretty dreadful, isn't it? Come, we'll move over to the fire. I'll make coffee in a minute. If you keep your nose clean, I might find a snifter of brandy to go with it.'

Vivian lowered herself into the rocking chair, lit two cigarettes and passed one to Susan who, perched on the stool, peered into the fire as if the future were written in the flames.

'I don't like it here,' Vivian said. 'I don't like not having a bathroom or washing my smalls in the kitchen sink or having to depend on my brother to supply us with necessities. But I'll put up with it for as long as it takes to keep Basil out of London. How bad are things in the city?'

'Bad,' said Susan. 'Very, very bad. The shelter at the crescent end of Salt Street was flattened. It might easily have been us.'

'Us?' said Vivian. 'Of course, Derek was with you.'

'He took me to dinner on Thursday, at the Dorchester.'

'Lucky you,' said Vivian. 'How was it? I mean, how was he?'

'He really is a gentleman. I'm surprised he's not married.'

'He says he has a girl somewhere, a Wren, but how that works . . .' Vivian shrugged.

'He told me it was over.'

'Perhaps it is.' Viv smoked in silence for half a minute. 'Have you heard from Danny lately?'

'Not lately, no.'

'Is *it* over, Susan?'

'I don't know. I'm so caught up in getting through each day I seldom think about Danny. Mr Boscombe's full of ideas and has no fear of anyone.'

'Don't tell me you're falling for your boss?' said Vivian. 'How utterly predictable. What is it about young women these days? They seem to think no man is out of reach.'

'I'm not in love with Walter Boscombe. I'm not in love with anyone which, in the middle of a war, is all to the good.'

'Let me ask you a not too serious question: if you met a man you really loved what would you give up for him?'

'I have no idea,' said Susan.

'Your job? Your career?'

'I doubt it,' Susan said. 'I think I'd try for a compromise.'

'Compromise.' Vivian savoured the word. 'I see.'

'We all have to compromise these days, don't we?'

'We do, indeed,' Vivian said. 'Now, here's another question for you: if I deliver a talk for this programme of yours, how much will my agreement raise your stock with Boscombe?'

'Quite a bit,' said Susan.

'Then you may tell your Mr Boscombe I'll do it, but only with a minimum of interference. I've no intention of becoming a mouthpiece for a man whose views I deplore.'

'What are the other conditions?'

'Basil will have to give his blessing.'

'Will he?'

'Yes, I'm sure he will.'

'Why?' said Susan.

'Because he loves me.'

'Oh,' said Susan, surprised. 'I never thought of that.'

'I'll bet you didn't,' said Vivian.

It was still raining when the taxi-cab crawled down the muddy track shortly after noon on Sunday but the wind had abated and the trees stood black and motionless against a pasteboard sky. In spite of the storm, she'd slept soundly in the camp cot. Vivian would have had her stay longer but trains were erratic and Susan, by then, was eager to get back to London.

'Nice time with your friends?' the cab driver asked, hoping, no doubt, for more gossip to pass on to his next passenger.

'Very nice, thank you,' Susan replied and, tipping her hat over her nose, pressed herself into a corner and pretended to sleep, a hint too broad for even a nosy cabby to ignore.

Spruce and well rested, she arrived at the Calcutta just after three on Monday afternoon. She was surprised to find Mr Boscombe not in his office but seated in her cubby typing on her typewriter.

He looked up, stripped a letter from the machine and, folding it, put it into his pocket. 'Well?' he said.

'She'll do it,' Susan said. 'She won't write to order, though. It's her script and she won't let anyone muck around with it. If you don't like it then you can tear up the contract and the deal's off.'

'What did you offer her?'

'Fifteen guineas and expenses.'

'Generous.'

'Vivian isn't interested in cash,' Susan said. 'If you must know, she's doing it for me.'

'You didn't bump into David Proudfoot when you were down there, by any chance?'

'I wasn't there long enough.'

'Did you tell Willets that he won't be coming back to *Speaking Up*?' Walter Boscombe said.

'I wouldn't worry about Basil,' Susan said. 'I doubt if he'll be back in harness for some time. He has a lung disease brought on, I think, by shock.'

'Another casualty of the war,' Walter Boscombe said. 'I take it she'll keep him out of London as long as possible?'

'I think that's her intention,' Susan said. 'Galley proofs of *Enemy in Our Midst* are due next week. If you want a set for yourself her agent Charlie Ames will arrange it. I also have her telephone number. She says you may call her when you've scheduled the broadcast.'

'Your friend Mrs Willets is being a lot more cooperative than I had anticipated. I was under the impression she was somewhat prickly.'

'She is prickly,' Susan said, 'but she's also patriotic.'

'Patriotic? Well, that is a surprise. Patriotism isn't held in high esteem by our intellectual elite these days.' He squeezed out from behind the desk. 'Apart from that, Susan, how was your weekend?'

'Damp.'

He laughed. 'You did well, though, very well. Thank you,' he said and put a hand on her shoulder.

It was the first time he'd touched her.

Somehow she felt it wouldn't be the last.

9

If there was one thing Archie Jackson enjoyed more than anything else it was paperwork. He was never happier than when locked away in his office with his pens and pencils, purchase journal, stores register, stock book and, joy of joys, the weekly trading account to keep him occupied. Pinned to the wall behind his desk was a bird's-eye plan of the canteen detailing every bay and alcove, every sink, draining board and stacking table, every urn, oven and boiling pan, all wonderfully devoid of women in aprons, bickering and sniggering; a picture, in other words, far removed from reality.

Back in his heyday in Salford, Archie had ruled the roost with a rod of iron by hiving off to his managers all the pettifogging complaints that the female staff threw up, but here in Orrell's he stood alone, his rod of iron turned, it seemed, to liquorice.

Never was this more apparent than on those Mondays – usually Mondays – when members of the Navy Board arrived to inspect progress on the top-secret work being done in Shed 3 and, as befitted their status, demand a silver service lunch.

It galled Archie to admit that while he might be able to tell Stilton from Red Leicester at thirty paces he could not for the life of him fold a linen napkin into a pyramid or place the cutlery in precisely the correct order; nor did he know, which Trudy Littlejohn claimed to do, what dishes would appeal to the refined palates of men used to dining in the best London clubs.

Archie's bids on both the home-brewed beer and the case of cider at the Spitfire Fund auction had fallen short and he was clear-eyed and clear-headed when he turned up to tackle the books that fateful morning. He had just stuck his nose into an analysis of invoice sheets when, with barely a knock, the office door was flung open and Trudy Littlejohn, forgoing her usual icy politeness, called out, 'They're coming. They're coming. The Navy Board are coming.'

'Oh, right,' said Archie, leaping up.

He placed a jar of pickled onions on top of the invoices in lieu of a paperweight and, fumbling in his trouser pocket for his keys, followed Mrs Littlejohn's long legs out into the canteen.

'Meat, Mr Jackson,' she shouted. 'We must have meat.'

'Certainly, Mrs Littlejohn,' Archie replied and, swerving, headed for the cold room, while Morven Hastie nudged her friend Breda, and, stepping boldly forth, announced her willingness to cook.

'Cook what?' said Trudy.

'Soup to start with,' said Morven. 'Then curry.'

'Curry?'

'Fish curry, Mrs Littlejohn,' Morven said. 'We've a slab of salt hake in the cold room. Boil it, flake it and Bob's your uncle. How are we for onions?'

'I'm sure we can find some somewhere.' Trudy peered suspiciously at the young woman. 'You wouldn't be planning on making anything too hot, would you?'

'Not me, Mrs Littlejohn. How many for lunch?'

'Twelve, I believe, is the usual number.'

'If we serve the curry in individual bowls with mashed spuds on the side we're off to the races,' Morven told her. 'I'll need two tins of pears and a jar of horseradish sauce.'

Trudy's eyes widened. 'For the curry?'

'For the soup,' said Morven. 'For the curry, chutney, sultanas, vinegar and curry powder – and carrots, of course.'

'Of course,' said Trudy Littlejohn. 'Mrs Hooper – Breda – would you be good enough to see that Morven gets what she wants.'

'No problem, Mrs Littlejohn,' said Breda obligingly, as if the incident of the red shoes had been entirely forgotten. 'Will you be requiring me to serve today?'

Naval officers, of whatever age and station, were not averse to having attractive young blondes with large busts leaning over them to fill a water glass or lift away an empty plate, a duty that Breda had diligently performed several times before.

'Yes, yes,' said Trudy Littlejohn. 'Find a fresh apron and a cap that fits and make sure your nails are clean,' then loped off to tell Mr Jackson to break out the hake.

'What're you up to, Morven?' Breda whispered. 'You're not gonna poison the Navy Board, are you?'

'I've too much respect for my own cooking to do a thing like that,' Morven answered, 'never mind the respect I have for the Senior Service. But . . .'

'But?' said Breda, frowning.

'Boy geniuses are fair game.'

Mitmee's 'Famous' soups came in metal jerry-cans, like petrol, and were guaranteed to please. Please some they no doubt did, for they were cheap enough for budget-conscious canteen managers and convenient enough for lazy chefs to decant without caring about taste. Morven couldn't deny that Mitmee's soups contained 'real' meat and vegetables and that the nutritive value, scaled on the label of every can, was scientifically accurate but she remained adamant that the industrial processes by which the soups were produced robbed them of any discernible flavour.

She had already done something – Morvie's little secret – with Mitmee's Oxtail that had beefed up the bland brown liquid to the point where factory hands, taste buds numbed by booze, cigarettes and too many lodging-house suppers, sat up and responded to a first spoonful with surprise, a second spoonful with delight and a third with expressions of such approval that Mrs Littlejohn and even placid Mrs Greevy were instantly on the defensive – and Morven was promptly removed from Soups and Gravies and sent back to Pies and Pastries where she could do less harm.

Trudy's motto, 'If they're hungry enough they'll eat anything,' went by the board when the Royal Navy hove into view and Morven's offer to whip up something extra special was one that Trudy could not, in conscience, refuse.

Tomato, pear and horseradish soup headed the menu that Trudy pecked out on a typewriter in the clerk's office in the hope that the naval officers would appreciate the subtle flavours and, if not, that fish curry and rhubarb tart would make up for any deficiencies in the starter.

While Trudy raced about typing menus, unpacking tablecloths and folding napkins, Morven calmly filled a cauldron with Mitmee's anaemic substitute for tomato soup and added mashed tinned pears and horseradish sauce to give the liquid bite. Rustling up lunch for a dozen was, it seemed, no problem for Morven who had been trained at Glasgow's famous Dough School and had worked in kitchens far worse than Orrell's before disappointment in love and an advert in *Caterer's Weekly* had brought her south to add her groats-worth to the war effort.

She washed the strips of hake, rinsed and refilled the pans and put the fish on the stove to boil. When that was almost done, she fried onions and carrots, added a quantity of stock, curry powder and a little, not too much, flour, which she stirred gently in her favourite pan, now and then skipping across the kitchen to apply a paddle to the soup.

Outside, unobserved by the kitchen staff, two long-bonneted motorcars arrived and a couple of high-ranking naval officers in dress uniform stepped from the cars into Shed No. 3. They were trailed by uniformed aides and two civilian gentlemen in dark overcoats. The soldiers on guard barely had time to salute before the whole shebang disappeared inside the shed and the door was bolted from within.

'How long? Oh, Lord, how long?' Trudy Littlejohn cried.

'Forty minutes,' Morven informed her. 'I hope they're not late.'

When it came to mess call men who selflessly served King and country, in whatever capacity, were seldom, if ever, late.

At five to noon the Navy Board contingent, accompanied by the civilians, the senior engineer, Mr Ferris, and three top boffins, including Dr Pepperdine, trooped across the yard and entered the side door of the canteen.

They detoured into a cloakroom that had been cleared of riff-raff then made their way to a long table against the east wall separated from the hoi polloi by a row of empty chairs and couple of potted plants that Mr Jackson had dug up from somewhere. The table setting was not quite the Ritz or the late-lamented Carlton, which had recently been reduced to rubble by a direct hit, but it represented a fair substitute for fine dining.

Four young women had been appointed to attend the guests, two to serve and two to clear. After much debate between Trudy and Mr Jackson, trolleys had been trundled out to ensure that the food arrived hot and that the business of clearing did not intrude upon the diners' deep discussions.

Breda waited patiently as a prayer was said – Mr Ferris, a staunch Methodist, did the honours – then wheeled her trolley from behind the serving counter and placed before each of the gentlemen on the west side of the table a plate of soup while another blonde built to scale did likewise for the blokes on the east.

Steve Pepperdine was flanked by an aide in uniform and an enigmatic civilian who, having shed his black hat and coat, appeared if not shabby at least quite ordinary and, Breda couldn't help but notice, apparently suffered from dandruff.

Stevie, of course, was in his element. He'd left his doctorate on the bench with his latest design for a stabilising gyroscope that would satisfy the demands of the Fleet Air Arm and was now intent on being the life and soul of the party by trotting out all the filthy jokes he couldn't possibly tell in mixed company.

'. . . and then, ha ha, the bear said to her . . .' He paused, irked, perhaps, at being interrupted on the punch line.

'Soup, Dr Pepperdine?' said Breda.

'Hot and spicy, is it?'

'Sir,' said Breda.

'Just the way I like it. Ladle it out, love.'

The aide had a dutiful smile on his face but the civilian's expression was neutral, bordering on sour.

'I say' – Steve Pepperdine wagged his spoon – 'aren't you the shoe woman? You are, aren't you? Hoh, yes. What a to-do that was.'

Breda served the civilian and moved on down the table, ears burning, while Dr Pepperdine regaled his fellow diners with an account of the Spitfire Auction and how nimbly his friend, Mrs Littlejohn, had spiked the guns of one of her 'gels' who was getting a bit above herself. Only the aide laughed, politely.

Breda trundled her empty trolley through the gate at the serving counter and shoved it down the aisle towards the range where Morven was filling bowls with curry.

'Pig!' Breda hissed.

'What's Stevie up to now?' said Morven.

'He's telling them all about me and the shoes.'

'Never mind.' Morven placed a steaming bowl directly into Breda's hands. 'Make sure our Steve gets this one. It's guaranteed to shut him up.'

'Hot and spicy, you mean?'

'Very hot and very spicy.'

'Just the way the beggar likes it,' Breda said and placed the bowl on the lowest shelf of the trolley to keep it safe for Steve.

'An excellent soup,' said one of the uniforms, dabbing his lips with a napkin. 'It's a great treat to run across institutional fare of such quality. Please convey my compliments to Mrs Littlejohn.'

Nods of agreement and murmurs of approval endorsed the officer's remark. The woman who was clearing plates looked confused and then, stopping just short of a curtsey, promised to deliver the message.

Breda advanced with the curry.

'Aaah!' said one of the civilians, emulating the Bisto boy. 'By George, that smells good. What is it, if I may ask?'

'Curry, sir, fish curry,' Breda informed him, putting out the bowls. 'It's a favourite with our patrons.'

'If it tastes as good as it smells, I'm not surprised,' said the civilian seated opposite Steve.

Breda drew Steve's bowl from the lower shelf of the trolley and placed it before him, then looked across the table at the man who'd just spoken. It had been six months since she'd last seen him. No trench-coat and trilby now but a smart three-piece dark blue suit with a subtle chalk stripe to the material and a handkerchief in the breast pocket. His hair had been barbered and he was shaved as smooth as a baby's bott but the features were unmistakable: the sharply pointed nose, the unrevealing eyes and the mouth that hovered on the verge of a smile, like, she thought, a crocodile's.

The prank that Morven and she were playing on Steve Pepperdine suddenly seemed childish. She was only vaguely aware that Dr Pepperdine, without waiting for the guests to be served, was already shovelling curry into his gob and puffing as the ground peppercorns that Morven had added to his bowl hit home.

'Is something wrong, Dr Pepperdine?' an aide asked. 'Don't you care for curry?'

'No, no,' Steve gasped. 'It's just – just 'ot.'

'Can't be too hot for me,' said Mr Ferris. 'When I was mining manganese in Goa for the Portuguese, the vindaloos melted your fillings. Come on, Steve. Tuck in. Put some hair on your chest.'

Swallowing hard and beginning to sweat, Stevie said, 'Yes, I've – I've had worse – better – hotter than this many a time.' Manfully, he shoved in another forkful and reached for the water jug.

Breda dispensed the last of the bowls and, not daring to look back, headed for the security of the kitchen.

'What's up with you?' said Morven. 'Don't tell me Stevie dropped dead? It wasn't that hot.'

'No,' Breda got out. 'It's one of the civilians. I've met him before. Jessop. He's the copper who put my mother in jail.'

'For what?'

'He said my mother was a spy but that was just to put the screws on me to tell 'im where me daddy was hiding. I got my mother out but they grabbed me daddy and sent 'im to Canada without a trial. The ship was sunk and 'e drowned.'

'Wow!' said Morven. 'No wonder you turned pale. What's this Jessop character doing with the navy?'

'He's Special Branch, I think.'

'I'll bet he's here to make sure our torpedoes are safe.'

'Why wouldn't they be?' said Breda.

''Cause there are Nazi agents everywhere. Some folk would sell their granny to the Germans for the right price.'

'Who? Who'd do a 'orrible thing like that?' Breda asked.

'I can think of one straight off,' Morven answered. 'Can't you?'

'Do you think Jessop recognised you?' Danny asked.

'He recognised me all right,' Breda answered. 'But 'e never said a word, not a bleedin' word.'

'Are you absolutely sure it was him?'

'It's not a face I'm liable to forget. Question is, what's he doing with the Navy Board?'

Danny lay back on the bed, nursing a mug of coffee.

She'd been relieved when he'd turned up at Shady Nook. She needed a friend to talk to, someone who knew her for what she was and all she'd been through. When she'd opened the carriage door he'd looked like a monk standing there, a monk from some poor order, with the torch in his hand and, tucked into his chest, a book some kind person at Wood Norton had given him to give to Billy.

It was snug in the carriage, rain drizzling gently on the roof and the fire crackling in the stove. Fed, watered and in his pyjamas, Billy lay on his stomach on the bunk, absorbed in the book that Danny had brought him: *The Boy's Book of Wonders*.

She doubted if Billy understood what half the pictures meant and he couldn't, as yet, read more than a few words. After Danny left, if Billy wasn't asleep by then, she'd squeeze in beside him and explain, as best she could, what the pictures were all about. She wished sometimes that someone would climb into bed with her and explain what everything was all about.

Danny said, 'Don't let it worry you, Breda. My guess, Jessop's on special detail with the navy tae check out the stuff your guys are up to in that shed. It's got nothin' to do with you, sweetheart. He was probably just as surprised as you were to see you.'

'I don't like it, Danny.'

'Every copper in the country is jumpy,' Danny went on. 'The Nazis are devious bastards at the best of times and these aren't the best of times.'

'They're not gonna blow up Orrell's, are they?'

'Naw, naw,' said Danny soothingly.

Breda moved from the table to the bed. She needed comfort, reassurance, a cuddle. He put the coffee mug down on the floor and wrapped an arm about her as if she were eight years old again. She glanced at Billy who was still absorbed in the mysteries of modern science then, in a whisper, said, 'If anything happens to me . . .'

'Nothin's gonna happen tae you.'

'If something does, something bad – promise me you'll look after Billy. Promise me, Danny.'

'All right,' Danny said, 'though why you'd want a

scrofulous wee gutter rat frae Glasgow to look after your kid I can't imagine.'

'You looked after me okay,' said Breda. 'You looked after us when nobody else gave much of a damn.'

'Couldn't get rid of you, could I?' Danny tried to make light of it. 'If anythin' happens to you, Breda, I'll take care o' the boy.'

'Promise?'

'I promise.'

'I wish you weren't going away.'

'Goin' away?'

'To this wedding.'

'It's only Coventry an' only for one night. And,' he added, 'I'm not there yet. Something's brewin'. Nobody seems to know what's in the wind but they're all pretty agitated. If big news breaks in the next week or two leave'll be cancelled, we'll be goin' nowhere an' Griff'll have to postpone his honeymoon.'

'Poor Griff. Poor Kate too.'

'Aye,' said Danny, without conviction. 'Be a shame, that.' He took his arm from around her and glanced at his wristwatch. 'Gotta go, Breda. You okay now?'

'I'm fine. I'm glad you came by.'

He picked up the coffee mug and drained the dregs. 'What happened tae the Pepperdine guy?'

'He went home early. Tummy upset.' Breda smoothed her skirt and cleared her throat. 'Bit mean of us, I suppose, but it serves 'im right. He's a pain in the backside. Everybody else thought the grub was great, by the way.'

'Even Jessop?'

'Bleedin' copper! We should 'ave poisoned 'im instead.'

Breda took Danny's coat from the peg by the door and

helped him into it. She watched him lean over Billy and ruffle the boy's hair.

'Good book?' Danny asked.

'Yus,' Billy answered, looking up. 'Fanks, Danny. What's 'at?'

Danny peered over his shoulder. 'It's a train.'

'Wiff propellers?'

'That's right. It's a railplane. They only made one,' Danny said. 'Then they didn't make any more. Maybe railplanes'll be runnin' everywhere by the time you're grown up.'

'After the war?'

'Aye, after the war.'

'When my daddy comes back?'

'Sure, when your dad comes back,' Danny said. 'See you, Billy.'

'Not if I see you first,' the little boy said, chuckling, and, rolling on to his stomach, returned to his book of wonders.

10

It came as no great surprise when Mr Boscombe invited her to lunch. She was, after all, a woman sufficiently experienced to assume that he not only admired her loyalty but had finally twigged that beneath the trim brown suit she had a figure too.

'Keep your hand on your purse, love,' Larry advised. 'You know what he's like.'

'No, I don't know what he's like,' Susan said. 'And this is my opportunity to find out.'

Larry shrugged. 'I just hope you don't live to regret it.'

'You're not jealous by any chance?'

'Absolutely not,' Larry said. 'Boscombe's not my type. Where's he taking you?'

'I have no idea,' said Susan.

The Monday night broadcast had ended on a high note when Mr Gillespie had finally extracted from Joe Kennedy, the departing American ambassador, a grudging admission that Roosevelt's opponent in the presidential race, Wendell Wilkie, did not share a policy of no appeasement to aggressor states.

On Monday night, too, remarkably, there had been no alerts, not one. Courtesy of Larry and his sister's motorcar, Susan had been home in bed in Salt Street shortly after two.

Rested, refreshed, bathed, scented and with not a hair out of place she treated herself to a cab next morning and was back at the Calcutta by a quarter to one o'clock to keep her lunch appointment with the boss.

Mr Boscombe was waiting at the pavement's edge, leaning nonchalantly against the bonnet of a Bentley that certainly hadn't come from the BBC's motor pool. He wore a two-piece lounge suit and silk scarf and, though the weather was uncertain, no overcoat or hat. He watched Susan emerge from the cab, one leg at a time. Flipping away his cigarette, he opened the front passenger door of the Bentley and ushered her into the plush wood- and leather-smelling interior. He came around the bonnet to the driver's door and slid behind the steering wheel, drew on a pair of fine leather gloves, fitting them over his thick fingers, and started the engine.

The car moved smoothly away from the kerb, tyres crunching on the sprinkling of broken glass that strewed the street. They passed a gutted shop, a greengrocer's, the shattered front of a tailor's shop with a dummy in a tuxedo staring blankly out at them, then braked to a sudden halt.

Barricades had been erected at the street's end and a notice-board stated: 'Danger. Unexploded bomb'. A crowd of spectators pressed against the ropes, ignoring not only the warning but the policemen who were trying to move them out of harm's way.

'Idiots!' Mr Boscombe shook his head. 'Total bloody idiots. Anything for a show, I suppose, but no sense, no sense at all.' He rested his arm on the rear of the seat, reversed the Bentley back down Scobie Street at high speed, executed a three-point turn and set off up Montford Street, heading north-west.

Susan let out her breath. 'May I ask where we're going?'

'To interview a potential contributor. Did Willets never take you on a hunting trip?'

Basil's contacts were mainly in Whitehall, Westminster and the upper echelons of Fleet Street with a few celebrated academics, like Professor Cobbold, thrown in. He lunched, dined and sipped sherry with all the right people but had guarded his connections jealously.

Susan said, 'I thought we were going for lunch.'

'We are. We're supping with the devil incarnate.'

'And where does the devil incarnate live?'

'Darkest Middlesex.'

'Where in darkest Middlesex?' Susan persisted.

'Redmain House, just outside Harrow.'

'Redmain House? Sir Peter Redmain's pile?'

'The very same. He went to school with my father and they served some time in India together, many moons ago.'

'But isn't he . . .'

'One of Herr Hitler's old chums? Of course, he is,' Mr Boscombe told her and, finding the way ahead clear, put his foot down on the gas.

If Susan had expected some wooded estate with a mile-long drive wending through parkland she was doomed to disappointment. She'd seen photographs of Redmain House in old copies of the *Tatler* and, at the time of the Mosley scandal, on the front pages of the *Mirror* and the *Mail*. It was one of the *Mirror* journalists who'd dug up the name Redmain's fellow subalterns in the Bengal Lancers had given him and in yellow press references thereafter he'd once more become 'Rogue' Redmain.

The house was no Georgian mansion in the midst of rolling fields but an ornate mid-Victorian pile at the end of a suburban street. It was protected by a small front garden that contained only weeds and laurel bushes. The iron gates had been removed, probably in a scrap metal drive, which made a mockery of the huge stone gateposts camouflaged with moss and lichen that had seemed so imposing in the *Tatler* photograph.

'Not exactly stately, is it?' Walter Boscombe nosed the Bentley between the gateposts. 'It should, I suppose, rightly be called Redmain's Retreat since the old bugger went to ground. I can't imagine Hess or von Ribbentrop setting up headquarters here when the great day comes.'

'The great day?' Susan said.

'When Adolf rides in state up the Mall.'

'Do you think that day will come?'

'Personally, no, I don't,' Mr Boscombe told her. 'But Redmain does. What's more, he's counting on it.'

He brought the car to rest by the steps that led up to the door, stripped off his driving gloves and tossed them on to the dash. He glanced at Susan and grinned. 'No doubt you're wondering what we're doing here and ten seconds after you meet Rogue Redmain, you'll wonder what on earth this doddering old fool can possibly contribute to *Speaking Up for Britain.* Well, Susan, don't be deceived. Redmain may give the impression he's senile but he's far from toothless, believe me.'

'What do you want me to do?'

'Sit quietly, smile modestly and say nothing. Redmain may be old but he still likes pretty young women.'

'Don't tell me I'm bait?'

'Window dressing, Mrs Cahill, window dressing. Bait would be someone ten years your junior dressed like Bo-Peep. Ah-hah! Stirrings in the den of iniquity. Time to go to work.'

The door was opened not by a butler but by a small,

wizened man dressed in a frock coat, baggy flannels and worn brown brogues who looked less like a rogue than a refugee. His hair, what remained of it, was combed forward across his forehead, Roman style. His eyes were weak and watery and a dewdrop clung to the tip of his nose. If he's setting out to give an appearance of demented eccentricity, Susan thought, then he's certainly succeeding.

In a whining little voice, he asked, 'Who might this be?'

'My assistant, Mrs Cahill,' Walter Boscombe answered and held out his hand in greeting. 'Kind of you to agree to meet us, sir. I realise how precious your time must be.'

'Precious, is it? How much are you going to pay me, Boscombe, for wasting my precious time, eh?' Ignoring Mr Boscombe's hand, he beckoned them to follow him inside.

The hall had the dank air of a mausoleum. A staircase soared up into the gloom. The bottom of the staircase was flanked by two half-naked female figures rendered in what might be marble or possibly painted plaster. Overhead hung a spidery chandelier with a single bulb in it. There were no furnishings of any kind in the hall and the walls were bare.

Saying nothing, Redmain crabbed across the hall, opened a heavy oak door and, without waiting for his guests, went on into the room beyond. Mr Boscombe placed a hand in the small of Susan's back, as if he feared that she might flee, and steered her into a gloomy, high-ceilinged drawing room.

Large windows with small glass panes had been blast-taped and two of the three were shuttered. The room smelled strongly of smoke. In the cavernous stone fireplace a handful of coal nuts smouldered. Several pieces of rococo furniture were scattered around the space and three spindly chairs were drawn up before a folding card table in the vicinity of the hearth.

Sir Peter Redmain had not entirely forgotten his manners. Ignoring Walter Boscombe, he detached Susan from her boss and, hand on her arm, led her to the far wall where a rectangle of pale wallpaper indicated where a painting had hung.

Looking up at the space, Redmain said, 'My Brueghel – Pieter not Jan – the tax people took that from me.'

Susan dutifully admired the patch of wallpaper and tried not to flinch when the old man groped for her hand. He drew her eight or ten paces to the left and looked up at another patch of pale wallpaper. 'My Rubens. Gone too.'

The old man's fingers stroked her wrist and a forefinger slipped up into her cuff as if he were feeling for her pulse. Pulling Susan after him, he crossed the width of the room and stopped by a framed picture hung in shadow on the interior wall.

'Eh, but they didn't get my Fragonard. I hid it away, you see.' He peered up fondly at the painting – a young girl in a forest setting – and, squeezing Susan's hand again, went on, 'I've others they don't know about downstairs. I'll show them to you later, if you wish. Would you like that?'

Susan opened her mouth to fashion a platitude that might deter the old man without actually insulting him but Mr Boscombe intervened. 'I doubt if we'll have time to view your collection, Sir Peter, fascinating though it may be. I'd rather like to get back to London before nightfall.'

To Susan's relief the old man released her hand and, turning, tugged on a frayed tapestry strap. 'You'll want to eat first, I suppose,' he said. 'It'll be plain fare, Boscombe, not what you're used to, but it's the best I can do with the scraps they've left me.'

The door opened and a woman in an old-fashioned ankle-length day-dress edged her way into the room carrying a wooden tray and, under her armpit, a bottle of wine.

'Good afternoon, Lady Redmain.' Walter Boscombe bowed. 'I rather thought you might still be out of the country. My father wishes to be remembered to you.'

Stooping over the card table, juggling tray and bottle, the woman looked up and smiled. 'Henry,' she said. 'Ah, dear Henry. I gather from reports in *The Times* that he's still making a thorough nuisance of himself.'

'He's just as bombastic as ever, if that's what you mean?' Mr Boscombe helped her unload plates and glasses from the tray. He slipped the bottle from under her arm and glanced at the label. 'A '33 Rhenish. Goes well with pilchards, does it? As I recall, 1933 was a very good year for you, Lady Redmain.'

She answered with another smile. 'Oh, you *are* your father's son, Walter. What if I were to tell you that this bottle came from Hindenburg's private cellar. Would that spoil your appetite?'

Walter Boscombe rolled the bottle over in his hands. 'Did it?'

'No, of course it didn't.' The woman laughed and, bearing the empty tray, headed for the door. 'I can't speak for the pilchards, though. Remember me to Henry.'

'Yes,' Walter Boscombe promised. 'I will.'

'I want to make it clear,' Basil Willets said, with as much puff as he could muster, 'that I am here under protest. There's nothing wrong with me that a few days' rest won't cure.'

The sister in the white cotton dress, head veil and heavy canvas apron did not contradict him. So far, to Basil's annoyance, she'd said nothing except, 'There,' and a few seconds later, 'Sit back.'

She had the commanding presence of a mother superior, though Baz suspected she was really an army officer with a rank that brooked no back-chat from anyone, especially male civilians. He was, he realised, seriously disadvantaged and, whether he liked it or not, totally at her mercy.

For a start he had trouble framing sentences because of his need to punctuate every other word with a laboured intake of breath; being naked to the waist didn't help his cause either. He was conscious of his skinny chest and sloping shoulders, ribs sticking out through paper-thin skin. He didn't need a doctor to tell him he'd lost weight. He'd never been muscular, like Derek, and lack of exercise down through the years had caused his belly to sag but, rationing or no rationing, the signs now indicated something more serious than poor diet and the inevitable predations of age.

'For God's sake, Basil, you're not *that* old,' Vivian had assured him. 'In any case, I didn't marry you for your bulging biceps. I married you for your intellect.'

'Not –' he panted, 'not – my – charm?'

There had been nothing charming about the state he'd found himself in that Monday morning. On attempting to get out of bed and shuffle to the lavatory, he'd been beset by such a bout of coughing that he'd fallen on all fours, leaking nastily from both ends.

An hour later David Proudfoot had turned up in a battered, mud-splattered lorry and had helped Vivian clean him up and get him dressed. He'd squeezed them into the lorry's cab and had driven four or five miles to Harveston Hall which was one of several large country houses near Hereford that served as convalescent homes for wounded soldiers and airmen.

'I'm not a soldier, you know,' Basil said. 'I shouldn't – be – taking up time that might better be spent on—'

'Quiet,' the woman said.

They were in an antechamber to a consulting room which in turn led into a waiting room furnished with armchairs and a sofa. Vivian was out there with her brother and heaven knows what they were saying about him. Viv hadn't even told him she was telephoning Proudfoot, had just gone ahead and done the deed while he'd been too debilitated to care. He felt better now, though the cold air in the cab of the lorry had brought on another coughing fit and his throat and chest still ached with the violence of the spasms.

He was seated on a four-legged stool, bare shoulders pressed against a screen covered in slightly sticky and decidedly chilly cellophane while the sister arranged a huge square-shaped camera against his chest. She moved the arms of the miniature crane from which the device was suspended an inch to the left, as if she were the captain of a submarine drawing a bead on a cruiser, then rapped out, 'Still,' and left him alone in the gelid light of the white-painted room while she nipped off behind a screen.

'Still,' came her sonorous voice. 'Still. Still.'

Basil held his breath, heard nothing, felt nothing, nothing that is but the dread that had gurgled in his stomach for days now, a gnawing, nagging fear that his career as a BBC producer was over and that poor Vivian would soon be wearing widow's weeds.

The sister returned, adjusted the camera and went off again. He waited, tensely, trying not to cough.

'Still.' If God were a female, Basil thought, that's what she'd sound like. 'Still. Still. Still.'

She returned once more and removed the camera, tipping it away on its weighted arms. Basil gagged, coughed and reached gladly for the cloth the woman held out. He spat into it and, fearfully, glanced at the result: dust-coloured phlegm, no blood, thank God. He folded the cloth and looked around for a place to put it.

The woman took it from him.

'Is it cancer?' he said. 'TB? What?'

'Dr Fleck will be with you when he's viewed the plates. You may dress now and return to the waiting room where, if you wish, you may smoke.'

Basil put on his clothes and tentatively opened the door of the consulting room – empty – made his way across it into the waiting room where Vivian was browsing through an ancient copy of *Country Life*. She tossed down the magazine and got to her feet.

There were three other people in the waiting room: a couple in their fifties and a young man in RAF service dress with a flight sergeant's stripes on his sleeve who shielded his face with his hand and, Basil thought, might even be crying.

Vivian had troubles enough of her own without involving herself in the misery of others. She stood close to Basil and whispered. 'What did they say?'

'Wait for plates.'

'How do you feel now?'

'Like a fraud, if you must know,' Basil answered. 'Where's your brother?'

'He had to make a delivery. Potatoes, I think. He'll be back in time to collect us, unless . . .'

'Unless what?'

'They decide to keep you in.'

'Keep me in?'

'For observation.'

'Over my dead body,' said Baz.

*

The pilchards lay on slices of cold toast. There was no sauce, no salad, no side dish of any kind, just fish on burned bread washed down with a Riesling that was too sweet for Susan's taste.

There was nothing sweet about the sudden turn in the conversation. Her boss's dislike of Rogue Redmain was all too obvious and soon after they were seated at the rickety little card table he went on the attack.

'You know why I'm here, Sir Peter. As I explained in my letter, I want you to give a talk about Hitler's objectives.'

Susan couldn't imagine the old man delivering anything worthwhile in the peevish voice that seemed so totally unsuited to broadcasting. She cut into the pilchard, dissected a bony fragment and put it in her mouth.

'What do I know about Hitler's objectives?' Redmain said. 'I haven't set foot in Berlin in two years. Your father saw to that.'

He rubbed knife and fork together as if he were sharpening a butcher's blade, dug into the fish on his plate, skewering and chewing with relish while he waited for Mr Boscombe to contradict him.

'He also kept you out of Brixton,' Mr Boscombe said.

'Oh, thank him, thank him most kindly,' Redmain said sarcastically. 'We'd be better off in Brixton, living on the fat of the land with our servants around us – like Mosley.'

'It wasn't my father who persuaded you to invest in German armaments and salt your profits in German banks. What was wrong with Switzerland?'

'I've never cared for the Swiss. I don't trust them.'

'You're broke – *if* you're broke, which I rather doubt – because of your own stupidity.' Giving up on the pilchards, Mr Boscombe pushed away his plate and lit a cigarette. 'If you were so damnably keen on the Third Reich why didn't you remain in Germany? I'm sure they'd have made you welcome.'

'Because I'm English, English to the core.'

'Wouldn't you like an opportunity to explain your – let's call it patriotism on my programme?'

'I've heard your programme, Boscombe. Jungle music played by Negroes to pander to Jews. As for that fellow who claims to have been at the Führer's elbow in the meeting with Franco – lies, blatant lies made up for propaganda.'

'I'm nothing,' Walter Boscombe said, 'if not even-handed. Come on my programme and refute the so-called lies. Within the bounds of security you may say exactly what you like. I'm sure you must have friends from the January Club who'd be delighted to hear their views expressed. The other side of the story, as it were.'

'Who sent you? Did that swine Liddell send you?'

'I represent the interests of the BBC, no other body. You may come down to our Soho studio for live broadcast or I can send a unit here to your house to record your talk. In any event, the fee will be one hundred pounds.'

Susan blinked.

'I'll tell you what might induce me to contribute to your blasted programme,' Redmain said, 'a promise to have my assets released by the tax authorities. In spite of what they say, I was never a member of the British Union of Fascists.'

'On the other hand, you were a member of the January Club.'

Rogue Redmain looked across the little table at Susan. 'If I record here in the house, will she come along with the unit?'

Walter Boscombe answered promptly, 'Mrs Cahill is a production assistant not a sound engineer. Besides, she's Jewish.'

Redmain sat back. 'Is it true what he says? *Are* you a Jew?'

Susan lied without compunction. 'Yes, I'm Jewish.'

'Another of your Hebrew tarts, Boscombe. I thought you'd had enough of those with the last one, the trouble-maker. What was her name – Shilberg's wife?'

Mr Boscombe refused to rise to the bait. 'I need your answer, Sir Peter.'

'I'd like some time to think about it.'

'You'd like time to make a few telephone calls, you mean. No,' Mr Boscombe said. 'I'm putting together my winter schedule and you're either on it or you're not. All I require is a nice fifteen-minute chat about the view from the Berchtesgaden and why you thought Hitler had the answer to all Germany's woes delivered in the sort of voice that will have half the hayseeds in America wagging their corncobs and agreeing with you.'

'What will Churchill have to say about that?'

'Churchill may be Prime Minister but he doesn't run the BBC. The worst that can happen is I'll be asked to resign. I wouldn't mind that one bit. There are plenty of other things I can do to keep the wolf from the door.'

Susan watched the old man wrestle with his conscience and his desire to be on the public stage once more. He straightened his stooped shoulders, dabbed at his nose and said, 'I know it's a trap, Boscombe, but if there's the faintest chance of casting a shadow of disrepute on you and your self-righteous family then, yes, I'll play along. I'll do your damned talk.'

'Good, that's good,' Mr Boscombe said. 'I'll have Mrs Cahill draw up a contract.'

'I don't need a contract. A handshake will do. I may be a traitor in your eyes but I'm still a man of my word.'

'Of course, you are. Of course,' Walter Boscombe said and offered the old man his hand to clinch their uneasy alliance.

They waited almost an hour. Vivian smoked one cigarette after another and Basil, growing ever more depressed, coughed with as much restraint as he could muster. The elderly couple were summoned by a nurse and did not return. The RAF sergeant remained locked in silent brooding until he too was summoned away. Vivian's attempts at conversation foundered on Basil's conviction that he was about to be handed a death sentence.

At one point, some forty minutes into the vigil, she put a hand on his back and said, 'Poor old sausage,' which childish phrase seemed to give him comfort.

Eventually the door of the consulting room flew open and a boyish-looking man wearing a short white cotton jacket over RAF blues bounded into the waiting room, a sheaf of grey and black negatives wobbling in his hand.

Vivian was near to nervous collapse by then and, snatching at Basil's hand, hauled him roughly to his feet.

'Mr – ah – Willets?'

'Yes,' said Vivian. 'We're Mr Willets.'

'David Proudfoot's friend?'

'His sister,' said Vivian.

'Step this way.' Dr Fleck led them into the consulting room and closed the door. 'How is David? Sorry I missed him. We used to play tennis together. Terrible cheat. Now' – he waggled the X-ray negatives casually – 'my guess is pleural empyema.'

'Your *guess*?' said Vivian.

'Fatal, I suppose,' said Basil.

'No,' said young Dr Fleck. 'Not necessarily. We're a long way from the scarring stage, though there is a small pocket of pus, I think, in the pleural cavity. Just as well David brought you in when he did.'

'Pus?' Basil said. 'Oh, God!'

'The X-rays are a little opaque so we may be okay,' Dr Fleck said. 'One or two questions, Mr – ah – Willets. Standard form.'

There was no desk in the consulting room, just a small table with a clean linen cloth and two empty enamel dishes upon it. Dr Fleck, Vivian noticed, wasn't sporting a stethoscope which deepened her suspicion that he wasn't a real doctor. She glanced round, found a wooden chair, scraped it out and plonked Basil down on it. She positioned herself directly behind him, facing the doctor.

'Any history of bronchitis in the family?'

'No,' Basil answered.

'Tuberculosis? Grandparents? Siblings? Cousins?'

'Not,' said Basil, 'to my knowledge.'

'Do you drink, Mr Willets?'

'In moder—'

'It's not alcohol,' Vivian said. 'Aren't you writing this down?'

'I don't have a pen. I'll write it up later. You're not a miner, are you? No, I thought not. Syphilis? Gonorrhoea?'

'He was blown up,' said Vivian, emphasising the *p*.

'Ah! Blast,' said Dr Fleck. 'Jolly good!'

'Blown up at the BBC,' Basil put in.

'What better place,' said Dr Fleck. 'Any other damage?'

'Ribs and shoulder,' Vivian informed him.

'Classic.' Dr Fleck's enthusiasm increased. 'Pulmonary abscess possible, not probable. We'll aspirate first then take a few more pictures to assist diagnosis. If we're lucky we won't have to remove any of those cracked ribs.'

Dry-mouthed, Vivian said, 'Will you keep him here?'

'Could ship him up to London if you prefer it but given what's happening in the capital I reckon he's better off where he is.'

'How long?' said Viv.

'Depends.' Dr Fleck shrugged. 'Two weeks, possibly three. Always a risk of complications. Better to be safe than sorry. You should have him home by Christmas.'

'Pardon?'

'Bad joke,' said Dr Fleck. 'Does he have pyjamas, dressing gown, toothbrush, that sort of thing?' Vivian shook her head. 'No problem. We'll find him something to be going on with.'

'I'll bring in everything he needs tonight.'

'Tomorrow would be better,' said Dr Fleck. 'Give him a chance to settle down, hmm.'

'I shouldn't be here,' Basil said. 'I'm not a soldier.'

'You're the next best thing,' the doctor assured him. 'One of our war wounded. Besides, any friend of David Proudfoot deserves the best attention we can give him.'

'What does my brother have to do with it?'

'Oh, I thought you knew,' said Dr Fleck, surprised. 'He owns Harveston Hall. It's only ours for the duration.'

The lorry, emptied of its load, lurched over rutted gravel. It was all Vivian could do to hold on to her seat while her brother, muffled in a grubby camel-coloured duffle coat, hunched over the steering wheel, eyes glued to the driveway. In spite of her resolve, the pain of parting had been too much to bear. She'd sobbed as they'd left the big square building behind whose curtained windows her husband was even now being put to bed by strangers.

At the gate a guard called out, 'Afternoon, Mr Proudfoot,' and the lorry passed through unchallenged.

It was a cloudy afternoon. When the lorry swung into the

country lane hedgerows swarmed around it and daylight became so scarce that her brother switched on the hooded headlamps.

'Tell you what,' David said, 'we'll pop over to the cottage. Pack a bag for Basil and I'll drop it off at the gate on my way home to Hackles. It isn't far, you know.'

'Why didn't you tell me you owned the Harveston place?'

'I didn't think you'd be interested.'

'How much land went with it?'

'Only forty acres.'

'Are you farming there too?'

'I am,' David Proudfoot said. 'By the way, before you get snotty about it, the Hall wasn't requisitioned. I offered it to the military three days after I signed the freehold.'

'When was this?'

'Beginning of the year.'

'What happened to the Ingrams?'

'They packed up and left for America. Texas, I think. Cyril Ingram's wife's an American. She wasn't going to hang around and wait for the storm troopers to arrive on her doorstep. Besides, she has two teenage sons and prefers them alive to dead.'

'In other words you got the estate for peanuts?'

'It was, shall we say, a sound investment.'

'Your house in Mayfair, was that part of the trade too?'

'Trade?' her brother said. 'I don't know what you mean?'

'You bought your way out of trouble, didn't you? You suddenly became a very good citizen, a flag-waving patriot. You hypocrite! What did your wife have to say about it?'

'Gwen and I are no longer together. Last I heard she was driving an ambulance in Chelsea and sharing digs with Roger Austin. Do you remember Austin?'

'No, I don't,' Vivian said. 'What about the girls?'

'Eleanor and I are not on the best of terms. She's in the ATS, Ordnance Corps. I'm not sure where she's stationed. Caro's a WAAF. She drops in from time to time.'

'Last I saw of them they were fund-raising for the BUF,' Vivian said. 'How times change.'

'And people change with them,' David reminded her.

'Who looks after you? Do you have another woman?'

'Dozens of them. Land girls. A housekeeper takes care of us and does the cooking. You might suppose it's all rather jolly but it isn't. It's damned hard work, if you must know.' He fiddled with the gear stick before he went on. 'I'm sorry about your husband, Vivian. Fleck's a good man, though. Basil will have the best of attention. I'd take you to lodge with me at Hackles but there just isn't room.'

'I'm grateful for what you've done for Basil and I don't mind staying at the cottage on my own. In any case, Baz will be home soon and I want to keep the place heated.'

'You're not going back to London then?'

'Permanently? No, not until Basil's fit and well.'

'I think,' her brother said, 'you're carrying independence too far, Viv. But you always were a stubborn cow. I'll send someone round tomorrow to stock you up and take you to visit Basil, though visiting in B Wing is restricted, I believe.'

'B Wing?'

'Bed rest required,' David said, and she knew he was lying. 'Incidentally, do you ever see anything of Susan Hooper?'

'She was down here at the weekend, a flying visit.'

'Really? And I missed her. How unfortunate.'

'She's married now, David.'

'To some bloke from Shadwell, no doubt.'

'To some bloke in the BBC.'

'What a waste.' David Proudfoot shook his head. 'What

an absolute waste.' He glanced at Vivian slyly in the faint light from the dashboard. 'Happily married, is she?'

'Ecstatically so,' said Vivian. 'You never had a chance with Susan, David. She was never going to fall for your nonsense.'

'She fell for Mercer Hughes, didn't she?'

'And look where that got her?'

'Does she know Mercer's back in England?'

'What? No, I'm sure she doesn't.'

'Well, he is. He's flying Hurricanes out of an airfield in Norfolk. I imagine he'd like to meet up with Susan again. Do you think she'd be interested in a nostalgic reunion with an old flame?'

'I doubt it,' Vivian said.

'Why not?'

'I just told you, she's happily married,' said Vivian.

'So you did now. So you did.'

Her father had been a staunch supporter of Oswald Mosley and a rare bird in the dockland communities. He'd had no notion what fascism was really all about and Ronnie and he had argued bitterly. What her father admired in Mosley was not his political credo but the false impression that he was somehow a man of the people, only with more money.

By the time she was twenty Susan had realised that what her father found most appealing in men like Mosley was their overbearing egotism. The magnetic attraction of power to the powerless was irresistible. The notion that small, inconsequential men, if properly led, might rearrange the structures of society had also been one of Vivian's favourite themes before she'd been side-tracked by issues of government incompetence.

Susan hadn't understood what true power meant until

she encountered Walter Boscombe. She had supposed it to be a feature of rank, of stripes on a sleeve, braid on a cap, cash in the bank. But that afternoon she'd received a glimpse of what lay behind Mr Boscombe's authority, that dark ocean of influence that lapped at the feet of the privileged.

Mr Boscombe did not start the engine immediately. He sat forward in the leather seat and watched Redmain close the door of the house and then, very softly, let out a whistle. 'I didn't suppose for a moment the old bastard would fall for it.'

'Is he doing it for the fee?' Susan asked.

'He isn't on his uppers by any means. I hope you weren't taken in by the performance?'

'No, I wasn't impressed – or convinced.'

'He won't show up at the studio looking like a tramp. He'll become Rogue Redmain the Bengal Lancer again, the Tory grandee fallen on hard times, the man, believe it or not, who once shared jokes and racing tips with the late King George and was in the running for Number Ten. *Sic transit gloria*, and all that. If he'd only kept his hands off young girls he wouldn't have been shipped off to Germany on some drummed-up diplomatic mission and fallen foul of Goebbels who, by the way, played him like a fiddle. Quite ironic, really. Goebbels hates capitalists and Redmain hates the proletariat.'

'And they both hate Jews.'

'Oh, yes, for quite different reasons they both hate Jews.'

'The *New Statesman* will have you hanged and quartered as soon as Redmain's name appears on the hand-outs.'

'The *Spectator* will do exactly the same. We might even be attacked in the *New York Times* and the *Washington Post*. I'll have a busy few days upstairs in Broadcasting House defending our right to free speech but by then it'll be too late and the governors won't dare pull the programme for fear of what the press will say.'

'It sounds,' Susan said, 'rather risky.'

'It most certainly is. But think of the audience we'll have for the broadcast, think of the postbag, the controversy. I'll handle the question and answer session myself. I know where most of the bodies are buried, you see, and, by God, I intend to roast him.' He tugged on his driving gloves. 'Are you cold?'

'A little.'

He started the engine and steered the Bentley backward through the stone gateposts. 'Used to be a nice little hotel halfway down the hill, if I recall. We might be a tad late for lunch but I'm sure they'll find us something to fill the aching void. Is that all right with you, Susan?'

'Absolutely fine,' she said and when he put an arm about her and drew her closer to him she was not inclined to resist.

11

Breda had never been one for calculated exercise. When she'd caught sight of the Hoxton Ramblers setting out on one of their epic hikes or members of the Tower Hamlets Cycling Club whirring along the Commercial Road she'd experienced no envy but had thought what fools they were for squandering all that energy.

Housework, chasing after Ronnie and Billy and serving in Stratton's had been exercise enough for her and she had more to worry about now than an inch round the hips and a sagging rear end. She was fit to cope with a long shift in Orrell's kitchens and a trek to and from Deaconsfield every weekday without wilting and ten minutes with her feet up, a cuppa on one hand and a ciggie in the other, invariably gave her second wind.

Billy, though, was a lively little boy and found the confinement of long winter evenings trying. Breda encouraged him to bounce about the railway carriage and, if the weather was dry and not too cold, help her draw water from the well or lug coal from the lean-to and even muck in with the weekly wash in the big wooden tub. In the evening she played pencil and paper games with him and, to improve his arithmetic, taught him the rudiments of gin rummy as a relief from endless rounds of snap and grandpa's whiskers.

As the nights became longer and the weather deteriorated

she saw less of Danny. All kinds of urgent stuff was coming down the wires that demanded extra hours from monitors and editors and even threatened to scupper Griff and Kate's wedding plans.

It had been a strangely peaceful week at Orrell's, however. Steve Pepperdine, though recovered from his gastric upset, was less ebullient than usual and Trudy, from whom Breda and Morven had expected trouble, appeared to have retreated into her shell, so much so that her arch-enemy, Archie Jackson, had been moved to enquire if she was quite well.

On Saturday afternoon Mr Pell took Billy off to watch Evesham Rovers play football against a scratch team from an army camp near Tewkesbury. Breda, Mrs Pell, Madge Gaydon and her girls queued at the food shops in town and, before dusk and heavy rain drove them home, shared a pot of tea in the Cambria tearoom.

It rained all night on Saturday. Come morning the Shady Nook track was black with mud and cloud lay low and sombre across the fields and distant hills. It wasn't the sort of weather to tempt Breda far from the warmth of the stove but by early afternoon Billy's restlessness was beginning to grate on her nerves. She put on his wellingtons, raincoat and balaclava and, with a warning not to go far, sent him out to see if Mr Gaydon's gang had started picking the Brussels sprouts in the field behind the coach.

She had barely settled to write a letter to her mother when Billy returned.

'Mum?'

'What?'

'There's a man out there.'

'You mean Mr Gaydon.'

'Another man.'

A subdued quality in her son's voice caused her to hurry to the door. She looked down at Billy, frowning.

'Where is 'e?'

'At the field gate. He asked me what me name was.'

'Did you tell him?'

Billy shook his head. 'I come straight 'ome.'

'Quite right,' said Breda, already reaching for her coat.

'I fink 'e might be a German,' Billy said.

'What makes you say that?'

'He's got a funny 'at on.'

Breda stepped from the coach and took her son's hand. 'Okay, let's go see what this cove's doing in our field.'

'Mr Gaydon's field.'

'Right,' Breda said. 'Mr Gaydon's field.'

The stranger wasn't wearing a coal-scuttle helmet but a deerstalker with the flaps tied up. He sported cord breeches, riding boots and a half-length coat in Cotswold green tweed. He should, by rights, have a shotgun tucked under his arm, Breda thought, to complete the picture of a country squire. He leaned on the bar of the field gate and watched Breda and Billy approach.

'That's a fine sturdy lad you have there, Mrs Hooper,' he said. 'I thought he might be yours.'

'You leave my boy alone. What you doing 'ere anyhow?'

'Out for a stroll, that's all,' Inspector Jessop said.

Breda kept the gate between her and the Special Branch man. 'My ma's in Ireland and you got nothing on me now, so bugger off. You're trespassing, you know.'

'Calm down, Mrs Hooper.'

'How'd you know where to find me?'

'I had no idea you were living in Evesham,' Jessop said, 'let alone working in Orrell's. Small world, isn't it?' He made no attempt to open the gate and remained leaning on the top bar. 'How do you like the country life?'

'What you want? What you doing 'ere?'

'Having a few days off,' Jessop said. 'I'm staying at a pretty little inn over at Tolmarsh. It's a relief to get out of London.'

'You ain't 'ere on no holiday.' Breda drew Billy behind her. 'Stay right where you are or – or I'll shout for Mr Gaydon.'

'Who's he? Is he the landowner?'

'Stop asking questions and just tell me what you're doing 'ere.'

'What happened to the café you used to run?'

'It went up in smoke,' said Breda.

'No one hurt, I trust?'

'None o' your damned business.' She lifted Billy, no light weight, into her arms. 'After what you done to my dad . . .'

'I didn't do anything to your dad, Mrs Hooper. Your dad cooked his own goose long before I came along. He was a bad lot, your father. What's more, you know it.'

'You didn't 'ave to drown 'im, though.'

'I didn't drown him. A German U-boat did that. It was just unfortunate he happened to be on the wrong ship at the wrong time.'

Billy clung to his mother, legs locked about her waist, an arm about her neck. He was old enough to know that something adult was happening, even if he didn't know what it was.

Breda said, 'I'm going 'ome now.'

'Wait,' said Jessop sharply.

'Why should I?'

He straightened. 'If you won't answer a few questions here and now, Mrs Hooper, I may have to call on you again.

I'm sure you wouldn't appreciate being disturbed in the middle of the night.'

'What sort of questions?'

'How long have you worked at Orrell's Engineering?'

'You can look it up on the books, can't you?'

'I'd prefer to have you tell me,' Jessop said.

Breda put Billy down but kept him close.

She said, 'Six weeks, thereabouts.'

'Have you made any friends in the kitchens?'

'I'm quite chummy with one or two.'

'Mrs Littlejohn, for instance?'

'She ain't no friend of mine.'

'How well do you know her?'

'Know she's a cow,' said Breda. 'Nobody likes 'er.'

'Nobody?' Mr Jessop raised an eyebrow.

'Well, yer. She's in thick with Mr Pepperdine.'

'Where does Mr Pepperdine live?'

'In the rectory in Shay Bridge with Trudy – Mrs Littlejohn – and her husband. Her husband's the vicar.'

'Do you think there's more going on between Dr Pepperdine and Mrs Littlejohn than meets the eye?'

'How would I know?' said Breda.

'Gossip,' the inspector suggested.

'What you doing with the navy? You work for the navy now?'

'I'm still my own man, Mrs Hooper, just a simple copper. Who *would* know about Mrs Littlejohn and Dr Pepperdine?'

'Miss Hastie might. She billets in Shay Bridge.'

'She's the Scot; am I right?'

'She's the one thinks you might be hunting for spies.'

'Does she now? What do you think?'

'I don't think you're in Evesham for the good of your

'ealth,' Breda said. 'I think you're interested in what goes on in Shed 3.'

'What does go on in Shed 3?'

'Haven't a bleedin' clue. Really, I haven't.'

'Who takes the tea trolley into Shed 3?'

'They don't 'ave no tea trolley. I think they've a kettle of their own but I've never set foot inside.'

'What about Mr Jackson? Does he go into Shed 3?'

'Archie's a food manager. He's got nothing to do with torpedoes. Anyway, he don't 'ave a special white pass so he'd never get past the guard,' said Breda. 'Why're you so interested in our canteen?'

Inspector Jessop held out his hand, palm uppermost. 'I do believe the rain's coming on again. I won't detain you further, Mrs Hooper. One thing, just before we part. I'd be mortally obliged if you wouldn't mention our conversation to anyone. I do mean anyone.'

'Careless talk costs lives, right?'

'Precisely,' said Inspector Jessop.

'All right,' Breda promised. 'Mum's the word,' and, out of habit, crossed her heart.

'What did he do then?' said Morven.

'Walked away. Didn't even come down by the road, just strolled off up the side of the field.'

'"Mortally obliged", that's exactly what he said to me,' said Morven. 'I was hardly round the corner from the church after evening service when he nabbed me.'

'Why didn't you scream?'

'I remembered him from Monday otherwise I'd have given him an earful. He fair gives me the willies, though. Is he dangerous?'

'Oh, yer,' said Breda, 'he's dangerous.'

Morven was rolling out a yard of pastry upon which Breda, almost absently, sprinkled a handful of flour now and then.

Apples, peeled, cored, sliced and simmering in cauldrons on the range filled the kitchen with a tangy aroma. The pastry bay was adjacent to the cold room but Archie and Trudy were presently closeted in the Reserve Equipment Store taking inventory of tableware, cleaning materials and linen.

The potato peeler was going full blast and with the general noise of food preparation echoing round the kitchen Breda and Morven's conversation was unlikely to be overheard. Even so, they kept their heads together and glanced over their shoulders as if they, not someone as yet unidentified, were trading state secrets.

'What did Billy say about it?' Morven asked.

'Billy still thinks he might be a Nazi in disguise.'

'Billy's not far wrong.' Morven plied the weighted roller vigorously. 'Bit of a wild coincidence him turning up here. Do you think it was just bad luck?'

'Yer, I do,' said Breda. 'I don't really think he's after me.'

'Is he after Trudy?'

'God knows!' Breda said. 'If Special Branch have sent 'im down 'ere then it can't be for nothing. If he's sniffing about behind Trudy's back then the finger must point at 'er.'

Morven nodded. 'Trudy's a funny sort of name, I've always thought. Don't know anybody else called Gertrude – except that actress and I think I heard she was Danish.'

'One or two Gerties down our way,' Breda admitted, 'but never did 'ear of a Trudy.' She moved closer. 'If you was a Nazi spy and wanted to find out what was going on in Shed 3 how would you go about it?'

'I'd seduce the top egg,' said Morven.

'And who's the top egg?'

'We both know the answer to that, don't we?' said Morven.

'Unless Stevie's the spy.'

'That twerp! The Nazis can't be that desperate.'

'The singing and dancing might be an act, a cover.'

'Aye, I saw that in a film once, I think,' said Morven. 'Peter Lorre was in it, or maybe it was Ronald Colman; one or the other.'

'How will Jessop know if Trudy's a spy?'

'Catch her with secret plans hidden away. Or a wireless. I've heard you need a wireless. Or messages,' said Morven. 'Messages hidden in holes.'

Breda, distracted, scattered a handful of flour over Morven's forearm. 'But that's only if Stevie's in on it. If Stevie's not in on it . . .'

'She's getting the dope from Stevie and passing it on.'

'To somebody else.'

'Who gives it to the Germans.'

'Now who could that be?' said Breda, just as Trudy and Mr Jackson emerged from the Equipment Store and, without exchanging a word, went their separate ways.

'Archie?' said Breda lightly.

'Don't be so daft,' said Morven and, shaking her head at her friend's foolishness, deftly fed a length of pastry into the cutter.

Breda saw neither hide nor hair of Mr Jessop in the course of the next week and had no opportunity to ask Danny's advice. The tide of news from Europe had reached high watermark and Danny, Griff and Kate were spending long hours in Wood Norton coping with the flood of propaganda that poured from the foreign stations.

The information that found its way from the monitors'

headphones to the editing table was not the same as the stuff that made newspaper headlines where prudent censorship and a need to keep up morale condensed the conflict to banner headlines: *Wop Air Defeat* or *Italy's Fight-Shy Navy Blasted* were front page eye-catchers while the grim statistics of Allied losses were hidden among adverts for Bird's custard and Rowntree's fruit gums.

The news of the Fleet Air Arm's daring raid on the Italian battle fleet in the harbour of Taranto first broke in the form of a bewildered announcement on Radio Frankfurt.

Wood Norton's translators pricked up their ears.

Within hours of the airborne torpedoes finding their 'sitting duck' targets the radio waves were crackling with information, true and false. In Wood Norton's M Unit pride in the outcome of the Taranto raid was tempered by exhaustion and in Silwyn Griffith and Kate Cottrell's case by fear that leave would be cancelled and their wedding plans scuppered.

'Hum,' said Mr Gregory, M Unit's supervisor, when Kate and Griff anxiously confronted him. 'Well, I can't have you scampering off for more than a day, that's for sure. We're overworked as it is. What time is the wedding?'

'Noon on Friday,' Griff replied.

'The best I can do is a shift and a half. Kate, you finish at seven on Thursday morning, don't you?'

Kate nodded.

'I'll need you back on the headphones by eight on Friday evening,' Mr Gregory said. 'Griffiths, you may knock off halfway through your day shift, say around midday Thursday and be back the same time as Kate, eight o'clock Friday evening.'

'The honeymoon . . .' Griff began.

'Will have to wait.'

'What about Danny?' Kate said.

'Cahill? Oh, yes, the best man.'

'Please.' Silwyn Griffith seldom begged. 'It's all arranged.'

Mr Gregory sighed. 'Oh, very well. Cahill too. Midday Thursday to eight Friday. But you'd better all be back on time. And no fuss when you leave. Just slip away quietly. Is that understood?'

'It is,' Silwyn said. 'Thank you, Mr Gregory,' then returned to the editors' room to impart the glad tidings to Danny.

On Thursday evening Breda had just put supper on the table and Billy, with a comic paper propped against the milk jug, had lifted his fork when the air-raid warning sounded. Although Shady Nook was off the beaten track the night sky was still and cloudless and the wail of the siren travelled across the fields as clearly as the cry of a vixen.

Billy lifted his head but showed no sign of panic. Patiently he adjusted the floppy pages of the comic paper and watched it slide again when the milk jug trembled once more. Then the sausage on his plate took on a life of its own, performed a little jig and might have danced off entirely if he hadn't speared it with his fork.

Breda placed the pot of mashed potato on the floor and turned off the Calor gas tap. Mr Gaydon had told her what to do in the event of an air raid: not to rush outside to seek shelter in the lean-to but to pull a mattress from the bunk and lie on the floor under it.

He had assured her that the German bombers who flew over Evesham weren't interested in market towns and if anything did come down from the sky it would only be a stray or a discard and the soft ground would absorb the blast. Much as Breda liked Mr Gaydon, on this score she didn't quite trust him. After all, he'd never witnessed the havoc a land-mine could cause or the effects of a parachute bomb exploding thirty feet above the ground.

She stood quite still, looking up at the curve of the roof of the coach while the vibrations increased and the wailing of the Deaconsfield siren was absorbed in the drone of the aeroplanes.

She'd heard planes go over before, now and then the snarl of a dogfight but never anything like this, not in Shadwell and certainly not in Evesham. The droning grew louder, denser until it seemed to reach down into her stomach.

'Oh, God!' she murmured. 'Oh, Jesus and Mary!'

She yanked open the stove and drenched the hot coals with milk from the jug, hauled the flock mattress from Billy's bunk, threw blankets on the floor and propped the mattress at an angle against the larder door.

'In,' she shouted. 'Billy, get in.'

Billy slithered from his seat and crawled into the space beneath the mattress. Breda turned off the lamp, opened the carriage door and stepped down on to the grass.

Looking up, she saw squadrons of German planes, shiny in the bright moonlight, spread across the sky: no sound but the impenetrable thunder of their engines, no gunfire, no popping from the ack-ack batteries against the hill, no whistle of falling bombs. Goering's pilots had bigger targets in their sights than Evesham. They were heading away from London, heading north towards Wolverhampton, Birmingham and Coventry.

'Oh, God!' Breda said again. 'Danny.'

There had been a delay at the change at Worcester and the boys were running late. They looked very dapper in dark suits and overcoats. Danny, at Griff's insistence, had even found a hat to wear, a dark grey fedora that Mr Pell said made him look like James Cagney. They each carried a respirator, a small suitcase and no other luggage for, knowing how crowded the trains would be, travelling light was the sensible thing to do.

'Do you know where we're goin', Griff?' Danny asked as they walked up the platform towards the station exit.

'The Gibson Hotel at the top of Broadgate. It's next to the big department store, apparently.'

'I thought you'd been here before?'

'Only once,' Griffiths said. 'Mr Cottrell had one of the teachers from the school pick me up in his motorcar. A flying visit for the Cottrells to make sure I didn't have horns and a tail.'

'When's your mother arrivin'?'

'She came up this morning. I called her and told her we'd have to leave soon after the service. She said she'd get in touch with the Cottrells and arrange a wedding dinner in the hotel tonight instead of a lunch after the service tomorrow.'

'So they're all here? Kate included?'

'Let's hope so,' Griff said. 'What time is it?'

'Ten past seven.' They stepped out into the darkened city. 'How far tae the hotel? Is it worth huntin' for a taxi?'

'Tram,' Griff said. 'According to Kate it's not far and the conductor will put us off right at the door of the hotel.'

'We could hoof it,' Danny suggested.

'In the dark,' said Griff. 'In a town we don't know. I don't think that's a good idea.' He glanced up. 'Particularly with a full moon and the sky as clear as a ruddy bell. I just hope the fat field marshal doesn't have malice on his mind, not until I've carried my blushing bride over the threshold.'

'What threshold?'

'M Unit's threshold, of course,' Griffiths said ruefully. 'Could that actually be our tramcar?'

'Is it pointin' the right way?'

'Looks like it.'

They moved away from the railway station out of the dim pool of light that didn't reach as far as the pavement's edge.

The tram was disgorging passengers at a broad corner, workers and one or two women stepping carefully down from the board. The tram was like something from a film, a phantom tram, defined by a faint blue glimmer that robbed the passengers of all identity. Griff put a foot on the board and addressed the conductor who was helping an elderly woman alight. 'Gibson's Hotel?'

The conductor was a large woman wrapped in a high-buttoned overcoat with a scarf around her throat and a transport cap perched on a knot of frizzy ginger hair.

'That's us.' She jangled her cash bag, winked and asked, not seriously, 'You looking for company?'

'He's got company.' Danny pulled himself up by the pole.

'I'm sure I could make room for two,' the woman said just as the siren wailed. No longer jocular, she shouted, 'All off, all off,' and vanished upstairs.

The tram jerked. A spray of white sparks flew from the overhead cable. The rim of the city centre was suddenly illuminated by falling flares. Buildings rose out of darkness, spires, pillars, chimneypots silhouetted against the first incendiary fires. The street filled with people. Fire tenders and pumps appeared, bells clanging. Four motorcycle dispatch riders roared around a corner. Griffiths pressed Danny back with his suitcase as the motorcyclists flew past and then, catching him by the arm, dragged him across the street into the doorway of a sandbagged shop.

A little girl, younger than Billy, tripped and fell sprawling on the cobbles. Her mother, already burdened by a babe in arms, screamed and sank to her knees. The swish-swish of incendiaries sounded overhead. A rain of phosphorus crackled on the rooftop. Griff and Danny ducked as two incendiaries rattled from the roof, kicked off the eaves and, spilling fire, splashed on to the pavement. Before Danny could move a woman in a tin hat and greatcoat plucked up the fallen child, caught the mother by the waist and whisked them away.

Griffith shouted, 'Looks like we'll have to walk.'

'Are you nuts?' Danny said, shouting too.

'It's that way, I reckon.' Griff pointed with the suitcase. 'These chaps know what they're doing. They're trained for it. They'll have the fires under control in no time. Come on, boyo. Shake a leg.'

They crept along the row of sandbagged shops. The tramcar was capped with burning phosphorus. Flames poured from the windows. The conductor beat at the stairs with a sack while an old man with a stick struggled to escape.

Danny held his suitcase over his head and followed Griffith up the Broadgate, now lit as bright as day. He heard the whine of falling bombs and pitched to the pavement a second before one exploded close to the railway station. A wave of dust, smoke and scorching heat fanned over him. Tramway wires snaked down. The tram lifted from the rails and settled at an angle, the conductor and the old man sprawling on the cobbles.

Griff hauled Danny to his feet.

'Are you hurt?'

'Naw.'

'Then let's get a move on.'

Griff was already running, overcoat flapping, hat and suitcase nowhere to be seen. A fire tender pulled out of a side street, swerved to avoid the streaming crowd then ploughed on towards the blaze that lit up the sky.

High-explosive bombs fell thick and fast.

Danny glimpsed a parachute bomb floating on to the roof of a church. His eyes smarted. His ears ached. He dropped his suitcase and, hands on knees, sought to suck air into his lungs. Then, lifting his head, he saw the department store up ahead, its windows filled with flames. Even as he watched, a neighbouring building erupted in a billowing cloud of smoke and the walls caved in, slumping not floor by floor but all of a piece.

Fragments of brick, concrete and glass rained down on him. No pause, no let-up. More bombs fell. A bus slammed into a house that was already a burning shell. The parachute bomb went off behind the church. A gas main jetted a spear of light up into the sky, one more beacon for the German bombardiers to aim at. The Broadgate was littered with debris and bodies, dead and injured. Instinct told him to run. Run where? He didn't know where the shelters were.

'Griffiths,' he yelled at the top of his voice. 'Griff.'

The Welshman was running towards the blazing store.

'Wait,' Danny shouted. 'Wait for me, Griff.'

He staggered to his feet, then, propelled by a massive explosion, was hurled into the air, catapulted into a wall of sandbags and blacked out.

PART THREE

Smoke and Mirrors

12

He had never written a love letter before. He wasn't even sure he was writing a love letter now. His letters to Grace Alvarez had been basic communiqués with censor-proof suggestions as to where and when they might meet. Given that he had slept with her, he wasn't churlish enough to neglect a little bit of sentiment now and then. Once he'd even quoted a few lines of a Herrick poem he'd found in the ship's copy of the *Oxford Book of Seventeenth-Century Verse* – a surprisingly well-thumbed copy at that – though he wasn't convinced that Grace, being of a practical nature, would appreciate rosebuds.

He'd signed his letters with the same chestnut as he signed his letters to his mother and sister, *With All My Love, Derek*, which seemed neither too effusive nor too restrained and was three whole words longer than Grace's tight and almost grudging, *Love, G.*

In fact, he hadn't written to or heard from Grace in months and when it came to composing letters to a woman who wasn't a blood relative he was definitely out of practice.

Dear Miss Hooper – scored out.

Dear Mrs Cahill – also scored out.

Susan – too curt.

Dear Susan. My Dear Susan. Dearest Susan. My Dearest Susan. He lit another Capstan, poured an inch of gin into his glass and, chin on hand, gloomily considered what impression he wished to convey. Hell's bells, he thought, if I'm having this much trouble with the form of address what's it going to be like when I get to the signature? He had no precedent for writing to a young woman, a young married woman with whom for no reason, base instinct excepted, he might be falling in love.

He took up his fountain pen again and printed, *Your Devoted Servant, Commander Derek R. Willets, R.N.*, then, snorting, crumpled the sheet and dropped it into the bucket under the kneehole desk.

It was quiet outside, too dashed quiet for Portsmouth. He could hear the tide lapping against the harbour wall, a sound usually dulled by familiarity. He thought he could hear a rating who'd had a drop too much to drink singing on the quay, but that, perhaps, was just 'the mermaids', the strange whispering melody that all sailors heard from time to time when the sea was calm and the night uncannily still. At least it wasn't an air-raid siren or the whine of a Stuka coming in to chance its arm in the moonlight.

This time tomorrow he would be steering for the Clyde to join the fleet. As a rule he looked forward to being at sea again but now there was regret at the thought of what or, rather, who he was leaving behind.

In twenty minutes or so his officers would arrive for briefing.

He put the gin to one side, ground out the cigarette and, taking up his pen once more, threw caution to the winds: *Dear Susan, I'm writing to say how much I enjoyed our time together both at and under the table. I hope we might meet again on my next spell of shore leave, whenever that might be, and make a proper occasion of it.*

It was just enough to declare his intentions without going

overboard. He stroked his chin, trying to come up with a witty remark to end on, but he could think of nothing that didn't sound facetious or far too suggestive. He took a deep breath, signed it, *Love, Derek*, and added a discreet little *x* below his name, half hoping that she wouldn't notice it.

Night after night London was taking a pasting, the blitz was spreading to other cities, the Allies were suffering reverses in the Mediterranean and food rationing had been tightened. Convoys from Canada, New Zealand and the United States were being blown apart by U-boats and it seemed as if Adolf's plan to starve Britain into submission might very well succeed. But Susan had never been happier. She had Mr Walter Boscombe to thank for that. Work was no longer a chore but a vocation. Long hours in the stuffy little office in the Soho studio were more than bread and butter, more than a rung on the ladder. It was as if the BBC really had become the nation's secret weapon and she a vital part of it.

'My God, you look terrible,' Vivian said. 'Are you sick?'

Susan yawned and hitched up her dressing gown.

'I'm fine, wonderful, never better. You're early. I didn't expect you for another couple of hours. I'd planned on meeting you at the station to take you to lunch, but . . .' She yawned again. 'How's Basil? Is he on the mend?'

This was the Vivian of old, smartly dressed, poised and professional, the London Vivian with her West End voice in tune. 'I'd hardly say he was on the mend, but he isn't going to die, at least not yet. There's talk of sending him home next week.'

She put down her valise, picked up the few pieces of mail that the postman had shoved through the letterbox and tossed them, without a glance, on the hall table.

'I came up on the milk train,' she continued. 'I thought there might be trouble with the connections but the worst of the damage is north of Hereford. God, what a pounding Coventry took. I swear, you could hear it in Gadney.' She looked around. 'We've been fortunate so far, I see. Who fixed the window?'

'Derek.'

'I can't have lunch with you, Susan. I'm meeting Charlie Ames at one o'clock to hand over corrected galleys for the new book. I'll be at the studio in ample time for Boscombe to put me through my paces. I assume you received the script.'

Susan gave her tousled hair a tug. 'We did and we're very pleased with it. Did you run through it with Basil?'

'He wasn't quite up to it.'

'Will he listen to the broadcast?'

'He's a patient in a military hospital, Susan, not the bloody Ritz. He'll be tucked up and fast asleep long before midnight. Don't stand about getting cold. I'll make myself some coffee and toast then I must be off. Do we have electricity?'

'Yes, but I'm not so sure about bread,' Susan said.

Vivian's early arrival had caught her off guard.

She was pleased to see her friend, of course, but wary about giving too much away. Vivian had disapproved of her affair with Bob Gaines and had thought she was betraying Danny out of malice. Nothing could have been further from the truth. Danny had married her on the rebound from a damaging relationship with Mercer Hughes and had helped her put her life back together, something for which she would always be grateful. Gratitude was no substitute for love, however. How could she explain to Viv, an old-school conservative, that she no longer needed a man to take care of her, particularly a husband?

She came out of the bathroom and went into her bedroom to dress. She could hear Vivian rattling about in the kitchen.

'Have you heard anything from Danny?' Vivian called out.

'Pardon?' Susan said, though she'd heard the question clearly.

'Danny? Any word from Danny?'

She finished dressing and went across the corner of the hall to the kitchen. 'No, not lately. Why do you ask?'

'I thought he was supposed to be at a wedding in Coventry.'

Susan said, 'Next week. I'm sure it's next week.'

'Well, I doubt if it'll be next week now, not in Coventry at any rate. His friend doesn't live in Coventry, does he?'

'Wood Norton. Groom and bride are both down there.'

'Just as well.' Vivian handed her a mug of coffee. 'By the way, you were right.'

'About what?'

'You are out of bread,' said Vivian.

Walter Boscombe well understood that within the primitive rules of warfare industrial towns and cities were considered fair game. The scale of the Luftwaffe's attack on Coventry had shaken him, though, the more so because he had no item on hand to cover the raid for Friday night's programme. He'd spent the best part of Thursday in his office in the Calcutta cobbling together an introductory piece to Vivian Proudfoot's talk.

He'd dined quietly on Thursday evening with his father and brother, Guy, in Guy's apartment in Albany and had spent the night there rather than returning to his flat in Sloane Square which had been 'dented' in a late October raid.

He had two appointments on Friday morning, one at Portland Place and the other in the cocktail bar of the

Charing Cross Hotel with a woman known only as Nadia. She had been an intimate friend of an MP who'd manipulated parliamentary privilege to avoid arrest and who still turned up, incredibly, in the House of Commons to post motions on the evils of internment which he saw as another manifestation of the Jewish conspiracy.

Walter returned to the Calcutta about three, dictated a few letters, then, with a dance band rehearsing on the stage outside, closed his office door and, feet on the desk, completed a final edit of the script before Vivian arrived at four o'clock.

Ten minutes of small talk about Willets's recuperation, the Coventry bombing, the hazards of rail travel and the hardships involved in living out of London, then he brought the script from his drawer and slid it across the desk.

'Do we announce you as Proudfoot or Willets? You're best known as Proudfoot. Would your husband be offended if we introduce you by your professional name?'

'I doubt it,' Vivian said.

'Proudfoot it is, then,' Walter said. 'May I ask you to read a paragraph or two while I time you for pace, then we'll trim the script a trifle . . .'

Vivian prickled. 'Trim what?'

Before Walter Boscombe could answer the telephone rang. With a grimace of apology he picked up the receiver and barked his name into it, then, softening, said, 'No, no, of course not.' He frowned across the desk at Vivian. 'I'll transfer – no, come to think of it, it might be best if Mrs Cahill took the call on the internal line. One moment.'

He placed the receiver on the desk, came swiftly around the desk and opened the door.

'Susan,' he called out loudly enough to make himself heard above the band. 'Susan, will you come here, please.'

She appeared at once from the cubby, notebook in hand.

'There's a call for you from the switchboard.'

'A call for me?' Susan said.

'It concerns your husband,' Walter Boscombe said.

Susan glanced from Walter to Vivian and then at the receiver on the desk. 'What about him?'

'I think you should speak to the person on the line,' Walter Boscombe said and, taking Vivian by the arm, led her out of the office to allow Susan Cahill a few bleak moments of privacy.

Breda didn't hear the details of the Luftwaffe's raid on Coventry until she reached Orrell's in the morning. Many employees had family in the city and the canteen hummed with speculation. There was nothing to be done except wait for news, good or bad. Breda got through the day in a haze of apprehension, serving food to grim-faced men who ate only to keep their strength up while waiting for someone to tell them if their loved ones were alive or dead.

That evening Mr Pell said he'd cycle to Wood Norton to see if anyone there had up-to-date news but Breda had told him she didn't think they'd let him through the gate.

Mrs Pell insisted that Billy and she stay for supper. They ate at the table in the living room and discussed the raid in whispers. Wireless bulletins made matters worse. Mrs Pell begged Breda to stay overnight but Breda used Billy as an excuse for returning to Shady Nook. She left soon after eight and walked with Billy through bright moonlight back to the railway coach, hoping that Danny would be seated on the doorstep puffing a ciggie, but doorstep and coach were empty.

There were several empty benches in Orrell's workshops too. Shortly after one o'clock, two policemen turned up and spoke with Mr Jackson. One of the young girls who worked at the sinks was called into Mr Jackson's office and, soon after, was led away in tears.

'Her sisters,' Trudy Littlejohn confided.

'Dead?' Morven asked.

'Yes, both dead.'

Breda wasn't Danny's wife or his sister and no one would come to Orrell's to tell her what had happened to him.

At shift's end she hurried to the Pells' house to find Billy seated at the table in the living room supping cocoa and quietly reading a comic paper.

'No word yet, Mrs Pell?' Breda asked.

'No, nothing. No news is good news, I suppose.'

The women were in the kitchen sipping tea when rapping on the back door made them jump. It wasn't a policeman or a warden but a youngish, fair-haired man wearing a raincoat, a soft hat and a long scarf. He had glasses on, very thick glasses that made his eyes seem small and mean.

He touched the brim of his hat. 'Mrs Pell?'

'I'm Mrs Pell.'

'May I come in?'

'Who are you?'

He produced a card in a blue celluloid holder and held it out for Mrs Pell to examine.

'Baker's my name. I'm the new district billeting officer. I believe you have vacancies. Two rooms, is it?'

'Vacancies?' said Mrs Pell dully.

The notebook in Baker's hand was also protected by blue celluloid. He flipped it open and squinted down at it.

'Two rooms. Three occupants,' he said. 'May I come in? I've a couple, both males, arriving by train from London this evening and nowhere to put them.'

'What are you saying?' Mrs Pell cried. 'Are you telling me . . .'

The billeting officer continued to study his notebook.

'One female. Cottrell. Two males sharing. Griffith and Cahill.' His mouth opened and his head jerked up. 'Oh!' he exclaimed. 'Oh, dear! Dear, dear, dear! You haven't been informed, have you? Been a mix-up somewhere, I'm afraid.' He hastily removed his hat. 'This isn't – I mean, it's not my fault.'

Then he stepped back and might have fled if Mrs Pell hadn't screamed, 'No vacancies here. No vacancies here,' and buried her face in her hands.

Walter Boscombe offered his arm and Vivian pulled out a chair for her to sit on but she had no need of support. She replaced the receiver on the cradle and rested on the edge of the desk.

'Danny's all right,' she said. 'That was a Mr Gregory telephoning from Wood Norton. Awfully kind of him.'

'Where is Danny?' Vivian said. 'Is he back in Evesham?'

'No, some place called Dudley. He's stuck there waiting for the railway line to re-open. Is Dudley near Coventry?'

'South of Wolverhampton?' Walter Boscombe told her.

'What's he doing there, I wonder?' Susan said. 'I must have got the wedding dates wrong, I suppose.'

'Susan, are you all right?' Vivian asked.

'Hmm, I'm fine. There's not much point in making tracks for Dudley. I've no intention of chasing all over the country now I know he's all right. If he needs me he can come up to London.'

'What about his friends?' Vivian asked. 'Are they safe too?'

'I really don't know,' Susan answered. 'They're Danny's

friends, not mine,' then, picking up her notebook, returned to her cubby next door.

A half-hour after the billeting officer beat an apologetic retreat a motorcar drew up at the pavement's edge and a man and a woman got out. Breda was in the kitchen heating soup for Billy who, now that the stranger had gone, had settled in Mr Pell's armchair in the living room to read his comic paper.

He'd been through too much upheaval recently not to realise that something bad was happening. It had worried him when Mrs Pell had screamed and if his mother had screamed too he'd have lost his composure completely. But his mother had drawn herself up, had folded her arms across her chest the way his gran used to do, and had told him in a very quiet voice to stay in the living room while she and Mrs Pell talked to the man.

The man hadn't come into the living room but he could hear Mrs Pell crying again and his mother saying, 'All right, all right, it's all right,' in a voice that meant it wasn't all right.

He'd thought of hiding behind the couch or under the dining table but there was nothing to hide from. Instead he'd curled up in Mr Pell's chair and tried to read his comic as if what was going on in the kitchen had nothing to do with him.

Later, he heard a car arrive and saw Mrs Pell at the window with the curtain pulled aside. He was tempted to shout out, 'Mind that light,' like the boys in class did but he didn't want to annoy Mrs Pell in case she started crying again.

Mrs Pell went out into the hall. His mother came out of the kitchen and crossed the corner of the living room to the front door. The front door was never used except by the postman and milkman and they never came in.

It worried him when he heard voices in the hall, a man's voice, deep and slow and posh, not Mr Pell or Mr Gaydon, not Danny either or Danny's friend who lived upstairs. When Mrs Pell came in to the living room she was crying. A man, a big, tall man who he'd never seen before had an arm around her and a woman he'd never seen before and his mummy came in after them.

He didn't know if he should give over the chair to Mrs Pell or the strange man or stay where he was.

'No,' he heard his mother say, 'he's mine.' She came forward, picked him up, turned him around and, sitting on the arm of Mr Pell's chair, held him tightly between her knees.

The man guided Mrs Pell to the table and pulled out a chair for her then he took the chair opposite, where Mr Pell usually sat. The woman in the green overcoat and beret stood behind Mrs Pell with a hand on her shoulder. Mrs Pell looked smaller than usual, crushed up like a piece of newspaper before you lit the fire with it. He could hear her crying, not loudly. He expected his mother to send him into the kitchen or upstairs to Danny's room but she didn't. He put his head back against her chest and heard her breathing. When he looked up he saw she was crying too.

The man reached out and took Mrs Pell's hands, his big hands round her small ones. 'I can only apologise once more,' he said. 'It simply didn't occur to me that Billeting would have confirmation before we did. My first thought was to inform Mrs Cahill, but no excuse will suffice for not calling on you. There's no question of the rooms being – of anyone else – I mean, until Danny gets back.'

'When will that be?' Mummy said.

'Tomorrow, we hope. It's a transport problem,' the man said.

Mummy sighed. Her chest heaved against his ear. 'Danny is all right, though?'

'I've spoken with him and, yes, he's all right.'

Mrs Pell pulled her hands across the table and looked up at the ceiling. 'What'll I do with her clothes?'

'Leave that to us, Mrs Pell,' the woman in the green overcoat said. 'We don't know who the next of kin might be but we'll make enquiries as soon as we can.'

'Her pretty clothes,' said Mrs Pell. 'All her pretty things.'

Billy heard the back door open and Mr Pell clumping and then the living room door opened and Mr Pell was there, looking this way and that at the strange man and woman in the room. Then Mr Pell used a bad word and nobody told him off for it. He came to the table, put an arm round Mrs Pell and hugged her.

Mrs Pell put her forehead against Mr Pell's forehead.

'Gone, dear. They've gone,' she said and began to cry again.

And Billy, without knowing why, began to cry too.

The waiters from the York Minster dining rooms in Dean Street arrived before Zach Gillespie had time to make good his escape. The waiters wore white jackets, black trousers, white shirts, bow-ties and tin helmets. They carried the buffet supper between them in a basket and, on Mr Boscombe's instruction, laid out the food on a table in front of the stage.

Precisely why Mr Boscombe had chosen that night to host a celebratory supper was not something he cared to explain. Smoked salmon, cooked meats and bread rolls fresh from the oven were washed down with champagne. It was warm in the underground cinema and, for the most part, quiet, the stale air scented by the sweet smell of Zach Gillespie's pipe tobacco.

Vivian's talk had gone very well. She'd sounded confident and assured, not bombastic. In crisp Canadian style, Zach Gillespie had read Mr Boscombe's carefully worded introduction and brought out all the points that Mr Boscombe wished emphasised in discussion afterwards. Elliot Kershaw, *The Times* Home Affairs correspondent, had topped off the programme with a poignant talk on St Michael whose cathedral in Coventry had been destroyed by the forces of evil but whose spirit of resistance was unquenchable.

No jazz tail-out, just five beats of silence before Mr Gillespie wished his listeners in North America God Speed and a good night's rest and switched off his microphone.

It was, or should have been, a pleasantly informal supper party, one that Susan would have revelled in if it hadn't been for the thought of Danny trapped in a town in the Midlands in circumstances she couldn't comprehend. She sipped champagne and tried to convince herself that Danny was having a whale of a time in a rest centre with his friends. Somehow, though, the image refused to congeal and she couldn't erase from her mind Elliot Kershaw's eulogy for a city in ruins.

'Why so pale and wan, fond lover?' Larry tickled her ear, the scarred ear, with his fingertip. 'We're up and running and off with a bang. Give's a smile, Susie pops, give us a flash of the old pearly whites, there's a good girl.'

Vivian said, 'She's concerned about her husband.'

'No, I'm not,' Susan retorted. 'Danny can take care of himself. He always falls on his feet.'

'Well, he has a long way to fall this time,' said Vivian. 'Did you really not know his friend's wedding was this week?'

'I probably did and I'd forgotten.'

She moved away, took a fork from a basket on the table and served herself two slices of cold roast beef. She held the glass in one hand and a plate in the other and, turning her back on Vivian and Larry, joined the group of three men.

Walter Boscombe glanced at her and blew cigarette smoke towards the ceiling. 'Kershaw here seems to believe we're up to something sinister and possibly illegal.'

'I didn't say illegal,' Elliot Kershaw corrected.

Mr Gillespie took the pipe from his mouth. 'What then?'

'Sailing close to the wind,' Kershaw told him. 'It's rumoured in Fleet Street, Walter, that you're giving Redmain wireless time to clear his name.'

'Clear his name? What on earth gave you and your gang that impression? Good God, man, I'm out to hang him, if I can.'

'Hardly worth the bother,' Kershaw said. 'He's a burned-out case.'

'Did he look like a burned-out case to you, Susan?' Walter Boscombe asked.

Without prompting, Susan delivered the answer he required. 'He certainly appears to be burned out but it struck me as an act, a sham. He's still up to the ears in it.'

Elliot Kershaw didn't look like a *Times* correspondent, more like a down-at-heel racing reporter for Danny's old paper, the *Star*. He was stocky in build with an out-of-shape nose and a shock of wiry grey hair that hadn't seen a comb in weeks. He lifted a thin slice of roast beef from his plate, folded, chewed and swallowed it, while giving Susan the once-over.

'Up to the ears in what, young lady?'

'Conspiring with fascist sympathisers.'

'Conspiring to do what, though? Bring down the government? Pave the way for an invasion? Lock up all the Jews the way we've locked up all the Italians?' Kershaw said. 'Does Redmain have a list of undesirables ready to hand to von Ribbentrop as soon as the Nazis take over Westminster?'

'I expect Ribbentrop already has such a list,' Mr Gillespie said.

'If he has,' Mr Boscombe put in, 'my name's bound to be on it.'

'What a conceited devil you are, Boscombe,' Elliot Kershaw said. 'Basically, you're nothing but a BBC producer with ideas above your station.' He paused, another slice of roast beef hanging from his fork. 'Or are you?'

'Am I what?'

'A not so humble employee of the BBC,' Kershaw said. 'If *Speaking Up for Britain* isn't propaganda then I don't know what it is. It may not be black propaganda but it's certainly a funny shade of grey. I think you're a tool . . .'

'I've been called that often enough,' Mr Boscombe put in.

'. . . a tool, shall we say, of a higher power. You're serving two masters, if you ask me.'

'What an imagination you have, Kershaw. On this form you could give our friend Dennis Wheatley a run for his money. Next thing you'll be telling me I'm in cahoots with MI5.' He laughed and wagged his cigarette in the journalist's face. 'If you publish one word of that ridiculous rubbish I'll sue your breeks off.'

'He would too,' said Zach Gillespie. 'Anything for a bit of free publicity, hmm, Walter?'

'You're darn tootin'.' Walter Boscombe put an arm about

Susan's waist and drew her to him. 'What do you think, Mrs Cahill? Do you think I'm an agent for MI5?'

'Absolutely,' Susan said, and laughed.

The glare over Chelsea indicated that the Luftwaffe had not been entirely absent from the skies over London when Mr Boscombe let Vivian and Susan off at the mouth of Salt Street Mews at half past four in the morning.

'Would you care to come in for a nightcap?' Susan invited.

'Not tonight, Susan, thank you,' Walter Boscombe said. 'Even secret agents do have to sleep some time.' He opened the passenger door for Vivian. 'Thank you again for a most illuminating talk. I'll have Susan forward anything interesting that comes out of the postbag, as well as your fee, of course. Oh, and please remember what we talked about. Give it some thought, if you will.'

'I will,' Vivian promised. 'Goodnight, Mr Boscombe,' and, taking Susan's arm, steered her into the mews.

As soon as they were safe within the house and had removed their coats and hats, Susan said, 'What was *that* all about?'

'That,' said Vivian, 'may well have been why I was invited to London in the first place.' She tested the electric switch and to her surprise saw the bulb in the hallway light up. 'God, but do I need a drink, a real drink, none of that fizzy French stuff. You?'

'If there's any whisky left in the decanter – yes, a tiddler.'

Puzzled, Susan followed Vivian into the living room and switched on the standard lamp. Vivian sank wearily on to the davenport, a glass of neat whisky in each hand, the decanter on the carpet between her feet.

She offered a glass to Susan, drank from the other and

leaned back against the cushions. 'If I wasn't catching an early morning train,' she said, 'I do believe I'd get stinko.'

'You haven't answered my question.'

Vivian sighed and closed her eyes. 'Bribery, that's what it is. Bribery, blackmail and corruption. Frankly, I wouldn't be at all surprised if the boss you seem so enamoured of, is, actually, an agent for some shifty government department.' She bent over, lifted the decanter, contemplated the whisky that remained within and put glass and decanter on the carpet. 'No,' she said. 'I'd better not.'

'What did Walter say to you?' Susan persisted. 'I'm not going to bed until you tell me.'

'He's a snake, that man,' said Vivian. 'What you see in him . . .'

'Vivian?'

'Given that you're now his pet lamb, no doubt you'll find out sooner or later.' She heaved herself to her feet and stretched. 'He wants me to set up a meeting with my brother.'

'David won't talk on the wireless.'

'David won't talk with his head in a bucket,' Vivian said. 'I told Boscombe as much, but he's very insistent, very persuasive, as you, no doubt, already know.'

Susan said, 'Can you do it? I mean, *will* you do it?'

'Betray my own flesh and blood in exchange for the promise of a decent job for my poor old husband when he's well again?' Vivian said. 'Of course, I will,' then, smirking, headed for the bathroom.

13

Danny was too proud to throw himself into her arms when she met him at the railway station but his expression said it all. He carried no case or gas-mask holder. The clothes he wore were not all his own: a pair of paint-stained flannels and a cheap raincoat buttoned up to the throat. She noticed he was limping a little, dragging his left foot. She linked his arm with hers and led him past the crowd at the bus stop before she said a word.

'Your Mr Gregory told me you might arrive this afternoon. He'll send someone down to see you tonight.'

'Who?' Danny said.

'I dunno. Someone. What 'appened to your leg?'

'Nothin''. It's okay.'

'Your face . . .'

'Scratches, that's all.'

Mr Gaydon had dropped by early that morning and had taken Billy up to the farm to play with the girls. Mr Pell had told her that he was too sick to work a Sunday shift, which meant he didn't want to leave Mrs Pell alone in case some other official arrived to upset her.

'Does Mrs Pell know about Griff and Kate?' Danny asked.

'Yer, she knows.' Breda hesitated. 'She wants to see you.'

He nodded.

Breda said, 'We can take the bus to the crossroads and . . .'

'We'll walk.'

'Danny, are you sure?'

'We'll walk,' he said again and, still without looking at her, tightened his grip on her arm.

In fading daylight the little row of council houses, backed by leafless trees, was stark and forbidding. Mr Pell was loitering by the gate. He didn't rush to greet them but waited until they reached the gate before he opened it.

The next-door neighbours had tried to engage him in conversation but he'd given them short shrift. The husband was still in the front garden, pretending to potter at his pea patch but really keeping a weather eye out for who or what might be coming down the road. They were a nosy couple and, having heard the news on the Deaconsfield grapevine, were deathly afraid that the next occupant of Mrs Pell's vacant room might be a black man or some bearded fellow who jabbered in a language they couldn't understand.

Mr Pell shook Danny's hand.

'I hope you're hungry, son,' he said. 'She's been at the stove all afternoon. Braised oxtail and apple dumplings.' He glanced over Danny's shoulder at Breda to make sure she wasn't about to crack. 'What happened to your face?'

'Glass.'

'Stitches?'

'Naw, no stitches. It's not as bad as it looks.' He prodded at his glasses which, Breda noticed, were scratched on the lenses and had one leg held on by a grubby strip of adhesive tape. 'Lucky I was wearin' the blinkers or it might've been worse.'

Mr Pell drew himself up. 'Are you ready for this, Danny?'

'Aye, I'm ready,' Danny said and, brushing past Mr Pell, made for the kitchen door.

'Have you had enough?' Mrs Pell said. 'There's more in the pot if you want it.'

'No, thanks. I'm stuffed.'

'Braised oxtail was always Silwyn's favourite.'

'You're right,' Danny said. 'It was.'

Seated in an armchair, Breda nursed a teacup and a cigarette. Mr Pell watched his wife untie her apron and fold it across the back of a chair. She poured tea into one of the floral cups that only appeared on special occasions, added a drop of milk and then, settling herself on the chair, drew the cup to her and tested the temperature of the tea with the tip of her tongue.

'Now, Danny,' she said, 'tell me all about it.'

'I can only tell you what the coppers told me,' Danny began. 'I was knocked out by bomb blast. Someone scraped me off the pavement an' dragged me tae a shelter. Then the shelter was hit with an incendiary. We rushed outside an' the ambulance people put some of us into the back of a lorry an' drove us out o' Coventry. The guy – it might've been a woman – who drove that lorry deserves a medal. Buildings were fallin' down around us and the road was pitted wi' craters. Stuff kept hittin' the top o' the lorry and two or three times we were blown sideways before we got tae the hospital in Dudley. The hospital was jam-packed, stretchers an' bodies in all the corridors. A doctor looked me over an' put me in a big room with women an' kiddies, all screaming an' crying.

'The bomb had ripped my coat and trousers off. All I had on was my shirt an' the jacket o' my blue suit. They gave me a blanket. A nurse came an' bathed my face an' picked out most o' the glass. My leg was swollen at the ankle but she said nothing appeared tae be broken. She helped me outside into a motorcar with three women an' a wee girl. We were driven tae a hall where there was tea and buns an' more blankets. After a bit, a man came round an' wrote my details on a pad. When I asked him about – well, you couldn't expect him tae know about that, I suppose.

'Next day the man with the pad an' two coppers came round. They told me the Gibson Hotel had been burned out and there were no survivors. The coppers had a list o' names. They were all on it: Mrs Griffiths, Mr and Mrs Cottrell an' Kate. They'd been trapped in the alley at the back o' the hotel.'

'What about Griff?' Mr Pell put in.

'Griff didn't get to the hotel,' Danny said. 'Firemen saw him go down in the street. There was nothing they could do for him. I wanted tae go tae the mortuary in Coventry to make sure, but they told me it wasn't safe. Anyway, I wasn't a relative. The police contacted Mr Gregory in Wood Norton and Silwyn's father in Wales. Mr Griffiths came over from Brecon with his sister tae take care of arrangements. There was nothin' for me tae do.'

Breda said quietly, 'When are the funerals?'

'Wednesday or Thursday. They're buryin' them all at once, all together, a mass grave.' He rubbed his hand over his face and tugged at his lip. 'Somebody from the BBC'll be there. Some big-wig.'

'Too much of a lord mayor's show for us,' said Mr Pell before his wife could speak. 'Better if we remember them where we knew them best, here in Deaconsfield.'

Danny pushed his chair back from the table and got to his feet. 'I'll need some clean clothes.' He looked up at the ceiling. 'I'd appreciate it if somebody would come up with me. Mr Pell?'

'Sure, son, sure.'

They went upstairs together.

Mrs Pell sat motionless at the table, the teacup held in both hands and listened to the clumping on the floor above and the muffled sound of voices, too faint to be audible.

At length, Breda said, 'I'll take 'im home with me tonight.'

'Whatever's best for Danny.' Mrs Pell glanced round at Breda. 'Unless you want to stay here, you and the little chap.'

'I don't think that's a good idea,' Breda said.

He switched on the lamp and closed the blackout curtain and, turning his back on Mr Pell, opened a drawer on the dressing table and brought out two clean shirts, underwear, socks and a tie. He laid them on his bed and took down his second best suit from the hanger on the hook behind the door. He tried not to look at the ratty old sheepskin coat, at the polished shoes that peeped out from beneath the bed or the three or four books that Griff had left on the bedside table, as if he'd have time for reading when Kate and he were wife and husband.

'Can I do anything to help?' Mr Pell asked.

Danny seated himself on the bed, hands between his knees, eyes fixed on the lamplight. 'They were trapped in the back alley when the hotel fell down,' he said. 'The copper said smoke killed them but he was just bein' tactful. I think they were burned tae death. If the train'd been on time we'd have been there too.'

'Danny . . .'

'Poor old Griff. It took a bloody German bomb tae shut the beggar up. Blew his head off. Shrapnel. Blew his head clean off. They only knew who he was by the cards in his pockets. Strangers, a year ago we were, strangers an' now . . .' He slapped his hands to his knees and got to his feet. 'I can't stay here. I know she'll want me to an' I know the billeting fee's useful but I just can't stay here.'

'Maybe in a day or two . . .'

'If Mr Gregory calls, tell him where I am.'

'With Breda and the boy at Shady Nook?'

'Aye,' Danny said. 'Tell him – tomorrow. I'll be in tomorrow for the eight o'clock shift. I'll pick up the rest of my things in a day or two once I know what's what at Wood Norton. Oh, one other thing, Mr Pell, a favour.'

'Whatever you need, Danny.'

'Can I borrow one of the bikes?'

An air-raid warning and the sound of distant explosions did not intimidate the hard-drinking crowd in the public bar of the York Minster or deter those of a less rambunctious disposition from enjoying their dinner in the restaurant upstairs. The solitary incendiary that fell on the building's sloping roof was pounced upon and gleefully extinguished by a team of Polish airmen who had volunteered to take first watch.

Polish was by no means the only language spoken in the Minster. French, Dutch, Hungarian and Greek mingled with a variety of English accents while, from the pavement outside, a melodic rendering of 'Shine Through my Dreams' by two tipsy subalterns from the Scots Guards and a Wren who was obviously Irish added to the bedlam.

Susan's heart had missed a beat when Walter Boscombe had invited her to supper. On the short walk from the Calcutta to Dean Street she almost managed to convince herself that he might be trying to lure her into bed.

The Minster's Belgian proprietor was scrupulous when

it came to enforcing blackout regulations. The doors, front and back, were weighted with stiff canvas curtains that hindered light from seeping out and fresh air from seeping in. Beer, spirits, several brands of tobacco and the untranslatable odour of sweat-stained serge created an atmosphere as thick as Channel fog. It was all Susan could do to hang on to Walter's hand as he climbed the steep stairs to the dining room where the sound of shouting and raucous singing was deadened by carpeted boards.

An elderly waiter cleared a route to a table for two, took coats and hats, pulled out chairs and handed Mr Boscombe a menu and a wine list. While Walter studied the wine list, Susan studied Walter. He was handsome, certainly, but in a brutish sort of way that many women, Susan among them, found attractive or, if not attractive, exciting. In the heady atmosphere of the Minster's upper room she found herself wondering if all she'd heard about Mr Boscombe's attributes as a lover were true.

A young man in Free French uniform appeared at her side. He had sleek black hair and a pencil moustache and carried his hat under his arm. He bowed to Susan then said something to Walter who, with a murmured apology, rose and, turning his back on the table, conversed in rapid French with the young officer for half a minute or so. The officer clicked his heels, bowed once more to Susan, and went off downstairs.

'Who,' Susan asked, 'was that?'

'One of de Gaulle's aides.' Walter Boscombe returned to studying the wine list. 'Somewhat of a fuss-pot – like his boss.'

'You do seem to know lots of interesting people.'

Mr Boscombe peered at her over the top of the wine list for a long moment, then, waving the card in the air, summoned the waiter and ordered a bottle of claret and two bowls of onion soup.

'The best soup in London,' he said, 'and, given the scarcity of onions, soon perhaps to be the last best soup in town.' He paused, still looking at her, and added, 'Make the most of it, Mrs Cahill, while the going's good. Yes, I do know quite a number of interesting people, people no more or less interesting than your friends. How well *do* you know David Proudfoot, for instance?'

At that moment she surrendered all pretence of being a naïve little girl from Shadwell. 'Well enough to know he's a crook and a lecher – which makes me wonder why you're pursuing him. I was under the impression the pro-fascist threat had evaporated when Mosley was sent to jail. Unless, of course, you're using *Speaking Up* to smoke out what the *Mirror* called "the rump of the resistance," by which I don't think they meant the French.'

'My brother thinks you have nice breasts.'

'I beg your pardon.'

'Given the choice between being complimented on their brains or their beauty the majority of women of my acquaintance will choose the latter. But I don't think that's you somehow.'

She watched the waiter uncork a bottle, Mr Boscombe conduct the ritual of tasting and the glasses being filled. 'Since you're obviously not flirting with me,' she said, 'perhaps you'd be good enough to tell me what you do want.'

'Kershaw's not far off the mark when he called *Speaking Up* grey propaganda. Public reaction to our broadcasts over the next few weeks will be divided, especially in the press, but I'm hoping to stir up interest in other quarters too.'

'What does this have to do with David Proudfoot?'

'Someone's protecting him, someone with influence.'

'And you want to find out who?'

'In a nutshell, Susan, yes.'

'Well, you can be sure he's not going to talk to you.'

'Which,' Walter Boscombe said, 'is where you come in.'

It was after dark before Fred Gaydon brought Billy home to Shady Nook. He'd nursed a vague notion that Breda and he might share more than a wink and a nudge, though he'd never played the field with other women before, mainly because the Evesham community was too tight-knit to get away with that sort of mischief undetected. Breda Hooper was a Cockney, though, a big city girl who, he was willing to bet, had a bit of a history and knew what was what. Her son was the stumbling block, the reason why he lusted only lightly after the statuesque widow. To impose himself on Breda would be a betrayal of the little boy's trust.

Even so he couldn't help but be disappointed when he saw the bicycle leaning against the side of the carriage and heard Billy call out, 'Danny's 'ere. Danny's back.'

Breda opened the door and Billy vanished into the railway carriage. He heard a man's voice, low and restrained, greet the boy before Breda stepped outside and closed the carriage door.

'Thanks, Fred,' she said. 'I hope 'e wasn't no trouble.'

'No trouble at all. Is – I mean, is Mr Cahill . . .'

'Danny,' Breda said. 'Yes, he's 'ere. He's staying over.' She moved a half-step closer. 'Do you mind?'

'Why would I mind?'

'He can't go back to the Pells, not yet anyway. You can understand 'ow he feels.'

'I'm not sure I can,' Fred Gaydon admitted. 'If Danny wants to billet here then it's no skin off my nose. What about you and Billy moving in with the Pells?'

'BBC accommodation ain't open to evacuees.'

'Not really my place to ask, Breda, but what about Danny's wife?'

'What about 'er?'

'Won't she – well, object?'

'She won't know nothing about it,' Breda said. 'Even if she did, she wouldn't care. She don't love 'im and never 'as.'

He hesitated. 'You do, don't you? Love him, I mean?'

''Course, I do.'

'Then he's a lucky fella,' Fred Gaydon said. 'A very lucky fella,' and reluctantly bade her goodnight.

Raiding that night was light and sporadic and Mr Boscombe sent her home in a taxi. She was mildly aggrieved that he hadn't considered her irresistible and that supper at the York Minster hadn't ended with a kiss but, rather ridiculously, with a handshake.

What had started out as simple infatuation with a complicated man had taken an unexpected turn. She sat back in the taxi-cab and tried to shake off the disappointment and come to terms with the fact that he wanted more from her than she could possibly have imagined. She was flattered and, at the same time, mortified and, on entering the empty mews house in Salt Street, felt unusually lonely.

She poured the last drops of Vivian's whisky into a clean glass, topped it up with water from the tap in the kitchen, then went into the office, switched on the lamp and, wrestling with her common sense, stared at the telephone on the desk.

There was no one she could feasibly call at this late hour. Even if Danny was at the editing table in Wood Norton, she decided it was highly unlikely she'd be allowed to talk with him. And Vivian? Vivian wasn't a solution to her problem but part of it.

She drank the watered whisky, left the empty glass on the desk, switched off the lamp and went into the hall.

It was only then she noticed the letter on the hall table, a stiff white envelope addressed to Mrs Susan Cahill. She took the envelope into her bedroom, switched on the bedside lamp and, seated on the bed, slit it open.

The letter within was neatly folded and not very long.

'Dear Susan,' it began and ended with a kiss, a tiny little *x* that seemed both brave and bashful.

The sentiments in between were inconsequential, though she did wonder what he meant by making an occasion of it. With another chap, a different type of chap, she might assume that he had something racier in mind than another dinner at the Dorchester.

She put the letter on the bed, went into the bathroom, washed her face and cleaned her teeth, then, in the bedroom, undressed and put on her nightgown.

She climbed into bed, lay back against the pillow, read Derek's letter once more, then, with the letter resting against her nose and a smile on her lips, gently drifted off to sleep.

14

'So,' Morven said, 'you've got him all to yourself at last.'

'It's not like you think it is,' Breda said. 'Danny ain't the sort to take advantage.'

'Must be a wee bit awkward, though, especially at bedtime.'

'Danny has Billy's bunk and Billy sleeps with me. Not the best arrangement but the only one what's proper.'

'Good for you, Breda,' Morven said. 'I couldn't share a room with a man who wasn't my husband and keep my hands to myself.'

They were seated at one end of the canteen table, polishing off sausage and egg pie.

After the curry incident Mrs Littlejohn had steered clear of the communal table. She ate dinner from a plate in the vegetable store or, failing that, in the kitchen wash-up. Archie's objections to her unsocial eating habits had been silenced by Trudy who may have lost her bark but when it came to dealing with Mr Jackson certainly hadn't lost her bite.

In her dealings with Stevie Pepperdine, however, she had become more circumspect. What went on in the vicarage between dusk and dawn was anybody's guess but, within working hours, Steve and Trudy deliberately ignored each other.

'No go with the billeting officer then?' Morven asked.

'Not a hope.' Breda shrugged. 'Danny can go back to Mrs Pell's any time but he can't take us with 'im since we're not BBC employees.'

'What about Billy?'

'Mrs Pell still takes 'im in before and after school and 'e goes up to the Gaydons on Saturday mornings. He's okay.'

'If you're ever stuck for a nanny just send for Auntie Morven.'

'I might 'old you to that, Morven,' Breda said, 'if I can persuade Danny to come out of 'is shell and take me to the works concert or, better still, the Christmas dance.'

'You can bring Billy to the concert,' Morven said, 'but on the night of the dance it's every woman for herself. By the by, have you seen any more of that cove from Special Branch? He didn't turn up with the Navy Board last Monday.'

'Maybe it's all blown over, whatever it was. Tell me,' Breda said, 'what's this concert in aid of? No, let me guess: the Spitfire Fund. Gonna cost me a fortune just to 'ear Stevie Pepperdine play his thingme, I expect. Who else does a turn?'

'Haven't a clue. This is the first ever Orrell's works concert,' Morven said, 'and with luck it'll be the last.'

'Aren't you going then?'

''Course I'm going,' said Morven. 'Wouldn't miss it for worlds.'

In spite of what Breda had told Morven, having Danny as a lodger was by no means all fun and games. He was attentive to Billy, played cards with him, read from the *Wonder Book* and tucked him up in bed. He ate whatever Breda put before him and pitched in with the chores, filling a bucket from the well, raking out the stove, replacing the Calor gas canister when it ran out and emptying the chemical toilet into a pit on the edge of the field, a job Breda hated.

He was, without doubt, handy to have around.

Trouble was that even when he was there, half the time he wasn't and would sit at the folding table, smoking a cigarette, nursing a teacup and staring into space.

'Penny for 'em, Danny?'

'Hmm?'

'What're you thinking about?'

'Aw, nothin' much. Work. The war. That's all.'

There were times in the first week of what Morven persisted in calling 'cohabitation' when Danny seemed more like a stranger than her oldest friend. He no longer dropped by the BBC Club in Evesham or took part in any of the social events that the monitoring unit put on. He pushed his bicycle down the muddy lane to the road, cycled through town to Wood Norton and returned by the same dreary route, passing Breda and Billy as they left for work and school or sometimes not seeing them at all.

'Concert?' he said, frowning. 'Where?'

'I just told you. Wasn't you listening? First Saturday in December in Shay Bridge church hall,' Breda informed him. 'They was thinking of putting it on in Orrell's canteen but the Navy Board drew the line at that. It's in aid of the Spitfire Fund. Mr Pepperdine's got it all organised. I thought you might like to come.'

'Well,' Danny said cautiously, 'if I'm not on duty . . .'

'How about the dance?'

'Dance? What dance?'

'Week later, same place. Band coming down from the RAF station at Ledington. Supposed to be top-notch.'

'I don't dance, Breda. You know that.'

'If you don't wanna be seen with me in public just say so.'

'It's not that.'

'Danny, you gotta get over it.' She lit a cigarette and blew out the match with enough force to make the wisp of hair on her forehead shiver. 'You're not the only one lost somebody.'

'You know I can't make promises.'

'I'm not asking for bleedin' promises. I just want you to spare a thought for me instead of thinking about 'er all the time. She's dead, Danny. Besides, she was never yours in the first place.'

'Oh,' he said, 'you mean Kate?'

'Who the heck do you think I mean?'

'I thought you meant Susan,' he said.

Radio critics were generally impressed by Vivian's talk but the editor of the *New Statesman* predicted that her contribution was only a softening-up exercise for high Tory malfeasance, a well-engineered plot to appease the beleaguered workers of Great Britain.

More gratifying was the transcript of a broadcast picked up by the monitoring unit in which a German announcer on the Zeesen transmitter took time off from sports reporting to mock the BBC for using a woman to berate Churchill, which, of course, was never Vivian's intention, as her husband was quick to point out.

'What in heaven's name gave Jerry the impression that Viv was on their side?' Basil waved the copy of the transcript and almost but not quite tipped the sheaf of clippings from his knee into the grate. 'Is this the only one from the German stations, Susan?'

'That's it, Basil,' Susan told him. 'The American papers

take quite the opposite view. I think you'll find the item from the *New York Times* particularly—'

'Yes, yes,' Basil said. 'I've absolutely no doubt your boss picked the polite ones just to placate me.'

'I don't see what you've got to do with it,' Vivian said. 'Nor do I see why Boscombe has any need to placate you.' Seated at the table in the cottage kitchen, mirror propped against a sauce bottle, she carefully applied lipstick. 'Given the transient nature of broadcasting and the other speakers Boscombe has lined up, my talk is a one-day wonder.'

'I thought it was supposed to publicise your book.'

'Oh, that!' Vivian pursed her lips and with the tip of her little finger smoothed out the rouge. 'April's a long way off, dear. With any luck, *Enemy in Our Midst* will sink without trace.'

'I thought you said it was your best book ever.'

'I've changed my mind. I'm not proud of *Enemy* after all.'

'Well, *I'm* proud of it,' Basil said. 'And I'm proud of you.'

He sat back in the rocking chair and protected the slippery sheaf of correspondence with his elbows as if the endorsement of total strangers was all he needed to confirm his opinion of his wife's talent. He was dressed in flannels, a shirt without a necktie, a woollen pullover and a dressing gown, for he had lost so much weight that even a whisper of night air chilled his bones. His lungs, however, were on the mend, thanks to the ministrations of Dr Fleck and his nurses. A month or so of rest and recuperation would see him firmly on his feet again if, that is, impatience and irascibility didn't do for him in the interim.

'I still can't understand why you're not manning the fort, Susan,' he said. 'Is there such a glut of producers hanging around this Soho picture house that Boscombe can afford to let you flit off on a Friday afternoon?'

Susan said, 'I've been agitating for a few days' leave and this, according to Mr Boscombe, will be my last chance to shake the shackles before Christmas.'

'Why didn't you go to Evesham to see your husband?'

Vivian got to her feet and smoothed her skirt over her hips. 'Because she came to see us instead. Now, do you have everything you need? There's broth in the pot. All you have to do is turn on the stove. There's a cooked chicken leg too under the big plate in the larder and bread . . .'

'I'm not helpless, you know.' Basil rocked a little in the chair, then, head cocked, asked, 'Does he know you're coming?'

'No, we're seizing the chance to drop in.'

'Why?' said Basil. 'Why go to all the expense of bringing a taxi away out here when all you have to do is lift the telephone and your brother will send a chap to collect you?'

'Yes,' said Vivian. 'In a muck cart.' She put on her hat and, bending, adjusted it in the hand mirror. 'Besides, he doesn't know Susan's here and I thought it would be a nice surprise. Doesn't David deserve a nice surprise after all he's done for us?'

'Pus in the pleural cavity does not equate with softening of the brain,' Basil said. 'You're up to something, Vivian. I'd like to know what it is?'

'An old friend of mine is back in Britain,' Susan put in quickly. 'I've reason to believe he may be staying with David over the weekend. To be perfectly honest, I'd like to see him again without – well, making too much of it.'

'Oh, God!' said Basil. 'An *affaire de coeur*, is it? Women!

I don't know! Dare I ask the fellow's name, or is that a secret too?'

'Mercer Hughes.'

'I was under the impression he'd fled the country in disgrace.'

'He did,' Vivian said, 'but he's back to do his bit. He's a pilot in the RAF.'

'Redemption, I suppose.' Basil nodded. 'Good luck to you, Susan. I just hope you've learned the lessons of the past and bear them in mind when you meet him again.'

'What's *that* supposed to mean?' said Vivian.

'Lord knows! I thought it sounded rather paternal.'

'Hah!' Vivian said and, with a last peek in the mirror, put on her coat. 'Say goodnight to Grandpa Willets, my dear, and let's be on our way,' then steered Susan outside to wait for the cab before her husband really put his foot in it.

It had been five years since last she'd set foot in Hackles and the war had brought many changes. The huge, white-washed, two-storey Tudor-style farmhouse had been camouflaged by dark green paint and the four gnarled wooden pillars that supported the front porch were all but hidden by sandbags. The windows were thickly curtained and only the grey-white smoke that rose from the tall chimneys would, Susan thought, be visible from the air.

Outbuildings too had been painted, including the barn that had housed David Proudfoot's library of esoteric books. The tennis lawn that fronted the house was criss-crossed with trenches and piled with heaps of earth. In the yard Susan glimpsed a tractor, a cart and two or three push-bikes. On the terrace several pieces of farm machinery were parked higgledy-piggledy.

The taxi drew up short of the terrace. Vivian paid the

cabby while Susan looked up wistfully at the darkened house. In spite of what she'd told Basil, the chances of Mercer Hughes being here were not far short of nil. Her relationship with Mercer had ended in tears. There was no room in her life for tears now. She reminded herself that she was here on a mission and must keep a cool head and her wits about her.

The taxi reversed into the yard, swung out and vanished into the darkness of the Hereford road. The corner of a curtain on a ground-floor window rose, showing a triangle of warm light and, screened by the bars that protected the glass, a face.

Vivian took Susan's arm and picked her way through the machinery to the sandbagged porch which, when a door opened, was outlined by a wedge of butter-coloured light.

'Dear God, David,' Vivian said, 'you've got everything here but tanks and a howitzer. Do you think the Nazis are plotting to invade Hackles?'

He wore a dinner suit, his stiff shirt front white in the gloom. 'Vivian?' he said. 'What the hell – what are you doing here? Susan? Susan Hooper? Is that you?'

'It's Cahill now.'

'Of course, it is. What a pleasant surprise.'

He took Susan by the hand and Vivian by the arm and guided them between the sandbags into the hall which, Susan noticed, was littered with fertiliser sacks and farming implements.

'Is Basil all right?'

'He's fine. Enjoying an evening on his own.'

'Then what – wait.' He returned to the porch, closed the doors and came back into the hall. 'It's not that I'm not pleased to see you both, but – well, what brings you here?'

'Boredom.' Vivian removed her overcoat and hat. 'Nursing

has never been my forte, David. To be frank, Susan's visit seemed like an ideal opportunity to take a breather, particularly as Basil's well enough to be left on his own. You don't mind, do you?'

'No, I don't – of course, I don't mind.'

Viv gestured to the passage that led to the kitchen. 'If you have guests, David, we won't intrude.'

'Actually, I do have guests.' He hesitated, then, with a lift of the shoulders, said, 'Come along. You may as well join us.' He led them down the long passageway that linked the hall to the kitchen. 'Eating informally saves heating the dining room,' he explained. 'I doubt if Gwen would approve. On the other hand we insist on evening dress. Doesn't do to let standards slip too far.'

A gust of warm air mingled with appetising smells wafted into the corridor when David opened the kitchen door. He stood back to let Vivian and Susan enter first.

The long oak kitchen table was set with linen cloths, candles in silver holders, shimmering glass, cutlery and china-ware. At the stove was a woman in a floral dress and apron and an elderly man in a brown cotton jacket: servants. A young woman in WAAF officer's uniform was filling plates with soup and passing them to the guests: Caroline, David's younger daughter.

Glancing up, Caro cried, 'Good Lord above! Susan Hooper, as I live and breathe. And Aunt Vivian, too. It's been ages, simply ages. Welcome to the Hackles soup kitchen.'

She balanced the ladle on the rim of the tureen and, tapping a young man on her left with the flat of her hand, instructed him to pop out to the drawing room and find something for her aunt and her friend to sit on.

Obviously used to taking orders, the young man pushed back his chair and slipped out through the kitchen's rear door which, Susan thought, suggested that he was familiar with the lie of the house. 'That's Bill, just my Bill,' Caro said and went back to dispensing soup.

Four men in dinner suits and four young women in evening dress were seated round the table. Caro was the only one in uniform. Mercer Hughes, thank God, wasn't present.

David said, 'My sister, Vivian Willets, and Mrs Susan Cahill. I assume no one will object if they join us for dinner. I think there's enough to go round. Peter, I believe you and Mrs Cahill are already acquainted.'

Clad in an expensive dinner suit, complete with cummerbund, there was nothing of the tramp about Sir Peter Redmain now. The whine had gone out of his voice too. He spoke with an insolent assurance. 'Ah, yes,' he said. 'Boscombe's little Jewess. Good evening to you, Mrs Cahill.'

'Good evening to you, Sir Peter,' Susan replied and, with an effort of will, managed to deliver a smile.

'You knew, didn't you? Why didn't you warn me?'

'Awkward, was it?'

'Awkward isn't the bleedin' word for it.'

'All right, Susan, no need to shout,' Walter Boscombe said.

'Throwing me, not to mention Vivian, straight into the lion's den was unforgivable.'

'How could I possibly have known that Redmain would be there? I was aware that he and Proudfoot were acquainted but I didn't imagine we'd be fortunate enough to catch them together.'

'It may have been fortunate for you but for Viv and me it was unadulterated torment.'

They were alone in Mr Boscombe's office on Sunday afternoon. Susan had called him from the cottage on

Saturday morning and had given him a piece of her mind over the telephone. He'd told her to sit tight in Gadney in case David Proudfoot showed up to try to persuade her to keep her mouth shut, but there had been no approach from Proudfoot, no contact at all.

Acting on Mr Boscombe's instruction, she'd caught the Sunday morning train from Hereford. On arriving in London she'd gone directly to the studio in Soho where he was waiting for her.

'So nothing was said, nothing pertinent?'

'About what?' Susan said.

'Vivian's broadcast, for example.'

'Everyone who'd heard it was suitably complimentary.'

'Redmain too?'

'Oh, he's good, he's very, very good. Cool as a cucumber. He's nothing like the decrepit wreck he pretends to be.'

'His wife wasn't with him, I take it?'

'Of course not. He was licking his chops at the prospect of doing whatever he does with the girls.'

'Tell me about the girls?'

'As far as I could make out they were all from posh schools and employed in various government departments. They had my number immediately. They knew I wasn't one of them. They knew I was "common" as soon as they clapped eyes on me. They also knew how to keep their mouths shut.'

'The men, what about the men?'

'The one called Bill is Caro Proudfoot's boyfriend, practically her bond serf. He's a pilot officer at Credenhill. Accounts section.'

'Surname?'

'Don't know. It wasn't mentioned.'

'The other men?' Walter Boscombe prompted.

'I didn't recognise them. The one introduced only as

George is about your age, perhaps a bit older. Viv told me later he's George Sabatini, the banker. He didn't look like an Italian to me and he spoke perfect English.'

'Eton English,' Mr Boscombe put in. 'His father hails from Milan originally but George and his sisters were raised in England. He has banking ties with Switzerland and several government contracts involving munitions. Proudfoot and he are old chums.'

'The other chap,' Susan went on, 'kept himself to himself. He didn't seem awfully pleased to see us, particularly when he heard I worked for the BBC. His name is Feaver. He has an unusual first name. Hansom, would it be?'

'Ransome,' Mr Boscombe corrected. 'Ransome Feaver, more commonly known as Willy. Eton, Cambridge. Fought – rather gallantly – in the Great War, but what he's been up to lately is a mystery. In fact, as you may have gathered, they're a mysterious bunch all round. What did Vivian make of them?'

'Viv did not approve,' Susan said. 'She's not very happy with you either, as it happens. What were we doing there, Walter? Was it really just coincidence that we stumbled in on what was supposed to be a very private dinner party?'

'I was aware that Proudfoot gave weekend parties but I certainly didn't intend to pitch you and Vivian into the middle of one. If Redmain was present then it's safe to assume they were vetting what he would say on *Speaking Up*.'

'Among other things,' said Susan.

'Quite! No indication that Redmain has changed his tune about appearing on the programme?'

'None. He asked me some fairly nifty questions about what you might expect of him,' Susan said. 'I told him I was sure you'd be pleased with whatever he chose to come up with.'

'How did he react to that?'

'He didn't believe me. None of them believed me,' Susan said. 'I don't blame them. Walter, what sort of game *are* you playing? First we have a spy on the programme. Next a radical sort of author, Vivian, and in a week's time we're going to treat our American cousins to a talk by a discredited old villain. Why are we washing our dirty linen in public? More to the point, why are the Director General and the Board of Trustees letting you get away with it?'

'In three words, Susan: Churchill hates traitors.'

'Well, that's no secret. We all hate traitors.'

'That may be so,' Walter Boscombe said, 'but, heaven knows, it's hard enough waging war against a ruthless foe without having to glance constantly over your shoulder to ensure that your friends aren't about to stab you in the back. Did Proudfoot proposition you?'

'Proposition . . .?'

'Sexually.'

Flustered, Susan said, 'I don't think I'm his type.'

'That's not what I heard.'

'If he ever did fancy me – I'm not saying he did – then he doesn't now. He's far too cagey to take up with someone working for the other side. Besides, he'd no opportunity. After we'd scoffed dinner and paid our respects, Vivian made our excuses. David whistled up a lackey to drive us home in a car similar to yours; a Daimler, I think.' She paused. 'Don't tell me you were hoping I'd become David Proudfoot's mistress just to supply you with ammunition for your damned campaign?'

'Nothing so crude,' said Walter Boscombe. 'I prefer to keep you pure and unsullied, Mrs Cahill. You're far too useful to hand over to a rat like David Proudfoot.'

'Am I useful?' said Susan, surprised. 'Am I, really?'

'One compliment is all you're going to get,' Walter Boscombe said. 'Stop batting your eyelashes like Shirley Temple and buzz off home. If you hear anything from Proudfoot or, for that matter, from Vivian please let me know.'

'What time do you need me tomorrow?'

'Three,' he said and, with a waggle of his fingers and what might have been a smile, dismissed her.

Danny had known it would happen sooner rather than later. The pressure on the monitoring unit had increased fourfold over the past few months and staff were being drafted in almost daily.

None the less, it shocked him to find Griff's chair at the editing table occupied by a middle-aged man whom Mr Gregory introduced as a former sub-editor from the *Yorkshire Post*. There were new girls in the monitoring hut too, one of whom occupied the cubicle where Kate had worked. Danny had no wish to meet her face to face and kept his head down and concentrated on his work.

He cycled through Evesham in frosty dawns and bitterly cold twilights, not caring whether it was wet or fine, day or night. He didn't call on the Pells, didn't pore over newspaper reports of the Coventry funerals or spare more than a passing thought for Griff's parents or whoever might be mourning the Cottrells. Lying in the bunk at night, knees drawn up, listening to Billy's soft little snores and Breda sighing in her sleep, he couldn't be entirely sure that he wasn't grieving for Susan, not Kate, that the orphan ache he'd carried with him all his days had found shape and form at last.

It had rained all day. The track to the railway carriage was thick with mud. He carried the bicycle balanced on his shoulder, propped it against the door of the lean-to and climbed into the coach's warm interior.

Breda was cooking on the little gas stove. She'd replaced her work jumper with a lime-green blouse that showed off her figure. She had tidied her hair too and fastened around her throat a cheap necklace of glass beads that he, Danny, had brought her from the Southwark Fair when she was no older than eleven or twelve.

She turned and gave him a smile, then, wiping her hands on her apron, seated herself on one bed while he sat on the other and unlaced his muddy shoes and eased them off.

'How's the ankle?'

'Okay. The swellin's nearly gone.'

He peeled off his wet stockings and Breda, standing, leaned over him to drape them on a loop of wire he'd rigged up beside the gas stove. She swayed a little. He put his hand on her thigh to steady her, but that was all there was to it. Seated on a blanket on the floor in his favourite corner, Billy was deciphering a simple story in a school reading book that had been handed out as homework.

Breda checked the contents of the pot before she resumed her seat. She gestured with her thumb. 'What should I do with it?'

The jacket of his blue suit hung from a wire hanger on the back of the larder door. The garment had been cleaned but the ragged tears and burned-edged holes in the material were all too obvious.

'Will it mend?' Danny asked.

'Nah, I doubt it.'

'Save the lining if it's any use,' Danny said, 'an' dump the rest.'

Fishing in her apron pocket, Breda brought out a neatly folded handkerchief. 'What about this? What'll I do with this?'

She opened the corners of the handkerchief and carefully

unwrapped the little parcel of tissue paper that the handkerchief contained. 'I found it in the top pocket of your jacket.'

'Kate's wedding ring,' said Danny. 'I'd forgotten I had it.'

'Should I send it to Mr Griffiths?'

'Naw,' Danny said. 'I'll take it tae him myself.'

'You're not gonna keep it, are you?'

'Just for a wee while, that's all,' he said and, wrapping the ring in tissue, hid it away in his trouser pocket.

15

'Well,' Vivian said, 'you certainly took your time getting here. I expected you about a week ago.'

David popped his head round the tailgate of the lorry and gave her one of the sunny smiles that, in his youth, had melted the heart of everyone from stony-faced matrons to irate landowners and which even she, the flinty sister, had found hard to resist. He reached into the back of the lorry and brought out a wooden apple crate piled high with groceries.

'How much do I owe you?' Vivian said.

'Compliments of the house. Where shall I put it?'

'Don't tempt me,' Vivian said.

She watched her brother place the crate carefully on the bonnet of the vehicle and, holding it steady with his elbow, flash the schoolboy smile once more. 'Is Basil at home?'

'No, he's out gathering mushrooms,' Vivian said. 'Of course, he's at home. Where else would he be?'

'Hasn't he been outside yet?'

'Not yet. He isn't too steady on his pins. I assume your intention is to exclude my dear husband from the conversation that thee and me are about to engage upon.' Viv tugged the cardigan over her shoulders. 'I'm not going to apologise, you know.'

'Why would you?' David said. 'My house is your—'

'Come off it,' Vivian said. 'You practically peed yourself when Susan and I gatecrashed your dinner party.'

'It wasn't quite what you suppose it to be, you know.'

'Musical beds, you mean?'

'Don't be such a prig, Viv. Haven't you learned yet that men are much easier to manipulate when young women are around?'

'More to the point, David, why are you entertaining traitors like Peter Redmain in the first place?'

'Just because we hold different opinions to you doesn't make us Quislings. Even that cuddly old Liberal, Lloyd George, doesn't believe we can win this war and a negotiated peace is all that will save us from annihilation. No one's suggesting he should be shot at dawn.'

'Comparing Redmain to Lloyd George is pushing it,' said Vivian. 'As for that other chap, Feaver, what's his little game?'

'I wish I could answer that,' David Proudfoot said. 'I truly do. I imagine Susan squeezed you for every drop of gossip about my house guests to carry back to her boss?'

'Naturally.'

'What I require from you now, Vivian, is a little reciprocity.'

'Whatever it is, no. I've no intention of becoming involved in your nefarious schemes, David.'

'One phone call, that's all. One simple call. Please.'

'To whom?'

'Susan.'

'Asking her to keep her mouth shut? It's too late for that.'

'I'm sure it is,' David said. 'Redmain's probably arriving at the studio about now. Take it from me, Redmain's talk will be as bland as tapioca. The question and answer session does present problems, however. Redmain will be at Boscombe's mercy.'

'And you need to make sure he doesn't leak your name?'

'On the contrary. I need to make sure, absolutely sure, that my name *is* leaked.'

'So you can sue the BBC?'

'Trust me, I'm not going to sue anyone. I don't care how Boscombe does it but I need Redmain to mention my name on air.'

'I don't understand.'

'You don't have to understand. In fact, the less you know the better,' David said, 'just promise me you'll do it.'

Vivian hesitated. In spite of what she'd told Susan, David *was* still her brother and he *had* been good to her. She'd known for years that he was a crook but, all evidence to the contrary, still had her doubts that he was a traitor.

She nodded. 'All right.'

He blew out his cheeks in relief. 'I wouldn't ask you to do it if it wasn't a matter of life and death. You won't let me down, sis?'

'No, I won't let you down.'

He nodded. 'Now, where do you want me to put the groceries?'

'I'll take the box indoors,' Vivian said.

'Are you sure you can manage?'

'Now that *is* a silly question,' Vivian said.

Sliding the apple box from the bonnet, she tucked it under one arm and, without another word, carried it into the cottage while her brother, tense and uncertain, watched her go.

Susan knocked on the door of Mr Boscombe's office and, without awaiting an invitation, threw open the door. He was seated at his desk reading a script with the lamp drawn close and his hands, like blinkers, clapped one to each side of his head.

He looked up. 'What?'

'Where is he?'

'Redmain? In the studio being voice-tested.'

'Do you have his script?'

'I'm reading it now. It is, as expected, complete flannel. Oh, it's not a bad talk if you're looking for a picturesque tour of pre-war Bavaria but he's giving nothing away.'

'No cracks? No hooks?'

'One or two small hand-holds I might get a grip on.'

'Does he know you're doing the interview?'

'Not yet. Redmain's not the only one who can play it close to the chest. What's wrong, Susan?'

'Vivian just called.'

He took his hands from his face, pushed away the desk lamp and sat back. 'Did she now? What did she want?'

'David Proudfoot wishes us – you – to make sure his name gets a mention on tonight's programme.'

Walter Boscombe frowned. 'Now let me get this clear: Proudfoot wants us to finger him by name with half a million witnesses listening in? Did he say why?'

'Only that it was a matter of life or death.'

'He's probably exaggerating,' Walter Boscombe said.

'Will you do it?'

'More a matter of can I do it,' Walter Boscombe said. 'It'll be tricky enough getting Redmain to say anything incriminating without luring him into name-dropping. Why would Proudfoot want to have his name linked to that gang, especially when he's already under surveillance?'

'Aren't they all under surveillance?'

'I'm not privy to that sort of information.'

'Of course, Proudfoot may not be one of them,' Susan said. 'Let's suppose David's an MI5 informer and his cover's in danger of being blown, how might he convince his colleagues he really is one of them? What better way than by having it confirmed by the BBC?'

'Now why didn't I think of that?' Walter said.

'Does it hold water?'

'It most certainly does,' said Walter. 'What a clever girl you are, Mrs Cahill. What a very clever girl.'

Rogue Redmain's talk ran under by twenty seconds. Zach Gillespie took in the slack by expanding his thanks while Walter Boscombe slipped into the studio and seated himself at the table.

The question and answer element of the programme was timed for nine minutes after which the audience would be treated to a recorded talk by Bernard Darwin on 'The Value of Sport in Wartime' to tamely round out the hour.

Susan listened to the exchange on the speaker in the sound engineer's room. She was more nervous than she had been in ages and puffed on the cigarette that Larry had thoughtfully provided as if her life depended upon it.

'So far this is ditchwater, Susie,' Larry muttered. 'I can't understand what the fuss is about. I've heard more controversial talks on *Children's Hour*.'

'Shush,' Susan said, 'and listen.'

'Skiing in Bavaria now,' Larry grumbled. 'What next?'

Walter Boscombe's voice was deep and richly toned and his ease of delivery contrasted with Redmain's clipped speech which sounded just a little too didactic and, at times, excitable.

'Did you ever ski with Dr Goebbels in Bavaria?'

'To the best of my knowledge Dr Goebbels does not ski.'

'With Reichsmarschall Goering, perhaps?'

'The Reichsmarschall doesn't ski either, or not often.'

'He's more of a hunter, is he not? Did you ever hunt with

the Reichsmarschall on those forest slopes you described so vividly in your talk, Sir Peter? Boars, I believe, are plentiful in Bavaria.'

'I never hunted with Goering, no.'

'I was under the impression you enjoyed country pursuits. Do you follow the pack, Sir Peter?'

'Follow the pack?'

'Ride to hounds.'

'No, I do not ride to hounds.'

'What *do* you do now that you're no longer free to travel?' Walter Boscombe asked casually. 'Do you farm?'

'Farm? No,' Rogue Redmain answered.

He's stumbling, Susan thought. She stubbed out her cigarette into the ashtray, nudged Larry and gave him a thumbs-up.

'But you do have farmers in your circle of friends?'

'What does farming have to do with Germany?'

The pause was perfect. Susan automatically counted the beats – one, three, five – before Mr Boscombe answered, 'That, I believe, is the question, Sir Peter. If you've no interest in agriculture what do you and your farmer friends have in common?'

'I told you, I have no farmer friends.'

'None? Not one?'

'Well, yes, I'm acquainted with Proudfoot . . .'

'Proudfoot?'

'David Proudfoot.'

'The Mosleyite?'

'The farmer. You said farmers. You said nothing about Oswald Mosley. I was never a Blackshirt, you know. You won't find my name on any of your lists.'

In the offices below the level of the studio telephones began to ring, faintly at first, then insistently.

'Fat's in the fire now,' Larry murmured.

Mr Boscombe's voice reached new levels of drollery. 'You may not have been a Blackshirt, Sir Peter, but you have the advantage of having spoken fairly recently with the leaders of the country with which we are at war. I assume you did not discuss farming with the German Chancellor. What was the substance of your conversations?'

'We talked mainly about painting.'

'In your informal meetings with Dr Goebbels what were the topics most favoured? The Four-Year Plan? The Communist menace? What to do with the Jews?'

Rogue Redmain was back on familiar ground. He had been asked similar questions in the witch hunt of fascist sympathisers that had followed Italy's entry into the war and had his answers off pat. The last few minutes of the discussion passed along predictable lines while, in the empty offices below, the telephones continued to ring.

Wireless reception in Gadney had never been of the best and that night, for no discernible reason, the Willets' set was acting up. Basil, for all his claims to expertise, was unable to find the station. He knelt on the floor in pyjamas and dressing gown, the heels of his slippers yawning, and, ear close to speaker, fiddled with the knobs that governed wavelength while Vivian loomed over him yelping, 'There! There! That's it. You've got it now, Basil,' just as the sweeping strings of a Viennese orchestra drowned out the North American Service once more.

Then, a half-hour into the broadcast, interference cleared and Walter Boscombe's voice came over loud and clear: '. . . *do you do now that you are no longer free to travel?*'

Basil sat back on his heels, Vivian leaning on his shoulder.

'. . . *have farmers in your circle of friends?*'

'Oh, clever, clever,' Vivian growled. 'Press on, press on.'

'*Proudfoot?*'

'*David Proudfoot.*'

Viv punched the air. 'Gotcha!'

A half-hour later, before Zach Gillespie had wished the American audience God speed, the telephone rang. Vivian, who had been expecting the call, answered it.

Her brother's first words were, 'Thank you.'

'You should really be thanking Susan, you know.'

'Let's hope I have the chance some time,' her brother said. 'Is there anything I can do to express my gratitude?'

'Apart from telling me what you're up to?'

'Apart from that.'

'You've done more than enough for Basil and me already, David,' Vivian said, 'but if you happened to have a spare typewriter lying around in your attic . . .'

'A typewriter? What on earth do you want with a typewriter? Do you have an idea for a new book?'

'Yes, a novel this time,' Vivian said. 'About spies.'

'I take it that's a joke?'

'No spies, David, I promise. What do I know about espionage?'

'No more than I do,' her brother said, then, hastily, 'I can't let you go without thanking you again. You saved a life, believe me. Goodnight, Vivian. Sleep well.'

'You too,' Vivian said, and hung up.

Basil appeared from the scullery carrying a glass of warm milk. He seated himself at the table, removed a small box from his dressing gown pocket and tipped from it two pills.

'What did David want at this hour? Was he furious at being linked to a collaborator?' he said. 'Surely, he's not blaming you for Boscombe's moment of madness?'

'Actually, he didn't seem to be unduly put out.'

'You watch, he'll be calling his lawyer first thing tomorrow.'

'I doubt it,' Vivian said. 'Take your pills and go to bed, dear.'

'Aren't you coming?'

'Not just yet,' Vivian said. 'I thought I'd write a letter to Susan. Won't take long,'

Basil placed two pills on his tongue and washed them down with milk. 'Boscombe's for the high jump, you know. I'd never have got away with the outrageous stunts he's pulled.' He sipped a little more milk. 'Is Susan having an affair with him?'

'With Walter Boscombe? I don't think so.'

'Can't blame me for asking, can you? She certainly hasn't been faithful to that long-suffering husband of hers. I rather liked Danny Cahill. I thought Susan very foolish to fall for Robert Gaines. I mean, if the marriage is well and truly on the rocks, she can surely do better than Walter Boscombe.'

'You're turning into a right old curmudgeon, Basil Willets.'

'It's probably the pills.' He finished the milk, pushed the glass away and rested his head on a hand. 'I had rather hoped that Derek and she might – oh, well, matchmaking was never my forte.'

Vivian said, 'If I were looking for a man to warm my cockles in the long hours of the night, I wouldn't choose a sailor.'

'Aren't sailors supposed to be hot stuff?'

'Absence may make the heart grow fonder but it doesn't do much for other parts of the female anatomy.'

'Sex, you mean,' Basil said. 'I can never quite get used to the idea that women aren't as modest as they were in my day.'

'Or, thankfully, as repressed.'

'Were you repressed, Vivian?'

'I dwelled in a constant fever of lust.'

'Are you serious?'

'Of course, I'm not serious,' Vivian said.

'You certainly didn't fancy me, did you?'

'Ah, Mr Willets,' Vivian said, kissing the top of his head, 'there you are wrong, quite wrong.'

He looked up, surprised. 'Really? I had no idea.'

'If I had thrown myself at you in those dim and distant summer days of our youth, what would you have done?'

'Run a mile.'

'Precisely,' Vivian said and, kissing him once more, went off to find her writing pad.

16

Breda was delighted when Danny negotiated a Saturday evening free of duty at Wood Norton and, with Billy by the hand and his landlady hanging on his arm, sallied forth to join the crowd that waited for the bus at Deaconsfield crossroads.

Danny was too considerate of her feelings to hint that he would rather not be crammed into a church hall full of machine-shop workers, their wives and children, not to mention a posse of local farmers who had been at the ale since the pubs opened at five and were, by seven o'clock, game for just about anything.

Two wardens and a constable had been posted to keep order and ensure that blackout regulations were observed. The lights in St John's church hall were dim but not too dim to read the programme, two hundred copies of which had been sold in lieu of tickets. The programme promised an accordionist, a ladies' choir, a song sketch entitled 'Daddy Wouldn't Buy Me a Bow-Wow', a cornet solo, a comic juggling act and, to bring the first half to a close, 'Mysterio the Magician', whose moniker caused Billy's eyes to light up.

'What'll 'e do, Auntie Morven? Will 'e saw a lady in 'alf?'

'If he does,' Morven answered, 'it better not be me. I'm wee enough as it is.' Dipping into her handbag, she brought out a bar of chocolate, broke it against her knee and, leaning over Breda's lap, offered a piece to Danny.

Breda had read enough cheap fiction to realise that blue eyes and brown meeting over a Five Boys chocolate bar might signal danger.

'Oy,' she said gruffly. 'Women and children first, if you please.'

Morven giggled. 'Sorry, my mistake,' and, picking a square from the wrapping, popped it into Billy's open mouth.

Trudy Littlejohn had coopted a 'gang' to help dress the stage and, on Saturday afternoon, manhandle the folding benches from the basement and set them up in the hall. The cornet player, the ladies' choir and the shopkeepers who put on the Bow-Wow sketch had been part of a Shay Bridge concert party before the war and were well known in the villages round about.

Dr Pepperdine had intended to open the show with a couple of numbers on his ukulele but Mrs Greevy had brought forth from under a bushel her twelve-year-old granddaughter, Sharon, who, wearing a pleated skirt, white ankle socks and a sequinned bolero and lugging an accordion bigger than she was, had auditioned in Orrell's canteen.

Little Sharon had demonstrated such a precocious aptitude for music that Stevie Pepperdine had grudgingly conceded the opening spot to the child and relegated his George Formby impersonation to the second half of the programme, by which time, he hoped, the audience would be generous enough not to make comparisons.

The jugglers were Orrell's employees: Charlie, a lathe-operator, and his girlfriend, Peggy, a packer. Their initial clumsiness was well rehearsed and a series of hilarious mishaps with balls, rings and rubber eggs concluded with a disciplined display of poise and balance with balls, rings and eggs all in the air at once, an act, Stevie felt sure, that would bring the house down.

Mysterio the Magician was another dish of fish. Mr Townsend had laboured in Shed No. 3 for almost a year with no suggestion that he had talents beyond the mere mathematical. He had lugubrious features, a cap of jet-black hair and delicate long-fingered hands. He lodged in a room in the Avon Hotel in Evesham and kept himself very much to himself. No one, least of all Steve, had an inkling that Mr Townsend had a secret life until he offered to present a magic act for the benefit of the Spitfire Fund.

Some act it was, too. He demonstrated it to Steve and Trudy in the empty hall late one evening three days before the concert and had brought up by hired van all his equipment, apart from a kitten that, he said, he would borrow from a chambermaid in the Avon for Saturday's performance. He wore a dinner suit under a voluminous black cloak lined in red silk, carried a silver-knobbed cane and sported the obligatory topper. He also brought with him a wardrobe that turned out to be an essential prop for his final trick, a variation of the lady vanishes.

The lady in question was – just had to be – Trudy.

'You're not putting me into a box, I hope?'

'No, madam,' Mysterio, in character, assured her. 'No box. Well, not a box as such.'

'What then?'

'A wardrobe.'

'I'm not awfully keen on enclosed spaces,' Trudy confessed.

'You won't be in there for long, I assure you.'

Such delights lay ahead for the audience that trooped into the Shay Bridge church hall that Saturday evening. Lady Ashcroft felt she'd stretched her tolerance of rude theatricals to the limit, however, and had begged a previous appointment and Bishop Bunce, or, rather, his secretary, had discovered another engagement hidden in the diary. The row of chairs immediately below the stage was, therefore, occupied by lesser lights, not least of whom was Agnes Croall, Shay Bridge's oldest citizen, who, at ninety-eight, still had most of her teeth and sufficient bite to chew the ear off anyone who crossed her. When she made it known, loudly, that she required a cushion Reverend Littlejohn instantly scampered off to find one.

The curtain that had covered the front of the stage had been turned into parachutes but the painted drapes at the rear remained, relics from a long-ago and best forgotten production of *Princess Ida*, by a touring company from Wales. Footlights and a spot had been connected by a couple of electricians from Orrell's. The first indication the audience had that the show was about to begin was the appearance of a beam of light that danced about the empty stage like Tinker Bell after a night on the tiles.

The drone of conversation changed to a mutter of anticipation. Danny glanced along the row and gave Breda a wink while Billy gaped at the dancing beam with his mouth open, another square of Morven's chocolate melting on his tongue.

The spotlight finally settled stage left.

The lights in the hall went off.

Squeals, cheers and whistles rang out.

Mrs Croall peevishly demanded to know what had happened to Reverend Littlejohn and her cushion.

Then, abruptly, the footlights flared and Steve Pepperdine, clad in a striped jacket and straw boater, pranced on stage accompanied by little Sharon Greevy and her accordion.

'Ladies and gentlemen,' he announced solemnly. 'Please be uprising for the National Anthem.'

The audience rose noisily. Standing rigidly to attention, the boater held by his trouser leg, Steve led the assembly in verse and chorus while the kid squeezed away on the box, her nimble fingers darting over buttons and keys.

The King having been duly acknowledged, the members of the audience sat down again while Steve introduced the Vale of Evesham's very own infant prodigy, Miss Sharon Greevy, who immediately plunged into a Spanish fandango that soon had everyone clapping and yelling, 'Olé.'

The talented little minx segued effortlessly into 'Beer Barrel Polka' which not only invited but demanded audience participation and set such a gloriously rowdy tone for the evening that only Steve's promise that Sharon would return later in the programme allowed her to make way for St John's Ladies' Choir's sweet if mannered rendition of Ralph Vaughan Williams's 'Linden Lea'.

There were fourteen ladies in the choir and a piano and pianist had to be trundled in from the wings, a noisy procedure less than smoothly accomplished that dampened the jovial mood, though the posse of tipsy farmers kept it going as best they could with an a cappella chorus of 'Roll Out the Barrel'.

In the midst of this hiatus a stealthy movement in the side aisle of the hall caught Breda's attention. She'd been craning to wipe chocolate from Billy's mouth with her handkerchief when she noticed the men slipping past: two police officers in uniform, two in trench-coats and soft hats.

'Morven?' she murmured.

'I see him,' Morven said.

'What's *he* doing 'ere?'

'Maybe he's going to give us a song,' Morven said as Inspector Jessop and his cohorts vanished backstage.

*

Four brass castors supported the wardrobe which, though it gave every appearance of being solid Victorian furniture, was made up of panels of light plyboard skilfully painted to resemble oak. Mysterio had made quite sure that the stage-hands who rolled the object into view put their backs into it, though any of them could have positioned it with one hand.

Mr Townsend's act up to then had been marked by a series of astonishing illusions, not least of which was the appearance on top of his head of a small black kitten lapping milk from a saucer, a feat made all the more remarkable by the fact that more than half the audience was willing to swear that Mysterio hadn't removed his topper since he'd stepped on stage.

The kitten was duly placed on the cane which Mysterio held at arm's length and which, amazingly, grew and grew – the cane not the kitten – until the poor beast, clinging on for dear life, was detached by Mysterio's 'glamorous assistant', Mrs Littlejohn, and slipped safely into a wicker basket.

Billy hadn't known what to make of it and had hidden his face in Morven's sleeve but even sceptics, like Danny, were impressed when Mysterio casually made the saucer of milk vanish into thin air.

Danny had seen something like the wardrobe trick before, though. He knew, or believed he did, that the device contained a sliding panel behind which, tall as she was, the Littlejohn woman would hide while Mysterio spun the wardrobe round to show the audience that it was empty. In all probability, Danny thought, he would then make the woman reappear and claim credit for what was, after all, just a well-constructed piece of carpentry.

He'd heard so many bad things from Breda about Trudy Littlejohn, that he was surprised to find she didn't breathe fire. In a sheathed black evening dress with her hair drawn up, she reminded him a wee bit of the 'strict mistresses' he'd encountered in his days as a crime reporter's assistant on the *Star*.

Breda and her perky Scottish friend were whispering, heads together. They had, in fact, been whispering throughout much of the show and seemed not so much disinterested in the acts as distracted by what might be going on backstage.

'What's up?' he'd asked.

'Nothing,' they'd answered in unison.

The wardrobe was now positioned centre stage, door wide open, the spot lighting up an empty interior.

'Has 'e got kitties in there?' Billy enquired apprehensively.

'Nah, nah, son, no more kitties.' Danny lifted the boy on to his knee to give him a better view. 'He's goin' tae make the lady in the black dress disappear.'

'Dead 'er?'

'What? No, no. It's just a trick. She'll be fine, you'll see.'

Mrs Trudy Littlejohn was not so sure. She'd rehearsed the moves with Mr Townsend. Nothing to it, he'd said, safe as houses, piece of cake, easy as pie. All she had to do was press her hand to the inside of the wardrobe and a panel would spring open. Rather a tight squeeze for a tall person, yes, but nothing that couldn't be managed.

Press again, the panel would close and he'd do the rest.

'How long will I be in there?'

'Two minutes.'

Trudy had hated enclosed spaces ever since her nanny had locked her in the boot cupboard for wetting her knickers. She enjoyed the spotlight, though, and having everyone look at her. From her stance in the wings she heard Mysterio say, 'Now I will call upon my assistant once more and seize the opportunity to thank Mrs Littlejohn for gallantly agreeing to undertake this dangerous illusion from which' – he covered the side of his mouth with the flat of his hand – 'from which three of my former assistants have so far failed to return.' Uneasy laughter, in which Trudy did not join; Steve patted her bottom to send her out into the spotlight and into the wardrobe. Mysterio concluded his introduction. The choir's piano player, offstage, struck four or five dramatic chords.

The wardrobe door closed.

Mrs Littlejohn pressed the panel and when it swung open stepped nimbly into the narrow space and closed the panel behind her. Arms by her sides, tummy tucked in, she closed her eyes and held her breath, waiting for the sway of the wardrobe that would indicate that her ordeal was almost over.

She braced herself, counting out the seconds in her head, but the wardrobe did not sway, did not rotate, and she realised that the door hadn't opened after all. She clenched her knees together and began counting the seconds again in the hope that Mysterio would iron out the hitch before she lost her nerve.

Then, muffled by plyboard, she heard Mysterio say, 'Oh, shit!'

Shrieking at the pitch of her voice, she hammered on the panel which stubbornly refused to open. She was still shrieking five seconds later when the first of the German Stukas swept over the church hall roof and the bombing raid began.

'Down,' Danny shouted. 'Down, all of you.' He dropped Billy between his knees and, hand cupped on the boy's head, pushed him beneath the bench. Dust sifted from the rafters and the light fittings swung wildly as a second plane passed overhead.

Whistles shrilled. An air-raid warning, cranked out on a hand-held siren, echoed throughout the hall, by which time the members of the audience were stampeding into the vestibule where a suffocating surge of bodies piled against a door locked by an over-zealous verger. The din within the hall failed to drown the deafening roar of the Stukas which, grazing the treetops, released a shower of incendiaries to pinpoint the target.

'Danny?' Breda calmly put the question. 'What's best?'

'Get under the bench,' Danny told her. 'Both of you.'

Ducking, Morven crawled under the bench and, encountering Billy, said, 'Fancy meeting you here.' Breda joined them and Danny began heaving empty benches on top of them, tent-shaped. 'All this for a shilling, eh?' Morven went on, nose resting against Billy's cheek. 'Now that's what I call a bargain.'

'I'm – I'm not scared,' said Billy. 'Are you scared?'

'Me? No,' said Morven, who had never been more scared in her life. 'It's nothing but a lot of noise. Right, Billy?'

'Rrr-right,' Billy agreed and tucked himself under her bosom.

Mrs Croall attempted to scramble on to the stage and might have made it too if an explosion in the vicinity of the church hadn't incited a fresh wave of panic.

The last Danny saw of Shay Bridge's venerable citizen she was scuttling off in the direction of the corridor, while Mysterio, fresh out of magic, pushed her aside and, clutching the basket that held the kitten, hurled himself into the crowd.

In the vestibule the verger finally found his keys. When he unlocked the front door the good folk of Shay Bridge poured out and scattered, scrambling over the churchyard wall and stumbling down the lane into the town.

In the hall, Danny stood his ground. He listened for more

explosions but none came. He doubted if this was a random attack, a stray shedding of bombs, and his first thought was that the BBC transmitter tower was the target and that when he returned to Wood Norton he would find nothing but matchwood where the monitoring huts had been.

Breda's face appeared below him. 'What's 'appening, Danny?'

'They're after somethin' for sure but it isn't Shay Bridge.'

'Orrell's,' Breda said. 'I'll bet they're after Orrell's.'

And Breda, for once, was right.

Swooning was not in Trudy Littlejohn's repertoire of dramatic gestures but she came perilously close when the wardrobe shook. She closed her eyes and clenched her teeth, waiting for the fiery blast that would dismember the wardrobe and dispatch her, all dirty, damp and dishevelled, upstairs to meet her Maker. Then the wardrobe tipped upright and a sliver of light showed at the top of the panel.

A man's voice said, 'Where the devil is she?'

'Here, here, I'm in here.'

'Hand me the axe.'

'No,' Trudy shouted. 'Wait.'

The panel swung open. Light flooded in. She fell into a man's arms and clung to the stranger whom she'd a vague recollection of having seen before.

'What do you want done with her, sir?'

'Cuff her, put on the blindfold and get her out to the van.'

'Will I put her in with Pepperdine, sir?'

'No, stick Pepperdine in the back of the car.'

'What about the husband, Inspector?'

'He's scarpered. I expect the bastard will be halfway to Berlin by now,' Inspector Jessop said.

'Berlin?' said Trudy, an instant before her arms were snapped behind her back and a sour-smelling cloth tied over her eyes. 'What's Stanley going to do in—'

It was all over a good five minutes before the Spitfires arrived to engage the enemy. There had been no damage to church or hall but a bomb had fallen on the far bank of the Shay close enough to the old bridge to shake its foundations and send stones from the parapet tumbling into the river.

No one was killed and there were few casualties, mainly cases of bruising and hysteria. Nevertheless, the folk of the Avon Vale had experienced their first real taste of blitzkrieg.

From west to east the sky was ablaze. Curtains of smoke hung above the trees and the stench of burning was strong. Among the strands of cloud that veiled the stars, the trail of the enemy raiders dissolved slowly and there was great fear that the bombers would return.

Ambulances appeared at the head of the lane. A female in uniform directed traffic. Just as Danny, carrying Billy, escorted Breda and Morven from the hall, a motorcycle rider skidded to a halt and, a moment later, the ambulances revved their engines and headed off down the Deaconsfield Road. Fire crews too were on the move; you could hear them clanging along the Ledington Road on the far side of the Shay.

Billy was too much in awe of what was happening to be afraid. He clung tightly to Danny, legs clasped about Danny's waist. Morven hoisted herself on to the wall and, perched there, shaded her eyes with her hand as if she were peering into the sun. Breda leaned against the stonework and gazed at the cloud of smoke that rose above what remained of Orrell's Engineering Works.

'They've gone,' Danny said. 'I don't think they'll be back. Sneak attack with no heavy bombers. In an' out before the scanners could plot them. Now our Spits are in the air, the Jerries won't hang around. They've done what they set out tae do.'

'Why did they want to bomb our factory?' Breda said. 'I mean, Mother o' God, do they not 'ave better things to do?'

'I hate to sound callous,' Morven said, 'but how are you going to get back to Deaconsfield? You can bet the roads are closed and you can hardly walk all that way.'

'I suppose we could shelter in the church,' Breda said.

'My landlady's an old cow but she's a greedy old cow,' Morven said. 'Slip her a few bob and she'll let us sleep in the parlour. You and Billy can have my bed, Breda.'

'Where'll you sleep?' Breda said.

'In the parlour with Danny.'

'How far away's your house?' Danny asked.

'Five minutes down the High Street,' Morven answered.

'Okay, we'll go there, if it's all right with Breda?' Danny said.

It was not all right with Breda but she had Billy to consider and spending the night on the floor of a chilly church wouldn't be good for him. 'Yer, it's all right with me.'

With Danny carrying Billy and Morven leading the way, they set off down the lane towards the High Street.

They'd gone no more than a few yards before Archie Jackson, swimming against the tide, came up the lane towards them, asking everyone he met, 'Have you seen Mrs Littlejohn? Have you seen Trudy?'

But no one had.

17

Many moons would pass before Trudy Littlejohn learned how lucky she'd been not to be sent to the holding centre for enemy agents at Ham where Dr Stephen Pepperdine wound up after his arrest. Camp 020 was under the command of Colonel 'Tin Eye' Stephens and what went on there was, literally, nobody's business.

Why Trudy escaped that fate was never explained. Indeed, nothing was ever explained. Only by putting together the few scraps of information that came her way was she able to piece together the events that led to her incarceration in St Jude's Home for Incurables, a discreet little country house near Malvern that had recently been purchased by the security services.

Here she was interrogated by Major Rupert 'Iron Hoof' Saunders and Special Branch officer Jessop, the short and the tall of security services 'breakers'. No violent hand was ever laid upon her. She was never whipped or beaten – that was not the British way – yet what happened in the cells of St Jude's would change Trudy for ever. She would never forget the ride out of Shay Bridge on that night in early December with a blindfold covering her eyes and one wrist manacled to a hook or handle on the wall of the vehicle so that every swerve and leap of the van tore at the muscles of her shoulder and made her cry out.

No word was addressed to her throughout the journey. She heard shuffling, a cough, the scratch of a match and smelled cigarette smoke. Whether the smoker was male or female, old or young, in uniform or civvies, she had no clue. When she called out, angrily at first then in a meek beseeching voice that no one in Orrell's canteen would have recognised, nobody answered.

When the van finally stopped Trudy was convinced they were about to take her out and shoot her. She kept repeating, 'No, No, No,' but no one paid any attention.

The manacle was removed. She was helped from the van. Cold air fanned her legs. She thrust her hands between her knees and trotted forward, still blindfolded. She stumbled on steps. A hand grabbed her elbow, steadied her, steered her across a length of squeaky linoleum and brought her to a halt.

A woman's voice said, 'Is she the wife?'

'She is,' a man's voice replied.

'What's wrong with her?'

'She had an accident.'

'Is she bleeding?'

'No, she wet herself.'

Trudy was led down a steep flight of steps and thrust into a cell. The cloth was removed. She was blind for a moment, blinking. There was nothing in the room, no furniture save a metal bucket with a wooden frame over it; no bed or cot, only a mattress on the floor and a single grey blanket; no windows, just a vent, the shape and size of a letterbox, high up on the wall and a single dim bulb in a wire cage screwed into the ceiling.

Trudy's knees buckled. She might have fallen to the concrete if the man hadn't held her upright. She recognised him now and was illogically relieved, as if the face were friendly not just familiar.

'I remember you,' she said. 'You're with the Navy Board.'

'No, Mrs Littlejohn, I'm not with the Navy Board.' He pushed her away. 'Take off your clothes.'

'Are you going to rape me?'

'Whatever gave you that idea?' Inspector Jessop said, then, stepping to the open door, called out, 'Phyllis, will you hurry it along, please. We don't have all night.'

Walter's choice of restaurant was unusual: a gloomy basement in Morton's Hotel – very second-rate – didn't seem like his natural habitat. Susan arrived by cab on the stroke of eight.

The cloakroom was unattended and the 'gentlemen' hanging about the bar at the top of the stairs reminded Susan of the corner boys who scouted for bookies outside dockland pubs, only they weren't boys but plump-bellied, middle-aged men in well-cut lounge suits. They gave her the glad eye as she passed along the line of the bar and, guided by a flickering sign that said *Rest*ant,* found the staircase and went down into the cavern below.

The wide, low-ceiled room had framed photographs lining the walls, mainly film stars and boxers, but the rest of the décor ran more to aspidistras and stewed tea in floral teapots.

To her surprise, and disappointment, Walter was not alone.

At the table with him was a robust-looking man a few years older than Walter. He was bald or almost so. What hair he had was cropped close to his skull. He wore a grey lounge suit, a florid silk necktie and gold cufflinks.

He rose, smiling, and introduced himself. 'Mrs Cahill, it's a pleasure to meet you. I'm Raymond Hall. Everyone calls me Ray.'

Walter helped her off with her overcoat and laid it neatly

across a vacant chair. 'Ray's with the Ministry of Information, one of those departments too ineffectual to deserve a name.'

He drew out a chair and only after she was seated, sat too.

The table was tucked into a corner. The cloth that covered it had not been changed that day and Susan guessed they weren't here for the cuisine.

'Are we on the carpet, Mr Hall?' she asked.

'Ray, I'm Ray to my friends.'

'Which doesn't answer my question.'

'I warned you, Ray,' Walter said. 'She's very sharp.'

'She is. She is,' Raymond Hall said. 'I'd better mind my Ps and Qs. No, Mrs Cahill, you are not on the carpet. There may be gnashing of teeth in the boardroom in Portland Place but the chaps in our sleepy little department are very pleased with what you've been up to.'

'I'm glad someone is,' Susan said. 'So far we've taken a shellacking from the press and it wouldn't surprise me if there are questions in the House about Redmain's gaffe.'

'I assure you there will be no questions in the House, if, by the House, you mean the Palace of Westminster.' Ray Hall glanced up as a waiter presented a menu in a grubby pink folder. 'Give us a moment or two, Terry, then bring us something to drink. A jar of red and another of white will do to begin with. And make sure the glasses are clean, there's a good lad.'

Susan watched the waiter depart, taking the menu with him.

'May I ask,' she said, 'exactly what is it about *Speaking Up for Britain* that pleases your chaps so much?'

'You don't believe in beating about the bush, do you, Mrs Cahill?' said the man from the ministry. 'What do *you* think appeals to us about *Speaking Up*?'

'Probably our choice of contributors.'

'Don't give away all our secrets, Susan,' Walter Boscombe said.

'You seem to know quite a lot about me,' said Susan. 'I expect you know I visited Hackles, where one of "your chaps" is presently pretending to be a true son of the soil and not a property owner with houses all over Mayfair.'

Raymond Hall showed no surprise. 'Is that an educated guess or did Proudfoot let something slip?'

'David Proudfoot wouldn't be one of your chaps for long if he let things slip. To put your mind at rest, Mr Hall, I don't share my educated guesses with anyone other than Mr Boscombe.'

'Not even your friend Vivian?'

'Not even Vivian.'

'Do you like working for the BBC, Susan?'

'I do. I like it very much.'

'In spite of all the bickering between the governors, the ministry and the government?'

'I don't move in those exalted circles,' Susan said, 'nor am I ever likely to. If it hadn't been for the war I doubt if I'd be sitting here talking to you.'

'Shadwell,' Raymond Hall said. 'Never would one guess that you came up from the East End, Mrs Cahill. Your voice is one of the best disguises I've ever seen, or, should I say, heard. But you're still an East End girl at heart, are you not?'

'Yes, I am – and not ashamed to admit it.'

'You don't like to be pushed around.'

'I like to think I'm fairly independent.'

'What does your husband have to say about that?'

'With due respect I don't think that's any of your business.'

'Quite right,' Raymond Hall conceded. 'I've pried enough for one evening. Let's quaff a glass or two of what passes for vino in this establishment and talk of less personal matters.'

'Before we do,' said Susan, 'may I ask just what it is you do in a Ministry of Information department so discreet that it doesn't even merit an acronym?'

'What do *you* think we do, Susan?'

She didn't answer at once. She had pushed her position to its limit and felt her confidence wane. She glanced at Walter whose expression gave nothing away. For months now she'd listened to learned men, and not so learned men, air their opinions in and out of the studio. She was familiar with the dialogue of political necessity, the coded language that underpinned rhetoric and she had learned the value of keeping something in reserve.

'Smoke and mirrors, Mr Hall,' she said at length. 'I think your department deals in smoke and mirrors.'

'Yep, that about sums it up,' he said, laughing. 'Now, you really must call me Ray.'

No sooner had she taken off her clothes than a woman appeared in the doorway bearing a long green cotton smock, a pair of clean grey knickers, a basin of warm water and a towel. The woman was in her early twenties but so stern and tightly buttoned that she might have been ten or a dozen years older. She had a grating regional accent that Trudy couldn't place.

'Wash yourself and get dressed,' the woman told her, then, carrying Trudy's shoes and all her clothes, left the cell without locking the door.

Trudy bathed as best she could, dried herself on the rough towel and slipped on the knickers and the smock. Hardly had she finished dressing before the door opened and the man who claimed he was not with the Navy Board strode into the cell. He had taken off his hat and trench-coat and carried a clipboard and a mug of hot tea that he placed carefully into Trudy's cupped hands. There being no chair or table in the cell, he balanced the clipboard across his forearm and prepared to begin his questioning.

Trudy pressed the tin mug to her breast and let the heat seep into her. 'Why am I here?' she said. 'Why have I been arrested?'

'I'll ask the questions,' the man said.

'What am I charged with?'

'Under the Emergency Powers Act governing the defence of the realm charges are no longer required to detain you. If sufficient evidence is found to bring you to trial you will be entitled to legal assistance to present your case at the Old Bailey but if you are found guilty of treasonable acts then you will face execution.'

Trudy sipped a mouthful of tea. It was strong and very hot, without milk or sweetening. She let the liquid trickle slowly down her throat, warming her a little.

She said, 'No, I won't. Even if I am guilty of something, God knows what, you'd never execute a woman.'

'Name, date and place of birth?'

Trudy sipped tea and tried not to shiver.

'Name, date and . . .'

She told him all he needed to know and watched him record her answers on a form. When he'd finished he took the mug and, without a word, went out of the cell and locked the door.

She felt better now, still afraid but no longer bewildered. She was determined not to fall apart again no matter what they did to unsettle her. When the overhead light suddenly went off, she let out a defiant cry of 'Hah!' and, groping, found the mattress and seated herself cross-legged upon it, the blanket over her shoulders.

It was too cold to sleep, which was probably just as well. Three or four minutes after the light went out it suddenly went on again. She listened, heard nothing. The silence was absolute and, in its way, more unnerving than the darkness. She waited, cross-legged like a swami and, sure enough, the light went out again.

She wondered where they'd taken Steve, who had warned Stanley, and why the security services assumed Stanley was heading for Germany, not Italy or Spain.

Five minutes passed.

The light went on once more.

Silence, dead silence.

She listened to her stomach rumbling. She'd had nothing to eat since an hour before the concert and even then it had only been a corned beef sandwich. She thought of soup, Morven Hastie's special vegetable broth, thick as porridge and twice as filling. Her stomach growled once more. She wondered how long they would keep her here and if they served breakfast and if so what it would be. Bread and dripping? Bread without the dripping, more like, and tea. Yes, surely there would be tea.

The door rattled and swung open.

In spite of her resolve to stay calm, Trudy stiffened.

It wasn't the man but a woman, not the young woman but a woman of her own age dressed in an ankle-length brown skirt and starched white shirt. She wore boots, Trudy noticed, black boots, not the kind sold by fashionable stores.

'Up,' the woman said.

Trudy rose to her feet. 'May I take the blanket?'

'No.'

'Do you have a comb I might borrow?'

The woman ignored the question and gestured with a hooked thumb to the open door. Two army sergeants escorted Trudy out into the passageway and along it. One of the soldiers threw open a double door to a room that lay at right angles to the corridor.

Bright light and the strong smell of tobacco smoke hit her. With the sergeants hard on her heels she squared her shoulders and stepped into the room.

'Prisoner, sah.'

'Thank you, Sergeant.'

The sergeants went out, closing the double door behind them. The woman with the boots took a seat on a chair in a corner of the room near to the door.

It was a large room. Boarded windows filled one wall. The wooden floor, Trudy noticed, was marked in faded white paint for a game; badminton, perhaps, a game she'd never played.

Dead ahead was a long table behind which were seated four men in army uniform, two in civilian clothing and a young woman who was probably a stenographer.

The principal prosecutor was a short, almost dwarf-like major with a severe limp. He advanced upon Trudy with an expression of such severity that it suggested fury. He carried a cane, not unlike Mysterio's cane only less rigid. For an instant Trudy thought he was about to hit her with it. When it came to bullying, however, she knew a thing or two and would not be cowed. She tightened her buttocks and threw out her chest, daring him, a major in the British army, to strike a defenceless woman.

'Are you Gertrude Alcock Littlejohn?'

If I'm not, Trudy thought, then you're in more trouble than I am. 'Yes,' she said.

He had a gravel voice, husky in the extreme. 'Where is he?'

'Where,' Trudy said, 'is who?'

'Your husband?'

'I imagine,' Trudy said, 'he's at home in Shay Bridge, looking everywhere for me.'

When he walked around her she could hear the thump as his foot struck the floorboards. She waited for the tip of the cane to lift her smock, for the smack of the cane across her bare thighs, then the major appeared at her side, his face close to her shoulder.

The whiff of shaving lotion mingled with the smell of tobacco on his breath. A vain man, a stickler, she thought, a martinet. God knows, she'd met enough of those, from bishops to curates, choir-masters to organists. The major peered up at her. How such a small man had ever obtained a commission she couldn't imagine.

The man who was not with the Navy Board rested his forearms on the table and asked, 'Where is he, Mrs Littlejohn? Where is your husband hiding?'

'I have no earthly idea,' Trudy answered.

'Liar!' the major snapped with enough force to send a little spray of spittle on to her cheek. 'Where does he go? Who are his friends? Where does he meet his contacts?'

The uniforms at the table were young, not one of them much over twenty-four or -five. They were alert and attentive, unlike the civilian couple who were, or pretended to be, bored. She had none of the information they wanted and she was not yet prepared to give up Stanley if it meant she must also give up Steve.

She watched the man who was not with the Navy Board amble round the table and prop his backside on the table's edge.

'It would be as well for you, Mrs Littlejohn, if you cooperate,' he said. 'Cooperation at this stage might keep you out of prison.'

'I'd help if I could,' Trudy said, 'but I honestly don't know what you're talking about.'

'Stubborn,' the major said. 'If you insist on doing it the hard way, Mrs Littlejohn, I'll be pleased to accommodate you.'

'I cannot tell you what I do not know,' said Trudy primly.

'Do you deny that you assisted your husband in obtaining information about the work that goes on in Orrell's Engineering sheds?' the major said. 'Do you deny that you helped your husband pass on this information to a foreign power to the detriment of our national interest?'

'I'm a canteen manager. I never go near the sheds.'

'How long have you known Dr Pepperdine?'

'Since he came to lodge with us in the vicarage,' Trudy replied. 'In – let me see – March of this year. Yes, March.'

'Who brought Dr Pepperdine into your home?'

'I think it must have been Stanley.'

'How long have you been married to – Stanley?'

'Six years.'

'Where did you meet him? Leiden, was it, or Heidelberg?'

'Norwich.'

It dawned on Trudy that they knew more about Stanley than she did, though one fact, it seemed, had so far escaped them.

'Your employment, your job in the Orrell's canteen,' the man who was not with the Navy Board said, 'who recommended you?'

'Steve – Dr Pepperdine heard they were looking for catering staff and put my name forward.'

'At your husband's request?'

'I don't think Stanley had anything to do with it.'

'Did Stanley put you in Pepperdine's bed?' the major said.

'I beg your pardon?'

'Did your husband brief you on what questions to ask during your coital encounters with Pepperdine? Was Pepperdine in league with your husband all along and you, Mrs Littlejohn, were simply, shall we say, compensation?'

They might give the impression that they had all the power and all the answers, but they were floundering too. They were as unsure of her as she was of them. They had bungled somewhere and were hell-bent on taking it out on her. She shifted her weight from one bare foot to the other and enjoyed a fleeting moment of triumph.

'Oh, is that what you think?' she heard herself say. 'Compensation? If only I had been. No, sir, I wasn't even that.' Then she took a deep breath and told them the truth. 'Steve Pepperdine wasn't *my* boyfriend. He wasn't *my* lover. He didn't sleep with me. He slept with Stanley.'

'Oh, Christ!' the man who was not with the Navy Board said, while the major opened his mouth and, finding nothing intelligent to say, closed it again with a snap.

The dismal meal in the Morton Hotel wound up ridiculously early. By half past nine the last sticky vestige of sponge pudding had been consumed, the cheese board ignored and the waiter's offer of a concessionary glass of vintage port rejected. Raymond Hall assured Susan that they would dine under more congenial circumstances next time they met and then, after settling the bill, departed.

Walter looked at her across the cheese board and raised not one but both eyebrows. 'I suppose we could brave the storm and go on for a drink, unless you've something more exciting to do.'

'I think I've had enough excitement for one evening,' Susan said. 'I didn't let you down, did I?'

'On the contrary.'

'What department *does* Mr Hall work for?'

'The British predilection for fuzziness has never been more apparent than in the relationship between the BBC and the Ministry of Information,' Walter said evasively. 'Thank God, we're still hanging on to the Calcutta, though it seems we'll be moved back into the Big House in January whether we like it or not.' He rose, lifted her overcoat from the chair and held it while she put it on. 'What's it to be? A drink somewhere or an early night?'

'I've a perfectly good bottle of Haig's at home.'

'Is that an invitation?'

'I do believe it is.'

'I trust,' he said, 'you're not intending to get me drunk and take advantage of me, by which I mean persuading me to tell you all sorts of things it's better you don't know.'

'For instance?'

'No,' he said. 'No, no. My lips, like yours, are sealed.'

Spotter planes had come in from the south-east early in the evening but had been driven off by British fighters. Since then heavy cloud had rolled in accompanied by teeming rain and the early warning had soon been followed by an all-clear that seemed to indicate that Goering's bomber crews were weathered in across the Channel. Cloud was down over London, the curtain of rain so low that the roof of the insurance building was invisible and the solitary searchlight from the Hyde Park basin probed disconsolately at empty air. Walter parked the Bentley in the street outside the mews and ran with her for the shelter of the house. Ten minutes later, with the electrical fire and lamps lighted, the atmosphere within the house was comfortable bearing on cosy.

Walter seemed quite at home lounging on Viv's davenport, sipping whisky and smoking. Susan was sufficiently relaxed to slip off her shoes and, with her legs tucked under her, settle into what Vivian called her 'Little Mermaid' pose in Basil's armchair.

'Shall I put on the wireless?' she asked.

'God, no.'

'We might be missing something important.'

'At this moment I don't care if Hitler invades Russia,' Walter said. 'My brother's right. He said you had nice breasts and you have.'

Susan raised her index finger from the glass and wagged it. 'I'm not going to let you put me off with flattery.'

Walter crossed his legs and sank further into the davenport's cushions. 'I'll make you a trade, Mrs Cahill. I'll tell you what you want to know.'

'In exchange for what?'

'Whatever you care to give,' Walter said. 'You were right on the nose about Proudfoot, by the way.'

'You mean, he is a spy.'

'Not exactly a spy,' Walter said. 'An informer. However much you may dislike him he's on our side. The powers that be are anxious that his reputation as a collaborator remains untarnished. Hence his insistence that we announce to the world his connection with Peter Redmain. That's all I can tell you, Susan.'

'I'll bet it's not.'

'It's all you're going to get out of me. I'm a humble cog in the intelligence machine, not one of the backroom boys.'

'And Mr Hall, Raymond Hall?'

'Oh, he is one of the backroom boys. There,' Walter said, 'I've told you more than I should. Now it's your turn.'

'My turn?'

He rose from the davenport, put his glass on the top of the cocktail cabinet and snuffed out his cigarette in the ashtray.

It was very deliberate, very smoothly done. She wondered how many times he'd done this before, how many women had felt, as she did, the magnetism of the man. Blood raced in her head and her heart was beating so fast that she could hardly draw breath. She watched him fan away smoke from the cigarette and dust the traces of whisky from his lips.

'You're not going to refuse me, Susan, are you?'

He would take her, she knew, without conscience; the little girl from Shadwell, the doe-eyed disciple with nice breasts, convenient and, to all intents and purposes, willing.

He put an arm about her and plucked her from the armchair. His hand felt huge, a bear paw sliding down her back. His thick fingers cupped her, crushing her dress into the cleft of her thighs. He pulled her against him, rubbing hard against her belly. There was nothing tender or teasing about his kisses. His tongue forced her lips apart. He did not thrust his tongue into her mouth, though, but flicked it against the tip of her tongue while his fingers tested the response between her legs.

'Wait,' she whispered. 'Not here. Let me slip into . . .'

He kissed her again, pushing her back against the armchair with enough force to make the chair shift. He held her raggedly upright and thrust his tongue into her mouth again, fingers digging deep into the pale, wet wisps of her underwear.

In the office across the hall the telephone rang.

'Shit!' he said and pulled away. 'I suppose you'll want to answer it in case it's your bloody husband.'

'Danny?' she said. 'Why would it . . .'

'Go, go,' he said testily. 'But don't be all night.'

Telephone calls at this hour were rare and a little frightening. Danny? Why would it be Danny? Minutes later and she would have been in the bedroom, pinned down and panting, and nothing would have stopped her then.

The ringing of the telephone echoed persistently in the hall.

Walter sloshed whisky into his glass and lit a cigarette.

'Answer the damned thing,' he told her.

She crossed the hall quickly, went into the office and switched on the desk lamp. She paused just long enough to adjust her dress then cautiously lifted the receiver.

'Susan?'

For an instant she felt as if she might faint.

'Derek? Derek, is that you?' she said. 'I thought you were . . .'

'Well, I'm not,' he said.

'Are you all right?'

'Yes, all in one piece.'

'What happened?'

'A minor mishap is the best way of putting it.'

'Where are you?'

'Not at liberty to say,' he told her, then added, 'Mother sends you her regards.'

She leaned into the desk, cupping the receiver in both hands. 'Scotland. My God, you're in Scotland.'

'Did you get my letter?'

'I did. I didn't know where – how to reply.'

'The line's cracking up,' he said. 'Not surprised in this filthy weather. Look, are you free on Tuesday?'

'Free?'

'For that dinner I promised you.'

'Are you coming up to London?'

'With luck and a following wind. Tuesday?'

'Yes,' she said, shouting through the crackle. 'Tuesday.'

'Till then.'

'Till then.'

Walter was waiting in the hall with his overcoat on.

'That was your sailor boy, wasn't it?'

'Yes.'

'I can readily compete with a husband,' he said, 'but a sailor home from the sea is a step too far.' He wrapped his scarf about his neck. 'I misjudged you, Susan. I thought you were a free spirit.'

'I'm sorry, Walter, truly sorry.'

'Don't be,' he said. 'Goodnight, Mrs Cahill.'

'Goodnight, Mr Boscombe.'

She watched him step out into the rain and quickly closed the door, then, with a little skip, headed back into the living room to pour herself a stiff drink and offer thanks for an intervention that came close to being divine.

PART FOUR

The Constant Star

18

Greenock was not a town famed for its architecture but from the centre of the river the view of the surrounding hills was quite spectacular. Somewhat less than spectacular was the sight of the poor old *Constant Star* all but invisible in the welter of cranes and scaffolding that bordered the crowded shipping lanes.

Derek couldn't make up his mind whether it was good luck or bad that had brought four German dive-bombers shrieking out of cloud cover just as the destroyer approached anchorage within the Clyde's boom defences.

The torpedo struck right aft and missed the shell room and magazine by inches, otherwise there would have been precious little left of the newly refitted ship. As it was they were damned fortunate there were few casualties and no fatalities, though the stern of the vessel was holed and damage to the steering gear meant that she had to be towed ignominiously through the fleet to the repair yard.

In the past six months the old tub had spent more time in refitting yards than she'd done at sea. The more bullish of Derek's young officers muttered about applying for a transfer to see some action before the blessed war was over. A hectic week removing ammunition and stores had kept them occupied, however, and an extra spell of shore leave tempered their impatience.

It came as no surprise that early estimates of damage indicated a delay of four to six weeks before the *Constant Star* would be fit for service. Derek expected to receive a cable reassigning him to another ship but captain, crew and the *Constant Star* were, it seemed, doomed to remain wedded each to the other whether Commander Willets liked it or not. As soon as he'd organised a rota for maintenance parties and a viable leave schedule for officers and ratings, he took himself off to his mother's house in nearby Troon.

From there, late on a pouring-wet Saturday night, he rang Susan and, early on Sunday morning, crammed himself into a railway train and eagerly headed south.

The Shay Bridge lodging house was not on the billeting list. Morven was the sole paying guest. Her landlady had given them supper and allowed Danny and Morven to sleep in the parlour while Breda and Billy squeezed into Morven's bed in the tiny front room.

The house, a bungalow, was situated in a cul-de-sac bounded by the river and close enough to the Ledington Road for the incessant rumble of traffic to keep Breda awake.

It seemed odd to be in Morven's bed in Morven's room with Morven's possessions round about: postcards from her family in Scotland propped on the dressing table, a framed photograph of a young man by a farm gate with sunlit hills in the background and, of all things, a scuffed, well-loved soft toy, not a teddy bear but a donkey, that lay on Morven's pillow together with a frilly, if somewhat impractical, night-dress that Morven whisked away before Billy was tucked into bed.

Try as she might, Breda could not sleep. Traffic on the roads reminded her of the problems she'd have to face come morning. She was also troubled by the notion that her dependable Danny might not be so dependable after all and that a blue-eyed blonde with a Scottish accent might yet be his downfall.

How callous, she thought, to be fretting about trivialities when just three miles away people were dead or dying.

'Breda.'

She opened her eyes. It was still pitch dark. Danny, fully dressed, crouched by the side of the bed.

'What time is it?'

'Just after six,' he told her. 'I'm goin' tae try to make it to Wood Norton.'

Breda sat up. 'What's that noise?'

'Rain,' Danny said. 'It's raining cats an' dogs.'

'How're you gonna get to Wood Norton?'

'Walk, if I have to. There might be a bus, you never know.'

'Have you 'ad something to eat?'

'Morven's makin' me somethin.'

'Is she now?' said Breda. 'I'd better get up.'

'Stay put,' Danny said. 'Morven'll find out what's happenin' down the road at Orrell's and come back for you.'

He leaned out of the darkness and kissed her, sloppily, somewhere in the vicinity of her mouth.

'Let the boy sleep till Morven comes back with news. We'll be all right, I'm sure,' he told her and at that moment Breda had no option but to believe him.

Six men had died in the attack. Twenty-three others, including five women from the packing department, had been injured. Corpses and wounded had been removed before Morven, Breda, Billy and Archie Jackson arrived at the gate. Archie had spent an uncomfortable night on the floor of the church along with thirty or so concert-goers who had been unable to get home to Evesham.

Orrell's security staff, wardens, soldiers and rescue crews had been hard at it since well before first light. The fire-bombs had been followed by a series of shuddering explosions in the field north of the factory. There had barely been time to sound the alarm and begin clearing the huts of night-shift workers before three Stukas circled over the tree line and, with the target well lighted, strafed the factory site and dropped more high-explosive bombs.

Shed No. 3 had suffered a direct hit. There was little left but a mountain of shattered brick and timber with, incongruously, a zinc-lined bath, in which testing had been carried out, sticking up like a fleshless arm. Fire had ravaged the roofs and walls of three of the four machine-shops but, thanks to prompt action by fire crews, aided by heavy rain, the blackened structures remained intact. The packing house was scorched but stable.

There was water everywhere. The tyres of the motorcars of the representatives of the Navy Board threw up great fans as they toured the perimeter. The hoses of the fire crews, snaking from EWS tanks, pumped water on smouldering shells and two huge craters in the tarmac just inside the fence were rapidly turning into lakes. The canteen building had lost a bit of one wall and a corner of the roof but, according to optimistic Archie, was still fit for purpose.

Breda was puzzled by the size of the crowd that gathered at the factory gate. She could understand why Orrell's employees had trailed out in the cold, grey, drizzling dawn but why half the population of Shay Bridge had abandoned the comforts of their air-raid shelters to gaze at a bomb site was beyond her comprehension; the same mentality, she supposed, that drove folk to tramp across empty fields to stare at a hole in the ground or a fragment of a German aeroplane that had fallen from the sky.

The main gate was guarded by soldiers and policemen; a farce, really, given that the barbed-wire fence that surrounded the site had been blown down and the gate to the delivery bay had vanished.

The crowd waited patiently while Navy Board officers consulted with fire chiefs and a couple of helmeted men in filthy overalls from the heavy rescue squad.

It was just as well she hadn't heeded Danny, Breda thought, and had got Billy out of bed early. Morven had hastened back to the bungalow with news that two buses and a small fleet of council vans were ferrying workers to the factory. There had just been time for Morven's landlady to grill some ham and stuff a boiled egg into Billy's mouth before they ran to catch the bus outside the Post Office and head, all three, for what was left of the engineering works.

Mr Pell was already in the crowd. He greeted them grimly but cheered up when he saw Billy and, to give the boy a better view, hoisted him on to his shoulders.

One of the younger naval officers, accompanied by a Wren, was checking time clock cards against lists supplied by the rescue squads and ambulance crews.

'Why won't they let us in?' Archie Jackson complained. 'I mean, we could help, couldn't we?'

'Safety first, I suppose,' said Mr Pell.

'The quicker I get started on stock-taking,' Archie went on, 'the sooner we'll be able to start serving.'

'Serving?' said Breda. 'You don't really think they'll keep this place open, do you?'

'Depends on the state of the machinery,' Mr Pell told her. 'They can shore up the sheds fast enough if they think it's worthwhile. It's important work we do here, you know.'

'Gyroscopes,' said Morven with a hint of scorn. 'Talking of which, has anybody seen Dr Pepperdine?'

'Or Mrs Littlejohn?' Breda added.

'I couldn't find Trudy anywhere,' Archie Jackson said. 'I even went by the vicarage this morning but it's all locked up, with a policeman at the gate.'

'A policeman?' said Breda, thinking of Inspector Jessop. 'Was 'e in uniform?'

'He was,' said Archie. 'Wouldn't tell me what he was doing there. In fact, he was downright rude.'

'No Stevie and no Trudy,' said Morven. 'Maybe they've run off together.'

'Don't say that,' Archie told her. 'Mrs Littlejohn's very good at her job and we'll need all the help we can get.'

'Particularly if there's no electricity, no gas and no water,' Morven said. 'I don't see any sign of a WVS mobile either. I'll bet those lads in the overalls could do with a nice bowl of soup.'

'And how're you gonna do that?' said Breda.

'Campfire cookery,' said Morven.

It was after nine before the Navy Board agreed to let the manager open the gate. By that time the crowd had thinned. The workforce was divided into two groups, one to clear debris, the other to report on the condition of the machines. Electricians and plumbers were detailed to help Water and Gas Board employees repair cables and pipes. Canteen staff were given the job of inspecting equipment, accessories and stores and to retrieve as many perishable items as possible before dirt and dampness ruined them.

Breda didn't know what to do for the best. She supposed she should take Billy home, but her inclination was to stay and help. Her mind was made up for her when Mr Pell walked boldly through the gate with Billy riding on his shoulders. After a few words with the manager, he lowered Billy to the ground and handed him over to Morven, a transfer of ownership to which Billy did not object in the least. There were other children on the site too and Mrs Greevy's granddaughter, Sharon, minus accordion, had brought along several of her school friends to help with the clearing up.

Mr Jackson led his troops around the flooded craters to the side door of the canteen and lined them up in military fashion. He delivered a terse little lecture on the need for caution, opened the side door, stepped inside and surveyed the mess within.

'How bad is it, Mr Jackson?' someone asked.

'It's not – er – good,' Archie answered and signalled his ladies to enter, one by one.

If Trudy hoped that her bombshell about her husband's sexual proclivities would get her off the hook, she was doomed to disappointment. The edge of the interrogation had been blunted, though, and there was a pause, a long pause, while the major conferred with the other officers at the table before questioning began again.

Back aching, feet and legs frozen and her bladder acting up, Trudy held her ground for well over an hour. In that time she learned by deduction that her husband was no mere homosexual who lived in fear of the law but a spy for and a collaborator with a coterie of Nazi sympathisers who were willing to sell, or even give away, precious information to the enemy.

Eventually the major ceased stumping up and down and returned to his seat behind the table and the man who was not with the Navy Board set about asking the same questions all over again. Trudy remained steadfast: I do not know where my husband is now. I do not know who he might turn to. I do not know the names of any of my husband's special friends. I do not speak German. We holidayed in Bournemouth and, once, in Llandudno. My parents live in Norwich. I have no sisters or brothers. I have never been to Heidelberg or Leiden. I did have a friend who came from Berne. He brought me shoes. Stanley did not know I had a Swiss friend. Yes, my friend was also my lover. He gave me shoes, red shoes. He did not meet Stanley. Bournemouth every summer. Once to Llandudno. I do not know where my husband is now.

She had no idea what time it was when one of the sergeants knocked on the double door and, on instruction, entered.

Everyone behind the long table sat up as if revitalised by the sergeant's smart salute. He advanced to the table and whispered something to the major. The major rose to his feet and then sat down again. The sergeant spoke again, the major answered curtly and dismissed him. The major spoke to one of the civilians. The civilian slouched across the table, threw up an arm and covered his face with his hand. The officers stirred and, with a scraping of chairs, turned their backs on Trudy and went into a huddle.

Trudy struggled hear what was being said but all she could make out was a humourless growl punctuated by the major's gravel voice repeating the same filthy word over and over again.

In due course the woman by the door was sent out. She returned with one of the sergeants. The woman and the sergeant, saying nothing, escorted Trudy, sore, stiff and cold, back to her cell.

As soon as the soldier and the woman left and the door closed Trudy straddled the wooden frame and relieved herself. Then she slumped on to the mattress, pulled the blanket up to her chin and stretched out her aching limbs.

The bulb in its cage in the ceiling flickered.

And the light went out.

Sunday was no day to go shopping but she knew she wouldn't have the time or the opportunity on Monday to queue at the local butcher's let alone hunt down groceries to feed a hungry sailor. She rose early, counted the money in her purse, found a shopping basket in a cupboard in the hall and, wrapped in one of Vivian's voluminous oilskins, set out for the nearest Tube station in the hope that some trains might be running.

It was after noon before she found herself in Shadwell, in Thornton Street, the narrow thoroughfare where her brother had learned his trade as a butcher in Herr Brauschmidt's High-Class Pork & Beef. Herr Brauschmidt had decamped to stay with his son in America and his shop now was no better than a fire-blackened ruin.

To Susan's astonishment, however, Herr Brauschmidt's arch-rival, Moses Gertler, was still in business. His neat little shop, just across the street, even had glass in the window and a freshly painted sign, *Kosher Butcher*, hanging from a bent pole over the doorway.

Naturally, a queue had formed on the pavement outside the shop, six or eight women and five or six children clutching ration books and shopping bags. Breda would have been more at home here than she was, Susan thought. Breda's main rival for Ronnie's favours had been Mr Gertler's daughter, Ruth, a dark-haired beauty who had persuaded Ronnie to join the International Brigade in Spain, a war that seemed like ancient history now.

Thornton Street, Pitt Street, Docklands Road and almost every other street in Shadwell was so broken and battered that her old stamping grounds were like an alien country into which she ventured at her peril. Susan turned up the collar of the oilskin and self-consciously joined the tail of the queue.

It hadn't been her intention to come as far as Thornton Street. She'd been heading for the Sunday market in Fawley Street where, blitz or not, she was sure the barrow boys would be out in force, and where, for a price, she might pick up a shank of something resembling mutton or, more likely, some tins of stew or pork sausages that had fallen off the back of a lorry and, if she were lucky, a jar of decent coffee and a packet of tea. She felt bad about encouraging black marketeers but her desire to stock the larder for Derek's arrival overcame her scruples.

'Susan? Susie Hooper, what on earth are you doing here?'

Gilt buttons and shoulder boards on the greatcoat displayed an officer's rank. The tricorn hat with its wreathed anchor badge sat jauntily on her dark hair.

'It's me – Ruth,' the woman said. 'Don't you recognise me?'

'Of course, I do,' Susan said, hiding her embarrassment. 'I just – I mean, I didn't realise you'd joined up.' Then, gathering herself, she added, 'Must say, you look frightfully smart in uniform.'

'The only reason I chose the Royal Navy was because of the uniform. With my colouring I look dreadful in khaki.' Ruth paused, smiling. 'Besides, the navy were very welcoming to a nice Jewish girl. What are you doing down this way, Susan? I heard you'd moved up in the world. The BBC, isn't it?'

'Yes.'

'Have you met Tommy Handley?'

'Not personally, no.'

Ruth Gertler put a hand on Susan's arm and lowered her voice. 'I was so, so sorry to hear about Ronnie. I really admired your brother. How's Breda? Is she managing to push on with her life?'

'She's in Evesham at present.'

'Good for her. If I had children I wouldn't stay in London.'

'Where are you stationed?'

'Plymouth, but I'm on the move to a new posting in Liverpool, which is why I've a few days' leave. Popped up to say hello to Dad and Mum and stuff myself full of what substitutes for veal pie.'

The women in the crowd were eavesdropping shamelessly. Two small girls in ragged jumpers stared up at the lady in the warm greatcoat and lovely hat, their mouths open in awe. Susan experienced a twinge of resentment not unmixed with guilt that she was not in uniform too.

'You still haven't told me what you're doing here,' said Second Officer Gertler.

'All right, I may as well confess. I'm on the scrounge for off-ration meat. I've a guest coming to stay for a day or two . . .'

'A feller?'

'Yes, a naval officer as it happens.'

'Ah-hah! The Senior Service strikes again,' Ruth Gertler said. 'Well, we can't have you standing out here. Come along and talk to Dad. I'm sure he'll be pleased to see you.'

Dark mutterings, scowls and hard stares did not deter Second Officer Gertler who, taking Susan by the arm, led her past the queue and into the shop, the door of which was guarded not by a man with a cleaver but by Ruth's formidable mother.

'Darling.' Mrs Gertler kissed her daughter on the lips. 'Who is this you have brought to see us?'

'You remember Susan Hooper. Ronnie's sister.'

'Sure I do, sure,' Mrs Gertler said and, with a wave of

her plump arm, admitted Susan into the holy of holies where Mr Gertler and a young boy were dismembering a chicken behind a glass counter that displayed, albeit sparsely, a tray of beef sausages and a row of small meat pies. Ruth Gertler dug Susan gently in the ribs.

'Manna from heaven?' she said.

'You can say that again,' said Susan.

The light in the cell had gone out but the vent high on the wall showed a thin strip of daylight and more light came from the open doorway. Groaning, Trudy uncoiled from the foetal position in which she'd slept and peered up at the woman who towered over her. She could see boots beneath the hem of the skirt and on the floor beside the boots a neatly folded pile of clothes, her clothes, her shoes perched on top.

'Get dressed,' the woman said.

'What – what time is it?'

'Get dressed,' the woman said again.

Trudy got to her feet. The woman watched, arms folded, but made no move to help her. Trudy was too numb to care about modesty. She peeled off the smock and knickers and dressed as quickly as she could, pulling on her underwear, garter belt, stockings and black sheath dress. She leaned against the wall, slipped on her shoes and stood up.

'Out,' the woman said.

'Where are you taking me?'

'Out.'

Trudy followed the woman into the corridor. No soldiers this time, just the surly female's hand in the small of her back steering her along the corridor past the double doors, across an empty hall floored with brown linoleum and into an office furnished with filing cabinets, a desk and several wooden chairs.

Tall windows looked down on a courtyard in which were parked two motorcars and a large black van. The man who was not with the Navy Board was seated behind the desk.

In that bleak room in wintry daylight he looked, Trudy thought, about as bad as she felt. He supped what smelled like coffee from a coronation mug and nibbled a piece of cold toast.

'Take a pew, Mrs Littlejohn,' he said. 'It's been a long night for all of us. I'd ask you how you slept but I think I know what your answer would be.' He pushed the plate of toast towards her. 'Help yourself. Coffee's on its way.'

Hardly were the words out of his mouth before the young stenographer appeared and placed a mug of coffee on the desk, together with a green cardboard folder.

'Will that be all, Inspector?'

'It will, Phyllis. Catch some sleep if you can.'

The young woman went away and closed the door behind her. Trudy reached for the coffee mug and drank gladly.

'What time is it?' she asked.

'Coming up for ten.'

'Really?' Trudy said. 'Sunday?'

'Sunday.'

'Have you found my husband?'

The inspector sighed and shook his head. 'Not yet. After you finish breakfast, Mrs Littlejohn, you're free to leave.'

'Free to leave?' Trudy said. 'Leave where?'

The inspector opened the green cardboard folder, took from it a long slip of paper and pushed it towards her. 'The nearest railway station is Malvern. We've drafted a rail voucher to Evesham which is as close as we can get you to Shay Bridge.'

'Are you kicking me out like *this*?' Trudy said. 'No overcoat, no hat, scarf or gloves. What am I supposed to do? Walk to the railway station and freeze to death on the road?'

'I'll find you a coat and drive you to the station.' He reached into a drawer in the desk, brought out a small metal cash box and fished from it two half-crowns. 'Five shillings should be enough to see you home.'

'Where am I going to go?' Trudy said. 'Who's going to take care of me now Stanley's gone? I can't go to my mother-in-law's house since she'll blame me for everything that's happened.'

'Strictly to satisfy my curiosity, Mrs Littlejohn,' the inspector said, 'when did you begin your affair with the Swiss bloke? Max Feldman's his name, I believe.'

'How did you find out about Max?'

The inspector smiled wearily. 'We're not as incompetent as some folk believe. How long did it last and when did it end?'

'It lasted six months and ended four years ago. He stopped writing to me and my letters to him were returned unopened. Do you happen to know where Max is now?'

'Alas, no,' the inspector said. 'The bookshop he owned in Berne closed in 1938 and he just – well, went elsewhere, I suppose.'

'He loved me, you know. He did love me.'

'I'm sure he did.'

'That's all I ever wanted,' Trudy said. 'To be loved. Why are you letting me go?'

'We've nothing to hold you on.'

'And Steve, Dr Pepperdine, will you release him too?'

The inspector didn't reply at once. He came around the desk and, standing close, placed a hand on her shoulder.

'I'm sorry to be the one to tell you this, Mrs Littlejohn, but Steve Pepperdine died early this morning.'

'Died?' Trudy heard herself say. 'Steve's dead? You shot him, didn't you? You bastards, you shot him.'

'No, Mrs Littlejohn,' the inspector said, 'he hanged himself,' and then, darting forward, caught her before she fell.

19

She was late in reaching the Calcutta. The nightly raid had wreaked havoc along the Euston Road and she'd hoofed it from the Tube station on the Piccadilly line lugging the laden shopping basket. She'd spent every last farthing on black market groceries and could not afford a cab fare. She hoped that Larry would be on call and she might borrow a shilling or two from him for, under the circumstances, asking Walter to subsidise her even to the tune of a bus fare was not a tactful thing to do.

She slipped quietly into the studio and scuttled into her cubby where she took off the awful oilskin, stowed the basket out of sight behind her desk and was in process of tidying her hair when, without knocking, Walter strode in.

'Ah! There you are. I apologise for dragging you in on a Sunday, but it's all hands to the pump.'

'I had some shopping to do and the Underground was . . . look, I'm sorry about last night.'

He carried a sheaf of scripts under his arm. He unloaded them on to her desk, fished out his case, found and lit a cigarette.

'Last night?' he said. 'Why, what happened last night?'

'It's more a question of what didn't happen last night.'

'Well, it won't happen again, Susan, you have my word.'

'Are you angry with me?'

'Not in the least. I may be an opportunist but I'm not an out-and-out cad. I can live perfectly well without you whimpering all over the place because I took advantage of you.'

'I am not the whimpering sort, Mr Boscombe.'

'No, you're not, are you? I apologise.' He placed a hand on the bundle of scripts. 'Friday's lot. Cattermole's lead piece on "The Press in the Third Reich" is very pertinent but a trifle over-exuberant. See if you can track him down at his weekend retreat and I'll have a chat with him.' Susan realised that he was not quite as diffident as he appeared to be. 'When's your sailor boy arriving?'

'I'm hoping to see him on Tuesday.'

'Do you want time off?'

'That won't be necessary.'

'I take it this *is* the same sailor: Basil Willets's brother?'

'Yes, of course.'

'I didn't think you were the sort to play the field,' Walter Boscombe said. 'Now don't fly off, Susan. I only have your interests at heart.'

'Provided they coincide with yours.'

'That goes without saying,' he said.

Basil was dozing in the armchair by the fire and Vivian was at the table pecking away on the typewriter that her brother had sent down when the sound of a motorcar engine caused them to lift their heads and exchange a glance.

'Who the devil can that be?' Basil said. 'I thought we were in for a quiet Sunday evening with the Home Service.'

'It's probably David. Who else could it be?'

'Open the door, dearest, and let's find out.'

A few minutes later a bedraggled Derek Willets, carrying a small suitcase, came into the cottage kitchen.

Basil struggled out of the armchair and shook his brother's

hand. 'Good to see you, old man. Forgive the question but why aren't you halfway to Canada at the helm of your destroyer?'

'She fell foul of a torpedo. She's in dock for repairs.'

'Many dead?' said Vivian.

'No,' Derek said. 'We were very fortunate. Nine injured, which isn't bad out of a crew of a hundred and thirty.' He put his suitcase on the floor and, crouching, opened it and brought out a bottle of brandy. 'To speed your recovery, Baz, and sweeten your temper.'

'How long will we have the pleasure of your company?'

'Not long enough,' said Derek. 'I must be off early tomorrow morning. I've a rendezvous with some chaps in the Admiralty who have questions to ask about my reports.'

'You're not in trouble, Derek, are you?' Vivian said.

'Good Lord, no.' He placed the bottle on the table. 'If someone were to offer me a snifter I wouldn't say no. I've had a long and dreary journey with changes at Preston and Crewe. Trains are so crowded these days. I couldn't find a place in first class and didn't have the gall to pull rank. Basil, how are you? You look a great deal better than last time I saw you.'

'I'll be back in harness by the first of the year. We'll move up to Salt Street soon after Christmas. Come on, off with that damp greatcoat. Vivian, do we have brandy glasses?'

'Don't make me laugh.' Vivian helped Derek off with his coat. 'We're lucky to have cups. I'll open a tin of stew for supper, which is the best I can do on short notice.'

'Anything at all will be fine,' Derek said. 'Mother sends you her fondest, Baz. She's rather miffed you haven't written.'

'Oh, I'll get around to it eventually.'

'Would it be safe to assume you're moored on the Clyde?'

Vivian called from the scullery. 'Or would that be classified as careless talk?'

'All talk about shipping's classified,' Derek said. 'The U-boats seem to have our number as it is. If too many merchant ships go to the bottom the war's as good as lost.'

Vivian brought three cups from the scullery and poured a measure of brandy into each. 'That won't happen, will it?'

'Unfortunately, it might,' Derek answered. 'However, I've an ulterior motive in coming all this way, apart from wishing to see you. Vivian, what's the state of affairs between Susan and her husband? It appears that the marriage might be over but I'd like to be sure.'

'Would you?' said Basil. 'Why?'

'I'm going up to London hoping to see Susan.'

'Well, you won't see much of her,' Basil said. 'She'll be slaving away on Boscombe's infernal programme all day.'

'Not all night, surely?' said Derek.

'You old devil,' Basil said. 'No, just some of the night.'

'Basil, shut up,' Vivian told him. 'What do you really know about Susan, Derek? Do you know, for instance, that she had a relationship with an American journalist this past summer? That was the beginning of the end of the marriage. Actually, I think it was slipping towards the rocks before that.'

'Go on,' Derek said.

'Danny was never right for Susan.'

'Why not?'

'She's ambitious, too ambitious for her own good,' Vivian said. 'You might – let's be blunt about it – you might have a fling with her but you're in no position to give her what she needs. What's the name of your ship?'

'The *Constant Star*.'

'How apt,' said Vivian. 'That's what our girl is searching

for: a constant star, a guiding light. You'd do well to bear that in mind.'

'Twaddle!' said Basil. 'We're in the middle of a bloody war. Nobody knows what tomorrow will bring. We could all be dead by Christmas. Heed my advice, old son, take what you can get, tip your hat and be on your way.'

'I didn't expect that from you,' Derek said. 'I always looked on you as a model of propriety.'

'What's the point in hanging on to values that no longer have any validity? Constant stars and guiding lights are all very well when you have a future to look to, but what future do you have, Derek? Next voyage out your damned boat could be at the bottom of the ocean, and you with it.'

'Basil Willets, how dare you!' Vivian snapped. 'That's an appalling thing to say.'

'It's no more than the truth. Am I not right, Derek?'

'You are. Of course, you are.'

'But you can't – repeat can't – let yourself think like that,' said Vivian. 'You have to believe there's a future or give up believing in anything.'

'What do you believe in, Vivian?' her husband asked. 'Oh, you're not going to say "love", are you?'

'What other possible reason could I have for squatting in a squalid little hovel in the middle of winter listening to you moaning?'

'She's got you there, Baz,' said Derek.

'I confess she has.' Basil sighed. 'Never mind, dearest. Some day we'll look back and tell ourselves just how much fun we had in this jolly old war.'

'You might,' said Vivian. 'I won't.' She poured a dash of brandy into her cup and turned her chair to face her brother-in-law. 'Falling in love in wartime is a mug's game. Falling in love with Susan Cahill will bring you nothing but heartache, Derek.'

'That's a risk I'm willing to take.'

'Hardly what a modern young woman wishes to hear,' said Basil. 'She wants you to beat your chest like King Kong and sweep her into your arms without a thought of consequence.'

'Shut up, Basil,' said Vivian once more. 'The thing is, Derek, it's not Susan's husband you have to worry about, it's her boss.'

'Boscombe?' said Basil. 'Surely Susan has more sense than to take up with a rotter like Walter Boscombe. The man's as transparent as a pane of glass.'

'I wouldn't be so sure of that,' Vivian said. 'He can offer Susan all sorts of things that Derek can't. I don't mean money. I mean the feeling that she's more important than she really is.'

'Susan won't fall for that waffle,' said Basil. 'She's not one of your flighty Bloomsbury crowd. She's a sensible East End girl. When it comes to it she'll pick the right man – and the right man's sitting right here with us. He's a commander in the Royal Navy, for Pete's sake. Once he puts on that uniform he can have any girl he wants just for the asking.'

'But he doesn't want just any girl, do you, Derek?' Vivian said. 'He happens to be in love with Susan Cahill.'

'In love?' Basil said. 'Is that true, Derek?'

'I think it might be,' Derek Willets admitted.

'Then tell her so,' Vivian said.

'And see where it gets you,' said Basil.

The rain had gone off but dust thickened the mist that crept from the fields and the acrid stench of smoke lingered across the site. Soldiers were ferried in from camps nearby and the din of lorries, pumps and a small mobile generator added to the clatter within the canteen. Wash-up and vegetable preparation sinks were cracked and pans from the equipment racks scattered hither and yon but the manager's office was undamaged and here Archie set up his headquarters.

Serving counters and tables were scrubbed, food in the cold store checked, tinned goods too. While this was being done a WVS mobile canteen prowled into the yard followed by a NAAFI wagon. Not to be outdone, Archie left Mrs Greevy in charge, hurried out into the yard and was spotted several minutes later on the pillion of a navy dispatch rider's motorcycle as it zoomed out of the gate. A half-hour later Archie returned in the cab of a Calor gas van from which four cylinders of liquid petroleum gas, a camp cooking range and two stoves were unloaded and set up by an agent of the local distributor who, Sunday or not, Archie had rooted out to aid the crisis.

Shortly thereafter, much to Archie's relief, fresh water spurted from the taps into the cracked sinks. Within minutes a tea urn was perched on one LPG stove and on the other a cauldron of Mitmee's vegetable soup. Thirty loaves, six dozen eggs and, oddly, twelve jars of mustard pickle were delivered from Archie's special suppliers just before noon. Cash changed hands and Archie, whistling cheerfully, chalked up a menu and announced that hot food would be served from half past twelve.

Morven had the temerity to enquire, 'Who's paying for all this, Mr Jackson?'

'The Navy Board, of course.'

'Do they know they're footing the bill?' said Breda.

'Not yet,' said Archie, unperturbed. 'I'll hand them the invoice just as soon as we're back in production.'

The children were fed first. They had a table to themselves

and made short work of the soup and a dish described as 'Cheese Monkey'. Though it tasted rather more of petrol and mustard pickle than it did of cheese, it went down well enough not just with the little guinea pigs but with weary men and women too.

Telephone wires brought down in the raid were repaired by mid-afternoon. Archie then spent a productive twenty minutes calling in more favours that resulted in deliveries of milk, potatoes, apples, four sacks of flour and another consignment of eggs, enough to keep the evening and night shifts nourished.

Out among the ruins, men laboured to retrieve machinery that might be repaired and, as the mist thickened and dusk settled over the site, Archie asked for volunteers to keep the canteen ticking over throughout the night. Breda and Billy were excused, of course, and Sharon Greevy's bold little schoolgirl band discouraged from staying late for there would be school next day, but Morven said she would hang on for one more shift and persuaded several of the unmarried women to join her.

In the canteen, among the thirty or so workers who were eating at the tables, a small committee had formed. Two wardens, a police inspector and a young, rather harassed naval lieutenant were debating how to ensure that blackout regulations were enforced and the hole in the canteen's roof and back wall covered.

'Tarpaulins,' said Archie from his stance behind the serving counter. 'If they can't find enough tarpaulins, I'm sure I can. There's no wind tonight and . . .'

His voice trailed off. Breda looked up from buttoning Billy's coat as Orrell's gateman and a soldier entered the kitchen by the side door. Slumped between them was a figure in a man's raincoat at least a half-size too small for her.

She wore no hat and her hair was plastered down across her brow. Beneath the raincoat the hem of a black dress showed like a mourning fringe.

'My dear good God!' said Archie. 'It's Trudy.'

'Do you know this woman, sir?' the soldier asked. 'She claims she's one of yours.'

'I told um,' the gateman said, 'but he wouldn't listen.'

'Yes, yes, damn it,' Mr Jackson said. 'She is one of ours.'

And Trudy, lifting her head, sobbed, 'Archie. Oh, Archie, help me, please,' and threw herself into his arms.

The rain had gone off but the night air was depressingly damp. In spite of his apprehension, Danny was relieved to step into the warmth of the BBC Club in Evesham's Greenhill Hotel. He imagined that Griff and Kate might be seated at their favourite table in the bar waiting for him to join them and experienced a melancholy moment at the realisation that he would never see either of them again.

They had formed a tight little trio, clannish and a bit standoffish. For that reason he'd made no other close friends in or out of the editing room.

Someone was playing the piano, Griff's piano. Danny was tempted to tell the young woman at the keys to shove off and make way for his Welsh pal who needed all the practice he could get. The thought cheered him; the memory of Griffith wrestling with Rachmaninoff, then, with a despairing cry of defeat, breaking into the 'Maple Leaf Rag' was surely one worth cherishing.

As usual at this time of the evening the bar was crowded with translators. Bearded Russian émigrés rubbed shoulders with pipe-smoking dons and a couple of Austrians who, Danny had heard, could decipher the most obscure contortions of German grammar. Two women at the bar, neither young nor pretty, were sufficiently expert in East European languages to be admitted to the inner circle of hard-drinking, chain-smoking intellectuals and far too grand to spare Danny a passing glance or make way for him at the counter.

Eventually he managed to catch the eye of the barman, secure a pint of bitter and retreat to a table by the door.

Most of the talk in the editing hut had concerned the raid on Shay Bridge. He'd already picked up enough gossip to satisfy himself that Orrell's Engineering Works hadn't been totally wiped out. How this sort of information floated into Wood Norton Hall was one of those puzzles to which no one seemed to have an answer, unless, that is, a foreign radio station had sprung the news before anyone in Whitehall or Westminster had got wind of it which, incredible as it seemed, was an occurrence not uncommon.

The raid had been directed only at the Navy Board's installation. Apart from a couple of high-explosive bombs that had strayed into fields north of Deaconsfield, damage had been confined to the Shay Bridge area. Mr Gregory's theory that someone had leaked word of what was going on at Orrell's to an enemy agent did not seem too far-fetched.

Danny glanced at his wristwatch. Breda and Billy would be home by now or taking refuge with the Pells. If he got a move on he might catch the service bus to Deaconsfield crossroads. He finished his pint and wandered into the foyer. He half hoped that the door to the secretary's office would be locked, for he hadn't quite made up his mind that what he was about to do was sensible.

The office door was open, however, and both the manager and the club secretary were visible within, drinking tea and, rather messily, munching sausage rolls.

Danny hovered.

'May I help you with something?' the secretary asked.

'Aye, it's – it's about the Christmas party?'

'Well, don't hang about in the hall. Come in.'

Danny stepped reluctantly into the office. He was, he knew, committed now. 'I was wondering if I could bring a guest.'

'You can bring your grandmother, if you like,' the secretary said, 'if you're willing to cough up for a double ticket.'

'How much is that?'

'Ten bob.'

'Steep,' said Danny, frowning.

'Free booze until ten thirty.' The manager winked. 'Hope your girlfriend's the thirsty sort.'

'She's not my girlfriend. She's my landlady.'

'You're Cahill, aren't you?' the manager said.

'Yeah, I am.'

'You're staying in a caravan on Gaydon's land.'

'What difference does that make?'

'None at all.' The manager hesitated. 'You were in Coventry, weren't you?'

'I was,' said Danny.

'Sorry to hear it,' the manager said. 'I mean . . .'

'I know what you mean,' said Danny.

The pause was just long enough to be respectful.

The secretary wiped crumbs from his waistcoat and opened a drawer in his desk. 'One ticket. Two persons. Ten bob, if you please.'

Danny took a banknote from his wallet, smoothed out the wrinkles and placed it on the desk. The ticket he received in exchange had been printed on a plain file card but someone had possessed enough festive spirit to stick a tiny silver star in the top corner.

'It's white tie and tails, you know,' the secretary told him.

'*What*?'

'Kidding, just kidding,' the secretary said.

'The only thing we insist on,' the manager said, 'is that you leave your horse at the door.'

'Very funny,' Danny said.

Carefully folding the ticket into his wallet, he left the couple in the office chuckling over their sausage rolls and hurried out into the street to catch the bus for home.

It hadn't seemed like Sunday. It hadn't seemed like any particular day at all; a day out of time. War itself did that to you, robbed you of familiar patterns and comforting habits. Back shifts, night shifts, air raids, nothing fixed, nothing assured, not even, it seemed, the certainty of having a job to go to tomorrow. Then, like a bolt from the blue, Trudy Littlejohn had staggered into the canteen dressed in a black dress and a man's coat and had pitched herself pathetically into Archie Jackson's arms, Archie had carried her off into his office and closed the door and suddenly you didn't even know who your enemies were any more.

The only news that emerged from Archie's office before Breda had to run to catch the bus was that Steve Pepperdine had been killed which, in itself, struck her as less tragic than bizarre.

Hadn't she just seen him prancing about in a boater and striped jacket behind the footlights in the church hall, playing the fool as usual? Hadn't she just watched Trudy stepping into a wardrobe and vanishing, unheard of until she reappeared, looking like death, eighteen or twenty hours later in the battered surroundings of Orrell's canteen? That wasn't magic, Breda thought, but a distortion of what passed for reality these days.

She'd been too tired to carry Billy from the bus stop to

the railway carriage but he'd had such a fine time being petted and praised by 'the big girls' that he'd trudged along beside her without complaint until they reached home.

She was so utterly weary that she didn't dare sit down or she'd never get up again. She tackled the iron stove first, cleaning out the ashes, lighting kindling and, kneeling, laying little lumps of coal on the recalcitrant flames. Next, she lit the Calor gas stove, filled a kettle from the tub and dumped the kettle on the ring.

Billy slumped on the bed, eyelids drooping. What he needed – what she needed – was a hot bath but that luxury, too, belonged to another time and place. She scrubbed his face and hands with a soapy cloth, dried him off, popped him into his pyjamas and kept him awake long enough to eat a slice of bread and jam and drink half a mug of milky cocoa before she tucked him into bed.

He was asleep before she kissed him goodnight.

She brushed his trousers, gave his shoes a polish, dug out a clean shirt, underwear and stockings and put them on the ledge for the morning. The air in the carriage was warming up. She took off her clothes and washed herself with the soapy cloth, put on her flannel nightgown and frayed old dressing gown.

She'd no idea when Danny would return. It wouldn't be the first time he'd drawn double duty and been out all night. She put out a tin of soup, another of beans and scraped a little butter on two slices of bread. She nibbled a slice of bread, drank tea and smoked a cigarette, prolonging the blissful moment when she'd turn down the lamp and slip in beside Billy, her own little hot-water bottle.

Forearms tucked under her bosom, forehead resting on the folding table, she had a fleeting vision of Steve Pepperdine and Trudy dancing together in Morven Hastie's bedroom while the cloth donkey danced on the pillow with Morven's frilly nightie.

She wakened abruptly.

Sitting up, she blinked at the blue glare of the gas ring reflected in the curve of the china mug on the table in front of her nose. Danny, at the Calor stove, was stirring the contents of a small pot. There was so much to tell him, so many questions to ask but she was so tired that all she could think of to say was, 'What's that you're making?'

'Beans,' Danny told her.

She watched him pour the beans on to a slice of bread and carry the plate to the table. He seated himself opposite her and began to eat. Then he paused.

'Hang on,' he said. 'I've got somethin' for you.' He fished his wallet from his pocket and brought out a folded card.

'What is it?' Breda said.

'Ticket for two tae a party, a Christmas party.'

'Where?'

'At the BBC Club.'

'Two?' said Breda.

'Sure, you an' me. The Gaydons'll look after Billy for the night, if you ask them.'

Breda peered dopily at the ticket's tiny silver star.

'A party at the BBC Club?' she said. 'Me, at the BBC Club, with you?'

'Something tae look forward to,' Danny said.

'Oh, my Gawd!' Breda was suddenly wide awake. 'What'll I wear? What can I possibly wear?'

Shaking his head ruefully, Danny went back to the beans.

It hadn't occurred to Susan that Derek still had a key to the house in the mews or that he might arrive unannounced in the wee small hours. She'd expected him to show up at lunchtime, hat in hand, to behave like a suitor not a lodger. She'd come to regard Viv's house as her own and while she was willing, very willing indeed, to share the accommodation with Commander Willets, she wished that he'd given her a little more notice of his early arrival.

She'd slept late on Monday morning and had rushed out at the last minute, leaving the bed unmade, a damp towel writhing on the bathroom floor and her unmentionables scattered across the bedroom carpet. She wasn't usually so untidy but her trip to Shadwell and her encounter with Ruth Gertler had disconcerted her, in addition to which she was excited at the prospect of seeing Derek again, though why one little letter had had that effect she couldn't explain.

Monday night's broadcast had gone off without a hitch. A news round-up, written and read by Mr Gillespie, was followed by a live talk on 'The Place of Prayer in Wartime', a talk that offered practical advice on coping with grief, suffering and loss from a bishop whose views would not have been out of place in the *Daily Worker*. The bishop, a convivial chap, had gone off with Walter for a noggin at one of Walter's clubs, and Larry, his sister's motorcar filled with BBC petrol, had dropped Susan off at the end of the mews.

She was still charged with nervous energy after the broadcast. She intended to sleep for a few hours and spend the morning primping and preening – Vivian's favourite slander – to be at her best for Derek's arrival. Now here he was, pottering about in the kitchen like a house-husband, like Basil, for heaven's sake, while she reeked of a smoky basement in Soho and looked about as attractive as a Gas Board navvy.

She took off her coat and hat and went into the kitchen.

No sweater and corduroys tonight: he wore his best blue trousers, a spotless white shirt with sleeves rolled up and collar undone and, as far as she could make out, had just finished washing the dishes that she'd left piled on the draining board. He dried his hands on a dishtowel, tossed it aside and in three strides crossed the kitchen and, before she could respond, kissed her.

'Those little pies in the larder were delicious. Where on earth did you find them, Susan?' he asked.

'Old friends in low places. Did you leave me some?'

'One, and even that was a sacrifice.'

'I have some beef sausages too, unless you've scoffed those as well. Will I cook for you? Are you hungry?'

'Oh, yes, I'm hungry,' he said.

Then, stooping, he swept his forearm behind her knees, caught her as she lost balance, lifted her in his arms, and carried her, unresisting, into the bedroom.

20

When it came to unravelling the mystery of what happened to Steve Pepperdine and why the Reverend Stanley Littlejohn had disappeared, the press were no help at all. There was no juice in spies and spying unless the case went to trial, no capital to be made from recording a death in custody or the seedy machinations of men who had succumbed to Nazi blackmail. The government had the power to suppress unedifying news and the barons of Fleet Street were well aware of it. No word, not one, appeared in print. Bishop Bunce may have been privy to the lurid details but he refused point-blank to allow the issue to be raised in synod and the parishioners of Shay Bridge St John's were obliged to share a clergyman with Ledington while the snug little rectory lay empty.

Stanley's widowed mother blamed Trudy for all that had gone wrong in the marriage and even succeeded in convincing herself that Stanley was on the run from Trudy not the law. Trudy's aged parents in Norwich were more forgiving, willing if not eager to offer their daughter refuge but for Trudy to return to the bosom of her family after years of relative freedom would have been the ultimate defeat.

Trudy's tears were not for Steve, the boyish show-off, or for the husband whom she had never loved, but for her own reputation, now irredeemably tainted by her role in the sinister ménage. There was no question of her remaining in the Navy Board's employ. Following her husband's lead she vanished from Shay Bridge without a word of farewell to anyone.

Two weeks after the Navy Board announced that Orrell's Engineering Works would continue in production, Mr Jackson negotiated a transfer to manage catering for a new munitions factory 'somewhere in Scotland'. He took Trudy with him as his housekeeper, thus fooling not only the Navy Board but also Inspector Jessop, who, by that time, had lost interest in Shay Bridge's *femme fatale* and had much bigger fish to fry.

A contrite Mrs Littlejohn might have considered leaving the red shoes on Breda's doorstep as a parting gift but contrition wasn't in Trudy's make-up. While she might surrender her future to doting Mr Jackson, there were certain aspects of her past that she wished to keep to herself, her brief, passionate affair with the bookseller of Berne among them.

Mr Jackson worked out his time as productively as possible, supervising clean-up, restocking and repairs. During reconstruction of the machine sheds, he saw to it that meals were provided round the clock for builders and staff and, leaning heavily on Miss Hastie, lunches for the Navy Board inspectors who were practically living on the site. What Archie did not do was reveal his plans for the future and, when asked, professed ignorance of Trudy's whereabouts, though, in fact, she was lodging temporarily with his father and sister in a council house in Salford.

If Morven's curiosity remained undimmed, Breda was too caught up in preparing for the Christmas party at the BBC Club to have more than a passing interest in Trudy's fate.

Breda was wary of Morven and Danny meeting too often and one benefit of Steve Pepperdine's demise was that the Spitfire Fund was closed and the works dance cancelled. Instead, she was going to the BBC Club at Danny's invitation and hoped that Morven would back off, if, that is, Morven had ever backed on in the first place.

'Have you decided what you're wearing yet?' Morven asked.

'Nope, not yet.'

'Haven't you got an evening dress?'

'Never 'ad an evening dress, not a proper one.'

'You could borrow mine but, even with alterations, you'd never fit into it,' said Morven. 'What about a nightie?'

'Are you nuts?'

'With the right sort of underskirt . . .'

'It's the BBC Club, Morven, not the bleedin' Windmill. I'm not giving Danny a showing-up by flaunting my attributes in a nightdress. Danny assures me it's a party, not a proper dance. He's not out there buying a dickey-bow and a stuffed shirt so I'll get away with a frock, like as not.'

'I've a nice stole if you fancy it.'

'Ermine?'

'Skunk, I think,' said Morven.

'In that case,' Breda said, 'I'll pass.'

'When is this party?'

'Next Saturday.'

'Who's looking after the wee chap?'

'The Gaydons will 'ave 'im for the night.'

'So you and Danny will be all alone in the moonlight. Ooo-ah!'

'Ooo-ah, yourself!' said Breda.

*

Susan had forgotten what it felt like to waken with a man by her side. She stretched her bare legs down the length of the bed and, shifting her weight, spooned herself into the line of Derek's body, her belly rubbing against his buttocks, breasts pressed to his shoulder blades, arms around his waist.

Derek had been surprisingly tender after the first fierce surge that had swept her off her feet. True, he'd pinned her to the bed, elbows digging into the pillow on each side of her head, their shoes knocking together somewhere below the equator, and had kissed her with undeniable ardour. But then he'd drawn back and had asked her if she wished him to stop. He didn't apologise; if he'd apologised it would, somehow, have made him seem weak or, at best, calculating.

She'd answered by cupping her hands behind his head, pulling him down and parting her lips in a kiss that had seemed to go on for ever. She'd opened her legs and let him fit himself between her knees, cradled on her skirt. She'd heard her shoe fall off and thud to the floor and her breath, and his breath too, becoming faster and faster. He didn't fumble to free himself or reach up to pull away her knickers, though she wouldn't have resisted if he had. He'd drawn back once more and had said, 'This isn't right, Susan. Would you like to make yourself more comfortable?'

'Yes,' she'd said. 'Yes, I would.'

He'd slipped from the bed, had given her his hand and helped her to her feet, had held her and kissed her and when at last he'd released her and she'd scampered off to the bathroom, he'd called out, 'Don't forget to come back.'

A sliver of daylight showed at the corner of the blackout curtain and the lamp in the living room was still alight. She had no idea what time it was. She felt him stir and, in a languorous state of arousal, pull her closer. She touched his shoulder with the tip of her tongue, tasting clean salt sweat.

'When are you expected at the office?' he asked.

'The office? Oh, I don't know. Does it matter?'

'I thought it might to you.'

'I'm probably late as it is. I'll call in sick. What about you?'

'I've done my duty – by the Admiralty, I mean.'

'Are we free to make a proper occasion of it then?'

'All day, if you like,' David said. 'Are you up for it?'

'The question is,' Susan said, 'are you?'

It was after one o'clock before the telephone rang which, Susan thought, showed great restraint on Walter Boscombe's part.

She lay flat on her back, one foot and one arm trapped under the weight of Commander Willets, RN, who was lying on his back too. She waited for the phone to stop ringing which, eventually, it did, then she extricated herself from Derek's clutches and, sitting up, reached for the clock on the bedside table.

Ten minutes past one.

The telephone began ringing again.

She ignored it.

It was chilly in the master bedroom. She reached for her dressing gown and, rising a little shakily, put it on and headed for the bathroom. By the time she came out of the bathroom the telephone had stopped ringing. She crossed into her bedroom to find something to wear, then went into the kitchen, put the kettle on the stove, lit the oven and, leaving the oven door open, crouched before it to warm herself. She had a slight headache: a small price to pay for the exertions of the night.

She was also hungry, famished, in fact.

Gathering herself, she went into the larder and brought out the bowl of Gertler's best beef sausages, a skinny packet of ham and four black market eggs. She was in the process of greasing the frying pan when the telephone started its infuriating clamour once more. She put the pan to one side and went out into the hall.

Derek was leaning in the doorway of the living room, struggling to light the cigarette that hung limply from his nether lip. Susan took the cigarette from his mouth, kissed him, put the cigarette back in place, struck a match and lit the ciggie.

'Good morning, sleepyhead,' she said and went into the office to answer the phone for no other reason than to shut it up.

'Susan, where the devil are you?'

'I'm sorry, Walter. I'm not feeling awfully well.'

'Flu, is it?'

'One of those – those female things.'

A pause, not quite long enough to be pregnant: 'I see.'

'If it's desperately urgent . . .' she began.

'I imagine we might stumble through without your assistance for once,' Mr Boscombe said. 'May I suggest you spend the rest of the day in bed.'

'You know, I think I might at that.'

A gruff, cynical, 'Huh,' then, 'Four o'clock tomorrow?'

'Absolutely,' Susan said.

'Without fail?'

'Without fail.'

She had never felt as well disposed towards anyone as she did towards Commander Derek Willets that winter afternoon in the kitchen of Vivian's house in Salt Street. Well disposed was, she realised, one of those polite expressions that had about as much relevance to two lovers sharing a late breakfast as that other misty word 'companionable'.

She said, 'I must admit you took me completely by surprise.'

'Really? And why is that?'

He was holding her hand, not gripping it tightly, just touching fingertips across the kitchen table.

'I thought you were too stuffy to do what you did.'

'My brother gave me some sound advice and for once I actually listened to him. He told me that women prefer men to be decisive.'

'Since when did Basil become an expert on affairs of the heart? He never struck me as having the right credentials for a matchmaker.'

'Basil's marriage – his first marriage – was as conservative as you could possibly imagine. He loved his wife and suffered greatly when she died, though, being a true blue Englishman, he hid his feelings behind a stiff upper lip and threw himself into his work. I think, looking back, he regretted that he'd wasted so much time in being polite that the passion had gone before Joan and he ever got anywhere near the bridal suite.'

'He didn't make that mistake with Vivian.'

'Times change, I suppose, and Baz with them.'

'What exactly did he tell you?' Susan said.

'He told me to beat my chest, like King Kong, pick you up and carry you off to my lair.'

'He didn't say that, did he?'

'In almost as many words.'

'He's obviously not himself these days.'

Derek took his hand from hers and sat back in the chair. She felt a little ripple of dread at the thought that this day, this night might be all they would ever have.

'Are any of us?' he said. 'I've never taken advantage before.'

'You didn't take advantage, darling.'

'Of the situation, of the war, I mean. You know what I am, Susan. You know what I do.'

'I don't want to think about it.'

'I'm not a young sub who, all evidence to the contrary, sincerely believes he's immortal.' He paused then said, 'I'm catching the eight forty from Euston tomorrow morning. Will you come to the station with me?'

'Of course, I will.'

'I don't want to sneak off like a thief in the night. I'd like you to say goodbye to me as if I were coming home again. It'll give me something to hang on to, even if it isn't true.'

'What,' Susan said, 'if it is true?'

'If I write, will you answer?'

'How do I do that?'

'Send your letters to Admiralty: name, rank and ship.'

'*Constant Star*?'

'That's it. I've no idea where we'll be sent but mail from home usually catches up with us somewhere. You've no idea what it would mean to me to hear from you.'

'Derek,' she said, 'are we talking about a future?'

'I do believe we are, Susan. At least, I am.'

'I'd be lying if I said I didn't think about the future too.'

'I hope that from now on I'm part of it,' Derek said.

'Oh, you are, you are. You will be.'

'Vivian thinks falling in love in wartime is a mug's game.'

'That only because she's been living with Basil, with his illness for too long,' Susan said. 'She's afraid she'll lose him. Being in love is probably the only thing that's keeping her going.'

'Better to have loved and lost than—'

She reached across the table and pressed a finger to his

lips. 'I may believe it, darling, but I'd rather not hear you say it. It's probably better not to tempt fate by making plans.'

'Talking of plans, I did promise to take you to dinner.'

'How can you even think of dinner? I'm absolutely stuffed.'

'You'll be hungry again soon,' he said. 'We'll go somewhere quiet and unpretentious nearby. A light supper and an early night would suit me. How about you?'

'Oh, yes, please,' Susan said. 'A very early night.'

Hardly had Danny put a foot into the railway carriage than Breda yelled, 'Out. Keep out.'

Dressing arrangements had been awkward but not *that* awkward. After all they'd lived cheek by jowl in her mother's house for nigh on fifteen years and neither had any secrets from the other. Breda had never been overly modest and in the middle of that self-aware phase that many young girls go through had swanned about in practically the all-together just to see what effect it might have on males of the species, including the lodger.

'It's bloody freezin' out here, Breed.' Danny leaned, shivering, against the wall of the coach. 'Hurry it up, will you?'

'Two minutes.'

Danny groaned, beat his arms across his chest and watched his breath gather in a cloud in front of his face. Then Billy stuck his head from the open door and said, 'She's got a new dress and you ain't supposed to see it till she's ready.'

The light of the paraffin lamp shed a patch of warmth on the frosted grass and the air from the coach held the savoury aroma of stew, tinned stew but stew none the less.

'Mind that light,' Billy intoned in his warden's voice then, giggling, went back indoors.

Danny had known that something was going on. There

had been furtive shufflings and a tucking away of sewing baskets and bits and pieces of ribbon and lace and he'd been warned not to open the drawer under Billy's bunk unless he wanted his head in his hands.

The warpaint had appeared too, little pots of powder and creams and a caked tray of stuff that looked like dried blood and the top of a jam jar in which Breda had conducted an experiment with soot as a substitute for mascara, an experiment, he gathered, that hadn't worked out too well.

He'd been tempted to remind Breda that this was not a fancy dress party, that turning up looking like Pocahontas would not endear her to members of the BBC's monitoring unit, though the engineers would probably love it. But, prudence personified, he'd kept his mouth shut.

He stamped his feet, beat his arms across his chest and reminded himself of the benevolent urge that had moved him to buy the damned ticket in the first place. At least the prospect of taking Breda out for an evening on the town, even if the town was Evesham, had had the desired effect of giving them both something to look forward to, if, that is, he didn't freeze to death in the interim.

'All rightee,' Breda called. 'I'm red-aaay.'

Danny sucked in a deep breath. He had no idea what to expect and, thus, expected the worst. He stepped into the coach prepared to lie gallantly in his teeth.

'Ta-rah!' Breda twirled as much as the limited space inside the railway coach allowed. 'Well, what do you think?'

What he thought, at that precise moment, did not bear repeating. His eyes opened wide, his throat thickened and it was several seconds before he could speak.

'Breda, what the heck have you done tae yourself?'

'Oh, Gawd! You don't like it.' She ceased twirling and slumped on the bed. 'I'm a mess, aren't I? An old bag trying to look like a young 'un again. I'm not going. You can take 'er instead.'

'Who, take who?'

'Morven. She won't embarrass you like I will.'

'Breda,' he said gruffly, 'stand up.'

She looked up at him, sniffing back tears. He caught her by the wrist, yanked her to her feet, then, stepping back, cleared floor space between the table and the stove.

'Do it again,' he said. 'Give us a bit of a twirl.'

'So you can laugh . . .'

'Just bloody do it.'

Billy was seated, cross-legged, in his corner by the iron stove, a strip of torn petticoat lace draped across his head. He watched his mother twirl once more, holding out the skirt that she'd spent hours sewing when Danny hadn't been there.

'Tell me the truth now, Danny,' Breda said. 'Don't lie.'

'You look . . .' Danny raked his vocabulary for exactly the right word, one that wouldn't convey to Breda just how desirable he found her in the clinging pastel print.

'Elegant,' he said at length. 'Really, really elegant.'

'You're only saying that.'

'In that rig-out, kid, you'll be the belle of the ball.'

'Elegant?' Breda said, looking down at herself. 'Nobody never called me that before.'

'Well, there's a first time for everything,' Danny said.

'So you think I'll do?'

'Aw, yeah,' said Danny sincerely. 'You'll do.'

All day long she'd walked around in a trance, numbed by the fear that she would never see him again, that the brusque unsentimental leave-taking in the busy railway station – a kiss, a hug, a wave from the open window as the train pulled out – would be the final scene in a banal playlet that would condemn her to live in the shadow of what might have been.

From Euston she'd returned to Salt Street where she'd stripped the bed, emptied ashtrays and swept carpets and, only when that was done, had bathed and changed and gone out again into the fading daylight and caught a bus to Soho.

Walter was lurking on the stairs that led up to the studio. He was seated with a script in his lap and a cigarette in his mouth while a dance band rehearsed on the stage and a team of electricians, whistling, rigged up lights as if, suddenly, the Calcutta had become a place of entertainment once more.

'What are they doing?' Susan asked.

'Damned if I know. Are you feeling better?'

'Yes, thank you.'

She waited for a sarcastic tail to his question. He said nothing, though, studied her, head on one side, squinting as cigarette smoke wreathed into his eyes. She was tempted to admit she hadn't been ill at all, that her sailor had been with her all day and all night – but Walter already knew that.

'Whatever they're up to,' he said at length, 'I wish they'd stop. I can hardly hear myself think.' He heaved himself from the stairs and thrust the script at her. 'Burnham had to pull out. Government business. Kingsley Wood is standing in with a talk on Air Defences, though, obviously, he's not giving much away. Would you type out the edit, please.'

'Of course.'

'By the way,' he said, 'that chap you met at Proudfoot's place, Feaver, Ransome Feaver . . .'

'What about him?'

'He's been arrested. Keep it under your hat for the time being.'

'Will he be brought to trial?'

'Possibly not. It depends on who he's willing to take down with him. In any case, the powers that be may not want their informers brought into a court of law.' He shrugged. 'None of our concern, really, now we've done our little bit.'

'Have we? I mean, did we?'

'We helped a little, shall we say. Susan, are you all right?'

'I'm fine, thank you,' she said, and crossing the floor, went into her office with Walter at her heels.

The orchestra had stopped playing. The electricians, their work done, stopped whistling. It was quiet in the studio with nothing but the faint chatter of a typewriter from one of the other cubbies and that muffled thumping from the street above as if someone were dancing on her grave.

Derek would be in Scotland by now. She wondered if he was thinking of her. She teased herself with the notion that something had happened, some minor accident that had brought him back to London, that the mews house would not be empty when she got home. And then she was crying, fists pressed into her cheeks. She rocked in her chair, sobbing helplessly, hurting too much to care what Walter thought of her.

'There, there,' he said sympathetically. 'Poor Susan,' and, when she'd cried herself out, gave her a handkerchief to dry her eyes before the business of setting up the week's programmes got properly under way.

21

Proceedings began as soon as the band assembled and, by way of tuning-up, rendered a version of the National Anthem while barmen, maids and those arty souls who were decorating the Christmas tree in the reception hall stood to attention and mumbled all the words they could remember.

The band was as close to a professional group as you would find outside London: six skilled musicians, two of whom, including the leader, had played with Jack Payne's radio orchestra before the war and were glad to be back on a bandstand with an audience to entertain. They were all attached to Wood Norton's BBC monitoring unit in various capacities and the tenor saxophonist and lead singer were expert engineers to whom tuning a microphone came naturally.

Mr Gregory and the other supervisors had arranged the rotas with care. Short of a major explosion of news, everyone on the roster would have an opportunity to quaff from the communal punch-bowl, play a few silly games that involved kissing or bumping backsides and, of course, dance to the strains of 'Pagan Serenade' or 'Under the Spanish Stars'.

By seven o'clock the bar was crowded and the lounge filling up.

Girls and boys from town had gathered outside the Greenhill to watch the lovely ladies and handsome gentlemen arrive by bus or, two or three eccentrics, on bicycles. There was quite a stir when Breda and Danny turned up in a farm cart driven by Mr Gaydon, and Breda, on Danny's hand, stepped down.

One young whippersnapper even had the temerity to whistle when Breda, doing her level best to appear elegant, almost lost her footing and flashed rather more stocking than she'd intended. Then, on Danny's arm, she ascended the steps and entered into the bright lights of the BBC Club where a small, elderly man, who looked disturbingly like her father, rushed forward, dangled a sprig of mistletoe over her head and kissed her.

'Down, Karl, down.' The manager yanked the little man away. 'My apologies. We shouldn't have invited him to collect tickets.'

'That's quite all right.' Breda struggled to regain her composure. 'Pleased to make your acquaintance.'

'Mrs Hooper, my landlady,' said Danny. 'Who gets the ticket?'

'Forget the ticket,' the manager said. 'Enjoy yourselves.'

'I'm sure we will,' said Breda as a florid-faced young man bounded out of the lounge with a cocktail glass in each hand and skidded to a halt in front of her.

'Good Lord, Daniel,' he said. 'Is this lovely creature really your landlady? What a dark horse you are. Mademoiselle, have a snort on me, or, rather, the house. If you provide board and lodging for this horrible Scotsman you probably need it.'

Breda accepted the proffered glass. 'What is it?'

'A special Hogsnorton cocktail that we call—'

'Best if Mrs Hooper doesn't know what we call it,' Danny said.

'Ah, yes, mustn't frighten the natives,' the chap said.

'Have you seen Ursula? She's in urgent need of refuelling, apparently.'

'Sorry, Roger,' Danny said. 'Try the ladies' powder room.'

'What a jolly good idea.'

Still clutching a glass, Roger scooted off across the hall.

Breda sniffed the cocktail's oily surface suspiciously.

'What's in this concoction, Danny?'

'Mostly gin, I think. Kate couldn't stand the stuff.'

'What *do* they call it?'

'Virgin's Bane,' Danny told her.

'Like Mother's Ruin?'

'Only worse.'

'Bloody 'ell!' said Breda and bravely drank it down.

Monitors and editors on late shift were sufficiently conscientious to stay sober but a number of those who, like Danny, weren't due at their posts until Sunday morning were less abstemious and one or two even got thoroughly plastered.

In addition to the lethal cocktail, a strong cider-based punch proved popular with party-goers as well as keg beer, bottled ale and plain old gin and tonic. It was perhaps as well that a fresh contingent of revellers arrived shortly after nine, when the rota changed, for as the evening progressed both games and dancing became more and more obstreperous.

Even the Teddy Bears' Picnic, a two-step familiar to all wireless engineers, who used a version to calibrate frequencies, degenerated into a kissing game in which Femi, a leggy Finn in a white satin evening gown, had to be rescued from the clutches of Karl, the elderly ticket-collector, whose nose came only to the level of Femi's cleavage but whose hands, it seemed, were perfectly aligned with her bottom.

Breda put all thought of a romantic evening out of mind. Topped up by two more glasses of Virgin's Bane, she shed both her inhibitions and her attempts at a Home Service accent and dragged Danny through foxtrot and quickstep as best she could, using her bosom as a buffer when all else failed.

She really came into her own, however, when Danny, bruised if not bleeding, collapsed into a chair by the wall near the door, fanning himself with both hands, just as the band struck up a few bars of 'Knees Up, Mother Brown', and Breda, Cockney spirit stirred, did a little jig in a vain attempt to rouse him.

'You've worn him out, Mrs Hooper,' said a voice behind her. 'I'd be honoured to take Cahill's place and give the poor lad a well-earned breather.'

They weren't strangers, not quite. She'd met him once before, on that dreadful afternoon in Mrs Pell's house when he'd arrived by motorcar to confirm that Griff and Kate Cottrell were dead. For an instant she was tempted to refuse, as if he, not the Jerries, had been responsible for the tragedy – then she realised how silly that was and graciously took Mr Gregory's arm and let him lead her out on to the crowded floor.

Crooner and trombonist claimed the lion's share of the microphone. The trumpet player, leering wickedly, produced a bowler hat with which he fashioned a muted voluntary while the couples, with much pushing and shoving, fell into line.

'Any Cockneys in the house?' the crooner called out.

'Yer.' Breda answered before she could stop herself. 'Me.'

'Give us a hand then, love, when we get to the chorus.'

Conscious that Mr Gregory, Danny's boss, was her partner, Breda checked a more exuberant reply and said, 'Delighted to oblige,' and the drummer clashed a cymbal, the crooner pulled the mike towards him and broke into the verse while the dancers flexed their knees and waited to stamp, kick and bawl out, *'Ee-aye, Ee-aye-oh,'* when the chorus came round.

One chorus followed another, the tempo increasing with

each until, one by one, the breathless and the blotto began to drop by the wayside and Breda realised that this was not a dance at all but a test of stamina, a challenge to youth and endurance. Giggling, she picked up her skirts, grabbed Mr Gregory's hand and, like a team of well-trained circus horses, they kicked in perfect unison while fugitives from M Unit, amazed at their supervisor's lack of decorum as well as his staying power, applauded.

Then it was just Femi, satin gown hitched up, and Breda dancing each to the other while the men fell away, panting, and the kicks became higher and higher and the band played faster and faster, then, with everyone in the hall, barmen and maids included, shouting one final, '*Ee-aye, Eey-aye-oh!*' the leader brought the number to a close and Breda and Femi, pearled with perspiration and barely able to breathe, fell into each other's arms and, in the spirit of the season, declared a well-fought truce.

'Whoof,' Breda gasped, hand to her chest. 'I ain't 'ad that much fun in years,' and, nudging Mr Gregory, added, 'You ain't such a bad old stick yourself.'

'You never bin darn the Old Kent Road of a Sat'day night, 'ave yer?' said Mr Gregory. 'Sarf Lunnin for me every time, where men is men and the women wears no bloomers.'

'Don't tell me you're from down that way,' said Breda.

'We all have to start somewhere,' Mr Gregory told her. 'Not a word to anyone, please, Mrs Hooper, or such authority as I do have will go up in smoke.'

'Our secret,' Breda promised and let him escort her back to the chair by the door where Danny, supping a pint of beer, waited.

He rose, nodded to Mr Gregory then passed the glass to Breda who, clutching it in both hands, drank greedily.

'Havin' a good time, sweetheart?' Danny asked.

'I certainly am,' Breda answered. 'How about you?'

'Great,' Danny said, 'just great,' and prudently retrieved the beer glass before she could wallop the lot.

By eleven o'clock a free bar and exhaustion were beginning to take their toll. The survivors were willing to sit about the lounge or sway on the dance floor and, with an odd tear or two to cool flushed cheeks, sing sentimental ballads while the saxophone played low and sweet and the drummer exchanged his sticks for brushes and the barman dimmed the lights.

In Breda's arms, Danny shuffled in soft, swaying circles, like an eddy in a stream. He held her very close, her cheek against his shoulder, the faint, not unpleasant aura of perfume and perspiration warm about her while the band played, 'No More Heartache, No More Tears'. And he wasn't sure whether what he felt was sadness or happiness or the first real stirrings of desire for a woman he'd known half his adult life.

'What's up with you?' Breda murmured.

He smiled and said, 'I was wonderin' whether I should kiss you now or later.'

'Why not both?' said Breda and pulled him closer still.

Danny had brought along a scarf to keep her warm while they waited at the pavement's edge for one of Evesham's few taxi-cabs which were doing a roaring trade that winter night.

The town lay dark, street lamps and houses blacked out but there was a shard of moon among the clouds and a blink of stars and Breda was far too happy to care about the darkness or the cold.

She clung to Danny as they moved up the queue for cabs and when their turn came and they were safe in the rear seat she wasted no time in kissing him. She had kissed him before, many times, but never like a first-time lover in the back seat of a taxi-cab. She sensed that he wanted her but might still slide away, slip into protecting her modesty or, like a brother, consider her taboo.

She was too astute to flirt and fumble, to remind him that she wasn't an innocent when it came to sex, that there had been many men – too many men – before Ronnie. She wondered if Danny was aware of that squad of casual lovers and afraid that he would have to compete with them. She didn't know how to tell him that she'd been properly loved by only one man, Ronnie, and that Ronnie, like Kate Cottrell, was dead.

She kissed him softly, their mouths meeting among the folds of the scarf, kissed him fondly while plotting how to convince him that Susan couldn't offer him half what she could and that living close together in a railway carriage could have only one possible outcome.

The cabby dropped them on Deaconsfield Road. They walked, hand in hand, along the lane and down the track, trailing the shaded torch beam. He stopped once and kissed her and she felt again the fear that he might only be humouring her and would turn aside and, without meaning to, rebuff her.

The interior of the coach was warm. She'd stoked the stove with coal nuts before they'd left and the poker soon brought the fire to life. She lit the paraffin lamp and took off her overcoat, hat and scarf while Danny, spectacles glinting like cat's eyes, went outside and drew fresh water from the depths of the well; clear, ice-cold water that Breda scooped up in a cup and drank to cleanse the taste of cocktails from her mouth.

The water made her throat ache and numbed her lips and when he kissed her it was like being kissed anew.

She raised an arm, found the key of the lamp and turned the wick down low and the carriage was lit by the flames in the coal in the stove and his fingers found the buttons at the top of her dress and the tie of the belt that held the dress at the waist and he tugged the top of the dress down and kissed the tops of her breasts and, in the soft red glow of the coal stove, took off her clothes.

Breda did nothing to help save kick away her shoes and, when he was ready, tilt her hips to take him into her and let Danny, her Danny, do the rest.

She'd slept so deeply that she hadn't heard him moving about. He was good that way, thoughtful, making no noise. He seated himself on the bunk at her feet and, when she sat up, held out a mug of tea and let her drink from it as if he were feeding a baby.

'We need a bigger bed,' he said.

'We need a bigger house,' said Breda.

'We could ask the Pells tae take us in. Billy could have a room tae himself an' we could share the big room. Mrs Pell wouldn't mind, even if it scandalised the neighbours. She'd claim the billeting fee for me an' we'd have more than enough between us to settle the balance.'

'Don't waste much time, do you, big boy?' Breda said. 'Now you've 'ad your way, seems once wasn't enough.' She took the mug from him and drank again. 'The crack of dawn ain't the best time to talk about anything sensible.'

'Once you've finished your tea, turn over an' catch another hour's kip. It's Sunday. Fred Gaydon won't bring Billy back till after breakfast at the earliest.'

'I do 'ave a bit of a sore head,' Breda admitted, then shook a warning finger. 'And no rude remarks from you, Mr Cahill. You know I don't like that sort of thing.'

'Once a prude, always a prude.'

'That's not what you said last night.'

'I wasn't quite myself last night.'

'Well, whoever you was, I hope 'e comes back soon.'

'I think you can count on it, sweetheart,' Danny said.

He took the mug and put it to one side then leaned over, slipped his hand beneath the tangle of blankets, gave her a squeeze and kissed her.

'Got tae go,' he said. 'I really do. You okay now?'

'Never been better,' Breda said, which, at that moment, was no more than the truth.

22

It was Larry who first put about the rumour that Mr Boscombe had personally ordered the raid that dropped the land-mine on the corner of Portland Place close to the front entrance of Broadcasting House. Even Larry would have baulked at making such a suggestion if there had been casualties in the Big House but mercifully there were only a few minor injuries.

The damage done to the building, though, was considerable. Fire and water wreaked havoc on the ground-floor reception hall and put many of the offices and studios that had just been repaired out of commission once more. After an emergency meeting of controllers and senior producers on Monday afternoon, Walter returned to the Calcutta and announced that the temporary Soho studio would remain their home for some time to come.

'A hot line to Goering, obviously,' Larry said. 'Given that our Walt's been agitating to stay put for weeks now it's too much of a coincidence otherwise.'

'Perhaps he persuaded Rogue Redmain to use his influence,' Susan said, 'and swop one of his dirty pictures for a land-mine.'

'You,' Larry said, 'are becoming far too cynical.'

'It's the company I keep,' said Susan.

In spite of the blitzkrieg that had reduced some parts of

London to a wasteland, Susan felt safe in the underground cubby. Her main concern was the progress of the war which, everyone now agreed, would be long and tough. The possibility of surrender or defeat was never mentioned, though it was always there, skulking, and the endless morale-boosting chatter, Susan thought, wasn't much more than a case of the Emperor's new clothes.

Derek was still in Greenock. She received a letter every day and, by one delivery, three at once, for he'd become an ardent correspondent. The letters were sprinkled with quotations from poets that Susan had never heard of; poems filled not with bells tolling, grim reapers or shadows on the shore but posies of flowers, lockets of hair and promises of everlasting spring. On the office typewriter she replied to each and every letter, giving Derek her all, her everything in a style leaning more to Ethel M. Dell than Virginia Woolf.

As long as the letters kept coming it was easy to pretend that Derek was safe and the *Constant Star*, laid up on the Clyde, would remain neglected by the Admiralty and ignored by the Luftwaffe. But when she passed down Oxford Street and saw the blackened shell of John Lewis department store or abruptly confronted a phalanx of fire tenders pumping water into what had been an office block she was forced to admit that all too soon the daily letters would dry up and Derek and the *Constant Star* would be out of touch, out of reach for weeks, months or years and that she, without her paper lover, would be alone again.

Which wasn't strictly true: Basil had been offered a post with Cecil Madden's Light Entertainment Service, though quite what the nature of his involvement would be had not been made clear. Vivian and he were planning to return to London just after Christmas and Susan would no longer have the house to herself.

On Wednesday, 11th December, the *Mirror* reported that two German spies had been hanged in Pentonville prison, an item that drew Susan up short. For a moment she wondered if they might be connected to David Proudfoot and the arrest of Ransome Feaver. Walter laughed and shook his head when she suggested it. Small fry, he assured her, German parachutists with a wireless set hidden in the grass, not collaborators, and went on to ask her what she was doing for Christmas.

She had no idea what she was doing for Christmas. If Viv and Basil changed their plans and came home early, she assumed they would eat together, fashion some kind of subdued celebration, listen to carols on the wireless, drink a little too much.

It crossed her mind that she might make another trip to Shadwell, stretch her acquaintance with Mr Gertler and scrounge a chicken or a tray of pies, but that was too much like begging and she put the idea out of mind. She also had a vague notion that she might catch a train to Scotland and Derek and she would have one last night together in a hotel. But trains, weather and her commitment to *Speaking Up* were against it and Derek had already told her that he'd be spending Christmas Day with his mother.

All these small concerns were put aside a week before Christmas when Walter invited her to lunch at the York Minster.

Dean Street had taken a bit of a pounding. A high-explosive bomb falling within range of the York Minster occasioned great concern in the cosmopolitan clientele until it was discovered that not one cask or flagon had been broken which was, of course, a piece of good fortune worthy of celebration. Scorched brickwork and a few boarded-up windows did not prevent service from continuing uninterrupted.

At a table for two in a corner of the dining room, Walter wasted no time in coming to the point. 'I've been offered the post of Deputy Director of North American Services, effective mid-January.'

'Congratulations,' Susan said. 'Is that the job you've been angling for all along?'

'Lord, no!' Walter said. 'They're trying to shunt me off into a cul-de-sac – not that Fifth Avenue is exactly that.'

'How responsible a position is it?'

'It's a fancy handle for listener research,' Walter informed her. 'I'll have a department to myself and access to influential people but it's still a passive post, more to do with re-broadcasting than original programming.'

'Turn it down,' Susan said.

'I'm not sure I can.'

'Oh, come on, Walter!' said Susan with a hint of exasperation. 'If the governors want rid of you why don't you force them to sack you? Did you push the propaganda too far?'

'Not far enough for some people.'

'Some people?' Susan said. 'You mean Raymond Hall, don't you? My God, Walter, are you really working for Ray Hall's department on the sly?'

He pursed his lips, raised his brows and looked almost, if not quite, guilty. 'I'm not saying I am and I'm not saying I'm not. Let's suppose, hypothetically, that happened to be the case, how would you feel about it?'

'Me? What's my opinion got to do with anything?'

'If I accept the New York posting I want you with me.'

'As your girlfriend, your mistress?'

'Don't be ridiculous. My personal assistant.'

America was a mystical land that, in her childish

imagination, had been inhabited by cowboys, gangsters and women in impossibly beautiful gowns. She knew better now, though traces of that fanciful image remained. Besides, she would have Walter to lean on and if she did wind up in his bed who in England would ever know?

'Susan, I need to be with someone I can trust.'

'Is that what that awful dinner in the Morton was all about? Was Raymond Hall sizing me up to see if I was – what – dependable?'

'Smart was Ray's assessment. Smart, perceptive and loyal,' Walter said. 'By the by, Ray's no longer attached to home security. He has, shall we say, a wider net to cast.'

'Are you asking me to become a spy?'

'You'll be an employee of the British Broadcasting Corporation first and foremost. Officially, my assistant. We'll be expected to meet the right people, attend the right parties, keep our eyes and ears open and give Ray, or one of his contacts, a nod if anything unusual comes to our attention.'

He put out his hand and lightly touched her fingers, rather as Derek had done over breakfast in the kitchen in Salt Street that morning after they'd first made love.

'There's far too much in-fighting going on with the European Service. It's almost impossible to tell who's behind the policy directives, whether it's the Foreign Office or the Ministry of Information or our own programme planners. The New York office is a way station at present but if America ever enters the war its importance will expand out of all measure and we'll be right on the spot when it does.'

'Meanwhile,' Susan said, 'you'll be answering to Ray Hall and whatever anonymous department he works for.'

'Instead of diffusing propaganda we'll be gathering it at source, providing raw material for our government to act upon. It's not much more than a glorified monitoring service, really.'

'Sophistry,' Susan stated.

'Now there's a big word for a Shadwell girl,' Walter said.

'Are you patronising me, Mr Boscombe?'

'Does it sound as if I'm patronising you? For heaven's sake, I'm offering you the opportunity of a lifetime. A responsible job with a decent rate of pay and a multitude of perks in the most exciting city in the world now that Paris has become a Nazi outpost. Is it the fact that you'd be serving two masters that bothers you?'

'It's not that, not really that. What will happen to *Speaking Up* after you leave? Will Basil be reinstated?'

'Basil's too traditional, too staid. He cares a mite too much about the BBC and what it used to stand for to cope with programmes being used as weapons of war. He'll be happier in Light Entertainment. Is it the sailor boy who's giving you pause?'

'Derek isn't a boy,' Susan said. 'He's the captain of a convoy destroyer and that's certainly no job for a boy.'

She expected him to tell her that waiting for a man who might not survive the next voyage or the one after was romantic fallacy. But Walter Boscombe was too shrewd to challenge her or point out that whatever feelings she had for Commander Willets might not survive two or three or four years of separation.

He raised his hand and the wine waiter came running as fast as his old legs would carry him. Walter took a great while studying the wine list, allowing Susan time to sort out the questions in her mind, then, having chosen, dismissed the waiter, leaned across the table and asked her point-blank.

'Well, Susan, are you with me, or not?'

'May I have a little while to think about it?'

'Of course, but I must insist that you don't discuss it with Vivian, Basil or Larry or, for that matter, with anyone.'

Susan nodded. 'When do you need an answer?'

'By the first of the year at the latest.'

'The first of the year it is,' she said as the waiter appeared bearing an ice bucket. 'Walter, what on earth did you order?'

'Champagne,' he said, 'a trifle prematurely, perhaps.'

Fifth Avenue was a far cry from Regent Street or Oxford Street or battered Portland Place. No more worries about air raids, ration cards, clothing allowances or if Hitler's Panzers would come growling up the Mall as soon as winter was over.

It's not as if I'll be leaving England for good or severing my ties with home and country, Susan told herself. I'll still be working for the BBC. My brother's dead, my father's in Limerick and my lover will be out of touch, if not out of mind, for months at a time. There's nothing to keep me in London, no ties that can't be broken. Derek will understand. And if he doesn't, too bad. It would be foolish to commit herself to waiting for a man whom she hardly knew, an affair that had barely begun and that might very well end in tears.

She was tempted to tell Larry her news. She knew, or thought she did, what he would say: 'Go, Susie pops, go.'

There was no reason not to. After all, it was what she'd always dreamed of: excitement, travel, another rung on the ladder of success, due recompense for all her hard work, her application, her dedication. And if it meant that she would have to sleep with Walter Boscombe, what harm in that? She was no innocent virgin. She was Susan Hooper Cahill, a woman of independent spirit.

There was nothing to stop her, nothing worthwhile.

She contemplated breaking her promise to Walter by calling Vivian for advice. She knew that Vivian and Basil would gang up to remind her what a rotter Boscombe was. She couldn't explain to them that there was more to the New York posting than met the eye, that she would be working not just for the BBC but also for the government, for the good of the country, a loyal and selfless citizen speaking up for Britain in the land of the free.

She knew she should seize this golden opportunity but niggling doubts remained, not concerning her competence, her ability to adapt or her ability to deceive but a vague melancholy suspicion that she might simply be running away.

Walter didn't ask and she didn't tell him.

All he said was, 'When will you be back?'

'Friday, mid-afternoon at the latest.'

'Very well,' he said and returned to reading the scripts that she'd dumped on his desk that morning.

There was no heating on the train. By the time she reached Evesham in early afternoon she was chilled to the bone. She had no idea where she might find Danny, if her BBC pass would get her through the gates of the monitoring unit at Wood Norton and, even if it did, if Danny would deign to speak with her. She hadn't seen him, hadn't written or called in the month since the Coventry bombing, and as the train pulled out of Paddington and rumbled through the bomb-scarred suburbs it occurred to her that she should at least have let him know she still cared.

Evesham High Street was surprisingly spacious; a broad thoroughfare with trees in the centre flanked by a medley of quaint old houses and modern buildings. There was much traffic about, motorcars, vans, horse-drawn carts and a number of young men and women riding bicycles. In summer she would probably have a view of fields, market gardens and distant hills but a still grey mist enveloped the town, a mist that, even in early afternoon, hinted at frost and a bitter night to come.

She found a tearoom not far from the station, warmed herself at a log fire, drank tea and ate a cheese and pickle sandwich. She'd come to Evesham with a purpose but no plan. The girl at the counter told her that Wood Norton lay on one side of town and Deaconsfield Road on the other. Sense told her to head for the BBC establishment but the monitoring unit was probably protected by armed guards and when a bus for Deaconsfield came into view she flagged it down, boarded and rode out through the mist to Danny's lodging, hoping that she might find him there.

Her apprehension increased as she walked from the crossroads through a spectral landscape accompanied only by the unfamiliar chug of a tractor and the mocking of rooks, unseen in the still grey mist. She had a half-notion that Breda might loom out of the mist and tell her that the news had been false, that Danny had died in Coventry and that she had been living for weeks in a dream.

The row of semi-detached council houses emerged, not a light to be seen in any of them. The gardens were trim, the hedges rimed with frost, the air tainted with the smell of wood smoke, coal smoke and cooking. She had never before been anywhere quite like it, not in Shadwell, London or Hereford; the sort of place where lives were lived quietly and inconspicuously, just the sort of place, she thought, where an unassuming man like her husband might feel at home.

The number was painted on the gate. The front lawn had been dug up. Small staves stuck in the cold earth like little grave markers suggested that something had been planted, some crop to feed the household in the spring. A paved path led down the side of the house. Her apprehension increased. She had no idea what she was doing here, prying or probing or trying, perhaps, to find an excuse for turning down an opportunity to put everything, including her crippled marriage, behind her.

Buried in the garden at the rear, the humped shape of an Anderson shelter was the only sign that war had affected the good folk of Deaconsfield. She knocked tentatively on the back door which, after a pause, opened a few inches.

The woman was small, pinched and pale. She wore a floral apron over a faded dress and a beret covered her greying hair.

'No vacancies,' she said and made to close the door.

'I'm looking for Danny, for Mr Cahill.'

'He don't live here.'

'Oh, I'm sorry. I must have the wrong address.'

'He don't live here any longer,' the woman said. 'What do you want with Danny? Who are you, anyway?'

'I'm his wife.'

'His wife from London?'

'Yes,' Susan said. 'I wonder if you'd be good enough to tell me where Mr Cahill's living now?'

'Is Danny expecting you?'

'No. I just happened to be . . .'

A face appeared at the woman's hip, a red-cheeked little face under a spiky mop of hair: Billy, her nephew. It had been three months since she'd said goodbye to him at Paddington but to judge by his scowl he was unsure who she was or, more likely, puzzled as to what she was doing here.

'Billy,' Susan said, 'don't you remember me?'

'Auntie Susie,' he said, and grinned.

*

If it had been up to Basil their bags would have been packed and ready to go soon after he received an official communiqué from the office of the Deputy Director General offering him a position as a producer in Light Entertainment which, the DDG felt, would be less taxing than a return to the American Service.

So eager was Basil to get back to London that he put up no resistance to 'losing' *Speaking Up*. He was well aware that illness had undermined his stamina and the grind of producing a thrice-weekly comments programme was beyond him. He was also cheered to receive a handwritten letter from Cecil Madden welcoming him to Light Entertainment's headquarters in the Criterion Theatre at Piccadilly Circus and tactfully enquiring when he felt he might be fit enough to join their rascally crew.

Vivian insisted that he be examined by Dr Fleck before they returned to the capital. She had begun work on another book – a different kind of book – and was already caught up in it. She had also found that she liked having her brother close at hand, for David had taken over the role of organiser and attended to the bothersome practicalities that distracted her from writing.

News of Susan came from Derek's letters, since Basil's reticent brother suddenly seemed to have found his voice.

'Love,' Vivian said. 'The idiot's fallen in love.'

'With Susan?' said Basil.

'Of course, with Susan.'

'He could do worse, I suppose.'

'At least he can't rush off and marry her, that's one thing to be thankful for,' Vivian said.

'Unless she asks her husband for a divorce.'

'What point would there be in that?' Vivian said. 'You don't know Susan Cahill like I do, Basil. She'll play two ends against the middle as long as it suits her. She can string Derek along for years without having to commit herself, provided she has a husband somewhere in the background. If someone better comes along, then she'll disconnect.'

'Disconnect?'

'Do what's best for her without regard for anyone else.'

'I wonder if he's been to bed with her yet?'

'It's high time you were back at work, dear, if only to stop you obsessing about sex.'

'I couldn't agree more,' Basil said. 'I can be ready to leave in an hour. How about you?'

'Not before Christmas.'

'What? For sex?'

'For London, you fool,' said Vivian.

It had been a long day for Breda at the counter in Orrell's canteen. Three sheds had been shored up, machinery installed and the staff had to cope not just with builders but also a full complement of machinists and packers, though, apparently, the boffins in Shed No. 3 had taken their top-secret experiments elsewhere now that the building had been destroyed and Dr Pepperdine had joined the ranks of the departed.

The mystery of how Steve Pepperdine had met his end and why the Reverend Littlejohn had also vanished provided an endless source of speculation that kept the girls entertained while they laboured at the sinks and pastry boards and, most especially, gathered to eat dinner. Haunting Archie Jackson with questions served no purpose for Archie had become, as Morven put it, as tight as the lid on a jar of pickles and twice as sour as the contents.

There was also another mystery for the girls to contend with. Who was the stranger who accompanied Archie round the canteen, making notes in a black-bound ledger? He was as skinny as a rake, well over six feet tall and padded about like a heron dabbing for frogs while he observed the daily routine and, with Archie whispering in his ear, scribbled in his book.

'Who is that man, Mr Jackson?'

'No one that concerns you, Miss Hastie.'

It was twenty past four when Breda arrived at the Pells' house and found her sister-in-law seated at the table in the living room sipping tea. She experienced a rush of resentment before she noticed that Susan was not her usual cocky self. She wore no make-up, had dark circles under her eyes and looked as if she'd been crying. She wore a half-length wool overcoat and one of those man-tailored suits that only came in slim fittings: a week ago Breda might have envied her, but not now.

Mrs Pell covered her embarrassment by pouring tea, handing Breda a cup and saucer and retreating to the kitchen.

'I didn't realise that his friends had been killed in the Coventry raid,' Susan began. 'It must have been awful for him.'

'It certainly was,' said Breda.

'Why didn't he tell me?'

'Why didn't you ask?'

'Well, I knew he was all right . . .' Susan trailed off lamely.

'And you was busy?'

'Actually, yes, I was.'

Breda balanced the saucer on the flat of her hand and drank daintily from one of Mrs Pell's 'special occasion' cups, though why Mrs P thought Danny's wife, dropping out of the blue, deserved the best floral china was puzzling. She might have gone at Susie if Billy hadn't been lying, tummy down, on the carpet in front of the fire with his nose in a school book and his ears pricked up.

Susan said, 'He's growing up fast.'

'Too bloomin' fast. Can't keep 'im in clothes.'

'Ronnie would be proud of him.'

Billy turned his head, alert at mention of his daddy's name.

Breda said quickly, 'Will be, will be proud of 'im – when 'e gets 'ome from overseas.'

'What? Yes, of course.' The blunder increased Susan's discomfort. 'I really came – I mean, I'm here to see Danny.'

'What if Danny don't want to see you?'

'He's still my husband, Breda. We have matters to discuss.'

'What matters?'

'Private matters.'

'Like a divorce?'

'No, not that,' Susan said. 'Where is he? The woman – Mrs Pell managed to avoid telling me where I might find him.'

'He's on duty at Wood Norton.'

'That's not what I meant, Breda. Is he with you?'

'Yer, he's with me; me and Billy.'

'Why doesn't he stay here?'

'You don't know nothin' about it, do you?' Breda said. 'You ain't never lost nobody you was close to.'

'I lost my brother, didn't I?'

Breda placed teacup and saucer on the table, fished in her coat pocket, brought out a crushed packet of Woodbine and lit a cigarette. She inhaled deeply and perched herself on an arm of Mr Pell's chair. Any tears Susie had been moved to shed had dried up. She had that spoiled expression on her biscuit again, lips pursed, head tilted back as if, even seated, Breda thought, she's looking down her nose at me.

Breda didn't want to talk about Ronnie. She wanted to keep Ronnie out of it, and not just for Billy's sake.

'How long you down 'ere for?' she asked.

'I'm due back at work tomorrow afternoon.'

'You can't stay with us. Ain't got no room.'

'The woman – Mrs Pell – has kindly offered to put me up for the night. Her rooms are empty, I believe.'

'You ain't sharin' with Danny, that's what you think.'

'It didn't even cross my mind.'

'I'll bet it didn't,' Breda said.

'What time does Danny come home?'

Breda shrugged. 'If he isn't held over, should be in about six.'

'Here?'

'Nope,' Breda said. 'My place. Our place.'

'Our place?'

'We're together now, Susie.'

'You mean, sharing accommodation?'

'I mean sharing everything.'

Susan scraped back her chair and got to her feet. 'I see.'

Thinking they were leaving, Billy closed his storybook and scuttled into the kitchen to find his schoolbag.

Breda said, 'If you wants to talk to Danny you'd best come with us. He won't come 'ere, specially if 'e's late. I'll feed you, then Danny can walk you back. Give you time to discuss your business.'

Susan took a step forward, glanced at the door of the kitchen, which Mrs Pell had tactfully closed, and hissed, 'If you think I'm going to stand by and let you take Danny from me . . .'

'I didn't take 'im, Susie,' Breda said. 'You gave 'im away.'

'What if I want him back?'

'Too bleedin' bad,' said Breda.

23

The Christmas party or, rather, its aftermath had changed everything. Danny Cahill was nobody's fool. The reason he'd chosen to deny Breda's feelings for him had more to do with a lingering sense of inadequacy than an absence of desire. He had resisted falling in love for too many years to suppose that rockets would soar and the earth shake if they ever so far forgot themselves as to tumble into bed together. He was, however, a red-blooded Scot and well aware that after fifteen years of striving to protect her from predatory males he was in danger of falling into that league himself.

There was also Billy to consider, the responsibility he owed to the boy, a moral responsibility, assumed in good faith.

This wasn't free-and-easy Shadwell and the last thing he wished to do was bring unmerited opprobrium down on Breda's head. He'd already had a quiet word with Mr Gregory who had sounded out the billeting officers who, in turn, conceded that, the exigencies of wartime notwithstanding, a married man living openly with a young widow was not something the BBC could condone, especially when a child of impressionable age was involved.

Dividing the accommodation offered by the Pells between a female evacuee and a member of the BBC's monitoring unit seemed like a sensible compromise; widow and child in one room, the editor in the other. Paperwork would take a few weeks to sort out but, assuming that the Pells and Mrs Hooper agreed to the arrangement, Mr Cahill, Mrs Hooper and her son would all move into the billet in Deaconsfield Road, public decency would be upheld and nobody could say a dickey-bird without appearing sanctimonious.

Danny was feeling particularly pleased with himself as he steered the bicycle down the frozen track to Shady Nook. He'd no doubt that Mr Pell would convince Mrs Pell that she would welcome having 'guests' again, particularly folk she knew, and that leasing out the rooms would not be disrespectful to the memory of Griff and Kate. He wasn't quite so sure how Breda would react. He intended to put it to her after Billy was asleep and point out the advantages of living in a house with running water, an indoor lavatory, electric light and a wireless.

Pedalling through town had ironed out the kinks that ten hours crouched at an editing table invariably induced. He was ready to do justice to supper, tuck Billy into bed and engage in a little connubial-style bliss with Breda. He propped the bicycle against the side of the coach, opened the door, stepped into the warmth of the railway carriage and almost tripped over his wife.

'What's up?' he asked in alarm. 'What's wrong?'

'Nothing,' Susan answered. 'Nothing much.'

'Is it your old man?'

'What makes you think that?'

'I know what a bigot he is and the Irish . . .'

'He's fine,' Susan said, 'as far as I know.'

'Then what are you doing here?'

'She came to see you,' Breda explained while stirring a pot on the iron stove. 'Says she needs to talk to you private.

I've fixed a bed for 'er at Mrs Pell's. You can walk 'er back there after we've ate.'

Susan was seated on the bunk, slender legs jutting into the aisle. Danny unwound his scarf, took off his coat and hung them on the peg. He was shaken by his wife's unannounced appearance. He'd taken no account of Susan when he'd been making his plans. Susan said, 'I was sorry to hear about your friends. Mrs Pell told me all about it. I hadn't realised it had been so bad.'

'Aye,' Danny said gravely, 'a sad time for all of us.'

'Kate – she wasn't your girl, though, was she?' Susan said.

'Naw, just a friend.' Danny shrugged. 'She was Griffiths's girl from the start. Not that it matters now.'

'Now you've found consolation elsewhere?' said Susan.

'Just as well he had somebody to console 'im,' said Breda, tapping the spoon against the rim of the pot. 'He had to 'ave somebody when 'e got back from Coventry.'

'You could have called me,' Susan said.

'You didn't know them,' Danny said.

'And you was busy,' said Breda again.

Knees on the cushion, back to the wall, Billy made himself as unobtrusive as possible. He was too young to appreciate the issues but he knew something was going on.

Susan said, 'Don't think I don't know how you've pushed me out of the picture.'

Breda plucked the spoon from the broth pot and waved it at her sister-in-law. 'You were too damned busy with your fancy friends to give Danny the time of day. What did you expect me to do?'

'Whoa, whoa, whoa.' Danny relieved Breda of the spoon. 'I'm not havin' any of this bickering, especially in front of – you know who. None of us have had much tae smile about these past three months but that's no excuse for squabblin'.'

'You're taking 'er side. I knew you'd take 'er side,' Breda said. 'All she 'as to do is show up and you . . .'

'I'm leaving,' Susan said, though she made no move to rise. 'As far as I'm concerned you can do what you like. I won't be here.'

'It's too early to go back tae Mrs Pell's,' Danny said. 'At least stay an' have somethin' to eat first.'

'No,' Susan said. 'I mean leaving England. I've been offered a post in the BBC's New York office.'

'Is Boscombe going too?' Danny said.

'Yes. I'll be his personal assistant.'

'Well, we all know what that—' Breda began.

'Breda,' Danny said firmly, 'be quiet.'

The pot on the coal stove bubbled. Scooping up a handful of her skirt, Breda wrapped it around her fingers, lifted the pot from the heat and placed it on the fold-down table.

'How long's the contract?' Danny asked.

'That hasn't been discussed.'

'It is a promotion, though?'

'Oh, yes.'

'You'll be in the tower in Fifth Avenue, I expect.'

'Yes.'

'Is this what you want, Susie?'

'I do believe it is.'

'Is New York overseas, Auntie Susie?' Billy asked.

'It's in America,' Susan told him.

'Maybe you'll meet Daddy.'

Susan brought him down on to her lap. 'America's a very big country so I wouldn't count on it, Billy.'

'But you never know, Auntie Susie,' said Billy. 'You never know what'll happen overseas.'

'You never know about anything these days,' said Breda and, opening the little cupboard above her son's head, brought out a cruet and four bowls. 'Since you're off to America, Susie, the least we can do is give you supper before you leave. Danny, pull out the stool.'

'Yes, dear,' said Danny and, with a misjudged wink at his wife, did exactly as he was told.

It was cold, so cold. Even with her collar turned up and her hat pulled down the air nipped at her ears and made the scars above the torn lobe tingle. She followed him in single file along the path between the hedgerows but when they came into the lane she took his arm. The mist had lifted a little but there were no lights to give it dimension and, oddly, she felt as if she were walking towards the sea or towards a cliff over which she might plunge if Danny and his shaded torch weren't there to guide her.

She said, 'I don't know how you can live like that.'

Surprised, he said, 'Like what?'

'In a place like that.'

'It's no palace, I'll admit, but then neither was Stratton's. Anyroads, I think we'll be lodging with the Pells soon after Christmas.'

The sound of their footsteps followed them as they came out into Deaconsfield Road. It was not much after nine but there were no snatches of music or a radio announcer's voice reading the news and, after London, the silence seemed unnatural.

'You're not going to leave her, Danny, are you?'

'Naw,' he said. 'It wouldn't be fair.'

'Fair to who – to whom?'

'Breda and Billy.'

'Don't be so damned noble. After all these years, Breda's finally got you where she wants you. Be man enough to admit it.'

'I'm in love with her, if that's what you mean.'

'You thought you were in love with me once.'

'I was. Still am, I suppose. But I was never the right man for you, Susan. Your old man spoiled you. He made you believe you were special. An' you are special – just not that special.'

'I'm sorry I let you down, Danny. Truly, I am.'

'I'm a big boy. I'll get over it. I *have* got over it,' he said. 'At least I can be sure Breda loves me for what I am, not just because I'm not somebody else.'

'Now you're just being cruel,' Susan said. 'Why don't you tell me the truth for once, tell me what you really think of me.'

'I think you're a bitch, if you must know.'

'That's it,' Susan said. 'That's what I came all this way to hear.'

'Burning your bridges; is that your game?' said Danny. 'Will you meet up with Gaines when you get tae New York?'

'I'm not that much of a fool – or that much of a bitch.'

'When do you leave?'

'Some time in January.'

He flashed the beam of the torch at the number on the gate. 'We're here.'

'Aren't you coming in with me?'

'Nope. I think I'd better get back.'

'To Breda.'

'Yep.'

'Danny, if you want a divorce . . .'

'What's the point?' he said. 'I intend tae stick with Breda with or without a wedding ring. I don't suppose you've got anyone lined up who wants tae make you an honest woman, not yet anyroads. If that happens – well, we'll talk about it then.'

'There are times when you're just too reasonable for your own good, Danny Cahill,' Susan said. 'Now, I think I'd better go in before I freeze to death.'

He hugged her, said softly. 'I hope you find what you're looking for over there, Susie. I really do.'

'Goodbye, Danny,' she said and, opening the gate, headed down the path to the kitchen door without once looking back.

Christmas cards were scattered on the floor of the hall in the mews house in Salt Street. She'd given no thought to the season and had posted cards only to her father and Derek. She suspected that Walter, Larry and Mr Gillespie would exchange small gifts before they left on Christmas Eve. She would buy something for each of them and a bottle of Scotch or brandy to welcome Vivian and Basil back from the country on the day after Boxing Day.

She'd no urge to decorate the house with sprigs of evergreen, even if she could find any; no need to scrape up traditional fare to consume on Christmas Day. It crossed her mind that Walter might invite her to lunch or dinner, though she took nothing for granted. For all she knew, he might be off with his father and brothers to spend Christmas on the Boscombe estate in Buckinghamshire.

She'd slept hardly at all in the bitterly cold bedroom in the council house in Deaconsfield in spite of the hot-water bottle and extra blankets that Mrs Pell had provided. It was just another uncomfortable room, haunted by the ghost of a young woman whom she'd never met and who, if she were honest, meant no more to her than the corpses that were pulled from the rubble after air raids.

The Pells, husband and wife, had spoken of the Cottrell girl and the Welshman, Griffiths, as if they were children who'd been plucked from this life by angels; spoke of Danny as if he were next door to a saint. Susan had been tempted to tell them the truth about her husband and her own harsh history but she was far too polite to give in to the impulse. She'd smiled, nodded indulgently and had pretended that all was as it should be until the cloying sentimentality had become too much and she'd pleaded exhaustion and been shown upstairs to the dismal little bedroom.

Optimism and a cavalier indifference to mortality had been sucked from her in the three long months since the handsome stranger from Bristol had been snuffed out in the listening room in Broadcasting House. All she could do now was run away from the woman she'd been, a woman who had given away her husband, had exchanged love for excitement and was not, after all, as special as she had once believed herself to be.

She sighed and, collecting the scattered cards from the hall floor, got to her feet. Eight cards addressed to Vivian, six to Basil, four to the Willets as a couple and one, just one, to her: a brown, official-looking envelope with her name printed in a hand she instantly recognised.

'Derek,' she said aloud.

Placing the other cards on the hall table, she carried her solitary trophy into the office and switched on the desk lamp. She slit the brown envelope carefully with a paper knife and slipped out the calendar, a single picture on stiff card with a little booklet of months and days attached to it by ribbons; an economy production that reflected wartime shortages.

She tilted the lampshade, studied the picture that Derek had chosen for her. The dark blue sky was lit by one huge star, a mammoth eight-point silvery star hanging over the sea upon which rode no cruiser or destroyer but a tiny sailing ship, its bows raised up and the wind behind it driving it into the waves. The boat looked so small, the sea so vast, that the great bright star seemed to be the only thing holding it steady on its course. The name on the little boat's bows was too small to read but she knew what it would be, what it should be or what Derek hoped she would make of it.

She turned the calendar over.

On the back he'd written: *Darling, I love you and miss you. To help you count the days until we can be together again. Derek.*

She stood motionless, calendar in hand, and wondered if it would be appropriate to cry or if that would be to give in to self-pity, an emotion of which Derek would surely disapprove.

Catching her breath, she slotted the calendar carefully into the envelope, carried it out into the hall and put it on top of the cards on the table by the door. Then she hurried into the bathroom to wash, change her clothes and make herself ready to catch a bus to Scobie Street and keep her promise to Walter to be back by mid-afternoon.

The conductor told her that it had been relatively quiet recently but he wasn't convinced that the Luftwaffe had done its worst and that the heavy nightly raids were tailing off. He said, chattily, that he'd a strange feeling in his water that Goering was just waiting for a clear night over Christmas to order his bombers out in force now that his pilots had had a breather.

It was certainly unusually calm in London that cold Friday afternoon. Shoppers were out in Oxford Street, barrow-boys, selling mainly cabbages and Brussels sprouts, had appeared from nowhere and the ringing sound of a Salvation Army brass quartet playing carols outside the Picture Palace near Oxford Circus served as a reminder that, blitz or no blitz, war or no war, Christmas was a time of celebration even if joy was in somewhat short supply.

Speaking Up would broadcast on Monday but not on the 25th. The schedule for the 27th had been sketched but not confirmed. Susan expected her desk to be strewn with unanswered letters and snappy little reminders from Walter who to chase up by telephone. Lack of sleep should have caught up with her but, surprisingly, she felt quite jaunty as she walked down Scobie Street, gas mask bumping against her hip, her 'emergency' overnight bag tucked under her arm.

Larry was standing outside the Calcutta chatting to a clean-cut young constable who may, or may not, have been on duty.

'His lordship's been looking for you, Susie,' Larry informed her. 'Have you been off sojourning some place swanky?'

'Evesham, that's all.'

'Giving your husband a Christmas treat, were you?'

'If I was, do you think I'd go telling you,' Susan said. 'Is he alone in the office?'

'All alone and palely loitering,' Larry said. 'Here, you could have him arrested for that, couldn't you, Colin?'

'Not,' said the constable, grinning, 'without reliable witnesses.'

'You'll find precious few of those round here,' said Larry and with a friendly tap to Susan's rear sent her on her way downstairs.

The stage was set up for a band rehearsal but as far as she could make out the musicians were in no hurry to begin. They were gathered around the snack bar, in a cloud of cigarette smoke, scoffing mince pies and sausage rolls and chattering like a bunch of old wives while the leader, in a cream-coloured evening jacket, patiently amused himself at the piano by improvising jazz chords on the melody of 'Silent Night'.

Walter's office door was firmly closed.

Susan went directly into her cubby, took off her coat and hat and left her bag and gas mask holder out of harm's way behind the desk. Then, after checking her watch against one of the studio clocks – ten minutes and twenty seconds past three o'clock – she knocked on the door of Walter's office and went in.

'I'm back,' she said brightly.

'So I can see,' said Walter. 'Not a moment too soon. Once that lot outside gets going we won't be able to hear ourselves think, let alone speak. Where's your notebook?'

'I'll fetch it in just a moment,' Susan told him.

He tipped back in the chair, knees braced against the edge of the desk, a cigarette purling smoke from a slot in the ashtray, a cup of something, probably tea, balanced precariously on the library's copy of *Who's Who*, 1938 edition.

'You've something to tell me, haven't you?' Walter said.

'Yes, actually, I have.'

He tucked his buttocks into the depths of the chair, planted his feet on the floor and leaned towards her, head cocked.

'Well,' he said. 'Out with it.'

'I've decided not to go to New York,' she heard herself say. 'I'm very grateful, Walter, but it's not for me.'

'May I ask why it's not for you?'

'I prefer to stay in London.'

He lifted the cigarette, drew smoke then stubbed it into the ashtray. If he was angry he gave no sign save for a slight tightening of the lips and one little twitch at the corner of his eye.

'What changed your mind? Who did you tell?'

'About serving two masters? No one. As for the offer of

a post in New York, I told my husband. He'll say nothing to anyone in or out of Wood Norton. He has no reason to.'

'Oh, I see. You went to Evesham, did you?'

'Where did you think I'd gone?'

He sighed, shrugged. 'Chasing your sailor boy.'

'I don't have to chase my sailor boy,' Susan said.

'He chases you, does he?'

'He doesn't have to,' Susan said. 'I'm not going anywhere.'

'Is there nothing I can say that'll change your mind?'

'No, Walter, there isn't. I don't expect you to understand.'

'Oh, but I do,' he said. 'Believe me, my dear Mrs Cahill, I do.' He looked at her for a long moment, not smiling, then said, 'I just think it's a pity your talent will be wasted here.'

'My talent for what?'

'Getting ahead,' he said, then, curtly, 'Now, fetch your notebook please and next week's schedule and let's see what we can do to stir up a little more sediment from the murky waters of the BBC before I take my leave.'

It was after five before she got back to the safety of her cubby. She closed the door as much as she dared to keep out the strains of 'Moonlight Serenade' and, picking up her bag from behind the desk, took out Derek's gift.

She'd no inclination to cry now, no room in her heart for regrets. She found a drawing-pin in her drawer, pulled out her chair, knelt on it and positioned the picture on the wall to the right of her desk where she could see it just by turning her head. She was tapping gently on the drawing-pin to coax it through the cardboard when Larry appeared behind her.

'Defacing Corporation property?' he said. 'The penalties for that sort of thing are severe.'

She glanced round. 'Really? Like what?'

'Being sent back to the typing pool in disgrace, I suppose.' He came closer and put out a hand to steady her which, because he was Larry, she didn't mind at all. 'Listen,' he muttered, 'there's a rumour going about that our Walter's moving on. Have you heard anything?'

She tried to look surprised. 'Heavens, no! Where did you get that piece of misinformation?'

'Gillespie had it from one of his Canadian chums who had it from someone in our New York office.'

Susan licked her thumb. 'New York? What on earth will Walter do in New York?'

'One dares hardly imagine,' Larry said. 'It seems the post of Deputy Director's up for grabs and I thought – well, I thought old Boscombe might want to take you with him.'

'No,' said Susan. 'In any case, I'm not sure I'd want to go.'

'I would,' Larry said, 'like a shot.'

'And leave England in the lurch. Surely not?'

He gave her his arm to help her down from the chair. 'In any event, the point's moot. I am but an 'umble engineer and they're ten for a cent in New York. If you haven't heard anything it's quite likely it's just another wild rumour fallen from the grapevine.' He turned to leave, then, pausing, glanced up at the calendar and nodded. 'I take it that next year has some significance for you – or, wait, is it the picture? Ah, yes, it's the picture, isn't it? Little boats against the storm, and all that. Mrs Cahill, I do believe you've got another feller, a sailor like as not.'

'I do believe you may be right, Mr Baines.'

'What a girl you are, Susie pops,' he said admiringly. 'What a girl, indeed,' then, shaking his head, sauntered out of the cubby and left her alone at last.

She slid the chair behind the desk, seated herself, placed her fingers lightly on the typewriter keys and, head up, looked at the picture, at the great shining star suspended not only above the little sailing boat but above her too.

At last I know who I am and where I am and what I must do.

I must wait for Derek to come home.

Just wait, she thought, wistfully . . .

In hope.

The Wayward Wife
Jessica Stirling

The war everyone dreaded has begun at last . . .

To Susan Cahill this war is more an adventure than a tragedy. Helped by a white lie about her marriage to Danny she has a new job as a producer's assistant at the BBC. And glamorous new friends, including one American war reporter who has made London his base and Susan his target.

Danny is also working for the BBC, sharing a room in a freezing farmhouse in Evesham, working long hours monitoring German radio broadcasts – and worrying about Susan.

Stuck in London when the blitz begins, Susan's sister-in-law Breda Hooper faces up to the worst with a small son at home and a husband in the fire service. Then her Italian father, hiding out from both the authorities and his former partners in crime, prepares to leave Breda a legacy as explosive as any German bomb.

'Stirling is a wonderful storyteller.' *Bookseller*

HODDER